A
Great Length
of Time

A Great Length of Time

of

Joyce Cherry Cresswell

Editing and design by Indigo Editing & Publications

Nurse and soldier cover image reprinted with the permission of Applewood Books, Publishers of *America's Living Past*, Carlisle, MA 01741.

USS Red Rover cover image reprinted with permission of the Navy Art Collection, Naval History and Heritage Command.

ISBN: 978-0-692-57226-9

For my great-grandmother,
a physician beloved by two generations.

When an ulcer has existed a great length of time, the constitution may possibly become so habituated to it, that the health may really suffer from its being healed.

—*A Dictionary of Practical Surgery,*
William Anderson, MD, 1823

Sir, you may place the slave where you please—you may dry up to your uttermost the fountains of his feelings, the springs of his thought—you may close upon his mind every avenue of knowledge and cloud it over with artificial night—you may yoke him to your labors as the ox which liveth only to work and worketh only to live—you may put him under any process, which, without destroying his value as a slave, will debase and crush him as a rational being—you may do this and the idea that he was born to be free will survive it all. It is allied to his hope of immortality—it is the ethereal part of his nature which oppression cannot reach; it is a torch lit up in his soul by the hand of the Deity and never meant to be extinguished by the hand of man.

—Rep. James McDowell, slaveholder
Virginia Slavery Debate, January 21, 1832
Virginia House of Delegates

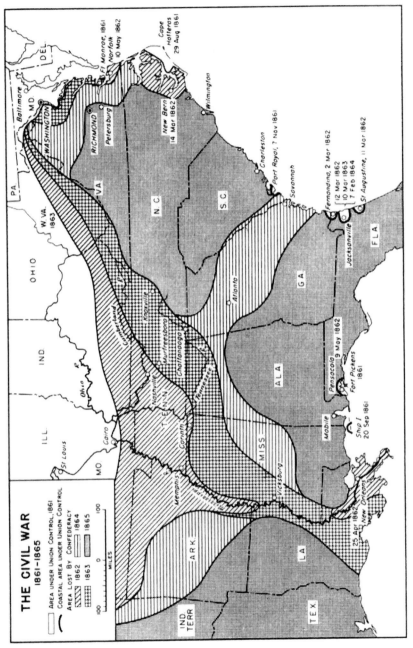

THE CIVIL WAR
1861-1865

Area under Union Control, 1861

Coastal area under Union Control

Area lost by Confederacy
1862   1864
1863   1865

MILES
100   0   100

Fr. Monroe, 1861
Norfolk
10 May 1862
Cape Hatteras
29 Aug 1861

New Bern
14 Mar 1862

Wilmington

Charleston

Port Royal, 7 Nov 1861

Savannah

Fernandina, 2 Mar 1862
12 Mar 1862
10 Mar 1863
7 Feb 1864
St Augustine, 11 Mar 1862

Jacksonville

Pensacola
9 May 1862

Fort Pickens
1861

Ship I.
20 Sep 1861

Mobile

New Orleans
25 Apr 1862

Vicksburg

Memphis

Corinth

Nashville

Murfreesboro

Chattanooga

Knoxville

Tennessee R.

Cumberland

Cairo

St Louis

Ohio R.

Baltimore

WASHINGTON

RICHMOND

Petersburg

DEL.

MD.

PA.

W. VA.
1863

OHIO

IND.

ILL.

MO.

VA.

N. C.

S. C.

GA.

ALA.

MISS.

FLA.

LA.

ARK.

TEX.

IND.
TERR.

TENN.

Atlanta

Image from the Perry-Castañeda Library Map Collection.

Key Historical Events, 1860–1866

November 6, 1860	Abraham Lincoln elected President of the United States
December 20, 1860	South Carolina secedes from the Union (first state to do so)
February 8, 1861	Seven seceded states form Confederate States of America
March 4, 1861	Lincoln inaugurated
April 12, 1861	Fort Sumter fired upon by South, Civil War begins
June 8, 1861	Tennessee joins Confederacy (last state to do so)
July 21, 1861	First Battle of Bull Run/Manassas (Confederate victory)
April 6–7, 1862	Battle of Shiloh/Pittsburg Landing (Union victory)
June 6, 1862	Memphis falls to Union, occupation begins
September 22, 1862	Lincoln announces he will emancipate slaves on January 1, 1863
January 1, 1863	Emancipation Proclamation goes into effect
Late May 1863	Siege of Vicksburg begins
July 1–3, 1863	Battle of Gettysburg (Union victory), last battle on northern soil
July 4, 1863	Vicksburg surrenders to Grant
July 13–17, 1863	Draft riots in New York City
November 19, 1863	Gettysburg Address
April 12, 1864	Fort Pillow massacre

June 1864–March 1865	Trench warfare encircles Richmond and Petersburg
June 10, 1864	Nathan Bedford Forrest surprises Union troops at Brice's Cross Roads
August–October 1864	Sheridan conducts scorched earth campaign against "Confederate Granary," the Shenandoah Valley
August 21, 1864	Nathan Bedford Forrest raids Memphis
September 1, 1864	Atlanta falls to Sherman
November 8, 1864	Lincoln wins re-election
November 15, 1864	Sherman begins "March to the Sea" from Atlanta to Savannah
December 21, 1864	Savannah falls to Sherman
February 17, 1865	Columbia falls to Sherman
March 4, 1865	Lincoln inaugurated for second term
April 2, 1865	Lee retreats from Richmond and Petersburg
April 9, 1865	Lee surrenders at Appomattox Court House
April 14, 1865	Lincoln assassinated
May 9, 1865	Nathan Bedford Forrest dismisses his troops
May 10, 1865	Jefferson Davis captured
June 23, 1865	Last Confederate general surrenders
November 6, 1865	Confederate Captain of CSS Shenandoah surrenders in London
August 20, 1866	Civil War declared over by President Andrew Johnson

Prologue

1855

THE TEENAGE GIRL HAD DIED FROM A TUMOR IN HER THROAT. HER body arrived from an orphanage whose trustees' enthusiasm for railroad stocks had made the expense of medical attention unfortunately quite impossible. The matron did what she could with plasters and tea. Once the girl took fully to bed, the ordeal was done in a week. The cadaver fee from the new women's medical college, while modest, would help offset the unfortunate affair with the B & R Railway.

The subject's hair was coarse and carrot red. Having long ago been cut short for the convenience of others, it now lay matted like a bird's nest upon her head. Her face was heart-shaped, defined by the widow's peak in the center of her forehead. Her perfectly straight teeth—her finest feature—were still creamy white when the ashen lips were forced back. Gray freckles spotted her nose. But for the tumor, which on the whole was rather a small thing—about the size of a wild strawberry—the girl might have found a boy, made lusty love, and raised a family.

The eight young women who gathered at the body had waited three years for this day. The papier-mâché cadaver had been packed away. The students now held lavender-scented handkerchiefs to their noses, their eyes wide with curiosity and traces of fear. The professor had led them in prayer, as he did before the opening of all new cadavers—one per graduating class. The student with the top marks would open the body and remove the suspected tumor. The rest would take the scalpel in their ordered turns. Some would faint.

Pushing her handkerchief into her apron pocket, the valedictorian took up the scalpel. She gently pressed the skin to find the ridges of the trachea with her fingertips. Leaning in, she made a vertical incision from under the jaw to that special spot, as her professor had said, where a locket might rest. A puff of foul air escaped from the cut, causing the others to cough quietly into their handkerchiefs. Parting the laceration with her fingers, she saw for the first time the distinctive rings of the trachea, something she had seen only in drawings and her mind's eye. The lifeless tissue was swollen, still pressing against the network of vessels and nerves that surrounded it. With her forefinger and thumb she grasped the normally hollow tube and squeezed, feeling the fatal resistance within. She looked at the professor, who raised his eyebrows in consent to the next step. Cutting into the trachea, she was pleased when the mass revealed itself. A clamor broke out around the table, and students pressed forward. The professor stepped close, hands clasped behind his waistcoat. "Ah, yes," he murmured, which was all the instruction they had learned to expect in their third year of medical college.

The student maneuvered the scalpel behind the tumor. She was eager to dissect it, to see its structure, to slice it and lay it upon the microscope. As she cut the growth from its host, she imagined the girl as a young mother, hanging laundry on a sunny day, winking at her husband as their redheaded children—a boy and a girl—chased chickens in the yard. Blue skies and waving grain washed her vision; a gentle breeze blew the sheets on the line.

The aspiring doctor placed the tumor in a ceramic dish, the tap of the scalpel startling her from her daydream. For a moment, she was confused, believing the girl now would rise from the table, healed. When she did not, the student sank to the floor in silence. Her classmates rushed around her, but she waved them off. She would learn that orphaned girls seldom found loving husbands or gave birth to carefree children. Nevertheless, she would always believe that this particular girl would have led a contented life but for a wild strawberry in her throat.

Chapter 1

A MONTH AFTER THE ANGUISH AT GETTYSBURG, A YOUNG WOMAN appeared at an army camp in the cornfields of Indiana. "I should like to serve the Union, sir," she said.

The man behind a heavy wooden desk glanced up. "That so?" he said. He scrawled his signature across the bottom of a document, returned his pen to its well, and sat back. His face was leathered and cracked. His hair hung in greasy strings over his ears. Above unremarkable hazel eyes, his brows erupted like thistles. From a coatrack behind him, a faded blue greatcoat, with its double row of brass buttons, proclaimed him an erstwhile leader of men.

"Rose Barnett, sir," the woman said, extending her hand. "Dr. Barnett."

He took the tips of her fingers in his calloused hand. "General Robert Temple," he said. "Doctor?"

"Yes, sir. Allopathic. I have practiced for five years in Chicago. I taught school for one year in New York, but it was not to my liking. I worked at a brass foundry for seven years."

The War of Rebellion—or, depending on one's point of view, the War of Northern Aggression—was more than two years running. When the ball had opened in the spring of '61, no one had expected more than a waltz or two. But here they were, three summers later, still dancing to ever more deadly tunes. "We didn't call for doctors," the general said. "Or teachers or foundry girls. We called for nurses."

"I am aware, sir. I thought perhaps additional doctors might be welcome." In fact, teachers and foundry girls were exactly what had been called for, as trained nurses were few and far between, but there was no gain in pointing that out.

"We especially didn't call for lady doctors. If there is such a thing." The general reached into his vest and retrieved a leather pouch of tobacco. "Sit down, miss. How old are you?"

"Twenty-nine, sir," Rose replied. "And some months."

"Close enough, I guess," he grumbled.

"I believe so, sir, with my experience." She had been traveling for ten days, visiting the aunts who had raised her in northern New York before returning west to this camp near the Ohio River. She had brought three dresses with her—two of dark linen for work and one of satin for special occasions. She had given careful thought to her costume today. Wishing to appear professional before an army officer, she had thought to wear a dispensary dress, but realizing she was in the end appealing to a man, she now sat across from General Temple in stunning emerald-green satin. A matching hair ribbon held her natural blond ringlets in perfect alignment as they brushed her shoulders. "I am fully degreed in medicine, sir. Together with a classmate, I established a dispensary for women and children, which we maintained in Chicago for five years."

"Lying-in," said the general, his gaze traveling the full topography of what he saw before him.

She did not blush or look away, as she knew he expected, but leveled her blue eyes back at him. "Principally, sir, but not exclusively. It has been my experience that once a child arrives in this world, it soon endures the croup or a fractured bone of some sort."

The general raised his unruly brows as if to signal she had him there. He took an ivory smoking pipe in his left hand. With a nail from his desk drawer, he dug at the blackened bowl and slammed its contents into his palm. He rolled his chair backward a few feet and stretched his arm precariously over its rocking back. For a moment Rose feared she might have to jump to catch him, but in a single motion he dumped the shavings into a spittoon, rapped the pipe against the edge, and rolled his chair back to the table, safe and sound.

"Battlefield's no ladies' dispensary, Miss Bartlett. You ever seen a war?"

"Barnett, sir. No, sir."

"I guessed not. Never shot an Indian, I suppose." He put the pipe in his mouth and sucked, creating a sound remarkably like the death rattle of an asthmatic. He coughed a deep, liquid cough and opened the pouch of tobacco. His nails were long and black with grime. "This conflict makes shooting Indians look like Sunday services," he said. "We've Gatling guns now, you know, not to mention the minié ball. Both turn boys to minced meat."

Rose had seen soldiers at the train stations in wheeled chairs and on stretchers, blinded and burned, with limbs reduced to oozing stumps. She had tried not to stare, but neither had she looked away. Always she had wondered, were the soldier her patient, would she have made the same choices? Army surgeons, it was said, were butchers, but she would not judge.

"I am of strong constitution," she said to the general, "and I am not afraid, sir." This last might have been an exaggeration, but it was short of a true lie. Blood did not disturb her. One could not deliver babies and be afraid of blood. And she had seen gruesome enough injuries from the harvester company in Chicago—injuries where limbs, and often lives, could not be saved.

The general pulled a thick string of tobacco from his pouch and packed it into the bowl of his pipe. "Oh, not now, I suspect," he said. "You're not afraid yet." He rose and stepped to the cold fireplace behind him. "Do you know why we're fighting this war, Miss Barnett?" He struck a parlor match on the hearth, held it to his pipe, and took several deep pulls of smoke. His face contorted with the effort. He tossed the match to the floor, ground it out with his boot, and kicked it into the fireplace. Smoke shot from his nostrils as he returned to the desk.

Rose said, "I think our president has made himself clear." The smoke smelled sweet and peppery.

"An abolitionist," the general said.

"You do not fashion yourself one, sir?"

5

"I am a military man, miss. A taker of orders. For two years I have been a Unionist, and now it seems I am an abolitionist as well."

"I should think it would relieve your burden, sir, to stand upon a noble cause."

"My burden will be relieved when the blood stops flowing, young lady." He spoke as if the war was somehow her fault.

"I do not presume to know why men must solve their differences with bloodshed, sir, nor how to stop them once they have begun."

"Nor do I, my dear. Nor do I." He sighed. "I admit we tricked the bastards into firing the first shot. We thought they wouldn't fight. But it was coming one way or the other." He squinted at Rose. "You're a trifle comely to be joining Miss Dix's crowd."

"I remind you, sir, I am a doctor. Miss Dix commands the nurses. And in any case, it is known she has relaxed her standards." She waited as he roared with laughter. While Dorothea Dix, Director of Nursing for the Union, had recruited many talented nurses, she was widely mocked for her decree that handsome women need not apply. Her idiosyncratic rules and tight-fisted bureaucracy had caused a bottleneck that drove commanders mad. "It is best, sir," Rose said, "not to judge a woman by her appearance. Both the plain and the not plain may have keen minds and a fever for the Union."

The general took a breath as if to laugh again but was seized instead by a fit of coughing. Rose stood to aid him, but he waved his hand at her to sit. At last he made a deep hacking sound and expectorated into the tarnished spittoon. The vessel was brass with a finely engraved pattern. Rose had burnished thousands of similar urns at the foundry while earning her fees for medical college. The gleaming pieces had left her hands as works of art. This was a humble end indeed for her industry.

Wiping his mouth on his sleeve, General Temple continued. "All these cowards rioting over the Enrollment Act, and here's a young lady begging to serve. Ironical. You must not be Irish."

"Actually, sir, my mother was Irish." Rose had never known her mother. Out of respect and not a small degree of sentimentality, she held her heritage close, regardless of public opinion.

The general blushed. "Beg pardon, miss."

"I do not condone the riots, sir, but would it not be better for every class to have an equal stake in the war? The newly arrived cannot afford to purchase substitutes; that is why they riot. What incentive have the rich to end a war, even a just one, when only the poor must fight it?"

"War is a tangle of ironies, Miss Barnett; the vagaries of conscription are among the least of them. Sadly, justness of cause impedes neither grief nor irony. In our quest to free the Southern black man, slave and free alike are lynched and murdered—not in the South, mind you, but in New York City. But if states won't send their quotas, the president must snatch boys by the collar, especially with desertions where they are." He chuckled. "At least the South did it first. It gives me no end of pleasure to see Jeff Davis calling up those spineless traitors. Of all the ironies, Southern conscription is the sweetest."

The general rose halfway from his chair and thoroughly rearranged the front of his trousers. Rose looked away. They were in the parlor of a two-story farmhouse that, with its glass windows and brick exterior, was far grander than the mud-chinked log homes she had seen elsewhere in Indiana. She wondered where the family was at this moment, whether they were staying with relatives or had bedded down with the army.

"Where were we?" the general asked, having retaken his seat. "Oh, yes. You wish to be an army surgeon." He drew on his pipe and studied her. "Being a surgeon takes a strong stomach and a stronger back. You are what, all of eight stone?"

"One hundred twenty American pounds, sir. I find that with the proper tools, most physical challenges are within my grasp."

"I am not speaking of levers and pulleys, Miss Barnett. Have you any experience in the art of amputation? I must know; the minié ball is a determined agent." He rocked his chair back and looked at her through half-shuttered eyes.

"As you suggest, sir, one becomes a surgeon through experience. During my medical studies, I observed an amputation of the leg, but at the dispensary we performed only the most rudimentary interventions." She did not add that she had been forbidden to enter the surgery rooms of Chicago's hospitals. "We lacked anesthesia, sir."

Surgery was as old as the hills, but until recently anesthesia had consisted of a swallow of brandy and four strong men. Cutting into the body to heal it required nothing so much as time, but precious little could be accomplished before even a thoroughly inebriated patient demanded a halt to the proceedings. By the time Rose was degreed in 1858, Queen Victoria had delivered her eighth and ninth children under the twilight of chloroform. Society had objected, committed as it was to the biblical imperative of female suffering, but if the Queen's soul was on her subjects' lips, physicians everywhere had thanked God for the advent of safe and effective anesthesia. Still, its administration was not a skill one learned from a book.

"We haven't that difficulty here," the general said. "The Sanitary Commission keeps us generously in ether and chloroform both." He leaned toward her, his eyes narrowed. "You're not one of those suffragists, are you?" he said. "We have enough on our hands."

"I hardly see that it matters, sir. With respect."

"Well, we don't need suffragists, but we do need nurses."

"I remind you, sir, I wish to serve as a surgeon."

The general's voice rose in pitch, as if he was speaking to a child. "I fear your enthusiasm leads you beyond your capacities, my dear. An army surgery is too hard a place for a woman, even a doctoress. I have three daughters of my own. I know what your sex can endure and what it cannot."

Rose realized now it was not she who stood before him but his daughters. She must make him imagine of her what he could not imagine of them. "I have attended many challenging births," she said, "which, although not the exact equivalent I admit, do require a high degree of professional judgment and tolerance. I can place stitches and remove buckshot. I have set two compound fractures; one survived. I am familiar with the stages of suppuration and the *materia medica*. I wish only to serve and further my skills, sir."

The general rubbed his eyes as if to push them out the back of his head. "The surgeons will not accept it. I am sorry." His voice had lost its sugary tone.

At last they had reached the truth. Rose had expected this, but she would not withdraw until every corner was explored. "Can you not order it, sir?"

"I am protecting you from your own folly," he sighed. "However, as you seem intent on serving, I have a hospital ship in Memphis that recently has lost half its lady nurses to cholera. The matron there is hollering for help."

She had erred in wearing the satin; black linen would have lessened her handicap, but it was too late now. She looked through a window to the pasture and fields beyond. A sea of soldiers milled about. Hundreds of horses nervously trampled the soil to dust in makeshift corrals. An American flag hung limp as if defeated in the rising waves of heat. She would not let an uninformed man determine her fate, not again. "I prefer to work in a surgery, sir."

The general struck the desk with his fist. Rose jumped. "The army has no obligation to school you, young lady!" he thundered. "We are at war. We do not need lady surgeons. We need lady nurses. To my eye, you would make a fine one, if you would but yield to the role!"

Rose did not shrink from his outburst. Her dispensary had been shuttered by men far more dangerous, more devious, than this common general, who seemed to wear his heart on his sleeve. But clearly he was not a man who embraced the new, the unfamiliar. If she agreed to his terms, she would at least be near a surgery. She could learn to care for wounds and watch firsthand as they healed—or failed to heal. Who knew what opportunities might arise? Perhaps a more forward-thinking man would apprentice her. She did not need General Temple's permission.

"I've no desire to antagonize you, sir," she said. "If nursing is the proficiency the Union requires of me at this time, I agree to the assignment."

"Bully!" the general exclaimed, rising and extending a hand across his desk. Rose did not take it quite yet, however.

"Might I inquire regarding the contract, sir?"

The general sank back into his chair. "Most of our nurses are volunteers, Miss Barnett."

"I am not a person of means, but I will accept a contract of twelve dollars per month. I believe that is what is paid to nurses—those who are paid."

The general rearranged his trousers again. "You know how to irritate a man, Miss Barnett. Just how can I help you?"

Rose suppressed a smile. "I am offering you my services as a nurse for twelve dollars per month," she said. "It seems a miserly sum for what is at stake, but I understand the Union's resources are thinly stretched."

The general sighed. "It seems you cannot be fooled," he said. "Twelve dollars it is."

"We are agreed," Rose said, rising and extending her hand. "Of course I shall employ my education whenever it obtains, sir. I should think Mr. Lincoln would be grateful to have one with greater training nursing his boys. No disrespect to the president, sir."

"None shall be conveyed," the general said, taking up his pen and scratching out their agreement. "I have no doubt your schooling will inform your efforts at every turn. I am also quite certain that your countenance will work wonders beyond what you imagine." He blotted the orders. "Captain Bayley with Company B will deliver you to the river. He heads south in an hour. Report to the cook." He pointed toward the camp at the edge of the pasture and handed her the document. "These are called orders. Don't lose them."

"Yes, sir."

"And one last thing, Miss Barnett."

"Sir?"

"You are a picture, but you will follow Miss Dix's parameters. Brown or black, and none of that hoop nonsense. A young man is easily moved."

"Thank you, sir. I shall have no difficulty complying."

"Good. Now leave me to my day. Boys are dying."

Near the stairs, Rose found a sewing room. She stepped inside, locked the door, and removed the green satin dress. She loosened her corset, took a deep breath, and slipped her dispensary dress over her head. Its soft, familiar shape brought a smile to her lips. She had long ago given up hoops. Except for their cooling effect in summer, the contraptions were impractical and, worse, degrading. They made it hard for a woman to be useful, let alone move about a medical dispensary.

Nevertheless, she could see why gentlemen were charmed by women who seemed to float on air. She enjoyed the illusion herself.

Her medical kit in one hand and valise in the other, she crossed the field behind the general's headquarters and approached a young soldier near the stable. "Can you show me to the Company B cook, sir?"

"Yes, ma'am, that I could do." The young man removed his drooping forage cap and repeated, "Yes, ma'am." He grinned from ear to ear but did not move.

"The cook?" Rose repeated.

"Oh, yes, ma'am. Follow me." He slapped his hat against his thigh as he tramped toward a cluster of tents upwind of the stables.

"Cookie!" he shouted. "You gotta see this." Turning to Rose, he said, "Sorry, ma'am, that don't sound good. I don't mean it. I mean, you, well…"

"I understand," Rose replied. "Is this the cook, then?" A portly man in a thin cotton shirt and blue woolen pants came from behind a tent, buttoning his fly.

"Yes, ma'am, that's him. Look, Cookie, ain't she fine?"

The cook had a boyish look with a round face and pink cheeks. The skin on his neck, dark red and glistening with sweat, reminded Rose of the bloody roast beef her aunts served each Christmas dinner.

"Git," the cook said.

The soldier gave Rose an up-and-down look before turning to go. At ten paces, he glanced over his shoulder and shook his head. "Damn," he said.

"Scuse Corporal Holt, ma'am. We've been a long time not seeing a female."

Rose gave a tight smile as the cook conducted his own scan of her person. "You'd be the nurse I heard about a whole one minute ago," he said, "now that we're just about packed up?"

"Yes, sir," she said. "General Temple said…" She heard pleading in her voice, a habit from childhood. She began again. "My orders are to join you to the Ohio, sir, where I will meet"—she pulled her papers from her apron pocket—"the USS *Redhawk*, sir, for transport to Memphis." Her hands shook as she held the orders out for the cook to examine. Was this how it was done?

He glanced at the papers and handed them back. "Let's get some things straight, me and you."

A slight lump rose in her throat as she retook her orders—proof of her purpose, her belonging—and slid them back into her pocket. Although mere words on paper, they already felt like a loyal friend. "I imagined some parameters might apply," she said.

"Don't know about that, but I know what I can tolerate and what I can't," he said.

"And what is intolerable to you, sir?"

"I will not be held back. These boys get hungry, and it's my job to feed them. You can set your watch by my comings and goings. I expect you to keep up."

"I will do my best, sir. It is but one day to the river, is it not?"

"One day or one hundred days, I won't be held back."

"No, sir, you shall not be delayed on my account."

"You'll be in the pantry, I guess. Come on." He led Rose around his tent. "Watch your step, ma'am," he said. He had used a small ditch as his latrine. In attempting to jump across, Rose lost her footing and fell, one hand landing an inch from his most recent deposit.

"Now that's what I mean," the cook said. "That's gonna put us behind."

"No, it shan't, sir," she said, scrambling to her feet and grabbing her cases.

The cook, blushing to his roots, mumbled apologies.

The pantry wagon was situated beneath an ancient white ash, its graceful branches and dappled shade offering the only absolution from the sultry day. The wagon was high sided and covered with a dingy canvas top. Tracings for six mules lay before it. Beside it stood boxes and bags of stores. Rose looked inside the wagon; already it seemed full.

"All this," she said, waving her arm at the supplies, "goes in there?"

"Yes, ma'am. All that and you, I'm told."

"You must have a system by now," she said.

"Yes, ma'am, except for the conveying of passengers. That will be a new challenge."

Although she wished to help, Rose stood aside. She studied the men as they loaded the wagon, the cook barking orders, younger men bragging and bullying, teasing each other, no doubt in exaggerated spirit due to her presence. She came from a world of women, a place of communion that, though often soiled with gossip and pettiness, she understood to its core. The world of men, with its winners and losers, confounded her.

An hour later, Rose sat on an immense bag of rice in the covered wagon, wedged among boxes of tinned peaches, hardtack, coffee, and smoked oysters. Pots and pans hung from the cart's frame, making what she judged to be an unwise and unnecessary racket. Otherwise, the wagon was a marvel of organization and order.

Rose appreciated order. Raised in western New York, she had spent her youth in scripturally dictated routine and self-denial. Her mother had died four days after giving birth to her. Her father, refusing to relinquish her even to his childless sister in Ohio, had fixed a leather sling between the wings of his plow and strapped in baby Rose with strips of homespun. There she rocked to the rhythms of the mule and the sound of hymns in her father's throat. The smells of her early years were still with her—manure, her father's sweat, the smell of rain on ready wheat. Even now the scents could trigger a rising in her gut strong enough at times to bring tears.

Rose could not recall her father's face, but she remembered the red stain on his shirt the day he coughed up blood. She was four. When she touched the wet spot, he shooed her away and she ran, stopping only at the neighbors' house a mile away. This, she knew, would anger him, as these people were unrepentant encroachers, each fall plowing an inch or two farther into their common road, enlarging themselves at her father's expense. Still, she ran there, and the wife came.

Once her father saw his blood on his child's hand, he lay down and did not rise again. The sister in Ohio having died by now in childbirth, two unmarried aunts were sent from Syracuse to care for Rose and her meager assets. Just fourteen and fifteen themselves, the sisters put Rose's father in the ground and sold the wheat land to the encroachers. They kept the house and a few acres behind the barn for a truck garden. They exchanged the mule for two buckboard ponies, which would have been about right in Rose's dead father's estimation, given the general worth of mules to horses. They ran chickens for eggs and kept a cow for milk. They observed the Sabbath and made certain Rose was schooled.

Neither woman ever married, a failure for which Rose often felt accountable. Both Grace and Fidelia enlisted in the holy wars against drink and slavery, although the suffrage movement, with its troubling social implications, did not enjoy their devotion. The weekly mail brought progressive newspapers and pamphlets into their home, with poems and essays and startling illustrations. Rose kept a handful of pamphlets under her mattress to read on Sunday afternoons when she should have been memorizing Scripture. What she read confused her, but the drawings of drunken gentlemen and half-naked slaves excited her in a way she neither understood nor resisted.

On one occasion they traveled to Rochester to hear an escaped slave tell his story. He was the first person of dark skin Rose had ever seen, other than the drawings in the pamphlets. His tales seemed fantastical until he turned around and removed his shirt. From the back of the lyceum, she could not actually see the scars, but she heard about them later. Several ladies had to be carried out.

The wagon stopped. A light rain was falling. The acidic odor of smoke stung Rose's nostrils. She slid to the rear of the wagon and peered out. A home had been burned; only its mud-brick chimney still stood. Chickens clucked stupidly in the steaming ashes. "Rebs," the cook called back to Rose. "Bastards all the way to Ohio by now." He shook his head and slapped the reigns. As Rose watched the ruined farmhouse recede into the distance, the taste of bile rose in her throat. She recalled General Temple's remark that she would be afraid.

The wagons halted again ten minutes later at the center of a small town. People were gathered near the smoking remains of what seemed to be the local bank. Rose dislodged her medical bag from between stacks of tinned oysters and climbed down from the wagon. She approached a group of men speaking to a Union officer.

"They was eight, ten times our number, Captain, but we sent them packing," one man was saying. There was nodding all around.

"I saw the evidence," the captain said, "north of here." Several men took to examining their boots. Keeping the fight on Southern soil was the cornerstone of Union strategy; everyone knew that. "I see they have relieved the bank of its burden as well," he added. He seemed to enjoy driving home the inadequacy of this hapless local militia.

"Excuse me, Captain," Rose said.

"What?" he barked, still glaring at the chastened home guards.

A man with a bandaged hand spoke to Rose. "Are you a nurse, ma'am? We've got a hurt boy. It's bad. Rebs chased his pa into the street, and he followed. They both got cut down. Pa died. The doc come up from Thurston, but the boy is pretty low."

The man pointed to a wood-framed house with a small garden beside it. Rose thanked him and went to the open door. Inside a woman knelt beside a kitchen fireplace, stirring rags in a cauldron of steaming, rust-colored water. A girl of about eight bounced a crying baby as two younger boys added wood to a thick carpet of orange coals. Even from outside, Rose could feel the heat of the fire. The woman stood, lifted the pot, and hefted the vessel into the coals. Embers flew, one landing on her dress. She brushed it off and wiped her forehead on her sleeve. Her shirt clung to her shoulders and chest above her corset. Trickles of sweat ran from her hairline. Her chestnut hair had once held a French braid, but now it had fallen into a jumble of knots that clung to her neck. When Rose knocked, the woman jumped and spun around, holding out the wet stick she had been using to stir the pot of rags. With a jerk of her head, she ordered the children to her side.

"Who are you?" she demanded. "What do you want? Git. Git." She waved the stick at Rose.

"I am a doctor, ma'am."

"That's a lie. Ain't no lady sawbones. That's a lie. You're reb." She raised the stick above her head. "Git."

"Ma, she's a lady," the girl shouted over the crying baby in her arms.

"I see that, June Louise. I ain't blind."

"Ma, if she ain't a reb, she can help Jimmy."

"And if she is?" The mother raised the stick higher. Her throat produced an animal's growl. "What if she is a reb?" she said, advancing toward Rose.

"Ma! She ain't no reb!" The little girl pulled on her mother's skirt, and the woman stopped advancing, but she did not lower the stick.

"We already had us a sawbones," she said. "Didn't do Jimmy no good to my mind."

"Ma, let her take a look at him," the girl said. "Can't hurt none."

"Sure as hell can," said the mother. She dropped the stick and fell to her knees weeping. "It can hurt. It can." Her children stepped away in silent witness. The baby on her sister's hip was the only one to reach out in response to her mother's grief. The woman's eyes scoured the room as if perhaps God would step through the ceiling and hear her appeal directly, then and there.

"Come on," the girl said to Rose, shifting the baby to her other hip. "He's upstairs." Rose stepped past the fallen mother and followed the girl down a short hallway. When the child opened the door to a steep flight of stairs, a stench engulfed them. Rose gagged and turned her head away.

"You get used to it," the girl said. She cocked her face toward the ceiling and shouted, "I'm bringing a lady up, Jimbo. Cover up."

Rose followed her toward the open-trussed attic, the heat and odor worsening as they climbed the stairs. At the top was a tiny room with a single window held open with a stick. Slices of blue sky showed through holes in the attic's roof that must have made it a frosty place in winter. With today's heat and humidity, the room was a different kind of unbearable.

A young man, naked but for a bandana draped over his developing manhood, lay on a blood-soaked mattress. Both of his legs were gone. Rose knelt at the foot of the mattress. She was careful to look only at the boy's face, not only to save him embarrassment but to give herself time to consider what her eyes had just seen. His face was on its way to handsome. His chin was square, and he had large brown eyes with remarkably long lashes. His skin was pimpled but not so badly that it would scar. He had only shaved a few times, she guessed, probably to polish up for church.

"You brought a lady up here?" the boy shouted at his little sister. He turned to Rose. "Who are you?" he demanded, placing his hands over the bandana.

She smiled at him, careful to keep her eyes on his face. She wondered if he had a sweetheart.

The girl spoke. "Jimmy, this here's a lady doctor. She can fix your legs."

"Git out. Git her out of here," he shouted.

"Are you Jimmy?" Rose asked, sitting back on her heels. He turned his head away. Now she looked down at the two oozing wounds. His right leg was a stump that ended about eight inches from his hip joint, but his left was nothing more than the socket of the hip itself. A flap of skin covered the leg stump, but the hip injury was still open, exuding corrosive fluids. The skin around it was gray. This putrefaction explained the dreadful odor.

She could see the blood still pumping in the open wound, swelling the femoral artery the surgeon had tied off, bleeding a little with every pump of the boy's heart. The fact that he was alive caused her a moment of panic, but when she realized he would, in fact, die—that she could not save him—her calm returned.

"It is very hot up here," she said. The girl was standing next to her. Rose looked up at her. "Can you bring us some water?" she asked. "And what is your name, honey?"

"June Louise," the girl said, bumping her hip in a rhythm against Rose's shoulder, making contact. "I go by Luey with most folks."

"May I call you Luey?"

"S'pose."

"Then can you please bring us each a cup of water, Luey?"

"I suppose so," the girl said. She did not move to leave Rose's side, but continued to rock against Rose's shoulder.

"You will not miss a thing," Rose said, "I promise. Just bring us that water right away, all right?" Rose put her arm around the girl and gently rubbed her back. "Be careful on the stairs."

"You sound like my ma." Luey turned, and with the baby still on her hip, she raced down the stairs as if Rose had asked for a demonstration of the most dangerous way she could possibly descend a set of steps.

"June Louise," her brother scolded, "you slow yourself down this minute!"

The door slammed in response.

Rose stood and stepped to the side of the bed. The boy did not turn away from her now but closed his eyes. His hands shook, holding down the bandana.

"Your little sister is sweet, but I cannot fix your legs," she said. "I am afraid they are gone for good."

The boy opened his eyes, but did not look up at Rose. "Tell me something I ain't already figured out."

"How about if we get you out of this attic?"

"How's that gonna fix them?"

"I thought we were agreed they cannot be repaired."

"What are you doing here, anyway? Doc already seen to me best he could." At last he looked at her, but he quickly glanced away again.

"I thought I might help you get settled. See if I can make those wounds a little more comfortable. Maybe help your ma out a bit. She seems worn thin."

"Don't you think I know that?" He began to cry. "It's my fault for running into the open. Pa told me not to, but I did it anyway."

Rose moved to the window. "There may be a storm today," she said. "Perhaps we will get some rain to cool things off." She turned back to the boy. He was wiping his nose on his hand and rubbing it on the mattress. "Sometimes," she said, "we do what comes naturally, even if it is not safe. You loved your pa."

"Well, lest you can turn a clock back and undo my foolishness, you might as well go on, get out of here," he said.

Rose knelt beside him and took a deep breath. Just a boy, he had made a terrible sacrifice. Perhaps it would help to make the small accommodation of formal address. "If you will allow me, sir," she said, "I believe I can lessen your suffering."

He steadied his eyes on hers for the first time. "I'm so hot," he pleaded.

"Yes, that is why I have ordered water. And if I may inquire, how is it that you are in this furnace of an attic?" Looking at the steep, narrow staircase, she asked, "How did you ever get up here?"

He shrugged. "Just woke up here. Guess ma knew I was going to stink to high heaven and told the boys to put me out of the way." He paused. "Rebs killed my pa." He began to cry again. "Sorry, ma'am."

"You must be heartsick from the loss of your father and your legs in the same day."

"It was just us home guards. Seemed like thousands of Johnnies."

"So I heard. You put a scare in them, though. I hear they skedaddled clear to Ohio."

"Yes, ma'am, they did. We did, we scared 'em."

"Mr. Lincoln will be glad to hear of it."

At last a smile parted his lips, and Rose felt there was hope for his spirits if not his body.

Luey was coming up the stairs with two cups of water and still carrying the baby. Rose wondered if the girl ever had a moment to read or play.

"Can you sit up?" Rose asked the boy. He could not sit fully upright; the amputation at his hip was too extreme, but there was benefit in asking something of him, even a small thing—benefit and respect in asking him to try. "Just a little," she said. "You can lay flat again after you drink." As she might lift a laboring woman, she slid her arm behind his back and grasped him under his wet armpit. She did not ask him to rise yet, giving him time to accept her arm there. His covering shifted, and he grabbed at it, groaning with the pain of even this slight movement. Rose looked away as he reordered things. When she felt he was settled, she signaled through a slight tug that it was time to sit.

"Just a little at a time," she said. With her other hand she folded his pillow in half and placed it below his shoulder blades. "How is that?"

He winced. "Well, ma'am, it don't feel any better yet, if I'm to be honest about it."

"No, I do not expect it to, but can you drink?" She gave him one of the cups, and he gulped it down in one single swallow. Rose longed to drink the second cup herself but instead handed it to him.

"Sips," she said. "You don't want to lose your breakfast over a cup of water."

"No, ma'am. I wouldn't want that. Not in front of you, leastways," he said.

Rose stayed with the family for two days. Neighbors moved the boy to a bed in the parlor from which he could see the garden. A sheet was hung for privacy. "You must leave the windows open, even if it rains," Rose told the mother and Luey. "The air must fully exchange every two hours."

She showed them how to flush the hip with tepid tea twice a day, pack it with charcoal and bind it gently against agents that might enter from the air. In the coming days he would develop a fever, become delirious and die. She left a three-day supply of laudanum, which would take him to the end. At least in the parlor he would be near his family and God's verdant earth. Perhaps there he might lift his head, however briefly, and feel pride rather than shame.

Chapter 2

Jimmy's cousin carried Rose by buckboard to a muddy spot on the Ohio River. A passing transport would take her to Memphis. Her driver was a sullen young man, or perhaps he was just frightened after what he had seen with his cousin. Only fifteen, he was safe from the draft for now, but what kind of pressure must be on him to enlist? He was not about to tell her, a stranger, and so they rode in silence to the river.

A ship was waiting. "Thank you for the safe delivery," Rose said as she climbed down from the wagon.

"Yep," the young man replied, slapping the reins against the horses' backs and turning them toward home.

The small landing was crowded with sailors. Some were bathing in the river; others played cards or napped. Most wore blue trousers, cut wide at the hem, and loose blouses with large, square collars that fell to their shoulder blades in back. Several stood at attention when Rose stepped among them. A very tall man greeted her. "Been expecting you, ma'am, if you be the nurse we were told to stop for."

"I am the nurse, yes," Rose said, the words feeling odd on her tongue.

"Let's get you aboard, then. Captain Mayden," he said, extending his hand in greeting. "And this lovely lady," he said, pointing toward the ship with his other hand, "is the USS *Redhawk*. She was the *Belinda*, but that wouldn't put much scare in the rebs, now, would it? Welcome aboard."

The ship, including its rear paddle wheel, was fully encased by steel plates. It rode low in the water, reminding Rose of the water skippers that had skimmed across the pond behind her family's barn. Two smokestacks framed the bow of the ship, their once gilded crowns now cracked and blackened with soot. Two simple steam pipes rose from the stern. Rose thought the huge front stacks only made the ship a better target, but embers had to go somewhere.

Captain Mayden led her to a sodden wood plank that extended from the muddy shore to an opening near the stern wheel. He offered his hand, but Rose could not take it, as her hands were full with her medical case, clothing satchel, skirt, and petticoats. The captain put two fingers to his mouth and produced a sharp whistle that brought forth several curious sailors. "Assist the lady," he ordered, and Rose felt her bags being whisked from her hands. She would have liked to keep the medical case, with its textbooks, laudanum drops, and opium powder, but it was too late now. She offered a hand and a tight smile to the captain, who led her up the plank to the ship where he began a leisurely stroll through the stifling enclosure of the main deck. The only light and fresh air beneath the cladding came through the side batteries where a dozen cannon circled the ship like chubby girls waiting to be asked to dance. The passages were low. Rose noticed the captain's forehead bore scabs and scars that testified either to forgetfulness or urgency.

The captain recited the ship's technical specifications like a husband boasting of his wife's endowments. After a half day's journey, Rose was exhausted. Feigning interest in the steam capacity and firepower of this seemingly ordinary vessel stretched her patience, but she gamely pressed on with enthusiastic throat noises, furrowed brow, and the occasional nod and smile. At last the captain led her into the fresh air of the top deck. A canvas roof provided shade from the sun. Sailors leaned against the gunwale, laughing, their eyes on Rose. The captain stopped beside what looked like a pair of cellar doors. He leaned over and, with a grunt, opened them to reveal a dark space below that indeed looked much like the root cellar she had known in her youth. Instead of the scent of fresh earth, however, the unmistakable perfume of urine floated up the short set of stairs. Two wooden planks hung by chains from opposite walls. One held a thin, torn mattress, moldy straw escaping from a hole in its striped ticking. On the other plank Rose saw a lantern and her two satchels.

"There're no windows, ma'am," said the captain. "You'll want to light that lantern there before I close you up. There're lucifers there." Next to the lantern lay a strip of wooden matches resembling a comb with missing teeth.

It was not yet dark, but Rose's body demanded sleep. She stepped down into the narrow space between the planks. The room was surprisingly cool despite the thickness of its air. She lit the lantern and said good night to the captain as he lowered the doors over her head. A bullet hole in one of the doors glowed like a tiny star. When she discovered a thunder mug beneath one of the beds, she realized she had forgotten to use the privy. Nor had she eaten since breakfast. Her stomach growled, but sleep would have to solve the problem.

She turned her back to the stairs and began unbuttoning her shirt. Glancing over her shoulder, she noticed that the bullet hole had gone dark. She was about to blow out the lantern when she heard a shout from the captain and a scuffling of feet. Keeping an eye on the hole, she pulled off her skirt and petticoats and removed her shirt and corset, followed by her chemise. She ran her hands up and over her breasts, relishing—as her friend, Chloe, had once remarked—their release from captivity. She dropped her nightgown over her head, then lowered her drawers, positioned the mug between her legs, and relieved herself. She replaced the cork and rolled it under the bed, then collapsed onto the straw mattress and, despite the fleeting thought that she might be in a quarantine cabin, let sleep take her.

She dreamed she was a slave. She had run off, and she knew, with that utter certitude that is the special province of dreams, that she would never run again, but would die an old woman, alone in an unheated hut, bent and hungry, her children and grandchildren and great-grandchildren sold off, every one. A faceless man whipped her naked back while with his other hand he gripped a child, her daughter, by her tiny arm. When the girl cried, the man shook her, saying, "Lookee there, child. You lookee." The scene changed. Now Rose was the child. The man's black, grimy fingernails dug into the flesh of her arm. The woman under the lash was her mother.

Rose woke, whimpering. Tears covered her face and pillow. The dream pulled at her. She wiped her eyes on the sleeve of her nightgown and sat up, shaking her head to dislodge the frightening images.

The bullet hole was bright, but she did not know if she had slept for a few moments or into the next day. The cabin had grown hot and damp. She lit the lantern and surveyed her dismal surroundings. One more night here would be plenty. She used the mug again, the smell of her own urine now filling the room.

A knock on the cabin door startled her. "Ma'am?" a young male voice called. "It's past noon, ma'am. Cap'n says to let you know."

Rose called back, "Yes, of course. I had no idea of the hour. I shall be out in five minutes."

"Cap'n says not to rush," the voice called back. "There's washing things here."

Without the cue of dawn to wake her, her body had taken the sleep it needed. She lifted the cabin door a crack and found a washbasin with cold water, a bar of gray soap, and a small rag. Taking them inside, she washed and then brushed her hair for the first time in days, the bristles of the brush against her scalp causing her skin to rise in gooseflesh. She tied her hair into a tight knot even though the austere treatment made the beauty of her evenly featured face all the more apparent. She pulled on her stockings, chemise and corset, petticoats, skirt, blouse, and apron. As she stepped out of her cabin, she felt a drip of sweat roll down the small of her back.

At some point in the night, they had gotten underway. They were in the center of a wide river. Rose had never been so far from land. The air smelled of smoke from the stacks, but the breeze from the moving ship felt glorious on her face. She walked to the steel dome that sheltered the officers' dining room, or "mess," as the captain had called it. Inside, a black man in civilian clothes and apron stood next to a cooking stove, a dishrag over his shoulder. With its protective cladding, the room was dark, lit only by lanterns and a narrow shaft of light that entered through the door.

"Good morning," she said.

"Ma'am."

"I appear to have slept through my breakfast and perhaps my lunch as well."

"Yes, ma'am. That you did, both. I got some lunch coffee left over here. Can I pour you some?"

"Please," she said. "Sleeping in that room, I had no idea it was so late in the day."

"You in the quarantine," he said.

"It seems so, yes." Her fleeting worry from the prior night now blossomed into a list of contagions to which the room might be host.

"That's a tight spot, all right. But you can no doubt get rested there."

"You have slept there?"

"Yes, ma'am. Most all of us been in the quarantine, one time or another."

Rose considered his statement and granted, "Disease does spread on a ship."

"Oh no, ma'am. The quarantine, mostly it's for sleeping off."

"I see. Well, I suppose that is good to hear," said Rose. She might rest easier tonight knowing that what lurked in the mattress was nothing worse than the common scourge of intemperance, to which she was certain she was immune.

"May I request something to eat?" she asked. "Cereal is fine."

"Well, you're in luck. No grits today, but I make a fine barley porridge."

"Yes, he does." The captain was standing behind her, so close that she jumped when he spoke. "I trust you are rested?"

"Yes, thank you. I had no idea of the time."

"Happens in that cabin."

"Well, I should like to be helpful to you today, sir," she said, "in consideration of the transport. Is there anything I can do for your men?"

As the cook set a bowl of stiff, cold cereal on the table, she and the captain took seats opposite each other. He rubbed his whiskered chin.

"Some of my boys got the clap," he said, looking evenly into Rose's eyes.

"I can examine them," she said, cutting the porridge with her spoon. "And how do you suppose they got the clap?" she asked as she took the cereal into her mouth and furrowed her brow in feigned concern.

"Well, I reckon they're just men being boys, or vice-ah-versa." The captain tipped his chair back, still looking at Rose.

"Do you have the clap, sir?" Rose returned his stare, as blank-faced as she could manage. She hated these conversations. Sometimes her patients' husbands had made similar remarks, usually while the wife was in the dressing room.

"Are you offering to take care of me?" The captain grinned.

"The treatment is not nearly as pleasant as the acquisition of the disease, sir, if you take my meaning. Most men bear it poorly, in fact."

"So I've heard," he said. He let down his chair. "No, I don't have the clap. As for my boys, we'll wait for Memphis to take care of them. I won't object to you offering a hand with a range of other complaints, though, long as you're here."

"All right, then, let's get started." Rose followed her last bite of barley with a gulp of coffee, glad the test was over.

When the captain announced that the lady nurse would see patients in the mess, a line formed on the top deck. She surmised that they came more for the spectacle than for medical care, and so she decided to walk the length of the line and pull out those actually in need. This way, every soldier would get a little feminine attention and those needing care would not have to wait behind the merely curious.

She was about halfway down the line, having sent three men inside, when she felt something tickle her forehead. She brushed away what she thought was an insect before she heard the sound of the gunshot. The men scattered like birds from a fence. Someone pushed her to the deck. "Git down, ma'am. Rebs are acting up today." A sailor fell next to her. He was shot through the neck. She recognized him. He had been next in line, and they had exchanged pleasantries. She had doubted he needed medical attention. He just wanted to look at her. Now a bullet had turned him from curious boy to a mother's grief. His heart, not yet knowing the situation, continued its work. Blood poured from the hole in his neck in rapid bursts. Rose placed her hand on the wound, but could only slow the inevitable, which came quickly. She had seen people die before, but this was her first death by gunshot. Except for the hole in his neck, the man was perfectly well. She was reminded of anatomy lab when the dead girl she had relieved of her fatal tumor had failed to rise. The racket of gunshots woke her from her daydream. An explosion rocked the boat and was followed by a cheer from below. Rose crawled to the gunwale and peered through a bullet hole. Sinking in the distance were the remains of a small fishing boat. It was upside down; three bodies floated in the water. They were dressed like farmers, not soldiers, and Rose wondered why they had so brazenly attacked the large ship. Yet she knew personally that they had fired the first shot. She touched her forehead and felt a crust of blood.

The captain called her from across the deck. Instinctively she stood to go to him, but he shouted, "Get down, ma'am!" She collapsed where she stood and crawled to him, climbing over another dead soldier and a man with a bleeding shoulder, her knees tangling in her skirt. A bullet had lodged in the palm of the captain's right hand as if he had reached out to catch it. The wound was ugly but not life threatening if cleaned soon.

"Damn guerillas," he cursed. Rose realized it had been foolish to line up the men on the open deck and that the captain knew this. Her presence on the ship had cost two men their lives. She felt dizzy and sick. She crawled away from the captain as she felt her breakfast coming up. He said nothing, for which she was grateful. She wiped her mouth on her apron and crawled back to sit beside the captain.

"Are there more?" she asked. "More guerillas?"

"There are always guerillas," he said, sounding weary. "Look, ma'am. Don't think that was your fault. They'd have shot us up regardless."

Rose smiled at his kindness. "A man near the officer's mess has died," she said, "and I saw another near the stack. One man has a wounded shoulder I can attend to. And there is your hand."

"Let's get the shoulder downstairs," he said, whistling for his men.

"My supplies are in my cabin," Rose said.

"Then get them," he replied.

Relieved to have a clear order, Rose crept across the deck to her cabin. As she struggled with the heavy doors, she imagined that a sniper might find satisfaction in putting a bullet through a Yankee woman, but no bullet came. She slid down the stairs and pulled her medical kit from under the bed. Reaching between her legs, she gathered the back of her skirt, pulled it forward, and tucked it into her waistband. She left the cabin, crossed the deck on all fours, and took the ladder to the deck below.

The man with the shoulder wound lay on a table, drinking from a flask of liquor. As Rose approached him, he attempted to smile, but fear showed in his wide eyes. She asked for lanterns and motioned for several men to stand near the table. Opening her kit, she removed a pair of tweezers, scissors, and a strand of horsehair. The man's eyes grew even larger, and his feet pushed against the table as if to escape. His friends held his legs, and the largest of them wrapped a muscled arm about his throat.

"Do I smell rum?" Rose asked with an intentional smile. The man nodded and closed his eyes. "I do not normally condone the consumption of intoxicants," she said, "but today I shall make an exception. You may have another swallow if you like. I have opium for the wound, and you may have some laudanum afterward. I am sorry to say the removal of the ball shall be unpleasant. If you are a religious man, you might seek assistance now." He became rigid as Rose bent over his shoulder. When she touched the wound, he cried and pulled away. Rose looked to the others to hold him. "I must probe. I am sorry," she said, and without waiting for permission, she pushed a finger into the wound. A guttural shriek rose from the man's throat, and he struggled against his friends' strong grip. Closing her eyes and feeling about in the wound, Rose imagined the shoulder as it appeared in her textbooks and as she had sketched it in dissection lab. The bone did not seem to be cracked or chipped. "You are lucky today," she said. "Only the flesh is torn. I have found the ball and must remove it." In a single motion, she inserted the tweezers and fished the ball from the soft tissues of his shoulder. He jumped with pain but relaxed and smiled when she held up the bullet for him to see. It was an old-fashioned musket ball, round and harmless, at least compared to the rifled minié ball, which would have tumbled and flattened, likely shattering his shoulder. She took up the man's hand and dropped the souvenir into his palm, closing his fingers around it. "Hold on to that for your grandchildren," she said as she ran her finger again in the track the ball had taken through his shoulder. Something loose and foreign rolled up under the pressure of her finger. With her tweezers she retrieved a wad of his shirt. Had she not found it, the wound would have festered and the patient likely would have died. "The worst is behind you," she said, "but I must do some stitching. After that you may have the laudanum." She threaded a curved needle with the length of horsehair. "He might need another swallow for this," she said to his friend, who put the rum to his lips. She sprinkled opium powder into the wound, pulled the sides together, and took the first stitch. As she did so, the man fainted, dropping the musket ball to the floor. She finished stitching and dressed the wound with a wet cloth. Then she woke him with salts that he might take his laudanum.

Rose stood on the bow of the *Redhawk* as the pilot squeezed the ship onto a crowded Memphis landing at the base of a wide cliff. The captain joined her. "How is your hand?" she asked.

"Good as new," he said. "Had a first-rate surgeon." He smiled. "And you? How is your war wound today?"

Rose touched the scab on her forehead where the bullet had passed. "I shall have something to remember the *Redhawk* by," she said. "A conversation piece."

"And fairly earned," he replied. "Look, there." He pointed to a ship at the north end of the landing. "There she is," he said. "The USS *Despain*, your new home."

The ship, with its giant sidewheel, towered over every other vessel. "It looks twice the size of the *Redhawk*," Rose said.

"That little lady carried a lot of cotton in her day. She's two hundred and forty-nine feet long, has a sixty-seven-foot beam, and rides twenty-seven feet above the water. Plus an extra six feet in the hold. She's a floating warehouse—or was. We snagged her when we got

Memphis." He chuckled. "We took her north, dressed her up like a painted lady, and ran her right back down here. Snugged her up against the landing just to rub their noses in it."

"Was the *Redhawk* in the battle for Memphis?" Rose asked.

"Yes, ma'am. It didn't last long, though. Mostly we carried injured up to Cairo."

Rose had been in Chicago when Memphis fell. The newspapers had described a ninety-minute spectacle of Union ironclad rammers broadsiding Confederate cottonclads, merchant ships reinforced with lengths of timber wrapped in cotton. Rose wondered if the homemade navy had entered the battle out of arrogance or desperation.

"I heard there was a picnic."

"Yes, ma'am. War watching."

Northern papers had mocked the people of Memphis for lunching on the bluff during the battle, but the elite of Washington City had done the same at the first battle of Bull Run. In both cases, the audience had been disappointed. Rose imagined crinolined ladies of both camps weeping into lace gloves as, one by one, they realized that war was neither dress ball nor picnic.

Seeing the ease with which their navy was dispatched, the privileged of Memphis had packed their things and moved inland, leaving some twenty thousand of their neighbors to cope with occupation. When the Yankees came ashore, shops and churches were shuttered. Banks were closed. The wharf was silent. But pragmatists and speculators were quick on the scene, and the city soon reopened. Now the Memphis landing was a chaos of sounds, sights, and smells that reminded Rose of the Haymarket in Chicago.

"That there," the captain was saying, pointing to a massive structure on the bluff, "is Gayoso House."

The building, fronted by six white columns, loomed over the bluff. "It looks like a Greek temple," Rose said.

"Marble bathtubs and full plumbing. Three hundred rooms."

"That's even bigger than the Tremont," Rose said. She only knew of Chicago's Tremont House because Republicans had stayed there when President Lincoln was nominated. She had never set foot in a hotel, even a small one.

"Yep. They say it's the best hotel on the Mississippi, maybe even the country. It's mostly a hospital now, though, and Union headquarters." He turned and pointed to the southern bluff. "And that," he said, "with the stripes and stars, is Fort Pickering. Most of the town of Memphis is up on the hill. This here," he said, waving his arm to indicate the landing area, "is for coming and going, loading and unloading." He pointed to the base of the cliff. "Those benches there, they're for ladies, if you ever want to sit of an evening."

On the dusty flats below, people of every age, dress, and color scurried like characters in a colossal tableau—women and children, beggars, hawkers, businessmen, and soldiers, most in Union blue but some in the gray or butternut of the paroled and oathed former rebel. Horses and mules with clanging tack rattled across the cobblestones. Dogs ran in packs, knocking over small children and startling horses. Steamships emitted shrieking whistles, and stevedores shouted orders at their mostly black laborers loading and unloading ships. A through-road connecting the flats to the top of the bluff carried a steady stream of buckboards, carriages, and pedestrians from town to the landing and back. Bales of cotton, sacks of wheat, and piles of logs waited to be loaded onto the half dozen Union merchant ships tied end-to-end along the muddy shore. Their captains would pilot the ships through guerilla-riddled waters to Northern markets where the Union would turn the goods into cash and the cash into ammunition that, if all went as planned, would find its way into Southern flesh. Six Union ironclads sat offshore ready to serve as escorts.

"Thank you for the transport, Captain," Rose said. "Do not neglect that dressing."

"No, ma'am. Thank you for patching me up," he replied, smiling and saluting her with his bandaged hand.

Moments later Rose stood beside the USS *Despain*. With its three full decks, the vessel looked like a floating hotel. She took a deep breath and, as if in a dream, saw her right foot touch the gangplank, then her left. Her legs pulled her forward until she stood on the deck of the ship.

A voice startled her. "You the lady I been waiting on?" An old man in uniform was walking toward her with a heavy limp. Deep crevices carved his sun-browned face; long tangles of thin, gray hair clung to his skull.

"I suppose so," she said. "Rose Barnett, sir." She handed him her orders.

He glanced at them and handed them back. "I thought they was sending a Virginia."

"My full name is Virginia Rose, sir, but I go by Rose."

"Just as well around here," he said. "Not as bad as Georgia, I suppose. Or South Carolina!" He laughed heartily at his joke.

Rose shared the name Virginia with her late mother and held it close to her heart, like a secret. Her father had not once called her by her first name, so grief-stricken was he at the loss of his wife—or so Rose had been told by her aunts. "And you are?" she asked the man.

"Rooster," he said. He placed his hand next to his mouth as if sharing a secret. His breath smelled of chewing tobacco; his teeth were brown. "I don't use my real handle, neither," he said with a wink.

She managed a slight smile. "And how did you come by *Rooster*?"

He crossed his arms as if he had hoped she would ask. "On Indian patrol one time, we was looking for Black Hawk and we run out of rations and I seen this chicken in the grass. I thought it was a prairie chicken, but there wasn't no flock around it, just one bird. Well, it was some sod farmer's coop rooster, run off. That's better eating any day, so I pulled out my shotgun, but Johnny Sloane, he dared me to get it with my pistol." He placed a hand on his cheek and shook his head. "Back then I could not disregard a dare." He chuckled. "The odds were poor, but I got him dead in the head. We had us a treat that night. No buckshot to break a tooth on, neither. Been Rooster ever since."

"I am glad you did not miss; you would have gone hungry."

"That's the downside of dares, yes, ma'am," Rooster replied. "So, let's get you up and running. You new to all this here?"

"I was baptized by fire on the way down. Guerillas in a fishing boat gave me this," she said, touching the scab on her forehead.

"Johnnie Reb's a bold one, especially them guerillas and bushwhackers. Stubborn, too."

"And your role here, Rooster?"

"Role, ma'am?"

"Your job?"

He threw his shoulders back. "Steward, ma'am. Well, second steward, on account I can't read them Latin words on the remedies, but every other way, I'm steward. Black Hawk himself got a chunk of my leg." He said this as if the Indian bore the blame for his want of Latin. "Can't walk or even ride much, but this here"—he waved his arm at the ship—"it gives me satisfaction. I got ladies under me, and I don't have to shoot Indians no more."

Rose produced a noncommittal hum in her throat, a mannerism she had cultivated for responding to the curious remarks of others. "So, I report to you?" she asked.

"Yes, ma'am." Rooster reached for her bags. Having anticipated the move, Rose held fast to her medical case and handed him her clothing satchel. He led her through a set of glossy blue doors. What she saw made her gasp. Four rows of hospital beds filled with men ran the length of the ship. Varnished wood columns with elaborate capitals supported the ceiling. Insect netting hung over each bed like enormous butterfly wings. Gauze-covered windows kept embers and smoke at bay while admitting a soft, hazy light.

From the walls, hand-painted tin signs ordered: "No Smoking!" "No Swearing!" "Quiet!" Rose doubted the rules were always obeyed, but today at least a quiet hum buzzed in the space. The ward reminded her of a ladies' tearoom she had once visited with her aunts, where she had been scolded for speaking too loudly. She smiled at the memory. "The environment seems sympathetic to healing," she said.

"They don't ask for sympathy, ma'am."

"Of course not. I mean the quiet," Rose replied. "The ward is quiet."

"Mostly," Rooster said. "By the time these boys get here, they're up to their craws in racket."

"How many beds are here?" she asked.

"Almost one hundred this deck, one twenty on third deck," Rooster said, pointing overhead. "Mostly fevers up there. Main deck, this one here, is surgeries."

Rose imagined the vast room filled with bales of cotton loaded floor to ceiling on this deck and two above, below and in the hold, heading for the mills of New England and the ports of New York and

Europe. And this was just one ship. For the first time she grasped the full muscle of Southern agriculture.

"She's got hot and cold water pipes," Rooster said as he began leading her down the corridor, "nine conveniences, six bathing showers, hydraulic hoists fore and aft, and a full laundry with its own boiler, you'll be glad to hear. The surgeons—there's ten of them—they're quartered next to the surgery." He pointed in the distance to a corner that was curtained off near a set of red double doors. "Down one, that's called 'first deck'," Rooster continued. "Sailors and their mess, engine and boilers and such. No sick wards down there. Topside, all the way up, that's Texas deck or top deck; it's for captain and officers and such. They got their mess up there, too. You know what a mess is, ma'am?"

Rose nodded as she struggled to grasp the geography of the massive vessel. "Where were these gentlemen wounded?"

"Vicksburg mostly, and Port Hudson. Some Jackson; we've been in and out of Jackson a few times. The action's been in Mississippi ever since we got Memphis, but it's slowed down since Vicksburg a month ago. We're heading there for another load once these boys get back on their feet. So to speak. I hope you like boat rides."

As she and Rooster walked, she kept her eyes on the red doors beside the surgeons' corner. A few men called out to her, but most lay quietly, doing the work of healing. Some groaned, a few wept. Several read Bibles. Male nurses walked the aisles feeding their patients, changing bandages, and helping them up to the privy. At a table half a dozen men played dominoes. The game stopped as she drew near. "Good day, gentlemen," she said, but while she might otherwise have engaged them, at this moment, she had eyes only for the doors she felt would lead her to the surgery.

As they approached the front of the ship, Rooster pointed to the doors. "This here's the surgery," he said.

Rose's heart raced in anticipation. In a moment she would see her first army surgery.

"Ladies not allowed," Rooster said, "excepting laundresses, a'course."

Rose felt as if she had been slapped. When General Temple had said that surgeons would not accept a woman as one of them, she

34

had not imagined literal, physical exclusion from the surgery. How could nurses assist if banned from this place? Just what would be her role here?

"You want a peek, while it's quiet?" Rooster was saying.

She nodded, grateful to him for stretching the rules. From his pocket he pulled a long leather strap with a key attached. The strap was tethered to his belt. "The boys like their laudanum, ma'am. Lock and key at all times." He unlocked the door and pushed it open. "After you, ma'am."

It would have been a respectable surgery even in a general hospital. The room held twelve wooden tables in two rows of six. At the head of each table stood a rolling cart stocked with the essentials for removing limbs and digging bullets—knives, saws, probes, tourniquets; sewing things; green and amber bottles of chloroform, whiskey, styptics; clay bowls and sponges; glass irrigating syringes; and roll upon roll of bandages, many seeming almost to blush from their pasts as skirts and petticoats.

But this was no ladies' tearoom. The joints and screws of every table showed the black tar of dried blood and human hair and offal. The floor was sticky despite the appearance of having been mopped. Swipe marks showed on the knives and tools that littered the carts. From hooks on the walls hung a dozen bloody leather aprons, some so thickly crusted Rose imagined them standing on their own and performing surgery. Above each hook, surnames had been scratched into the paint—a roll call of surgeons who had served here.

Windows covered with heavy iron mesh offered light and ventilation and at least the illusion of safety from stray bullets. "I know what you're thinking, ma'am," Rooster said. "These here walls are insulated with straw bales and steel plate. The worst thing ever got through these windows was a ember or two." He pointed to half a dozen burn scars on the floor of the surgery. "Ain't no minié balls coming in here, 'cept what the boys bring in, if you know what I mean."

"Thank you, Rooster," she replied. "Hospital ships are not to be fired upon, is that correct?"

"Yes, ma'am, generally. That and these walls keeps it pretty safe around here."

Rose smiled at his eagerness to reassure her. "And where are the surgeons now?" she asked.

"They'd be in town, ma'am."

"That way?" Rose said, pointing to where she thought Memphis lay. She had uncharacteristically lost her sense of direction.

"No, ma'am, town is over there," Rooster replied, pointing the opposite way. "Lots of folks, they get turned round on a ship, but not me, never."

"Apparently I am of the majority, then," said Rose. "And when will the surgeons return?"

"I would say tomorrow morning, maybe the next. Cutting's pretty well done on this batch. Finished up last night."

"I see. What occupies the surgeons in town?"

"Occupies?"

"What are their duties there?"

"Well, they's enjoying the sights and such, ma'am." Rooster cleared his throat.

Rose knew that saloons and places of amusement had spread like lice over Memphis. She could guess what sights were being enjoyed at that moment by the men she hoped would mentor her. "Thank you for showing me the surgery, Rooster. Can you assist me in locating my quarters?"

"Follow me. I'll get you there." As they left the surgery, Rooster made a small ceremony of locking the door behind them. Smiling at Rose, he dropped the key into his pocket and patted it with his hand. Several empty beds stood just outside the surgery in a wide corridor. "This is for coming around," Rooster said.

"Do you mean waking after surgery?"

"Yes, ma'am. Boys need to be watched, coming around. Lots of hurling goes on in here. Somebody's got to be here to catch it."

"And who does that?"

"Well, I got no sense of smell, so I spend a lot of time here. Better me than somebody burdened by it."

He walked to a ladder that led to the deck below. He descended backward then reached upward. "Hand me that satchel, ma'am. Nothing will happen to it, I promise."

The air below was stale and warm. Portholes yielded a feeble light but little ventilation. Rooster lit a lantern, which he swung toward a set of padlocked doors. "Supplies and medicine," he said. "And ice. Also locked. Lock and key!" Across from the storeroom, two small rooms sat opposite each other at the head of a long hallway. Rooster opened the door to the room on their right. "Home sweet home," he said.

The cabin's single porthole opened outward about six inches. Two bunks, an upper and a lower, hung from the wall. Each bed had a thin mattress covered with a blue wool blanket. The lower bunk possessed a pillow in a case embroidered with the words *He maketh me to lie down in green pastures*. Rose wondered how far from home this other nurse was and how long it would take to become friends.

Half a dozen hooks for clothing were screwed into the wall. Two wooden crates sat beneath them, one empty, the other filled with a woman's things. A wood shingle, perhaps meant as a writing surface, had been nailed to the wall beneath the porthole. It was small but perhaps, Rose thought, could hold a cup of wildflowers.

"Lock's good and sturdy," Rooster said, pointing to a slide that looked anything but solid should a burly shoulder decide to challenge it.

"Thank you, Rooster," she said as he placed her bags on the upper bunk. "Where might the others be at this hour?"

"Washin', I suppose."

"Why don't you take me to them so I can be of assistance?" Although she was bone tired, she wished to make an agreeable first impression with the group. She was uneasy about leaving her medical case behind, but if medication was stolen from a nurse's cabin, then it would just have to be a lesson hard-learned, as her Aunt Fidelia used to say.

They began to walk the long hall toward the back of the ship. Rooster opened the door to a room that held a furnace, engine, and boilers. "Gets noisy down here when we're running," he shouted, even though all was quiet. An immense rod connected the engine to the still paddlewheel. Two men sat twenty feet up on the paddle, making repairs. Others stacked wood near the furnace.

On the other side of the walkway, Rooster pointed to a long, narrow space with an opening but no door. "Sailors' quarters," Rooster said. Rose glanced inside and saw dozens of hammocks suspended in racks of three the entire length and width of the space. A few sailors swung in their beds. Some whistled. Across the way, in a dining hall, a handful of men played cards; a few read letters or books. To a man, they raised their heads and stared as she passed.

At the end of the hallway, three tall steps rose to a swinging door. Rooster helped Rose up and pushed open the door to an outer deck. "Ladies first," he said. Eager for fresh air, Rose breathed deeply only to be met by the distinctive odor of blood-soaked steam. They had entered a laundry. She should have known. The need for clean linens at war would be extraordinary. She had not considered this component of the work and felt a brief sense of despair at the thought of spending her days in this place, at this labor. At the dispensary, she and Chloe had washed bandages and sheets on Sundays after service. It had been an all-day chore that neither of them enjoyed. She hoped her turn in the ship's laundry would not come more than once a week.

A narrow canvas fly lent a strip of shade to the area near the door. The rest of the deck stood open to a white-hot sky. A spider's web of wires stretched over two thirds of the space, holding sheets, bandages, and tunics. A string of long, silver wash troughs ran around the perimeter of the deck. Beside each sink were buckets of sand for grinding stains.

A woman sat cross-legged by the first basin. A hideous scar bloomed where an ear should have been. With a rusted machete, she scraped blood from a blanket spread before her on the deck then drew the blade across the edge of a slop bucket swarming with flies. In her trough a wet sheet had formed a deep-maroon bubble. She rose and poked the bubble with a stick then returned to her scraping. She looked up at Rose through hooded eyes and spread her lips in an imitation of a smile.

The nurse at one trough dropped an armload of clean bandages into a basket, which she carried to a stove in the center of the deck. There another woman lowered them into a cauldron of boiling water. Nearby three young girls worked a wringer almost as large as the stove.

One child fed a corner of wet fabric into the rollers, another turned the crank, and the third directed the fabric into a basket for hanging.

Rooster shouted, "This here's your new girl!" The other nurses glanced her way but did not extend greetings. Before Rose could introduce herself, something exploded behind her. She yelped and collapsed into a crouch, arms over her head. When she looked up, the woman with the machete was chuckling and shaking her head. Embarrassed, Rose cautiously turned to see the source of the blast. A cast-iron boiler the size and approximate shape of a milk cow had blown off a feeder pipe that came from a rain barrel on the deck above. Water—cold water—was spurting everywhere. Someone stepped in to reattach the water supply, and it was she who finally spoke to Rose. "I'm Maggie," she said, twisting a junction in the pipe. "And this"—she pointed toward the boiler with her thumb—"is Daisy. She has bad days and worse days, like most milkers."

Rose smiled, relieved to be safe and to be acknowledged by one of the others. Maggie pointed to the woman at the stove. "That's Celia," she said. "She's in charge."

"Thank you, Maggie. My name is Rose. I will ask her for instructions."

Celia glanced at Rose briefly before looking at Maggie. "You talk to her," she said, with a jerk of her head.

Rose felt like a mouse between two cats, but whatever was between these two women, she would learn it in time. "We need to hang what's in the wringer basket," Maggie said. "And it looks like Laila could use some fresh water." The second trough was making the gurgling sound of an emptying drain. As the deck was cantilevered from the stern of the ship, Rose guessed that the troughs dumped directly into the river—a troublesome arrangement.

Rose turned to Rooster, still standing by the swinging door. "Thank you for the kind welcome," she said. "I must get to my task. I shall see you again soon."

"I will look forward upon it," he said, bowing deeply from the waist. He disappeared into the ship's interior.

"What's up his beak?" Celia grumbled when he had gone. "I'll hang those," she sighed, looking at Maggie and pointing to the basket of wrung sheets. "Let her see if she can handle Daisy."

Maggie set her mouth to a frown but picked up a bucket and stepped to the boiler. Rose followed her there. "First you pull the hot, which is at the top," Maggie said. "Stay alert. She spits." Just as she said this, the spigot coughed and sprayed hot water. She jumped back and cursed.

"Are you all right?" Rose asked. "Are you burned?"

"I'm fine," Maggie sighed, rubbing her hand over her neck. "She didn't make a liar of me."

Maggie held the bucket under the spigot again, turning the handle on and off until the hot water flowed smoothly again. "Fill it three-quarters full," she said, "then add some cold. Just enough to take the boil off." She bent and held the bucket beneath a spigot on the broken pipe she had just repaired. "It takes eighteen pails to fill a trough." She handed the water to Rose and nodded toward the second washing station.

Rose and Maggie filled Laila's trough while Laila shaved soap into the water with a knife. As they emptied the eighteenth bucket, the woman with one ear lifted the sheet from the first trough and dropped it into Laila's fresh, clean water. "Can't you wait even a moment?" Laila snapped. Rose supposed Laila might want a minute to enjoy the clean water—perhaps to splash her face—before her neighbor broke its spell. Even so, there was beauty in the feathers of blood now swirling across the water's surface.

"We can empty some lines," Maggie was saying, pointing to dry linens hanging nearby. She pulled down a sheet and handed one end to Rose. Each taking their corners, they began the work of folding. This was the part Rose had always enjoyed with Chloe.

"It seems like dancing," she said, "like a reel." She stepped toward Maggie to match a set of corners, their fingers touching lightly. Maggie held the top and Rose bent to slide hers into the bottom fold before stepping up to meet Maggie's fingers again.

"We lack a fiddler," Maggie replied with a smile and a quick step.

Sheet by sheet, bandage by bandage, they folded and stacked laundry. After a time, Celia and the others left the deck, but Rose and Maggie stayed on, offering to hang the last batch of wet linens. Rose was exhausted, but she had not spoken to another woman, other than Jimmy's poor mother, since leaving New York. Maggie was pleasant company.

"Thank you for helping," Maggie said. "Most are not so ready to lend a hand."

"Surely everyone does her share," Rose replied.

Maggie pulled another batch of dry bandages from the lines. Holding them to her chest, she turned to Rose and said, "I am not a nurse, Miss Barnett."

Rose stared at her, uncertain for a moment what she had just heard. "What do you mean you are not a nurse?"

Maggie shrugged. "I'm a laundress. That's what I mean."

Rose rested her hand on a stack of bandages. "You...you and Celia both?" she asked.

Maggie nodded.

"Everyone?" Rose waved her arm to indicate the entire space. "Some, perhaps," she said, thinking of the woman with the missing ear.

"All," Maggie replied.

Rose scanned the deck as if her peers might be hiding from her in jest. "But where are the nurses, if you are not one of them?"

"You will find them on the wards caring for the men, although some, I hear, are in town visiting the marshal's wife. She is celebrating a new baby, and they are staying the night."

Rose laughed. "I have just spent the afternoon doing laundry when I could have been having tea?" she exclaimed.

"You're not angry, ma'am?"

"No, no! It is ironical, is all."

"You just jumped in. I hardly knew what to do!" Maggie said.

"How did you know I was a nurse? Have I a scarlet *N* on my forehead?" Rose reached up and felt the scab from the bullet. "I suppose I do have something scarlet there," she said.

"How did you not know we were laundresses? This is a laundry, after all."

"I have done washing all my life. It never occurred to me it was someone else's job. Rooster brought me here, and you seemed to be expecting me."

"A laundress, yes, named Virginia. Not a nurse named Rose."

"Oh, dear. I have made a muddle," Rose said. "My full name is Virginia Rose, but I am not a laundress. Poor Rooster. I shall have to apologize."

An awkward silence descended. Maggie began folding the bandages she had just pulled from the line.

"I suppose I should go in search of my own kind," Rose said.

"They are probably on third deck, giving special diet." The gaiety in Maggie's voice was gone. Her eyes no longer met Rose's. "You'll find the nurses' cabin on the Texas. Take the main ladder by the storeroom, and when you get to the first deck, cross to port and take the ladder to the top. Nurses' quarters are at the stern. You can't miss them."

"I got lost at Texas," Rose said with forced levity.

"The top," Maggie said, shrugging. "You'll get the hang of it." She lifted her head from her work and yielded a slight smile.

"Well, thank you for the reel, in any case," Rose said.

Maggie bobbed a quick curtsey. "Likewise," she replied, dropping her eyes and returning to her bandages.

Rose stepped carefully down the tall steps Rooster had helped her scale earlier. In a single afternoon, she had made a friend and managed to lose her. She felt every sailor's eyes on her as she walked toward the front of the ship. She stepped into the room where she had dropped her satchels. Finding Celia there, she bid her good evening. "Yes, ma'am," Celia replied. Rose returned a tight smile and nodded. She took her bags and in a few minutes' time somehow found the top deck, the Texas. At the far end she saw what could only be the nurses' cabin, its gauzed windows framed by shiny black shutters. She stood at the door for several moments before entering, summoning the strength to start again. Finally, she grasped the door handle and swung it open. She was relieved to find the room empty.

A dozen beds rimmed the room, each encircled with insect netting. Five of the beds were dressed in faded counterpanes; one was tightly encased in a blue wool army blanket. The rest sat naked to their springs. The room smelled of cleansing sulfur. Spreading her nightgown over the nearest set of springs, she removed her boots, slid under the netting, and fell instantly asleep.

Chapter 3

ROSE WOKE WITH THE FIRST BLUSH OF DAYLIGHT. A STEAMBOAT WHIS-
tled nearby. She was stiff from sleeping on the uneven springs, but the
room brought a smile to her lips. The walls, ceiling, and floors were
painted a clean, glossy white. A gilded garland encircled the ceiling.
The capitals of the support pillars were filigreed in blue and gold.
She noticed a narrow door in one corner of the square room, which
she guessed might contain a privy. Next to it was a washbasin with
plumbing tubes. She ducked beneath her netting and swung her feet
to the floor. Even in the warm air, the painted floor felt cool on the
soles of her bare feet.

As she rose, the bed creaked, startling her. At the same instant,
the ship rocked slightly, and she lost her balance. Her arms flew outward, hitting an apple crate that held a cup of water, which in turn
flew through the air and dumped its contents through an insect net
onto an older woman's sleeping face. The woman shrieked and sat
up, sputtering.

"I am so sorry," Rose whispered, glancing around the room. Three
other women still slept; she feared waking them too. The older woman
reached out from under her netting, her arms flailing toward the crate.

"Your spectacles," Rose whispered. "Let me get them." She reached
under the woman's bed and handed her the glasses. The woman tucked

the metal ends behind her ears, lifted her netting, and, stretching out her neck like a curious goose, examined Rose from head to toe.

"I am so sorry, ma'am. I was trying to be quiet, and instead I have made a mess." Rose knelt to pick up the cup and mop the water from the floor with her nightgown.

"Indeed," said the woman. "Leave it. It's only water." At the same time, she aggressively brushed droplets from her wool blanket as if it was not at all only water. A deep frown engaged her mouth.

"How do you do, then?" Rose said. She extended a damp hand in greeting. "Rose Barnett."

The woman used Rose's hand to pull herself out of bed, finishing up toe-to-toe and nose-to-nose before her. She was of similar height but twice the girth.

"From?"

"Chicago, or rather, Indiana. I came in through the Indiana Home Guard. Also, Philadelphia and Connecticut. And New York. Originally, western New York."

"A vagabond."

"I am on my own," Rose said. "My parents died when I was small."

The woman raised her eyebrows. She continued to stand so close to Rose they were almost touching. She wore a long-sleeved brown flannel nightgown with a high, ruffled collar and a nightcap. She had been sweating overnight, and strands of gray hair clung to her neck. Her lips were thin from age, constituting just a slit in her face. She had no eyebrows. Her breath smelled like silage.

"I am Mother Pennoyer." She spoke directly into Rose's face. "You may call me 'Mother.' As far as you are concerned, this is my home and you are its guest." She turned to make up her bed, tucking and stretching the linens tightly. "You will make your bed daily," she said over her shoulder. "It is the secret to happiness."

"That is my habit, ma'am."

"You must be very happy, then." Mother Pennoyer brushed the last few drops of water from her blanket, fluffed her pillow, and arranged the net around her bed. Turning to the three others who were by now quite awake, she commanded, "Up, ladies." To Rose she said, "We do not languish in the linens here. Up, up!" She clapped her hands three times, turned, strode to the narrow door, and disappeared behind it.

One of the other nurses, an older woman of the African race, looked Rose up and down before stepping behind one of two dressing screens. A young woman who Rose thought might still be a teenager extended her hand. "I'm Elizabeth," she said. "And that"—she nodded toward the privy door—"is Mother Pennoyer. Rhymes with 'annoy her.'" Giggling, she stepped behind the other screen.

"I'm Holly," the last woman said. She stood three inches shorter than Rose, who just reached sixty-two inches herself.

"Like the tree?" Rose asked.

Holly laughed. "I was born on Christmas Eve, but my sister already was 'Mary,' and my father said that, while the world might endure a million Marys, our family could tolerate only one."

"I like it," Rose said with a smile. "A floral name, like mine."

"We have something in common," Holly said. She seemed close in age to Rose, with curly, dark hair. To her gray eyes nature had added a golden starburst, as if a candle glowed within her. Her smile was quick and generous.

"So how many are we, Nurse Holly?" Rose asked with a smile.

"With Mother, we've been eleven, but four left after Martha died of typhus last month. Three had cholera, and Samantha went to pieces when her last boy died at Vicksburg. Mother sent for her parents to take her home to Cincinnati." Holly twisted a handkerchief in her hands, and the corners of her mouth turned down. "Samantha's husband died earlier. She has lost everyone now." Tears began to run down her cheeks. "You learn to take one step at a time," she said, wiping her eyes. "If that step is to weep, then you weep." Her tears ceased as quickly as they had begun. "With you, we are back to seven female nurses. As Vicksburg is taken, we are unlikely to receive replacements. The fight will move east now, although we will be troubled by guerillas. And illness, of course."

"Where are the other two nurses? I count only five with myself."

The older woman stepped from behind the dressing screen. "Hobnobbin'," she said. She was dressed in a long-sleeved, black cotton dress with a high collar and a white apron. She had tied a blue scarf around her sphere of graying hair, the ends of which had been worked into four short twists, two beneath each ear. When the woman offered her hand in greeting, Rose's eyes lingered on the dark creases of her palm and the line where her skin turned from cream to brown. Looking up, she saw wariness in the woman's eyes as their hands came together. "Able," said the woman. "Able Stone."

"My pleasure," said Rose. "Rose Barnett. And where is your home, Miss Stone?"

With her other palm, Able patted the top of their clasped hands. "We'll see if we get there, you and I," she said, dropping Rose's hand before turning abruptly and leaving the cabin.

"She's private," Holly said. "She is risking more than the rest of us."

"But she is with the army."

"And as bound to this ship as to any master. Memphis is a dangerous place."

"I would like to know her."

"That will be her choice, not yours. Engage her as she comes," Holly said. "Do not pry, lest she accuse you of treating her as a specimen."

Rose tucked the advice away. "What did she mean by hobnobbing?" she asked. "Where are the other nurses?"

"Ashore," Holly said. "There are only two more."

"Ashore at this hour?"

Elizabeth, who had been quietly observing from her bed, became animated. "At Mayfield," she said. "They stayed overnight. The house is immense." She opened her eyes wide and whispered, "It belonged to a slaver!"

Holly said, "Mrs. Spalding, the marshal's wife, is confined. We were asked to provide companionship. Only two could be accommodated, so Able and Elizabeth and I volunteered to stay behind. And Mother, of course."

"I see," said Rose, doubting that Able had made any choice at all but wondering why Holly had declined. Certainly Elizabeth would not have volunteered to stay behind, yet here she was. "When do we expect their return?"

"The odds here are wondrous!" Elizabeth exclaimed.

"Don't be a child, Elizabeth," Holly said. "You are a nurse now." To Rose she replied, "Everyone should be accounted for within the hour."

"I only mean that there are many gentlemen about," Elizabeth said, pouting.

"Excuse us," Holly said to Rose. She put an arm around Elizabeth. "Let's get to breakfast and stop counting soldiers, shall we?"

The water closet door opened. Mother Pennoyer stepped out, exclaiming, "Where are my nurses?"

Rose rushed in behind her. A weak light filtered through high, gauzed windows. Where she had expected a nice chamber pot or a hole in a board, as on the *Redhawk*, here she found a true porcelain toilet. A chain hung from a wooden reservoir overhead. Rose had never used a plumbed toilet. She sat to relieve herself. A basket on the platform held squares of thin, unprinted newspaper, which she assumed were for drying. Upon standing, she pulled the chain and watched with curiosity as water from the reservoir flooded the bowl, washing everything away through a flap at the base.

A handwritten note tacked to the wall read, "Please refill reservoir before leaving." A foot pump lever sat beside the toilet. She placed her bare toes on it and pushed gently. Nothing happened. She looked about for instructions but did not see any. Surely this was the lever mentioned. If the other nurses could pump the device, she could as well. She placed the full ball of her foot on the lever and braced herself against the door. She pushed. The lever yielded, and the sound of water moving up the pipe made her sigh with relief. She gave three more hefty pumps, keeping an eye on the reservoir, lest it overflow. To incapacitate this lovely device after having spent her first day in the laundry would be an inauspicious start. She hoped four pumps were adequate. She would ask Holly later.

To the right of the toilet was a small door. Behind it stood a three-legged metal contraption with an overhead reservoir and a round, shallow tub at the base. This must be the bathing shower Rooster had mentioned. Rose thought of her patients in Chicago, their skin scaled and crusted with months of soil. She counseled bathing, but few could spare even the few pennies it took to enter the public bathhouse. Instead they washed from a pot at home, if at all; they did not own bathing tubs, let alone showers such as this. Rose studied the device. Perhaps bathing in it might feel something like standing in a rain shower. Hopefully, one would not catch a draft.

When Rose stepped out of the water closet, Holly and Elizabeth were gone. Mother Pennoyer stood by the sideboard with a broom in hand. Rose could hear two female voices chattering and giggling behind the dressing screens, over the tops of which were draped black nursing gowns.

"Ladies!" Mother Pennoyer barked at the screens. "There are men to be nursed. Go nurse them."

"Yes, ma'am," the voices returned in unison. The dark dresses disappeared and in a moment were replaced by what the women must have worn ashore—cotton gowns, one a pink stripe and one a robin's-egg blue. It was said that a flash of calico could arouse male fluids in ways that were disadvantageous to healing. Rose thought the idea specious and that a little color might improve a patient's humor, but she did agree that the lifting of men's spirits was a matter of some delicacy.

The two women came from behind the screens, folding their shore dresses and placing them in the apple crates next to their beds. One slipped a collapsed set of hoops beneath her bed. Mother Pennoyer shook her head and ordered them to the wards.

Alone with Mother Pennoyer, Rose made small talk. "Memphis seems a busy place," she said.

"It was good sized when we took it a year ago," said Mother Pennoyer. "We have overrun it with our army, not to mention the contraband that pour in."

"Contraband? Tennessee slaves are not emancipated. Is it not dangerous for runaways here?"

"They think they are safe behind Union lines, but they are not. Both the free and those that have run are grabbed here every day, right under the noses of Union pickets. I can't let Able go abroad for a moment without an escort. The town is crawling with slavers."

That the Emancipation Proclamation applied only to rebel states—but not to Southern territory under federal control, such as Memphis—confounded Rose. "It is not clear to me," she said, "how emancipation can unfold piecemeal, with different rules for different places."

"A partial dose seldom cures when the full measure is called for," Mother Pennoyer replied. "But that is not for nurses to decide."

"Where do the fugitives live? Surely not in town."

"Men of age enlist, generally. The women and children, the old, and the lazy collect in camps below the fort. The largest is on President's Island. Camp Dixie they call it."

"Have they sturdy homes there?"

"A few have built cottages, more like huts, I would call them. There are some old cotton warehouses that serve in the coldest weather, but the stench drives most to choose tents. Sanitation is disgraceful, especially in the rain, of course, and pestilence abounds. 'Tis not a life of comfort, but they choose it over what they had."

"As would I, I suppose," said Rose. "Have they medical care?"

"They have their own hospital at the fort. The Sanitary Commission sees to it; you needn't worry." Mother Pennoyer cleared her throat. "They say that now the river is ours, the fight is nearly done, but whoever says so does not know the South. These people will have their way, no matter the sense of it."

"And we will have ours," Rose replied instinctually. Rigidity in others could cause Rose to argue for argument's sake.

Mother Pennoyer's brow furrowed. "Surely you do not equate the two causes."

"I do not, of course. I only observe their passion in the matter." Hoping to avoid a quarrel, she pointed to the closet. "That is a lovely convenience."

"The Sanitary Commission is good to us." Mother Pennoyer sniffed loudly, thoroughly, through her narrow nostrils. Rose imagined that she snored at night.

"Does it empty to the river?"

"The output collects in a vessel that is dragged downstream. To my mind, we are only borrowing trouble, especially now that we possess the lower river. The engineers say the river cleanses the effluvia. You may count the cases of cholera and reach your own conclusion." She sniffed again.

"Surely the surgeons are aware."

"It is cutting they know, that is all." Mother Pennoyer set aside the broom and stepped to a cupboard from which she retrieved two porcelain cups. Both were emblazoned with the insignia of the *Despain*, a blue image of a side-wheeler over the golden rod of Caduceus. From a wooden box she took a pitcher of the same design and poured water into each cup, handing one to Rose. The water was clear, but still Rose hesitated.

"You needn't worry," Mother Pennoyer said. "Our filters are quite effective."

Rose raised the cup to her lips. Icy water bathed her throat. She tipped the cup high, finishing in two swallows. "It is cold," she said. "I have not tasted cold water in some time. It reminds me of the spring near my home in New York."

Mother Pennoyer poured her another cup. "What our Southern friends would not give for ice," she said. She turned her own cup in her hand, inspecting the insignia. "We know they will not trade slavery for it," she said, raising her eyebrows and drinking the water in a single swallow. "'Tis their sorrow," she continued. "When they concede, they shall have ice again."

There was pridefulness in this woman's voice, as if she held her opinions like conquered territory. "The water has a fine taste," Rose said. "How is it supplied?"

"We've cisterns," Mother Pennoyer said, pointing to three huge wooden casks on the deck, each taller than two men. "The rain catchment above the pilot house feeds to all three barrels. You will see the piping if you look."

Rose peered through the gauzed windows at the water supply system that served the huge ship. "And when the weather does not oblige?" she asked. "What then? I should fear that all the sand in the Sahara could not filter the Mississippi."

Mother Pennoyer frowned. "Are you given to hyperbole, Nurse Barnett?"

"No, ma'am," Rose said. Deciding to take a chance on humor, she added, "But I have been known to succumb to metaphor." She smiled and watched Mother Pennoyer's face carefully. In her experience, severe individuals often became even more so in the face of wit. Better to learn the woman's disposition now.

Mother Pennoyer compressed her lips into a small pucker and continued as if Rose had not spoken. "There are wells in the city," she said, "but too often they have been allowed to abut a cesspit. We take up water from tributaries, principally the Wolf. Never the Mississippi." She took up the broom again. Something about the way she swept reminded Rose of Aunt Fidelia, a woman whose bark was generally worse than her bite.

"There are some essentials we must discuss, Nurse Barnett."

"Of course," Rose said, glad to be past the pleasantries.

"Volunteerism," Mother Pennoyer said, "is the cornerstone of our work here." She had taken the broom to the far side of the room, as if to distance herself from what she was about to say.

"I am uncertain of your meaning, ma'am," Rose replied. "I believe you know that I am engaged under contract. I am not of independent means."

"You have not allowed me to finish," Mother Pennoyer said, poking the broom aggressively into a corner. "I was about to add that, while volunteers are well-meaning, they can be disorganized in a crisis and, worse, at times dangerous. Some are simply empty-headed. It shall be a relief to have one with experience among us, as I understand you to have."

Rose was relieved. "Thank you, ma'am. I do, yes, have experience."

"Nevertheless," Mother Pennoyer continued, as if she could not allow Rose the smallest advantage, "I know you consider yourself a doctor, but I will not have you holding it over my nurses. They have much to teach you."

Rose resisted the urge to say that she was, in fact, a doctor, that her three years in medical college were not a figment of her imagination. And although tempted to remark in jest upon the dubious reputation of doctors in general, she squelched the urge. Even self-deprecating humor seemed unwelcome in this woman's world. "I am here to learn, ma'am," she replied, guessing her deference would be silently noted.

Mother Pennoyer set down the broom and took a chair across from Rose. "Good. Now that that is out of the way," she said, "there are a few other things."

Rose straightened her posture to indicate her full attention.

"You may think you are prepared," Mother Pennoyer said, "but you are not. No one is." She paused, took a breath as if to speak, and paused again. At last she said, "Men are quick enough to start a war, but they do not consider how to clean it up. They act as if they don't know what happens when boys shoot at each other." She closed her eyes and lowered her voice to a near whisper. "Do not mistake me. I am no Copperhead. But you will find the wounds horrific. Due to inattention in the field, they have often festered. You will see maggots. If you find you cannot bear it, you must say so early rather than fail at your duties slowly. We do not have time for young women to feign bravery. If you are not up to it, go home. It is less a disgrace to leave than to stay and do harm."

"Yes, ma'am," Rose replied. She had heard a similar speech her first day in medical college, although her education had been a largely bloodless affair involving the memorization of anatomy and remedies. It was true that she had reacted poorly once, but from disappointment, not squeamishness. She did not expect to be alarmed by what she might see on the *Despain*. "Thank you for your kindness," she said. "Should such a day come, 'tis a comfort to know I shall not be harshly judged."

Mother Pennoyer frowned, as if she felt she had been misunderstood. "Second," she said, "Memphis is the headquarters of the Union's western front. General Sherman has been here for a year now, although I expect he will move east soon. He is currently resting in Mississippi with his family. Recruits and now conscripts—an entirely different beast—arrive here daily by the thousands." She pulled a handkerchief from her sleeve and coughed into it. "They bring their inclinations with them, which, if you listen to the generals, must be catered to." She ran a hand across her belly as if experiencing physical pain. "I have the pledge of the head surgeon that conditions resulting from self-indulgence," she said, "are not the concern of the female nursing staff."

Rose smiled, remembering her exchange with the captain of the *Redhawk*.

"You are amused?"

"A little. I could have used your assistance on the *Redhawk*."

"I am sorry to hear that. We are in a man's world." Mother Pennoyer pulled a folded handbill from her pocket and handed it to Rose. "Avoid town. If you must go, take your orders with you. Unaccompanied females are presumed to be seeking temporary employment." Her eyelids fluttered closed again.

Rose opened the flyer. Scripted in a large hand across the top were the words *Ladies of Memphis!* Below were rules of female behavior as defined by the Union. On pain of arrest, all women would carry identification and evidence of status at all times. Public women would submit to regular medical examination and, where required, report to the women's wing of Memphis General Hospital until cleared for return to work. Cribs and hotels were to submit to inspection and display Union-issued certificates of cleanliness in their front windows. Peep shows, burlesque halls, and saloons were for the enjoyment of men only, female employees excepted. Public women were forbidden to ride horseback for pleasure, walk in the town square, or visit the New Memphis Theater. Lastly, all ladies of Memphis were forbidden from sharing this broadsheet with any male person.

"A man's world, indeed," Rose said handing the document back to Mother Pennoyer. "One aspect of the order does catch my attention, however. I have heard the Union offers treatment for public women. So it is true?"

"Sadly, yes."

"I am sorry for the women," Rose said, "but glad they receive care." She had long ago pledged to speak up on behalf of those who could not do so themselves.

Mother Pennoyer frowned. "Better to clean the hen house than burn it down?" she asked.

"Something like that," Rose said.

"I am of the burning camp," Mother Pennoyer said.

"Yes, ma'am." She was not surprised by Mother Pennoyer's response, but her time in Chicago had taught her that women rarely chose degraded lives. Rose advised her patients—married or not, private and public—to use the fountain syringe, with small doses of carbolic acid, both before and after, to protect their health. But the method was not foolproof, especially for those required to yield with great frequency. Inspection and treatment seemed the least the army could do.

"The ship has two hundred beds," Mother Pennoyer was saying. "Twice that with pallets. There are ten Union general hospitals on shore with five thousand beds. Some are in converted warehouses, but we hold Memphis Hospital as well as the State Female College and Gayoso House. Eruptive fevers are kept apart from the intermittent. Smallpox is taken to Memphis Hospital. Camp fever comes and goes with the season. We raise pestilence tents as the need arises. As for surgery, we see mainly second cuts, but we receive fresh wounded as well, usually from local skirmishes with guerillas and some from across the river. We will likely retrieve some boys from Vicksburg soon, although I expect it to be our last trip."

"I shall look forward to it," Rose said. "I am eager to see the lower Mississippi."

"You are not on holiday, Nurse Barnett."

"No, ma'am."

"Now go find Nurse Lane and append yourself to her."

"Nurse Lane?"

"Holly. The one with common sense."

Rose left Mother Pennoyer still sweeping the clean floor and went below to look for Rooster. She found him outdoors on the deck. "May I speak to you?" she asked.

"Yes, ma'am," Rooster said, "you may." His mouth turned down, and he shook his head. "My fault entirely, ma'am."

"I am so sorry," Rose said. "I should have been more clear."

"My mistake, not reading the orders right, ma'am. Sorry I delivered you to the wrong post."

"Well, I enjoyed the tour," Rose said, smiling.

"You'll keep the surgery to yourself?" Rooster asked, as much with his eyes as his words.

"Of course. I would not wish to cause you trouble." She touched his elbow and saw him visibly relax.

"Then we are about as even as we can get, ma'am. Good of you to come by."

Rose thanked him and entered the surgical ward, glad to have the misunderstanding behind her. Near the doors a young man lay in deep sleep, perhaps unconscious. On a chalkboard above his bed were written the hope-shattering words *belly wound* with the prior day's date. Viscera could seldom be mended. She was surprised he had made it as far as the ship. She wondered if the surgeons had even tried to help or simply put him there to die. The young man's fingertips were blue. His breaths were very far apart. He would die that day.

Rose wondered what his mother was doing at this spiritual counterpoint to the moment when she had pushed him into the world. It was Monday, washing day for women everywhere. Perhaps she was carrying water from a stream in a rusty bucket. Perhaps her other children had died and this boy was her last. Or perhaps his sisters were skipping beside their mother, helping her keep her mind off her absent son. Had he been a quiet boy, a tender child, tied to his mother's heart? Or a ruffian, full of bluster and false courage? He must have been brave to have been shot in the belly—pushing forward toward the enemy. She hoped his passage would be smooth and that he was not in fact his mother's last child.

"Nurse Barnett!" Mother Pennoyer's voice startled her as Rose realized her name had been said more than once. She looked up from the dying soldier.

"Yes, ma'am?" she replied.

"Are you given to daydreaming?"

"I am sorry. I did not hear you. I was considering the soldier's situation." She paused. "Yes, I was daydreaming, ma'am. I am caught." She smiled, hoping to earn respect by admitting her error.

"The boy deserted," Mother Pennoyer said without sympathy. "He lies here by his own hand."

Rose's breath caught in her throat; she felt the blood leave her face.

"Do not invent what you cannot know, Nurse. Pickets tried to stop him. He even called out for them to watch. He is a coward. I suggest you help a patriot." She swept her arm toward the room full of soldiers.

"Yes, ma'am," Rose replied. Even a deserter had a mother. Surely they mourned like any other, perhaps even more deeply. Would not the one who watched a child grow be the one least surprised by cowardice, the one most likely to understand it?

Mother Pennoyer was summoning Holly to join them. "Keep her with you today," she ordered, leveling her eyes at Rose. "Report to me her shortcomings as well as her aptitudes."

"Yes, ma'am," Holly said as Mother Pennoyer turned away.

"Excuse me, ma'am," Rose said before the matron could get far. "Shall I write to the family?"

Mother Pennoyer sighed as if exhausted. "The fort commander will contact the family. Do not become entangled where you do not belong, Nurse Barnett. He deserted and took his life. Sadly, that is his record." She turned and walked away.

"It is harsh, I know," said Holly.

"'Tis more than harsh," said Rose. "It is cruel. I wish only to assure his family that his last hours were peaceful. Consider his poor mother hearing just the hard facts!"

"His commander is required to report the circumstances."

"But can we not also offer sympathy?"

"The army does not encourage sympathy toward deserters."

"Mr. Lincoln pardons them daily!"

"To the dismay of his generals. Come with me for now, and I will ask Mother Pennoyer to let you send a letter. She may allow it after the matter has cooled."

"Thank you," said Rose. "I suppose it bodes ill for me to lose my heart over my first case, and a deserter at that."

"Most of us began like you," Holly said. "Well, perhaps not quite so dramatically, over a handsome young deserter." Holly smiled and took Rose by the arm away from the unfortunate young man. "Now, did I hear you are a doctoress?"

Rose was grateful for Holly's kindness. "Yes, in Chicago," she said, "but here I shall serve as nurse."

"Why have you left the city?"

Rose hesitated, filtering through the jumble of events and emotions that had led to this moment. Choosing consistency, she said, "I wish to become a surgeon."

"I hope you do not expect your job here to take you to the surgery," Holly said. "Male nurses assist there. Women are left to bandaging and fevers."

"So I have been told, repeatedly. Still, perhaps someone will apprentice me. If not, then I shall study how the body heals while I change dressings."

"Did you work alone? You are very brave to live in such a wild city!"

Rose laughed. "The place is not so wild once you become accustomed to it, though it is growing rapidly and is quite crowded. I shared the dispensary with a friend from medical college. She was raised in Chicago. Her father owns a stockyard and granary. He helped us rent a two-story house near the rail yard. The dispensary was on the first floor; we lived upstairs. Our patients were women and children, chiefly, and the occasional husband. City life is expensive. The men work on the docks and in the rail yards. Their wives must work also, as domestics or, more often now, in factories. They take their children with them, for supervision as well as to bring in extra wages. Sometimes a child's hand would be caught in the gears or belts of a machine, or worse, they would fall under a train while playing at the yards unsupervised. The only way to save them was to remove the injured hand or leg, but we had neither the experience nor the anesthesia for the work. We would send them to the public hospital, but we were not allowed to assist or even observe. I hope to learn from the surgeons here so I can care for my patients in the future."

"I am sure you did your best," Holly said.

"'Tis not my best until I have acquired the skills to do the full job."

"Did you deliver babies as well? I would think a doctress well suited to such a task."

"Where there are women, there are babies," Rose replied. She hesitated for a moment before adding, "I am sorry to say that many of our patients were unmarried." She stopped to let Holly absorb the words. How she replied would reveal much.

"Public women?" Holly asked. "Or family girls? What is worse?"

"Family girls, chiefly," said Rose. "They are often just arrived from the country. It is a hard first lesson for them, and they often end up as public women in the end. The orphanages are overflowing."

"How sad to be alone and fallen. And to lose one's child as well!" Rose was relieved to hear sympathy from Holly. Few could resist judging a friendless woman. "And you lived independently, serving these women?" Holly asked.

"The clinic was not a charity. We asked our patients to pay something, however little. If women are to practice medicine, we must be paid for our expertise and training, just as men are. And while Chloe did not need to earn her way, I did. Many paid us in eggs or vegetables from window boxes—and I confess asking no questions when a bill was met with a leg of lamb! But we did well enough for five years."

Holly's eyebrows came together. "I think it best to ask payment. I know I should not like to take charity, for my pride. I would rather pay something."

"Such was our thinking."

"So here you are in the army. How does your partner manage without you?"

They had walked the full length of the ward and now stood on the deck. The sun occasionally burned through the dense white sky, its rays stinging but fresh compared to the heavy indoor air. "The dispensary is closed," Rose said.

"No! What happened?" Holly asked.

Rose had not told the full story to anyone yet, not even to her aunts. They had seemed to accept the half-truth that she had joined the army to fight for abolition. Now, far away on a ship in Memphis, she gave in to the pleasure of telling the full truth at last.

"Two men from city hall came to the dispensary last spring," she said. "They said that practicing medicine was detrimental to our health—mine and Chloe's!—and that we must desist. They were very clear about that last part. We ignored them, but brawny stevedores began appearing at our patients' homes. They told husbands not to let their wives come to us nor bring their children. The doctors formed a private association and placed advertisements in the ladies' pages warning women not to take chances with their children's health and always to look for what they called the 'Shield of Quality in All Things Medical'!" She shook her head. "The shield was just the letters of their club embossed on tin plates. But of course, they would not allow us to join the club, nor would they give us the shield to place in our window. Without the shield and without our married patients, we could not pay our bills."

"They forced you out? That is horrid!"

"So you know my secret. I was run out of town." Rose laughed, finding humor in the tale for the first time. "I needed work, so I joined the army. Still, I do wish to help the colored race, and I very much want to be a surgeon someday—a surgeon of the chest."

"There is little of that here," Holly replied. "Chest cases do not survive, as a rule. It is amputations we see for the most part."

"Still, it is surgery. I plan to study in Paris after the war. They are far ahead of us. For now, I am happy to help as I can, right here. And where are you from? What brings you to the army?"

Holly looked over her shoulder before whispering, "I am from Maryland. But I am a Unionist, I swear it!"

Rose laughed. "To be from a border state is a delicate matter indeed," she said, smiling.

"I am the youngest of twelve," Holly said. "Pa is a tanner, but his lungs are worn out from it." She hesitated. "And I was married before…"

"Before?" Rose replied.

Holly nodded, pulling a handkerchief from her apron. "He died at Shiloh," she said. Looking down at her hands, she added, "He was reb."

Many brothers and cousins had taken different paths, but for a man and wife to split in such a way, Rose thought, must be excruciating. "I am so sorry," she said.

"He is buried there, at Shiloh. I hope to move him back to Maryland. If he can be found." She wiped her eyes and the tears ceased as if under order to do so. "In any case," she added with rebounding cheer, "I am here under contract, as you are. I send my wages home to my father and mother. You see? You are not alone."

"We are nurses at arms, then," Rose said, touched by this small woman's fortitude. "But I warn you, I shall need instruction."

Holly placed a finger to her cheek, all signs of her grief now hidden away. "Ah, nursing—how shall I describe it? We are the feeders of those who will not eat—that is, we are cajolers. And chaplains. Barbers and poets. We clip the locks of dead soldiers and write soaring verse to grieving mothers. We calm the furies of opiated men who see ghosts in their midst. We distinguish one fever from the next and force nostrums down unwilling throats. We are sister, fiancée, and mother all at once. I have been on this ship for a year. From day to day I know not whether I am Juliet or Portia or Ophelia."

"Do you enjoy Shakespeare?" asked Rose.

"Oh, yes. I once saw *Romeo and Juliet* played out on a stage," Holly replied.

"When I was a teacher, I read the sonnets to my students, but they preferred Robinson Crusoe, of course. Since leaving teaching, I have read only textbooks and Latin primers."

"Now that you are aboard a ship, a primer on blue language may be called for."

Rose laughed. "That would be something."

Maggie was walking toward them with a stack of clean bandages. Rose called to her and offered to take the dressings. Maggie looked first to Holly, who smiled and extended her arms. "Yes, let us help," she said. "It will allow me to show Nurse Barnett the linen closet."

"Thank you, ma'am," Maggie said. She looked at Rose. "Nice to see you again," she said.

"How do you know Maggie already?" Holly asked as she led Rose inside to a supply pantry.

"We met last evening," Rose said. "Rooster mistook me for a laundress, and I spent the afternoon washing linens."

"Excuse me?"

"I know it sounds preposterous, but I have washed laundry all my life, even at the dispensary. It did not occur to me someone else might do it. Which proves my point! I clearly do not understand my role here. You must help me!"

Holly's laugh was a four-note trill that reminded Rose of the eastern meadowlark that had flourished in the fields of her youth. "You do seem in need of tutoring," Holly agreed, "although being kind to the laundresses is a clever first step. What would we do without clean linens?" She opened a door to neat piles of clean sheets, bandages, and nightshirts. "So, what is nursing? That is your question?"

"I suppose so."

"I can tell you what it is not. It is not cutting off a leg."

"That is not all doctors do," Rose said, placing her stack of bandages next to Holly's.

"I challenge you to distinguish nurse from doctor, but for the cutting," Holly replied.

"Oh, there is so much more! Medicine has become a true science," Rose said, "more in Europe than here, but we are advancing. We are searching out the biological causes of disease and keeping records of results to compare remedies."

"It is better than letting and cupping, I grant you. What midwife do you know would bleed a woman? It is absurd!"

"Exactly! The guesswork of the past is replaced by logic and deduction."

"But will doctors actually change? The surgeon general has removed calomel from the supply table—he says it has been proved unsafe—and yet our chief surgeon continues to order it."

"A doctor's mind is not easily swayed, I concede," said Rose. "But I myself have used calomel to advantage. And you know that midwives have as well. Most of us take change poorly at first."

"Perhaps calomel is not the best example."

"Perhaps it is the perfect example. It matters not who orders it. What matters is its tested efficacy. Despite its occasional benefits, if it offers more harm than good, perhaps we are better off without it."

"That kind of thinking will not stand you well with Dr. York," said Holly. "If you wish to enter the man's world of medicine, you may need to temper your opinions."

Rose reached out and took Holly's hands in hers. "First," she said, "it shall not be a man's world forever, although I grant that men will not yield easily. They say women's minds cannot endure the rigors of science, but that is rubbish! Why should I not be both woman and scientist? Women have been healers since the beginning of time."

"Women are not allowed on the battlefield, you know. Is that what you seek? But for the guerillas, we are far behind the lines here."

"I would not object to working in the field, as I understand the better surgeons are there."

"I have heard the field surgeons are only farm boys who know how to butcher a hog," said Holly.

"'Tis hyperbole," Rose replied.

Holly shrugged. "Men have told me what they see, waiting in line to be cut upon. It seems the chloroform does not work. Patients thrash about and cry throughout their surgeries. Even here on the ship, we hear them. It is horrible."

"Yet do they remember the surgery afterward?"

"Some do, others do not."

"I would put to you that it is the dosing, and not the anesthesia that is wanting. It is a difficult skill to master. This is what I wish to learn!"

"Most of the surgeries here are second cuts. The quickness of the field operations followed by the journey here lead to pyemia in most cases."

"How do they travel here?"

"Most by the river, as we have been busy at Vicksburg, but some come overland by ambulance wagon or train. Many walk in from local skirmishes. And the ill, of course, emerge from the camps and ships and town—everywhere. You must be prepared for the mundane. Knowing one fever from the next is our biggest challenge. I assume your training has prepared you to quickly name an illness and its remedy, but I would put Mother Pennoyer up against you any day."

"I am glad to hear she is more than just a mother hen."

"She is irascible but competent." Holly turned her eyes to meet Rose's. "As long as you also bring your heart to the task, I believe you will make a fine nurse."

They exchanged smiles, closed the linen cupboard, and looked out over the ward. Male and female nurses buzzed about the room. "And what of the male nurses?" Rose asked. "Do they bring their hearts to the task?"

"It is their backs they bring, but many find themselves suited to it, yes. It is not uncommon, however, for their nerve to desert them, even here. Many are sent by their commanders because they can take no more of the field. They are treated roughly at times by the patients."

Rose looked again at the ward full of men, more men than she had ever seen in one place in her life. How did the male body respond to illness and injury? The question left her eager with curiosity.

"And second?" said Holly. "Earlier you said, 'first.' I am wondering what your second point was."

Rose thought for a moment. "I believe I was about to say, as my second point, that you do not know me if you expect me to temper my opinions."

"That is something I may need to report to Mother Pennoyer," Holly said, smiling, "although I have a feeling it shall report itself soon enough."

The suicide patient died that afternoon. Mother Pennoyer allowed Rose to compose her first letter of condolence.

Chapter 4

A WEEK AFTER ROSE'S ARRIVAL IN MEMPHIS, THE CAPTAIN OF THE *Despain* announced that they would go south to retrieve Union wounded from Vicksburg. Captain Weirhard Fuchs was a tall man from the border state of Kentucky. Balding, with an unfortunate chin and sloping shoulders, he gave the look of a turtle, especially in profile. His cabin aide seemed unusually feminine. It was rumored, in fact, that the young man was not a man at all but a woman the captain used for his pleasure. Fuchs's men despised him, especially when he attempted to befriend them with tales of his barefoot childhood in Appalachia. They did his bidding, but only to the minimum degree. Behind his back they mispronounced his name, combining its suggestive syllables into crude jokes. He held neither their affection nor their respect.

In preparation for the trip, the *Despain* was to be emptied of its patients. Those unable to travel were moved ashore. All who could be moved were sent north on cargo barges, most without even a canvas shade against the heat or rain. Men were carried to the transports and rolled off their litters onto open decks where they lay like giant catches of fish writhing in the sun. By the time the men arrived at Cairo's general hospital, their conditions would have worsened in every way. Many who would have lived had they stayed in Memphis surely would die.

It fell to the chief surgeon, Dr. York, to decide readiness for travel. He moved from bed to bed cursorily examining each patient before deciding whether to ship him north or move him ashore. Most begged to be sent north. Rose longed to warn them, to plead with them to stay in Memphis a bit longer, but she stayed silent. Mother Pennoyer followed the surgeon, interjecting her own opinions as they moved from bed to bed and between decks. Rose was encouraged that, while never soliciting the nurse's opinion, the surgeon seemed to listen thoughtfully when she spoke. If there was not cordiality between them, there seemed to be respect. He did not appear to be a braggart, as she had heard would be the case among the surgeons, but neither did he seem an affable man. He nodded greetings only to the captain and other surgeons. Now, as she watched him consign these men to their fates, she saw neither pity nor disdain, only a trained mind efficiently performing its duties.

Rose was stocking medications with Able on the second deck when they steamed out of Memphis. As the surrender at Vicksburg was so recent, an ironclad joined them.

"Hospital ships are supposed to be off limits," Able said, "but guerillas don't care about that kind of thing."

"Sometimes it confounds me that war has rules," Rose replied. "But I am not sorry to be on a hospital ship."

"White men's rules, that's all."

"What do you mean?"

"It's like when a black man shows up in Yankee territory and they take to calling him contraband. Don't get me wrong; I'm glad you alls want to hold onto us. It's a fine enough rule, but it still leaves us as property. Just a white man's rule for a white man's problem. They want to shoot at hospital ships or not shoot at hospital ships, makes no difference to the black man."

"Has the *Despain* been fired on?"

"Not yet, but General Forrest makes his own rules."

"I suppose war with rules is better than war without," Rose replied. "But if we can stop ourselves from firing on hospital ships, why can we not stop firing on all ships?"

"You a Copperhead?" Able asked, looking at Rose sideways.

"I tend to seek middle ground," Rose said with a shrug.

"If there was middle ground for finding, Mr. Lincoln would have stumbled on it by now. A great compromiser, he is, but he's the Joshua we've been given. I do believe the wall will fall this time. Lord knows it's our turn."

"I pray you are right." Rose said farewell to Able and took the ladder to the second deck, wondering if it was possible to believe in the cause but not the fight.

The ship was running well in the channel. A rainsquall had blown through, leaving the atmosphere in the ship heavy and damp. Rose stepped out onto the deck where the air, even though humid and warm, at least was fresh. Holly stood at the bow. The ship's headwind had caused a ring of brown curls to escape her braid. Rose called her name, and she turned and smiled, but when Rose reached the railing, she found that Holly had been weeping.

"What is it?" she asked.

"Nothing," Holly said.

"It appears to be something," Rose replied.

Holly took a deep breath and shook her head, looking into the distance where a flock of long-necked, white birds flew low over the water. The sun was warm. The only sound was the paddlewheel's soft, rhythmic churn in the water. "It is so beautiful here," Holly murmured, "away from all of it." She turned to Rose. Tears ran down her cheeks. "I was in Memphis at first," she said, "treating fevers and changing dressings. But three months ago, we went downriver and anchored north of Vicksburg. It was Hell on earth. I am sorry; I can think of no other word for it."

"And now you are headed there again."

Holly nodded. "There was awful fighting before the siege began in May. Men came to the ship directly from the field. The wounds were unspeakable—limbs hanging by shreds of flesh and blood vessels, eyes gouged out. When it rained, the mud mixed with their blood and dried like mortar in the wounds."

Rose touched her shoulder. "You needn't speak of it if it troubles you."

"But that is the point! Everyone saw the same things, but no one will say so. Everyone seems jolly, but it is an act. I have seen with our patients that those who tell their stories fare better than those who do not. Should the same not apply to nurses? But if Mother Pennoyer sees my distress, she will send me home!"

"I will listen," Rose said, "and I shall keep your secret." She took Holly's hand in hers and led her to a footlocker out of the sun. "Tell me," she said gently.

Holly's eyes searched Rose's face as if looking for safety. "The cutting," she said, "was furious. Arms and legs were just thrown into piles. Once I saw a wedding ring on a hand in a pile, and I thought to remove it to return it to the man's wife. But it was too tight." A single chuckle escaped her throat, jostling another round of tears over their banks. "I remember thinking that his wife must have been a good cook. I was struggling with it, I suppose. I just wanted the ring! But Mother Pennoyer pulled me away and slapped my face." Deep sobs now shook her body. Rose put an arm around her but did not shush her.

"Once we surrounded the city, the artillery took over. The casualties declined, as both sides were dug in, but the rebels had a cannon called 'Whistling Dick.' It made the most dreadful squeal. They shot it out over the river. It was never near enough to hit us, but it stopped the blood in your veins." She shook her head vigorously as if to dislodge the sound from within.

"I have read that people in Vicksburg live in caves," Rose said.

Holly nodded. "The city wasn't safe," she said. "But I think they have moved home now."

"One woman, I hear, had her servants—as she called them—dig a cave with three bedrooms and a parlor, and she even installed her piano so her children could continue their lessons."

"I have heard similar tales." Holly nodded, smiling.

"But the meat on their tables is mule." Rose made a face, and Holly laughed.

"Yes," Holly said. "It is said the price is dear and the taste is muddy, but one grows accustomed!" She laughed again.

"It is good to see you smile," Rose said.

"I imagine cave life was less grand than most let on," Holly said. "I am sorry for anyone who must pretend to favor mule meat."

"How long was the siege?" Rose asked.

"Almost seven weeks. In June we blew a hole in their earthworks east of town, but then our own men were sent into the crater! They were trapped like fish in a barrel. It took our engineers two days to lay a bridge to get them out. What wounded we did get were already in suppuration." Tears came to Holly's eyes again. "Then a week later," she said, shrugging, "Pemberton surrendered. I have heard his men begged him to do it, lest they starve to death. They say Grant took no prisoners so he would not have to feed them."

"I have heard as much," Rose said. "What is more cruel, a bullet or an empty belly?"

"A few take the bullet," Holly said, "but all endure hunger, civilian and soldier alike." She wiped her eyes and her voice grew hard. "The starvation of Vicksburg is no accident," she said. "I fear we shall see it again. Grant holds the city as an example to the rest of the South, but he does not know his enemy. They do not wish to be schooled by us."

Rose considered the implications of a dozen more Vicksburgs across the South. She had been thinking of going ashore once they arrived. Now she knew she must do so.

At Milliken's Bend, two of the ship's four boilers broke down. The *Despain* limped into port an hour late. The landing was full of men lying or sitting in the sun, waiting to be taken north. The nurses went ashore to begin sorting the ill from the injured. Many needed second cuts, and camp fever of every sort raged among them. Surgeons began work on the most gravely hurt. Late in the afternoon two ambulances arrived from Jackson with freshly wounded. Litter bearers climbed inside to remove the stretchers from their swinging leather straps. One man had suffered a belly wound. Rose approached him before he was taken aboard. He struggled to place his shivering hands over his wound, as if covering his private parts. The hole was in the right side of his belly; if the upper bowel could be saved, Rose thought, he could still eliminate. But the long ambulance ride had taken its toll; his abdomen was full of fecal matter. Even if the bowel could be stitched, the mess in his belly was impossible to clean. The man's breaths were gasping. He could not speak but begged for relief with his eyes. Mother

Pennoyer ordered him to surgery. It was a kindness, Rose thought, to send him there where he could have hope. But a moment later the stretcher bearers carried him off the ship again. The surgeons had objected to the odor. Mother Pennoyer, flush with anger, pointed to the ship and ordered the man installed on Able's ward. She told Able to bandage the man's belly as best she could and administer a stimulant. As she gave her orders, the terrified man attempted to sit up, causing a distracted bearer to drop a corner of the stretcher. The man fell to the ground. Able was first to reach him.

"He's passed, ma'am," she said to Mother Pennoyer.

"Praise God," Mother Pennoyer said, directing a venomous gaze at the man who had dropped the stretcher. "What else do you have for us?"

The chastised litter bearers removed the last man from the ambulance with exaggerated care. He had sustained injuries to all four limbs. Field surgeons had removed both of his feet, but gangrene and maggots had invaded. He was insensible with fever. Early in the war, surgeons had followed the traditional approach of allowing wounds to heal naturally, but they had soon learned that gangrene could kill while they waited. The preferred approach now was to detach the wound—and its limb—from the body with as much dispatch as circumstances allowed.

Rose was not surprised when Dr. York pointed to the man and declared, "The limbs must be removed. All of them. Why it has not been done before now, I cannot surmise."

"Poor bastard," someone muttered.

"It's no one's idea of a picnic," Dr. York snapped. "Do you wish the man to die?"

"If it was me, yes," said another surgeon.

"Might as well take his pecker while you're at it," a male nurse uttered.

"Who has made that wretched remark?" Dr. York shouted. "The man has a mind, hasn't he?"

"But, how's he gonna…you know?" another surgeon asked, gesturing with a flip of his hand.

"He's not the only man with that confoundment, now, is he?" Dr. York replied. Turning to a young male nurse who looked about to weep, Dr. York said, "Mr. Edwards, you have kept your counsel. You will assist. It appears my fellow surgeons have not the stomach to save this man's life."

Edwards swallowed hard. "Sorry," he said to the others, his voice cracking and his eyes on the ground. "Orders." He stepped forward and relieved the lead stretcher bearer of his load as Dr. York took up the rear.

"His fever will assist us," Dr. York announced. "You may be light-handed with the chloroform. We shall leave at least six inches of femur each side, so that he may balance in sitting up." Turning back to others, he said, "You see? I am not the sadist you think me."

One by one the surgeons and male nurses followed him into the surgery. Rose ached to join them. She watched the door swing shut behind the last man then turned to comfort a panicked soldier with a missing arm.

The repairs to the boilers would require the *Despain* to stay in Vicksburg for three days. When Rose asked permission to go ashore, Mother Pennoyer's response was immediate and predictable. "The battlefield is not for women," she said.

"Yet we are here," Rose said.

"I repeat myself, Nurse Barnett. This is not a holiday."

"I cannot merely read about the war in the newspapers," Rose replied. "If I am to understand it, I must see it firsthand."

"War is not woman's business."

"With respect, ma'am, I believe the women of Vicksburg would disagree."

Mother Pennoyer's eyes opened to their full fury. "Do not lecture me, young lady. You know my meaning."

"But I do not know it. Women both north and south are losing sons and husbands and brothers every day. Women's futures are in tatters. It is our business. We pay a price too."

"That price is to forebear, not to interfere."

"I do not seek to interfere, just to understand," Rose said. She thought of the ancient Greek tale of women refusing their men until they stopped warring. The comedy had endured because of its basic truths about the relations of the sexes but perhaps also because of its intriguing suggestion that women should indeed interfere.

"As you are employed by the army, you must secure the captain's blessing," Mother Pennoyer said, looking at Rose as if the devil himself stood before her.

"Yes, ma'am. I appreciate your concern for my safety. I shall not stay long."

"Do not make us rescue you," Mother Pennoyer said.

"No, ma'am." Rose smiled inwardly at the notion of the old woman wandering the town calling her name.

Captain Fuchs was in his cabin playing poker with his assistant when she pled her case. "If you wish," he said, his eyes on his cards. The assistant appeared to be very young. He had no sign of a beard, and his fingers were as delicate as a woman's. Rose remembered the rumors she had heard. The assistant stared at Rose with narrow, unflinching eyes.

"Thank you, sir," Rose said, eager to leave the disagreeable scene.

Holly's reaction mirrored Mother Pennoyer's. "Oh, Rose. Do not put such visions in your head."

"I know it would be difficult for you, but I need to go. I wish to see what has been done in my name," Rose said.

"One does not always give in to one's desires," Holly advised.

"So you think me a voyeur?"

"Perhaps. There is only misery there. I pray you are ready for it." Holly shook her head, seeming to know Rose well enough already to realize it was futile to argue.

"Contrary to Mother's assessment," Rose assured her, "I do not consider this a holiday. However, I do confess a curiosity about the caves."

"And who shall comfort you in the middle of the night upon your return?" Holly said. She waved her hand toward the shore. "Go, see your caves."

Although the day was still warm, Rose took a shawl against mosquitoes and passed down the gangplank to the landing. It had rained recently, settling the dust and leaving small puddles behind. It felt wonderful to be on land again, alone and away from the busyness of the crowded ship. She climbed to a vantage point above the city. Below her, men carried their comrades on stretchers between warehouses and the docks. The normal sounds of a city rose on the humid air—men shouting, wagons rumbling, dogs barking. She followed a path into the hills, along a bony ridge east of the city. Before long she found her first cave. Someone had filled it in, but garbage still littered the area. Rats scattered as she approached. The opening faced east, away from the river, away from the shelling.

She pressed on until she came to a cluster of caves. Some had been filled in; a few remained open. Canvas awnings still covered the entrances where families ate and neighbors visited. Twice a day, Rose had heard, the shelling stopped while the Union guns cooled. Families emerged from their caves to cook their meals, let their children play and visit with neighbors. The ruts of rocking chairs were still visible in the hard pan. She stepped inside a cave. A child's shoe had been left behind; otherwise the space was empty except for animal droppings. The cave was shaped like a T, with a short entry and one room to each side at the back. The opening was high enough for her to stand, but the ceiling sloped steadily downward until, to enter what must have served as bedrooms, she would have to crawl on all fours. Light entered only at the front; the small rooms in back were dark shadows. Rose shuddered at the thought of living and sleeping here. She hurried out of the cave, gasping for air.

She followed the trail into a densely forested area behind a high ridge. There were no caves here, nor city sounds. There was only the land as God had made it, only birdsong and the soft rap of a woodpecker. As a child she had loved chasing flickers through the woods. She had once seen the huge ivory bill, but she loved the smaller, less fearsome flicker best. Instinctively now she turned toward the tapping, as if hearing the voice of an old friend. She walked toward the sound, searching the woods for a red head or a white rump flashing in flight. Distracted from the trail, she tripped on a tree root and fell to her hands and knees. She sat back, feeling foolish. The palms of her hands stung; one was bleeding. She could no longer hear the woodpecker.

As she stood to dust herself off, a piece of cloth caught her eye at the edge of the trail. It might have been blue at one time but now was sun-bleached, dishwater gray. She stepped closer. It was a hair ribbon. She knelt down and brushed aside the soil and forest debris that concealed it under a thorny bush. Who had it belonged to? She tugged on the ribbon. Something snake-like flew past her face. She shrieked and fell backward, landing again on her sore palms. Then she laughed. It was only a plait of hair—a braid, tied with a ribbon. She smiled at her fright until overcome by a thought more dreadful than her fear of snakes. Where was the owner of the braid? Both knowing and dreading what she might find, Rose gingerly lifted the branches of the prickly bush.

She had held a skull before, but only in the laboratory. This one, lying face down in the underbrush, was smaller than the other, lighter. It had been thoroughly cleaned by the creatures of the forest. She bent to lift it, preparing herself for the eye sockets. They would be huge. They were always a surprise. She turned the skull over in her hands and was startled not by the eyes but the mouth. Shrieking, she threw it back into the bush. It was the skull of a child, and its double row of teeth gave it an appearance more monstrous than human. A nervous laugh escaped Rose's throat. Who would have thought that beneath the endearing face of a baby lurked such a ghoulish countenance, that the ivory glory of a child's smile disguised such a hideous secret? Still, she thought, lifting the skull again and running her fingers over the crowded jumble of teeth, the human mouth was elegantly designed.

Where was the rest of this child? Rose set the skull beside the trail and searched the surrounding vegetation but found nothing. She clambered down an embankment into the sloping woods below. With a tree branch, she stirred the underbrush, moving steadily downhill two or three paces at a time. When at last she looked up, she could no longer see the trail. She had found nothing, and her temper rose. She had no desire to be the object of a search by Mother Pennoyer. Annoyed with herself, she turned back.

She had left no path. She began climbing upward, but the hill sometimes flattened out and sometimes seemed much steeper than she recalled. She told herself that if she just climbed steadily upward, she was sure to find the trail again, but when she reached a rocky outcropping she did not recall, fear replaced frustration. Where was she?

Her heart began to beat wildly, as if trying to escape her chest. From her gut a stinging heat spread through her body, and she began to perspire heavily. She became dizzy. Her stomach roiled, and she bent over in dry heaves.

Rose had seen panic many times. There came a time in every delivery when the woman was certain she was dying. She would grow irrational, demanding to leave the dispensary, announcing she had decided not to give birth after all. Often she vomited. Rose, knowing she might do something foolish, lowered herself to the forest floor. She closed her eyes and leaned back against the rocks, forcing herself to take several deep, intentional breaths. She had long considered the breath a healing agent. She used it often with her patients. Now she was the patient. When at last she opened her eyes, she was calm again. She stood and gingerly resumed her climb. She felt tender, hurt, but her mind was clear. A few moments later, from the corner of her eye, she saw the white flash of a pile of bones.

The death had been violent, quick. The clavicle and one side of the rib cage were crushed. A small femur and a tiny pelvis rested nearby. Deep gouges—teeth marks?—defaced the bones. Rose rocked back on her heels. How could a child be taken by wild animals? She must have wandered away from a cave. Just how would a mother watch a curious child in the wild? How could she keep her safe? Or worse, was the child abandoned, left to survive on her own, more animal than human? Rose had cared for discarded children in the city; surely it could happen here too, especially during war. But something told her otherwise, something said that, whatever had drawn this child to her fate in these woods—curiosity, hardship, or accident—someone missed her. The ribbon said it. The ribbon in her hair said someone had loved this child.

Rose placed the remains in her shawl, tied it into a stork's bundle, and struggled upward through the brush. She found the trail near where she had left the skull and braid. She knew the way home now. Spreading her shawl on the ground, she aligned the bones as nature would have them, that they might lie together properly one last time. She thought of the skeleton that had hung in the lecture hall at school. The students had named him Professor Bones, and they had grown accustomed to his kindly, gentle presence in their lecture hall. There was nothing kind or gentle about the ravaged partial skeleton she assembled here. It was, if anything, all too similar to that of the pitiful soldier they had taken on board earlier today.

As she placed the broken rib cage next to the skull, she noticed a string of bony protuberances along the ribs moving upward from back to front. These would be the rosary beads of rickets, something she had felt many times with her hands but had never seen with her eyes. The femur confirmed her guess. It bowed outward, and its head was compressed at a strange angle. The child's bones had been soft, her legs too weak to hold her body. She would have walked, but poorly. One of Rose's professors believed that wheat in the diet could prevent rickets, but others had dismissed the idea. They felt a doctor's role was healing the sick, not fussing over a child's porridge. Yet, Rose thought now, here was a child who, due to war, had likely spent half of her short life in perpetual hunger. Did not the rickets tell the story?

Rose gathered the corners of the shawl, the bones falling into a jumble in the center. She had seen enough of the unintended consequences of war for now. As she began her descent to the ship, she let slip the tears that had been demanding her attention.

Holly was with a patient when Rose arrived at her side. Touching Rose's dusty, tear-stained cheek, she shook her head. "You should not have gone ashore. What is this?" she asked, pointing to the bundle in Rose's arms.

"A child," Rose said. "We cannot help her now, other than to find her kin and a spot in the earth."

"You poor thing," Holly said, embracing Rose. "I must finish with this patient, but stay here and I will help you."

Rose nodded and clutched the child to her chest, swaying as if rocking a baby. She watched Holly greet the soldier. He did not reply but lay flat in his bed, his eyes fixed on the ceiling.

"His head's shot," said the soldier in the next bed. "Not bullet shot, skeered shot. He don't do nothin' but stare. Don't talk, not a'tall. Sometimes he eats, but that's the whole of it, and even that ain't much."

"Do you know him?" Holly asked.

"No, ma'am. Cap'n just sent me out with him, get him out the way."

The soldier at issue did not stir.

"I can see his affliction," said Holly to the talking soldier. "'Tis nostalgia. And what may be yours?"

"The chills, ma'am. Got rained on."

Holly felt his forehead. "Your cheeks are flushed, soldier. Is that common for you?"

"No'm. But I knowed a man once had cheeks like a lady's. A brute, he was. Making up, I suppose."

"This is not your normal coloring," Holly repeated, "pink of cheek?"

"I have a swarthy tone, ma'am. A few mamas back was some Shawnee, they tell me."

"I think you shall live. The fever will burn off the vapor you have taken from the rain. It shall only take a day or two."

"I've a powerful headache, ma'am."

Rose spoke reflexively. "It is the action of the fever. You must endure it."

Holly said, "I shall order you tincture of willow. It will relieve the pain but still allow the fever to do its work." To Rose she whispered, "You needn't skimp on remedies here. There is plenty."

"What about him?" the soldier was saying, gesturing toward his neighbor.

"How long has he been so?" Holly asked.

"Since we blew the crater, some weeks back."

"Does anything relieve him?" Holly asked.

"We tried fright, ma'am. We sneaked up on him and even slapped his face and poured cold water on him, yet he don't come out of it. Like I said, he eats sometimes, if you put a spoon to his mouth."

Holly turned to Rose. "We see this. The surgeons can do nothing. Stimulants may be attempted, but their result is temporary. I have already given a purgative."

"What do we do in such cases?" Rose asked.

"Locate his family and have him retrieved."

"And how do they fare, these men?"

"Some awaken upon the sight and sound of their loved ones. Those we return to the field. The others, perhaps over time they recover, but we do not hear of it if they do."

"It seems a pity to wake him only to send him back to the front," Rose replied.

Able was passing. "If he doesn't go back, somebody else does," she said.

Mother Pennoyer was calling to Holly. "Able," Holly said, "will you please stay with our patient and Nurse Barnett until I return? I shall just be a moment."

Able turned to face Rose. "What do you have there?" she asked. "I heard you went to town."

"A child," Rose said. "Remains of a child, from the hills." She lifted a corner of the shawl.

Able shook her head. "That child needs burying."

"Yes," Rose said. She felt the bones against her arms, knobby under the shawl. "She needs rest."

"Give her to me," Able said, extending her arms. She slid her hands under the shawl, lifting the bundle gently, pulling it from Rose to her own bosom. She closed her eyes and began to hum something from a hymnal, something Rose knew but could not name.

Holly returned with instructions. "Mother says to take the child to the marshal," she said.

"Can we not take a day to inquire?" Rose asked. She envisioned the child being thrown into a mass grave, forever unknown. "Can we not search for her family? Surely they have missed her." She imagined a mother tying the ribbon to her child's hair, unaware it would be the last time she would perform the simple, caring ritual.

"The ship is repaired," Holly replied. "We are leaving in the morning."

Rose looked down at the shawl and imagined the child alive and at play. Had she been a compliant little girl, or had she been headstrong, wriggling with impatience while her mother braided her hair? "Let us see what the marshal will agree to," she sighed. "Come with me?" she pleaded.

"We cannot all go. Mother will have a fit," Holly said.

"I'll go," Able said. "I have a bad case of cabin fever."

A line of supplicants filled the Vicksburg marshal's office. Rose and Able waited among the vanquished, people ready to swear allegiance to the United States so that they might work and feed their children again. One by one they addressed the marshal, whose job it was to ferret out the pretenders, although he challenged no one. Each interview ended with him cocking his head toward his clerk, whereupon the petitioner would turn, fling an arm over his head and pledge his troth to the enemy. Rose noticed that most, after signing the half sheet of paper, stuffed it into their pockets as if putting a snake there.

When at last she and Able reached the marshal's desk, he began as with the others: "Is it your desire…" But when Rose laid the shawl upon his desk and lifted its corners, the marshal stopped. "What is this?" he asked, suspicion in his voice.

"A child, sir," Rose replied. "I am with the *Despain*. I came across these remains in the hills. I am hoping you can find her family, that she might be properly buried."

The marshal was an older gentleman with white hair and a short red beard. If not fully mindful toward those who had gone before Rose, he had been respectful, but the package now before him seemed to raise his bile. "Ma'am, you know I can't take that on. Look at all these people." He waved at the civilians filling the room and extending out the door.

"I understand there is much to attend to, sir, but she is a child. She mustn't lie with soldiers." Snickers broke out behind her; Rose regretted her choice of words. The marshal banged a gavel and signaled for his clerk to remove the remains from the desk.

"Who said anything about soldiers? Have you seen the pile of dead civilians out there? It's summertime, in case your nose hadn't noticed." The buzz in the room ceased; two men stomped out, mumbling something about respect.

"She is only a child, sir. To bury her so roughly, even with civilians…"

"Are you saying a rebel child deserves better than our boys?" the marshal demanded. "Because if you are, you are out of line, ma'am."

"No, sir, of course not," she said, "but as the child is in an advanced state…" She lowered her voice. "There is no odor, sir. Mightn't we delay a few days, to make inquiry?"

"And if we don't find family?"

"A chaplain could lay her to rest, sir. Perhaps in a churchyard, properly marked."

"Cemeteries have been filled for some time now, ma'am."

"She does not require a large space, sir."

The marshal rubbed his eyes hard then looked up at Rose. "Ma'am," he pleaded. He looked again at the shawl, which dangled like a sack of rocks at his clerk's side. Rose remained quiet, giving him time to come to the right decision, but it was not the marshal who spoke next. A woman's voice rose from the center of the crowd behind her. "I'll put the child in the ground." A tiny, sunbaked woman made her way to the desk. Her stringy white hair was yellowed from age and hunger. "My husband was preacher here till he got kilt by all y'all," she said. "The child is ours. We'll bury her. Don't know that we can find her folks, but we'll do it suitable." She walked to the marshal's desk and put her hand out toward the clerk. He glanced at the marshal, who nodded.

"A fine resolution," the marshal said. "Thank you, ma'am."

The woman took the bundle not in her arms but by one hand upon the gathered cloth, as the clerk had done. Turning to Rose, she said, "Not to offend, but she should be prayed over by her own." The woman's eyes then moved to Able, scanning her up and down. Able was silent, her eyes focused in the distance. Turning back to Rose, the woman said, "I do thank you, ma'am, for your trouble. Can I keep the shawl?"

"Yes, of course," Rose said. She had bought the shawl with her first earnings as a doctor. She would miss it.

It was late when Rose and Able returned to the ship. They went to the mess for supper. "That was a good thing you did," Able said.

"I am glad she will have a service," Rose replied. "But 'tis cruel in the extreme, how she died—first to starve, and then to be taken by dogs. What have we done? What has our country done?"

"Children didn't start this thing," Able said, "but they've been growing up and running things just like their mamas and daddies for near on two hundred and fifty years. I have seen children do some wicked things."

"Still, you cannot blame a child for war!"

"They learn what they watch," Able said. She shook her head. "After this, they're going to grow up hating black folks even more than they do already. Not that the fight doesn't need fighting. It's a no-win situation, is all."

There was silence between them, as if to say more was too painful for either to bear. Both had finished their meals, but their shared experience now kept them at the table. Finally Rose ventured, "Will you tell me where you are from?"

Able sighed and clasped her hands on the table. "There's no 'from' for black folks, Nurse Barnett," she said.

"Holly said you have lived in Boston."

"If you know the answer, why did you ask?"

"Were you born there?" Rose pushed on.

"Am I free? That's what you mean." Able raised her eyebrows and stared at Rose until Rose averted her eyes.

"Is it wrong to ask?" Rose asked.

"Not wrong so much as dishonest, how you did it. You want to know if I'm free, ask me if I'm free."

"Would you answer me?"

"Before today, no."

"Will you now?"

Able shifted in her chair, frowning. "I saw where Paul Revere took his ride, and that gave me gooseflesh," she said. "My mistress showed me that."

"Are you free now?" Rose said.

"No, ma'am, not by the law. Even by Mr. Lincoln's rules I am still property. I'm run away, contraband." Able pushed her plate aside and looked around the room, empty now except for the two of them. "Most white people just want to hear the gore. They like getting all lathered up with pity, but you won't get that trash from me. Whatever I've seen, that's my private business to tell or not." She leveled her eyes at Rose across the table. "Between us," she said.

"Agreed," Rose replied. She thought of the pamphlets she had kept hidden in her room as a child. Did she in fact find pleasure in looking at them? Why had she kept them hidden?

"I was a wedding present," Able said. "Miss Lady Boston had a daddy owned a shipping fleet between Boston and Liverpool. All those Irish up north? Her daddy shipped them in. She got swept off her feet by a Georgia indigo planter come to Boston one day to see about shipping some dye to England. She married him and went south, but she did not care for it one bit. Missed her mama. So, middle of one night, she wakes me up, and next thing I know we're on a boat to Boston." Able laughed. "She was a rascal. Ran off with the kids, the silver, and the house slave. The worst of it was the silver, of course." She chuckled again. Then the smile left her face. "From day one she promised to get my freedom papers from her husband, but when it came down to it, I guess she was too proud to ask him. Even with slavery illegal in Boston, I needed it in writing. I told her I'd stay on for wages, but somehow those papers just never materialized. When the war started, I slipped out one night and joined the army. Now here I am back in slave land, a two-time runaway."

"Do you miss Boston?"

Able looked past Rose as if she could see Boston just on the other side of the ship. "I miss the libraries," she said. "People there take their reading seriously." She looked back at Rose. "But I don't miss the cold. And I surely don't miss slavehood." She was silent again, taking time, as if the words threatened to spill out randomly, out of her control. "I was eighteen when she got me. She was twenty. She had lady friends in Boston, but she never remarried. It was just her and me and three babies. We talked. She taught me to read. We read to each other after supper most nights. Sometimes we played chess." Able's voice cracked but no tears appeared. She cleared her throat. "Like I said, she showed me the sights. But I waited on those papers for twenty-two years. She played me. If the war hadn't come along, I'd still be 'yes-ma'am-ing' that bitch." She looked at Rose, her stare and silence indicating she would not apologize for the distasteful word. "Now you know. Between us."

"Between us," Rose promised. She had endless questions but knew to be glad for what Able had shared. "You are a good nurse," she said.

"When the boys will let me touch them. That's one thing about Southern folks. They're not indisposed to our touch. Northerns, they got an unholy fear of the dark."

"I cannot say you are wrong."

"I'm not wrong," Able said. "Why, Southern ladies hand us their brand-new babies for suckling so they can get their figures back. No Northern woman would do that. Anyway, Miss Boston's third child was born sick. I cared for it. Had to clear its lungs by pounding on his back every day. I was sorry for the child, I was. He died when he was eight, and I won't deny we both grieved hard over it. After that, all talk of papers went out like a snuffed candle. In the end, I had to let her and those children go, despite it all. Sometimes I don't know what I was thinking, leaving. It's dangerous down here, but it's bad up north too. Different kind of bad. Two-faced." She shrugged and stood to leave. "I like the paycheck here."

Rose laughed. "I feel the same about the paycheck." In her prayers that night, she asked for understanding. How was it, she prayed, that the price of Able's freedom could be a little girl's life? As she fell asleep, she imagined the child's mother braiding her daughter's hair, tying the ribbon and shooing her out the door.

Chapter 5

NEXT MORNING THE *DESPAIN* WEIGHED ANCHOR FOR MEMPHIS, HEAVY with its burden of sick and injured Union soldiers. The river was low from the hot summer, the channel elusive. Rose had heard that Captain Fuchs gained his position through a friend on the Sanitary Commission and that his piloting was not what it should be, especially in low water. On the third day they twice ran aground. Each time, Negro laborers were sent to dig the ship out from the heavy mud, wading waist deep in the swampy fringes of the river. While thus halted, the ship was swarmed by mosquitoes, shortening everyone's tempers. Only the laborers, Rose noted, worked without complaint or remark.

The ship reached Memphis on the sixth day, two days behind schedule. The nostalgia patient's family had arrived. He was not one who woke at the sound of his mother's voice, for which Rose was grateful.

The full amputee was on Rose's ward. He lay feverish and barely conscious as she kept his wounds dusted with bromide. Her sorrow about the child in Vicksburg faded as she ministered to the living, especially this man, but she feared for him when he awoke. Already she had seen men wake in terror as their minds grasped their situations. Some showed a nervous paralysis, staring at their bandaged stumps, closing and opening their eyes, seeing but not understanding, looking for what was not there. Many wept. Others cursed—what the nurses called a "blue waking." A few days later, this man's waking was very blue indeed.

Rose heard the chaos from two decks up in the nurses' cabin. She dressed quickly and took the ladder to the main deck. The night nurses, Elizabeth and Charlene, were pleading with the man to be calm, but whenever they approached, he growled at them like a dog. His teeth were bared, and foam had collected in the corners of his lips. Several days' growth of beard and matted hair gave him a fierce appearance. Rose sent Charlene to fetch Mother Pennoyer.

Rose's attempts to calm him were met with shouting and cursing. She was glad when Mother Pennoyer arrived. "I will manage this," she announced as she entered the ward. A cluster of nurses, male and female, parted to let her through.

"Who did this to me?" the soldier growled, rocking from side to side. "I'll kill the bastard! The son-of-a-bitch!"

"Young man," Mother Pennoyer admonished. "There are ladies present. And you are disturbing other patients." She laid her hands on his chest, holding him down.

"Get your hands off of me, you old biddy!"

She jerked back. "Sir, there is no need for such language."

"Get away!" he replied, violently rocking until his bed began to clatter along the deck. "All of you!" He looked at each nurse in turn. "All of you, get out of my sight. Whores!" He hacked and spit, the discharge landing on Mother Pennoyer's chest.

She left it in place and pointed to it. "Is this how a gentleman thanks those who do the Lord's work on his behalf?" She was opening her mouth to speak again when another wad landed on her cheek. This time she wiped it away with her apron. "Laudanum," she said to Charlene, "forty drops. You will feel better soon, sir." She turned and began cooing at the soldier in the adjacent bed as if he would show how it was done. "How does the Lord find you on this fine morning?" she asked, but the soldier rolled over, pulled his blanket about his shoulders, and closed his eyes. Mother Pennoyer lifted her chin and left the ward.

When Charlene returned with the medicine, the limbless man twisted his head and locked his lips against her. Rose offered to try, and she took the dropper. "Sir," she said, "the medicine will alleviate your physical discomfort, if not the other."

"Who did this?" he shouted. As he spoke, she wished to squirt the medicine into his open mouth, but he would not speak to her again if she tricked him. Instead, she held the dropper high, by her shoulder, where he could see it.

"I am sorry for your situation," she said. "The surgery was demanded."

He had exhausted himself now; his voice was calmer but his words were still angry. "Only a butcher does this," he said, spitting onto the floor. His shock was masking his pain, but he would need the laudanum soon.

"Sir, if I could ask you to cease expectorating, it would be a help to the others. If you could try."

"Others ain't been butchered up like a hog. Spit's all I got left, lady."

"I admit it may appear hopeless from your point of view, but might I suggest you still have your wits? You shall need them now more than ever. I should think you would wish to secure them."

"I never had what you call 'wits,' lady. Now I got nothing. Nothing but drool." He spit again on the floor.

The patient on his far side barked, "Cut it out, Parrott. Ain't us blowed you to bits."

"Shut your trap, Kellogg. Just shut up, you son-of-a-bitch."

"Who you calling a bitch, Parrott?" Kellogg threw back his blanket and jumped from his bed. Forgetting he had lost a leg, he fell to the floor.

"Serves you right," Parrott jeered. "And don't call me that no more. You damned well know my name is Sallers."

Nurses rushed to lift the fallen Kellogg as he mocked his neighbor. "At least I got a leg to stand on." The nurses tucked him into bed and admonished him to be silent. Rose could not help grinning at his joke.

She addressed the full amputee again. "Mr. Sallers?" she said, but he did not reply.

"He's our gun man," said a soldier across the way. "Had him a Parrott gun."

"You shut up, Quaker. Lady, I don't know what the hell you want. Leave me alone."

"It would be my regret to do so, sir, but if you like, I will leave you, just as soon as you ingest your remedy. It will ease your suffering."

"Just shoot me."

"Please, sir. Do not even jest about such a thing."

"What does it matter to you? Get it the hell over with. Even a damned horse is entitled to that."

"You are not a horse, sir," Rose said.

"I am less than a horse! A horse can run and feed itself and carry a load. A horse can take a shit without laying in its own filth. A horse can fuck another horse. I am not even a horse."

Rose tried to imagine herself in the man's position. Pity, dependency, others' disgust—all the indignities he now faced—would be anathema to her. A shiver ran down her spine. If she gave him a large enough dose of the laudanum she held in her hand, he would go to sleep and not wake up. It seemed kinder than a bullet—kinder, perhaps, than the life before him.

"Take this," Rose said, pushing the medicine into Elizabeth's hands. She walked rapidly to the end of the ward and out onto the deck. She could hear the soldier screaming, "Just shoot me! Shoot me!"

Rose dropped to the deck, gasping for air. She hugged her knees to her chest and rocked back and forth. A hand touched her back, and she turned to see Maggie kneeling beside her. "What is it?" Maggie asked.

"I cannot do this job," Rose said, beginning to weep. "I am not safe."

"What do you mean you're not safe?"

"I could hurt someone."

"You wouldn't hurt a tick."

Rose's anger flared at Maggie's dismissal. "You do not know! How would you know? All you have to do is wash bandages!"

"It is tiresome, trust me," Maggie replied kindly. "I know my burden is different. Nurses do suffer from what they carry."

"I am not strong enough for this," Rose said.

"You seem plenty hardy to me. You would not be a doctor otherwise."

"You do not live inside my head, Maggie."

"No, but I should like to spend an afternoon there sometime," she replied with a soft smile.

Rose extended an arm around her friend. "Thank you, Maggie. I think you would be surprised how little you might find there." She took a handkerchief from her pocket and wiped her eyes and nose. Holding up the damp scrap of cloth, she said, "A nurse's most essential tool."

"I think you are getting the hang of things." Maggie smiled.

"I am sorry I spoke to you cruelly," Rose said.

"Don't be," Maggie said. "You were having an honest cry."

When Rose entered the ward the next morning, the man was still asleep. She went to him and brushed his hair from his forehead. "It's the gun he's mad about," said the man across the aisle.

"What happened?" Rose asked.

"His gun gave out. Parrotts especially, they just reach a point when they've had it, and they blow."

"Were you there?"

"Close enough. The whole team on that cannon was killed, except Parrott. It didn't help that we was led straight into a two-sided ambush. Those of us here, we got caught by shrapnel from Parrott's gun—me and Kellogg and Langstreth—but for the guys on the gun, Parrott's the lucky one."

"I am not sure he sees it that way. And your arm?"

"I was coming back from the medical tent. Piece of the gun must have got it—sliced it off clean." He looked at the bandaged stump of his left arm. "He loved that gun. Rubbed it down every day, just like a horse. Prettiest gun in the battery. It just gave out is all. Guns are like people that way; you can shine up the outside, but inside there's still cracks."

"What is his real name?" Rose asked.

"Sallers, Willard Sallers. I think he likes Parrott better, though it don't sound like it anymore. Lord, he was proud of that gun." The soldier closed his eyes. When tears found their way to his cheeks, he tried to wipe them away with both hands, whimpering when his bandaged stump hit his chin.

"Thank you, soldier," Rose said to him. She stepped toward him and rested her hand briefly on his knee. Nurses were allowed a light touch to the knee, when there was one, to comfort without suggestion. The soldier nodded but did not open his eyes.

When the man called Parrott woke toward noon, he and his neighbor, Kellogg, engaged in another shouting match. "You and your pissing gun," said Kellogg. "If I didn't know you had such a tiny dick, I'd say you fucked that gun every night. Probably put those cracks in it yourself from all your miserable humping."

"Shut your pie hole," another man shouted at Kellogg.

"Shut yours, nancy boy!" someone yelled.

Parrott shouted above them all. "Somebody do me a favor and put me out of my misery. I don't want to listen to you bastards carry on about that damn gun."

At first Rose hoped that Parrott's joining in the banter meant he was rebounding, but when he kept it up into the evening, long after the rest had disengaged, she knew his recovery would be long. The next day was dark with rain. Much of the ward was sleeping when Rose approached with a stool and asked if she could sit with him.

"You ain't really asking."

"If you say no, I will leave, but you can be sure I will ask again," she said.

"Then sit away. Let's get it over with."

Rose settled on her stool. "Do I understand you operated a Parrott gun?" she asked.

"Yes, ma'am. She blew up." This was the first time he had answered a question directly and with civility. Rose felt encouraged.

"I hear you are a good gunman."

"Not good enough."

"It is not your fault your weapon was fatigued."

"It's my job to know that gun inside and out. I killed my own men."

"The soldier across the way, with the cut left arm. Who is that?"

"Quaker? Hell of a guy."

"Quaker told me about your gun. He said you took good care of it and that you are not to blame."

"Well, I don't have to worry about keeping no damned cannon pretty now, do I? Just don't call me Parrott no more."

"Well, then, Sergeant Sallers, how can I help you today?"

"You can shoot me."

"Please, sir, do not say that. 'Tis a sin to take another's life, and an equal sin to take one's own. 'Tis murder in either case."

"Now, I won't be taking my own life, will I?"

Rose did not answer him.

"Thought not. And as for sinning, what is war besides murder?"

"God does not condemn those who fight in his name," Rose said. The words spilled by rote from her tongue but felt highly inadequate to the task.

"Last I heard, rebels was Christians too. They God's warriors?"

It was a question she had asked herself many times, how both sides could invoke God as their leader. "It is confounding," she said, "but we cannot know his ways." She felt like a coward. "Would you like me to call a chaplain?"

"I'd rather a word with the generals. From what I hear, we were sent into an ambush to settle a bet between the muckety-mucks."

Rose had heard the rumor too. If true, the orders were treasonable. Look what they had cost just this one man. "But you, sir, must take pride in your service," she offered.

"Shoot me, then, and call me a hero."

"I think not today. You will feel better in spirit as your outward injuries heal. You must take one step at a time."

The man shouted at her, "In case you haven't noticed, I don't take steps anymore, lady."

"I am sorry for my choice of words, sir, but please at least consider the others. Be patient, and quiet, for your fellows. Please." She touched him lightly on the shoulder. He calmed himself and emitted a sigh of surrender.

"Ma'am?" he said.

"Yes, sergeant?"

"I need to use the privy."

"I will call a male nurse," she said. "Can you take care of it at your bed?"

"I think not."

"That is good news," she said. She felt relief that his body was recovering, but she felt her own emotions plunge as she thought of the nurse carrying him and holding him over the seat, handling him, and cleaning him. She would call Rooster; his gentle banter might distract the man. Rooster was a favorite among the patients. He often sat up with those who could not sleep, sharing wild stories of his army days, showing off the wound he had gotten from Black Hawk's tomahawk. He had once told Rose that for a time he lived with the Oglala and even took a wife. When she died of cholera, he returned to the army on the condition he would not have to shoot at anyone, especially Indians, ever again. The army had agreed.

"I will ask the steward to help you," she said to Parrott. "It will be painful. Please speak up if you wish additional laudanum after."

At night, Parrott moaned in pain and often woke shouting for relief. Orders were to give him as much narcotic as he requested. Laudable pus flowed well from his wounds, especially from his right leg. His mood continued to cycle. If anything, Rose felt that as he gained physical strength, his mental state worsened. He continued to shout and curse, especially at night, begging even in his sleep for someone to shoot him.

In two weeks' time, it was clear that he would live. Dr. York lessened the laudanum, which meant Parrott spent more hours alert and angry. His despair afflicted the entire ward. The space would be humming with its tearoom calm when, without warning, the ugly words, his dreadful invocation, would erupt. Everyone would stiffen, and conversations would stop. Sometimes instead of shouting the words, he moaned at full volume; the nurses were divided on whether this was an improvement. Sometimes the other men mocked him, the entire ward ringing with the dreadful chant, "Shoot him, shoot him, shoot him."

Patients began to say the ship was cursed, and indeed, healing slowed, and the pace of death increased. Nurses dragged themselves out of bed in the mornings, reluctant to go to the surgery ward. Petty quarrels and spats among the nurses broke out over who used someone's hairbrush or what had happened to a treasured pebble. An assistant surgeon threw a scalpel in anger, hitting a male nurse in the eye. The surgery lost not only the victim but the perpetrator, who spent a week in the brig. The chaplain from Gayoso House tried to reach Parrott through the example of Job, but he was spit upon and declined to return.

While Parrott napped one afternoon, Rose approached Quaker. She asked about his name.

"I was brought up Quaker, that's all," he said with a shrug.

"Why have you not deferred? Or found a substitute?"

"In '62, we was all volunteers. No need for substitutes back then. Anyway, I was showing my pa I was grown up to a man. At sixteen." He shook his head, the corners of his mouth turning up slightly.

"I do not mean to judge you," said Rose, "but how do you reconcile your upbringing with soldiering?"

"Sixteen, you don't think like that. Still, it only took me two minutes at Shiloh to know I wasn't meant for killing. I hid under a rock and cried like a baby. Sergeant dragged me back to the front without my rifle."

"You might have been shot."

"More likely by my sarge than Johnny reb. It's peculiar, but the boys stood up for me—most of them. Not Langstreth; he wanted me shot, but that's just him. I couldn't blow a bugle to get past St. Peter, so Parrott, he convinced the sergeant to put me on litters." He smiled. His young eyes were framed by laugh lines, as if he had spent his youth in continuous hilarity.

"It seems a reasonable compromise," she nodded, "but it is still quite dangerous."

"Friends ain't cowards, ma'am. We just look for another way, is all. It's funny; I admit being scared that first day, but since being on litters, I ain't been scared at all."

"It takes considerable courage to be on the field with a stretcher as your only weapon."

He shrugged. "I'm used to it now. Where the courage is at is in the choosing." He swallowed, his Adam's apple bobbing. "Sometimes I got to say no. I don't pretend I don't see them, like some carriers do. I talk to them, tell them straight out. That's the hardest part." He paused and looked at his bandaged arm. "Not saying I'm sorry to have lost this arm."

"Are you going home?"

"My pa ain't forgive me yet. Probably stay with the army if they'll have me. I won't lie, though. I do want off the field." He shook his head, struggling against tears, the laugh lines faded to shadows.

"You mustn't ruminate," Rose said. "It leads to melancholy."

"Why shouldn't it?" he said, fixing Rose with his eyes. "What's more melancholy than war? And it ain't just the killing. First the marching takes your wits. You walk and you walk, day and night. When you do stop, you can hardly lay down, your hips and back ache so. They drive you like cattle, half the time with bad rations, rain and sun, never telling you where you're going. You forage, but you're too tired to pluck a chicken even if you find one. Wild onions and hardtack is about it. And then all of a sudden, when you can't hardly take another step, Johnny shows up and all Hell breaks loose. Sorry, ma'am."

"It's all right, soldier. It is just a word, not a bullet."

Where most men left their pain inside, unspoken, this one's words seemed to need spilling. "The noise gets you first," he continued. "It's a vile racket. Not just the guns. The rebs, they have this yell, it turns your innards to water. And the stock, even the mules panic. I saw one kick a buckboard to a thousand pieces laying there with a slug in its shoulder, eyes rolling around like marbles, just strapped to that wagon." He reached behind his pillow and pulled out a pistol. "I end it quick as I can."

Rose was still not used to the sight of a weapon; she pulled back. "You should not have that on the ward," she said in a low voice. "The steward should have taken it when you came aboard. You need to report it." While the rule was for patients' weapons to be tagged and stored, personal weapons—often family treasures hidden deep in haversacks—were often missed or let slide.

Rose pointed to the *No Weapons* sign. "Even a Friend must follow the rules," she chided.

"I am caught," Quaker said with a smile. "I'd be afraid to lose it. Bought it that first day I run off; been with me ever since. But I guess

I won't be needing it anymore." He looked at the revolver almost, Rose thought, with love in his eyes.

"We shall take good care of it, I promise," Rose said. "I will send the steward for it."

"Yes, ma'am." He grinned as he tucked the pistol back under his pillow.

Rose felt she would stay another moment to let the sting of her admonishment wear off. "So, what shall we do with our friend over there?" she asked.

"Parrott? He's in a tough spot, no question."

"God must have a plan for him; he is alive."

"God has a plan for everybody, ma'am, but he don't share it with me. I'm just glad I ain't Mr. Lincoln. I don't care for his plan, not what I've seen of it so far anyways."

Rose laughed. "Do you know anything of his family?"

"Mr. Lincoln's?"

"Mr. Sallers's family."

"Oh. We come up together in New York."

The two words of her home state were music to Rose's ears. "I am from Seneca County, near the Finger Lakes," she said with a smile. "Where were you raised?"

"Up-country," he replied.

"Not so near to me, but I think we can call ourselves neighbors, don't you?"

"Yes, ma'am, I suppose that's fair." He smiled.

"So, neighbor, what do you know of Mr. Sallers's family?"

"His pa owns a mine. Sallers Mining. Big outfit. Parrott being the only son, he was next in line."

"Well, there you are. Neither arms nor legs are required to calculate the coal in a vein and order it dug out."

"Iron ore, ma'am, not coal. And you might think it, but I doubt they'll put him to the task now."

"Why would that be?"

Quaker lowered his voice. "They're high, ma'am, best I can say it. Proud."

"I am sorry to hear that." Rose worried for these maimed young men with long lives ahead of them. If their families did not take pride in their service, what would become of them? "You grew up together?"

Quaker nodded, pointing his good arm at Parrott and two others. "Him and me and Kellogg next to him, and Langstreth, down there at the far end. Langstreth, he's a bully. Kellogg too sometimes. But Parrott's okay, especially for a brat. He likes shenanigans—just little stuff like ghost whistling and such." Quaker shook his head, laughing. "He'd get switched for it, but nothing stopped him. He's pretty rugged for a rich kid. Maybe due to it, who knows?" He looked over at his friend. "Funny how war levels things." His chin quivered, and he swallowed hard. "It was Parrott's idea. All four of us could have stayed and worked in the mine, but we were all too big for that. We run off together one night." Suddenly he began to weep. "I'm sorry, ma'am."

Rose let him cry for a moment, watchful of his nervous state. Despite his tears, he was better for the conversation, but she would create a diversion. "Does Mr. Sallers have a sweetheart?" she asked.

Quaker wiped his nose on his good arm. "He was caught by the mercantile's girl in high school. He has some letters in his pocket, but there's no commitment. I doubt one will be forthcoming now."

In the exciting days after Fort Sumter, young women had made pledges they now were finding difficult to keep. To be a wife was one thing, but a lifelong nursemaid was something else altogether. In North and South alike a dance of rectitude was taking place—the broken man offering to withdraw, the young woman declining the offer. Only where no official engagement obtained was there room for retraction.

"Only a very steadfast girl would continue now," said Rose. "'Tis such a sad case."

Quaker wiped his nose again. "He'll get over it, ma'am. What choice does he have?"

"He seems to think there is a choice. He would have us shoot him."

"That's not a choice. That's coward."

"If he was dead, would he care whether we thought him a coward?"

"All men care how the world remembers them," Quaker said. "Especially soldiers."

"Then we shall pray his family takes him in, that he might go down as the hero he is."

"They'll take him in, but he won't be running no company."

Rose imagined Sergeant Sallers, Parrott, living out his life in an attic bedroom, kept out of sight, tended by servants or perhaps a sister who would forego her own happiness to care for him. She thought of all the lives touched by this one man's tragedy, the children who would not be born to him or to the dutiful sister, and tried to comprehend the tragedy magnified by the tens of thousands, North and South.

"What shall be your legacy, Private Quaker?" she asked, attempting to cheer not only him but herself.

"I suppose, as a Friend, I would like to go down as a peacemaker," he said.

"That is a challenge in these times."

"That is what will make it a legacy."

"I hope you are successful," said Rose, rising to go. "For now, if you could lift the pall from this ward, that would bring some peace."

"I would try, ma'am," Quaker said, "if I knew how."

Very late that night, Rose was woken by the sound of a gunshot. When another followed, and then another, she grabbed a shawl and ran to the ward, still in her nightgown. When she arrived, her first instinct was to flee. She turned and ran directly into Dr. York. Reluctantly she turned back and followed him into the ward. The sight was no better the second time. Parrott lay dead, a bullet through his heart. Atop him lay Langstreth, shot in the head, a pistol hanging from his hand. And at the foot of the bed lay Quaker, the back of his head gone, his gun beside him. Pandemonium ensued. Nurses screamed and wept. Mother Pennoyer appeared with Holly beside her. Dr. York examined the bodies and shook his head. Captain Fuchs arrived last.

"Who did this?" he demanded.

The ward went silent until Kellogg began to speak. "Langstreth come from the far end," he said, his chin beginning to tremble, his words halting. "When I seen he had a gun…." He paused and swallowed. "When I seen the gun, I thought about calling him out, I did, but what if he shot me?"

"Langstreth shot Parrott?" Captain Fuchs asked.

"Yes, sir."

"Who shot the other two?"

Kellogg began to weep. "The shot woke everybody up, and Quaker, he got up and he walked right by me to Parrott's bed, and he says to Langstreth, 'You are your mother's ever-living bastard,' and he shot him. Then…" Kellogg's face became a mask of pain. "Then he put the gun in his mouth and shot himself." He broke down in wracking sobs. "Quaker shouldn't have been the one had to do that."

"Get them out of here," the captain barked. He turned and left the ward.

Rooster called the corpse crew to remove the bodies. Mother Pennoyer told her stunned nurses to attend their patients, many of whom had risen from their beds and now were struggling to return. Some muttered that the curse was finally lifted.

One very young patient, a drummer, had remained in his bed. He was crying and calling for his mother. Rose went to him. He seemed so tiny in the bed. His knee had been shattered by a minié ball. He had lost his right leg. The sutures had festered; a second cut was necessary. He wept like the child he was. Rose sat on his bed and pulled him to her. She wrapped her arms around his small back and felt his body quake as he released his fear and pain in heaving sobs. He clung to her and burrowed his face in her bosom, as he must have done in his mother's arms. Perhaps she had secretly treasured these moments, as only a mother might, loving her child's fear for the way it made him need her, until the moment passed and he pulled away, brave again. Rose held the boy until he let go. His tears stopped, and he wiped his nose on his sleeve. He did not thank her. Instead, he lay down, placed an arm over his eyes, and turned his head away. Rose stood and tucked his blankets about him. "You will see your ma soon," she said. The boy did not answer.

The ward was quiet now. Nurses were finished settling patients, and the bodies were gone. Maggie and Celia were on their knees wiping the blood from the painted floor and ringing sponges into bloody buckets. The beds sat empty, stripped to their springs.

Rose found Holly standing alone on the deck. The sun was rising. The two women embraced, weeping in the other's arms. They sat on a rigging trunk, bearing the shock together. At last Holly said, "It's probably for the best."

Rose turned to her. "How can you say such a thing?"

Holly tried to take Rose's hand, but she pulled away.

"I just mean for Parrott," Holly said gently, "not for Quaker. It is very sad for Quaker."

Rose felt the heat of anger flood over her. "And Langstreth, he is not worth noting?"

"He was a bully," Holly said.

"Even a bully is God's child."

Holly raised her voice. "Why can you not see what is before you? We are at war. Some will live and others will die. Would you have two Quakers die so Langstreth might live? Why can you not see the good here?"

"I see nothing good in two murders and a suicide."

"You must learn to apportion your grief, Rose."

"That is a callous remark!"

"I am not callous toward Parrott or Quaker. 'Tis a shame for them. But, yes, the world is better off without Langstreth. I for one am glad he is gone, and I predict the pall shall lift from this ship."

"Do you not mean, now we are rid of Parrott?"

"To be honest, yes," Holly exclaimed. "There, I have said it. Does it satisfy you?"

Rose looked away. "It was my fault," she whispered.

Holly took Rose's shoulder and turned her around. "How can you say such a thing?"

"I knew Quaker had a gun," Rose said. "I forgot to tell Rooster to pick it up." Her confession was like a brief, cool rain on her anger. She began to sob in remorse.

"Oh, Rosie," Holly said, embracing her. "Nothing would have stopped Langstreth."

Rose was not ready for forgiveness. "Had I remembered to tell Rooster, two more deaths would have been averted."

"It is not your fault Quaker kept his pistol. The wards are awash in weapons; you know that."

"It was my job to report it," Rose insisted.

"Then I am at fault as well," said Holly, "as Langstreth was in my section of the ward."

"But I knew Quaker had a pistol!"

"He and every other soldier. You must forgive yourself, Rose. You could not have known this would happen." She put an arm around Rose's shoulder, guiding her to the ladder and up to the nurses' cabin to prepare for the day.

As Rose crawled into bed that night, she remembered Quaker's desire to be a peacemaker. Had he achieved that after all? Could violence bring peace? Her last, ambiguous thought before falling into an exhausted sleep was that she would never have to hear Parrott beg to be shot again.

Chapter 6

IN OCTOBER A UNION SOLDIER ARRIVED WHO HAD BEEN HIT BY AN old-fashioned musket ball. To the glee of the surgeons, it had lodged in his umbilicus. The ball was removed in an easy surgery, and the area was carefully stitched to erase almost all proof of the man's connection to his mother. This last touch the surgeons found particularly hilarious.

The man called out to Rose one day as she passed by. "Hand me my tin, if you will, Nurse." In the crate beside his bed, a snuff box rested on his boots. Rose handed him the small, rusty container, whose cover he removed with unsteady hands. The box held only a photograph of a woman and child.

"Your family?" Rose asked.

He nodded, touching the image with his fingertips.

"Where are they?"

He paused. "They've passed," he said, his voice unsteady. "Last winter, the flu. We moved from Little Rock to St. Louis right after Christmas last year. It didn't make no difference whether you was Yankee or reb in St. Louis, and Lula's second brother lived there. I was running from the draft, was what I was doing. Then Lula and little John passed, and I didn't see much to live for no more. I volunteered for Uncle Abe just to get out of town. Should have went to Oregon."

"General Sherman has lost a son also," Rose said "Recently. After Vicksburg, he called his family to him on the Big Black, south of there. The child took ill, and by the time they reached Memphis, the doctors could not help. The general walks about at night, like a ghost. I have seen him. It is more, it seems, than a father should be asked to bear, but with every hurt the Lord does send us strength."

"Sherman is a lunatic," the soldier replied. "He admits it. I am not that." The man seemed aggrieved at being compared to his superior.

"He suffers from melancholia," Rose said. "The strain of war brings it out. You are bereaved, but you do not seem a lunatic, no."

"Sometimes I wish I was. I might take it into my own hands to join my family."

With all the unwanted death around her, Rose had little patience for this man's wish to die. "'Tis the opium talking," she said. "Is there anything I can get for you?"

"There is one thing," he said, replacing the photograph and putting the lid on the box. Rose reached out to take it, but he held it to his chest. "Could you look into the progress of a friend?" he asked. "Sergeant Johnson. He's in surgery. Could you let me know how he fares?"

"Of course."

"He is my wife's brother."

"I shall inquire immediately, then," Rose said, glad to have an errand to distract her from this man's pain.

Rose had not entered the surgery since the day Rooster showed her around the ship. Female nurses wishing to inquire about a patient were expected to wait until a male nurse or doctor emerged from the room. Rose found the rule ridiculous and humiliating. The protocol was explained as a way of shielding female nurses from the grim realities of surgery, but what of those who did not wish to be shielded? And were laundresses not women, after all?

She approached the surgery, her hand reaching up and pushing the left door inward, as if of its own volition. She took two steps and was inside. She stood silently, unnoticed. Only three operations were in progress, the two nearest her appearing to be second cuts for gangrene.

"Excuse me, Doctors," she said. "Can you tell me how the patient Johnson fares? His brother-in-law wishes to know his condition."

The surgeons and male nurses looked at her and then to Dr. York. "Get out," he said quietly.

"Sir, I only wish to inquire on behalf of a patient. He is anxious about his brother, sir."

"The surgery is off limits to females. Out." He waved his arms, shooing her as if she were a stray cat. The others smirked.

Rose turned and left the surgery, fuming. The rule was ridiculous. Maggie and Celia were expected to carry linens in and out, but a female nurse could not enter to discuss a patient. It was not only illogical but bad medicine. She went to the deck to clear her head. Mother Pennoyer approached her there.

"Did I see you enter the surgery, Nurse Barnett?"

"You did," Rose replied. "I was seeking a report on a patient who is kin to one on my ward. He requested it."

"It is not your place."

"So Dr. York made clear."

"And so I am making clear," Mother Pennoyer said. "I warned you to mind yourself."

"I was not about to amputate! I merely asked a question."

"Mind your tone," Mother Pennoyer said. "It is a boundary you will respect."

"It shall be breached someday," Rose said under her breath.

"What do you say, young lady?"

"I say, the boundary shall be breached someday."

"Today is not that day. Return to your ward; you are needed there. As a nurse." Mother Pennoyer adopted a false cheer. "I believe we have a case of shingles," she said, "something new."

That evening Rose approached Dr. York after supper. If she was ever to enter the surgery again, she would need him on her side. He was smoking a cigar and reading a newspaper. Although she was certain he saw her, she had to clear her throat to gain his attention.

"I apologize for entering surgery today," she said.

"It is no place for a woman," Dr. York replied.

"I understand that is the rule, yet the logic behind it eludes me. Do we not care for the same patients, the same wounds?"

"It is a difference of degree," he said, snapping his newspaper and returning his focus there.

"Do you fear we shall take the vapors?" Rose said. Her tone was disrespectful, which she regretted, yet speaking back to this man felt like scratching an itch.

The doctor put his newspaper down. "Miss…?" he asked.

"Barnett," Rose replied.

"Miss Barnett, I fear nothing, for women shall not enter my surgery."

"And laundresses? What are they?"

"Let me rephrase. Ladies shall not enter my surgery. I assume you consider yourself thus." He turned his eyes back to his newspaper.

Strategic retreat was in order. "I am sorry, Doctor. I came to apologize, not to rekindle the fire."

A moment of quiet unfolded between them. Their eyes met. "And I should not raise my voice to a lady," he said. "It is a bad habit." As if sensing he had gone too far, he added roughly, "It carries over from my work."

But it was too late. Rose would not let this moment of contrition go unharvested. "I am degreed in medicine, sir," she said. "I have observed several surgeries, and I have conducted small procedures in my dispensary. I know well how to stitch a wound. I seek to become a surgeon myself one day."

"Bully," he said, rattling his paper. "Stay out of my surgery."

"Yes, sir," Rose replied, suppressing a smile.

The following morning Rose returned to her patient. "I am so sorry," she said. "I was unable to secure a report on your brother."

"His surgeon came by last evening. All is well. I am in your debt."

"Dr. York?"

"I did not catch his name, but he said the operation went well and we must only wait for suppuration. Levi may still lose more of his arm, but we hope for the best."

"Perhaps his bark is worse than his bite," Rose murmured.

"What's that?"

"Nothing. You are brighter today," Rose said.

"Am I?"

"You are sitting up, and you are hopeful for your brother."

"Well, if those are the measures, then I suppose you are correct. But do not forget where I am headed next—back to the field."

"Let us not worry trouble. May I listen to your lungs, sir?"

"I am sure they would not mind the attention," he said. He turned his head appropriately to the side.

She bent over him, placing her wooden tube stethoscope to his chest. "Breathe in, please."

Across the aisle, a soldier who was enjoying his laudanum called out, "I am next," to which Rose replied, "I will send for Mother Pennoyer."

"Not that! Anything but that!" the soldier mugged for his ward mates. Laughter ruffled through the ward. Rose returned her attention to her patient.

"Your lungs are clear," she said. "Sometimes the chloroform can cloud them, but you are fine. The surgery was brief. I think you might take a walk today, if you care to."

"Not today. Can you hand me my tin, please?"

"Of course," said Rose, handing him what was left of his family. "Whenever you are ready. There is no rush."

New recruits and conscripts were pouring into Memphis by the train-load. Everyone knew the Union was preparing to push into the deep South. Since their loss at Gettysburg, the Confederacy had seemed resigned to the idea that the war would take place on their soil. It would be their cities and farms at risk, their people who suffered, their homes that burned. Rose remembered with sadness Holly's prediction that there would be many more Vicksburgs.

Along with soldiers came camp fever of every sort. To relieve local facilities, the *Despain* was ordered to transport pestilence cases north to Cairo until they were well enough to be shipped back to the front. Surgery patients were moved ashore, and pallets were laid between the beds, doubling the number of patients aboard. The trip would take two days if they kept the channel. As they would be in the upper waters now, the odds favored easy going.

Dr. York did not hide his distaste for the errand. The wiping of brows held no appeal for him. When a contingent of wounded arrived in Memphis the night before departure, he ensured his surgery got its share. He wished, he said, for his men to gain experience in cutting while under way. Mother Pennoyer just sighed. With a double load of vomiting, delirious men, she remarked to Rose, she did not need wounded to care for as well.

Two hours into the trip, Maggie appeared at Rose's side holding an armload of bloody linen. "The surgeon wants you. You'll be surprised." She cocked her head toward the surgery. "Go!"

"Who?" she asked. "Which surgeon?"

"York," Maggie replied. "He is asking for you! You will see." She winked mysteriously and skipped away.

Rose wanted to gather her skirts and run to the surgery, but she would not give Dr. York the satisfaction. She walked with purpose, greeting patients along the way. Three beds shy of the swinging doors, a man asked for a treat from the kitchen.

"Private Taylor," she admonished, placing her hands on her hips. "I am surprised at you. You know you are on special diet for one more day." She wagged a finger at him. "You shall have your egg as soon as you are legal and not a moment before. What would your mother think of me?" She did not wait for a reply; what he really wanted was her attention, and she had given that. She turned and in a few paces was inside the surgery.

A half dozen injured men on stretchers lined the walls; every table held a patient. The floor was slick with blood and human tissue. Doctors shouted at the male nurses to move that thing and bring this other. Laborers shuffled through the muck, gathering severed limbs into dripping baskets to be dumped at Cairo. Patients shrieked, even under anesthesia, and strained against their leather straps. Laundresses gathered bloody linens. Male nurses ran about with instruments, colliding at times with others, while surgeons shouted into the din.

"Who has Dr. Yardley's calipers?"

"You lent them to me!"

"You are mistaken, sir!"

"No, you are mistaken!" Calipers flew through the air. A surgeon caught them and went back to his work. A wooden tray of tools crashed to the floor. The same surgeon shouted profanity at the nurse who fell to his knees to retrieve the tools. The doctor, impatient, bent and grabbed the device he needed from the floor and began cutting upon the arm of an unconscious man.

Two soldiers were having legs removed and another a minié ball dug from his buttock. On one table a man thrashed wildly. Rose thought perhaps Dr. York wished her to calm this man. He was large, wider than the table. His leg was severely injured. It was not smashed from a minié ball but rather had been sheared off cleanly, as if from an explosion. The doctors would cut a few inches higher and create a tidy flap. He would suffer nothing worse than what the enemy had ordained. Ironically, in his terror, he shouted, "My leg must remain! It must remain!" Finally he fell silent as the anesthetic took hold.

Rose saw Dr. York at the last table on the far side of the room, his back to the rest. He was the oldest of the surgeons, with long hair he combed across his bald pate. The end of his nose was swollen, perhaps a sign that alcohol played more of a role in his life than it should. Rose had heard that the other doctors excluded him from their group. He ate alone, with only the occasional company of Captain Fuchs. She felt that perhaps it was no wonder he had been short with her, being under the pressure of leading a group of young, brash surgeons who couldn't be bothered to share a tipple with him at the end of the day.

"Am I still needed, sir?"

He was alone with his patient in a cocoon of calm. He did not reply to her question.

"Sir? You called me?"

"Step here, Nurse," he said.

Rose moved closer.

"Nearer."

She stepped in until her shoulder and hip almost touched his. The patient had a wound to his left wrist. Amputation was called for. "I require an assistant," Dr. York said.

His sudden change of heart confounded Rose until he pulled back the soldier's shirt. There, bound in muslin, were two distinctly female breasts. Rose caught her breath. The surgeon grabbed her wrist, and she nodded in silent understanding.

The woman's face was brown from the sun. An inch of what on a man would have been a short, curly beard grew on both sides of her upper jaw. Her hair was cut short, almost to nothing. Her fingernails were thoroughly chewed, and the palms of both hands were cracked and callused. She could pass for a man easily and apparently had for some time. Now she would pay a man's price.

"No one else has seen this?" Rose whispered.

"I suspect she walked in," Dr. York replied. "I have not asked her; she was put under before I knew. Stand right here next to me, but do not crowd me." He grasped Rose by her two arms and moved her to stand at the woman's shoulder. He took his position at the patient's hip. "The tray is there," he said, pointing to the rolling cart to Rose's right. "When I ask for something, hand it to me. Immediately, not in a week."

"Yes, sir."

"Please prepare the patient," he said, turning away, "while I strap her below."

Rose did not know the correct preparation, but delay would be dangerous for both her patient and her career. She drew from her apron the scissors she normally used to cut locks of hair from dead soldiers. She cut the woman's shirt entirely from her arm, opened the side seam of the shirt, and folded it back across the woman's chest. For greater access in case of emergency, she decided to cut through the muslin, even at the risk of fully exposing the breasts. At the last snip of the binding, the left breast relaxed to reveal its nipple. For a moment Rose thought she should have left the cloth in place, but it was too late. She folded the muslin to cover the woman as best she could. Then she wrapped a leather strap around the woman's chest, lashing her to the table.

"The patient is ready," she said. Dr. York returned to his place beside her, having tied the woman's ankles and hips to the table. Rose was relieved when he did not comment on the patient's presentation.

In the field, someone—perhaps the woman herself—had placed a tourniquet on her forearm and wrapped the wrist with lint and wood ash. The wound was not severe, but maggots had hatched and the arm already showed signs of gangrene. Perhaps if she had been a man, Rose thought, she would have come by wagon and her hand might have been saved. Sometimes, especially with hands, broken bones and fragments could be removed and the wound sewn up, leaving the appendage useless but whole in appearance. But such surgery was possible only before suppuration set in. Now that three or four days had passed, the sole question was how high the surgeon would cut.

The woman stirred. "She must be still," Dr. York said.

Rose turned to retrieve the anesthetic.

"Now," Dr. York snapped.

With her left hand, Rose placed the cone over the woman's nose and mouth, and with her right she reached for the chloroform on the cart. She bit the cork with her teeth and unsteadily dripped the liquid onto the paper cup. The boat rocked, and a stream of chloroform poured forth onto the cone and the patient's face.

"Well, that ought to do it," Dr. York said, taking the cone away. "Let us hope she survives your care."

"I am sorry, sir. I am left-handed."

"You must work to correct that if you hope to be a surgeon."

"Yes, sir," Rose replied, encouraged at least by the implications of his remark.

"Now look here. One must determine the correct distance to cut from the initial insult," Dr. York began, turning the woman's arm over to inspect it. He pointed to a red streak on her forearm. "See how the poison has traveled up the arm? Although the wound is only to the wrist, we must assert ourselves above the elbow, where we are certain to encounter succulent tissue."

"That is assertive, indeed," Rose said.

Dr. York looked at her. "They call us butchers, but they do not know the circumstances. They are idiots if they think we've time for conservative measures here. She has waited too long as it is." He turned back to the table. "Tourniquet," he said.

Rose handed him the band of leather with its metal screw mechanism. She had not applied such a tourniquet before. She had learned the strap-and-rod method.

"The pad of the tourniquet must be placed with maximum pressure upon the brachial artery," he said.

Rose ran her fingers along the inner part of the woman's upper arm until she felt the pulse. "Here," she said.

"Place it so," he said, reaching in front of her with the tourniquet to slip the end of the strap through the tightening screw. The screw mechanism was ingenious, Rose thought, as she watched its metal teeth bite into the leather, creating a firm band around the woman's arm.

"Scalpel, two inch," said Dr. York. There would be no fulminant speeches here. The tray held several knives. One had the look of a barber's razor; another was curved and sharp on both edges. Most notable was a saw such as one might use to trim a tree. The two-inch scalpel, with its wooden handle and swollen blade, was the most familiar to Rose. With her right hand, she lifted it from the cart, transferred it to her left hand and handed it to the doctor.

"One motion," he said. "Reach, give. One motion."

"Yes, sir. Have I chosen the correct knife?"

"Yes. The assistant now draws up the integuments." Before he could ask her if she knew the term, Rose clasped her hands around the woman's arm below the tourniquet and pulled the skin and flesh upward and taut. He looked up, and their eyes met in understanding.

With the scalpel, Dr. York traced a ring upon the skin of the woman's arm, two inches above the elbow. A small red line appeared as the skin opened, and a moan escaped the woman's throat. "One penetrates only the skin," he said, "as the next step is to detach the fascia between skin and muscle, although only to a trivial extent. Hand me the third knife from left."

Rose gave him the razor-like scalpel. He flicked his thumb against the blade and handed it back. "Sharpen it."

A flat hone lay on the cart. Rose whisked the knife against it.

"You must expectorate upon the stone," he said. "You are wasting time."

Rose spit on the hone and slipped the knife against it several times before handing it back to him.

"This knife must be sharpened immediately before each use. Others may be sharpened weekly."

"Yes, sir."

The arm was bleeding heavily despite the tourniquet. Rose mopped it with a sponge, which she rinsed in a basin of water.

Dr. York inserted one corner of the knife between the skin and muscle and with short, semicircular bursts separated the two from each other around the full circumference of the arm. "It is like skinning an apple," he said, as he folded back two inches of skin from the underlying muscle. "The fascia is painful to heal, but separating it is essential if we are to fashion a healthy flap and prevent protrusion of the bone. One has little time for such things in the field, but here we may do it properly."

He bent the woman's arm at the elbow. "For the front cut only, we hold the arm thusly," he said. "Muscle is cut only in the relaxed position, never the extended. We will locate and tie off the brachial artery as we go and sever the bronchial vein from the bone in a single oblique cut. Some would cut the artery now and ligate it later, but if done correctly, ligation prior to severance reduces blood loss. It is my preference. Four by one quarter."

Rose was unsure which knife he meant. "The length is called first, the width second," he said when she hesitated. Rose handed him the narrow, pointed knife. Beginning where the skin lay folded, he slipped the sharp tip into the muscle of the upper arm. The patient rose against her restraints but did not cry out. "We cut at an upward angle," he said, inserting his fingers as he cut. "I am feeling ahead in order to stop short of the artery. Irrigate this." With a glass plunger, Rose pulled pink water from the bowl and squirted it into the wound. The action cleared away much of the blood, making the vessels and tissues easier to see.

"I have it," Dr. York said, his fingers just under the skin. "Tie, please, quickly." From the tray Rose lifted a spool of silk thread, cut a length, and handed it to him. She watched as he threaded it beneath and around the artery, tying a tight knot. "You must be careful not to damage the sheath, else you risk hemorrhage," he said. Before Rose could reply, he sliced the flesh clear to the bone. "Now to the artery," he said. The rapidity and certitude with which he worked was astonishing.

The patient, despite her double dose of anesthesia, began to moan and twist about. Rose felt relief that she had not overdosed her first patient. As if she had spoken out loud, Dr. York remarked, "She cannot withstand additional anesthesia. We must hurry."

He worked from front to back, separating the muscle from the entire circumference of the bone. Rose tied vessels as he instructed. All the while the patient struggled. "Notice that I have cut the front tissue obliquely while the back is cut square to the bone," he said. "'Tis not the choice of all surgeons, but in my opinion it leaves a more functional stump. It is more important in the leg than the arm, but it is the method I follow regardless."

He pointed to two linen strips on the cart. "Wrap the linen above the wound. Stand at her head and pull," he said. Rose did as she was told. The muscle and flesh of the woman's upper arm retracted, revealing the bone. The action caused the patient to open her eyes just as Dr. York took up the saw. She fainted and went still. "Your good fortune," he said to Rose.

He placed his left hand under the patient's elbow. "The limb must be supported against the work of the saw," he said. "Ordinarily, a second assistant would assist, but in this case the surgeon must provide the resistance." The saw had a pistol grip and a wide blade. Laying it against the exposed bone, Dr. York said, "As the pulling motion is more stable than the pushing, I begin by drawing the blade away from the body." He demonstrated, pulling the saw gently across the bone, making only the slightest mark. Then he pulled a second time and a third. "Now that the line is made, the pushing-pulling motion begins, ending always with the latter." He began a slow, deliberate back-and-forth motion with the saw. "It is not a matter of strength but of keeping one's tools sharp. One cuts gently and slowly, with long, sweeping motions. Were we to cut like butchers, as people say, the bone would splinter, and all hope would be lost."

He shifted his left hand beneath the elbow. "While the limb must be braced against the action of the saw, the cut must be allowed to open slightly, else the blade become lodged. Mind you, if you drop the limb too far, the lower bone will splinter and you shall have all kinds of misery." Rose watched as the blade slowly disappeared into the bone with only the slightest of margins through which to travel. "We have passed through the marrow and entered the lower cortical bone." He pulled the saw twice then cut back and forth for three strokes. "Now we prepare ourselves for the ending," he said. "The final cut is what type of motion?"

"A pulling motion, away from the body," Rose replied.

"Correct," he said. He pulled the saw one last stroke and lifted the arm away from its host. It seemed to Rose that the severed limb floated up from the woman's body like a specter, but the vision vanished when Dr. York dropped it to the floor and kicked it beneath the table. "You may relax the retraction slightly," he said. Rose eased the pressure on the strips of cloth. "Rasp," he said. Rose moved the ends of the cloth to her right hand, reached across her body, and retrieved the rasp from the cart. She handed it to Dr. York, and he began to smooth the edges of the newly cut bone. "It is imperative you clear even the smallest bone fragments from the tissue," he said. He inserted a finger between skin and muscle, and between muscle and bone, sliding it around every part of the wound, only once retrieving a bone fragment the size of a grain of sand. "With bullet wounds, you must feel for scraps of fabric as well," he said.

"Yes, sir," Rose said, recalling the surgery she had performed on the *Redhawk*. She knew to search for foreign matter in wounds.

At last Dr. York said, "'Tis the best we can hope for. Relax the tissue entirely and slowly release the tourniquet."

Rose slowly reversed the screw of the tourniquet, and blood flowed back into the tied vessels. There was seepage but no squirting of blood. She looked at Dr. York and he nodded. "Now the stump," he said.

The deeply angular cut on the front of the arm had left him ample tissue to pull to the back, where it would be sewn in place. "Now we are in want of the feminine skills," he said. "I shall show you a few stitches, and you will finish."

Rose's hands shook as she threaded the curved needle and gave it to the surgeon. "Now you become nervous?" he asked, raising his eyebrows.

"I am comprehending, sir, all that has happened in the last thirty minutes."

"Well, look here. Stitching is a simple matter. Even a child could do it. Leave each end open for suppuration, and otherwise, simply sew it closed like the sleeve on a shirt. I dare say this young woman's mother has a fair deal of shirt mending in her future. There. The flap is placed. You will finish."

Rose had placed many stitches in her time at the dispensary. "You do not tie off each suture separately?" she asked.

"Personal taste," he said. "It is quicker not to."

Rose took the needle from him. "I shall keep her in my ward," she said, "to maintain her secret."

"Yes," said Dr. York. "Let us not have a freak show. You may give her a whiff if you like, to ease the stitching. A whiff."

"And for dressing, sir?"

"Wet cold. Add some bromide to the solution. Laudanum only when she is fully alert." Turning from her, he shouted, "Where is my next patient?"

He walked to another table, where a surgeon was struggling with a delirious man. Rose held the cone above the woman's face and, with her left hand, let a single drop of chloroform fall onto the paper. She counted to five and lifted the cone away. The tendons of the woman's neck, which had been taut and distended, now relaxed under full sedation. Rose placed the point of the needle on the woman's flesh and pushed. The needle went in and came out, drawing blood with it, but her patient did not stir. Rose tied off each suture separately, as she had been taught. Then she dressed the wound and laid a sheet over the woman. Later she would bathe and rebind her, and place her in a clean nightshirt. She guessed the woman would not object to a man's tunic.

She signaled a male nurse to help her move the patient to the corridor. With the ship overfull with contagious men, the surgery patients Dr. York had brought aboard at the last minute were to stay there until Cairo, but she must make an exception in this case. She sent for Maggie.

"Didn't I tell you?" Maggie said, grinning with excitement. "He let you cut, didn't he?"

"He let me hand him instruments," Rose said, "and do some stitching."

"I knew it!" Maggie said.

Rose felt herself blush. "Maggie, dear," she said, containing her own excitement by moving forward, "do you know that spot in my ward where the water closet juts out?"

"Behind the closet?"

"Our special patient needs privacy. Can we fit a bed there?"

"That spot is Rooster's personal jumble, you know."

"I think he will help us. Can you find him?"

"My pleasure," she said, grinning from ear to ear.

As Maggie turned to go, Rose gave her hand a quick squeeze. "Thank you, Mags," she said, a lump rising in her throat. "Thanks for understanding."

"I'm not sure I do understand, but I know you do," Maggie said, leaving the corridor.

The patient had begun to stir. Her eyes fluttered open then closed again. Suddenly she sat up and vomited. The sheet fell from her chest, and her torn shirt fell open. Her eyes darted about in terror. Rose drew the soiled sheet around her. The woman retched again. In her stupor she kept trying to move her left arm to cover her breast, but she had only a stump, and it pained her. From her throat came a deep groan. Rose wrapped her arms around her.

"It is all right. No one knows," she whispered into the woman's ear. "I will clean it." Rose glanced over her shoulder to see if anyone was watching, but the general hubbub of the ship went on as usual. The other patients in the corridor were sleeping. Rose laid a towel over the woman's chest, removed the soiled sheet, and covered her with a fresh one. As she finished, Rooster approached.

"What's this I hear about making up a bunk behind the closet?" he asked.

"I know it is a bother, Rooster, but every space is taken. We are stuffed to the gills."

"I thought surgeries were staying in the corridor."

If she wanted Rooster's help, she would need to confide in him. "The patient is a woman," she whispered.

"A lady soldier?" he whispered back.

"Shhhh. We must be quiet about it."

"I'll say," Rooster replied. He whistled through his lips. "I never seen that before. Heard of it, but never seen it."

"Will you help me move her?"

"Was it you that took her arm, then, her being, you know, a her?"

"I assisted Dr. York is all," Rose said.

"That's something else I never seen before," he said, still whispering. "A lady surgeon. Red-letter day." He grinned. "What do you need?"

Rooster and Maggie emptied the area behind the closet, finagled a true bed into the space, and set up a screen. Maggie dressed the bed and laid out a fresh tunic. Rose watched as the two of them, communicating only with their eyes, silently moved the woman to the private corner.

After they had gone, Rose approached the bed. "You may open your eyes," she whispered. "You have been hurt. I am sorry, but we were required to remove your arm."

The patient opened her eyes and tried to pull her blankets up, her stump flailing. She did not speak.

"I know your secret," Rose said, keeping her voice low. "Only a few of us know. We will be discreet, I promise."

The woman stared at Rose, still without speaking.

"I am sorry about your arm," Rose said. "The surgery was successful in every way. We do not expect fever, although one can never predict. I have given orders not to wake you. As long as your eyes are closed, you may avoid intercourse with others. I will announce myself when I am present. Only I will tend you."

The woman nodded and closed her eyes.

"We will be in Cairo tomorrow, and I will speak to the matron there. Right now we must bathe you and get you into a nightshirt. It will be painful."

The woman opened her eyes again and looked at Rose, then at the ceiling.

"Can you sit up?" Rose put her hand behind the woman's shoulders to assist her. "When the pain is very bad, there is laudanum. Dr. York prefers his patients to clear the chloroform before giving it. I am sorry." This was a peculiarity of Dr. York's with which Rose disagreed. Many surgeons administered the drug before the patient came to consciousness, but he would not allow it. She felt he was overly cautious. In her experience those who received their first dose while still unconscious woke with less pain and did better overall. Nevertheless, she must follow orders. "Let us get you bathed."

Maggie had left two large basins of warm water, a new bar of soap, and a rubber bathing mat to protect the bed. Rose pulled the privacy screen closer.

"Will you tell me your name?" she asked as she lifted the woman to slide the bath mat beneath her. "Mine is Rose."

"Roberta," the woman said. Her voice was ragged from disuse and thirst. With her remaining arm, she helped Rose arrange the mat.

"All right, Roberta. We need to bathe you, but first, can you drink just a sip of this water?" Roberta took the cup Rose offered her and drank it down in two gulps. Knowing she was likely to do so, Rose had poured only a small amount into the cup. "Good," she said. "Next time you must sip. Now let us turn you round and get this shirt the rest of the way off." As Rose undressed her, Roberta tried to cover herself. Her right arm was effective, and her left might have been somewhat so except for the pain of moving it. Several times she gasped as Rose worked to remove the shirt. Once the shirt was off, the binding tumbled down as well.

Roberta's breasts were young and round. In contrast to her craggy, brown face, they were soft and untouched by the sun, although spotted with grime. Unlike those of Rose's patients in Chicago, they were not stretched from the demands of pregnancy and feeding. Rose dipped a sponge into one of the basins. As she squeezed the warm water over her patient's back, Roberta closed her eyes and sighed.

"I'll do it," she said, reaching up with her good arm and resting her hand atop Rose's for a brief moment. Rose relinquished the sponge and turned around. Every few moments, Roberta made a slight noise with her throat, drawing Rose's attention to rinse and return the sponge. "Can I wash below?" Roberta asked.

"Of course," Rose said.

"I need help with my trousers and drawers," Roberta said.

"Of course," Rose said. For the rest of her life, this woman would struggle with her underthings. Rose removed Roberta's boots, then unbuttoned the fly of her trousers. She averted her eyes as she pulled at the trousers. How had this woman kept her secret? How had she relieved herself and managed her monthlies surrounded by soldiers? When the drawers were off, she rinsed the sponge and handed it to Roberta. "Scrub away," she said, turning around to give her privacy.

"I am finished," Roberta said at last. "Stem to stern and in between."

Rose turned to hand her a towel. Roberta's body was now pink from scrubbing. "Let me know when you are ready for binding," Rose said. This was something else Roberta would need help with now. Would a husband do such a thing? "How shall we bind you?" Rose asked. "I am afraid I am ignorant of it."

"Cheesecloth is best, but it's scarce as watermelon in winter these days."

"Cheese is seldom had here," Rose said. "There is a dairy on Island Ten, but it all goes to milk, I believe. We have linen for bandaging. Would that do?"

"That'll do fine."

"You must be tired," Rose said, helping Roberta lie back on the bed, pulling the sheet to her chin. "Rest and I shall return with the binding and clean underthings. Remember to keep your eyes closed."

Roberta laid her right arm across the sheet covering her naked body and closed her eyes. Rose added a wool blanket, knowing the bath may have chilled her.

At supper Rose found Dr. York sitting alone and asked to join him. With a mouth full of oyster stew, he nodded and slid back his chair to stand. Rose pulled out the chair on the other side of the table, and Dr. York retook his seat. He swallowed and wiped his mouth with a napkin. Rose wasn't sure what she wanted to say. She gave him a half smile, raised her eyebrows, and looked away.

"Thank you for your help today," Dr. York said, still chewing.

"I wanted to thank you," Rose said, barely above a whisper. She summoned the courage to look directly at him. He was watching her. When their eyes met, she looked away. "It was kind of you," she said.

"It seemed appropriate," he replied.

"Kind in two ways, I mean." He lay down his spoon and gave her his attention. "It was kind of you to protect her secret," Rose said.

"I've no desire to see her arrested, although I dare say I wonder about the scruples of a woman who goes about in such a way."

"She is like Joan of Arc," said Rose.

"Were she my daughter, I would lock her up." The surgeon picked up his spoon and began to eat his stew again, chewing the oysters with vigor.

"I daresay, were she your daughter, she might be a doctor," Rose replied, hoping to break the tension between them.

"Then I should lock her up for that," Dr. York said.

Rose blushed. "You would lock me up, then?" she said.

"Only my own child. I have no concern either way about your virtue, Miss Barnett. None whatsoever."

If he did not wish to be polite, she at least would be true to her mission. "You were twice kind, just the same," said Rose.

"And how is that, Miss Barnett? I am unaccustomed to being told I am kind at all, let alone doubly so. If I was kind to your little Joan of Arc, how else was I so?"

His stubbornness had flustered her. She hesitated, searching for words. At last she said, "I am grateful." The remark was far from the speech she had planned, a speech in which her gratitude was offset by a statement of her qualifications and interest in performing further surgeries, a statement carefully designed to lead him to conclude that he needed her assistance. These things went unsaid.

"Ahhhhh, so you think I was being kind to you."

Rose pushed back her chair and stood to leave, the heat of embarrassment rising within her. "Forgive me," she said.

"No, forgive me," he replied, standing and extending his hand. "I did not mean to be disagreeable. You have paid me a compliment, and I have reacted rudely. Please, sit down."

Rose warily retook her seat, watching his face for clues to hidden intent. She did not know what to say next. She looked at her hands, feeling somehow she was no longer in control of her own gift of gratitude. She must sit here and wait for whatever would happen.

"My surgeon's deportment gets the better of me at times," Dr. York was saying. "Thank you for joining me. I am honored."

"I wish to express my appreciation, that is all." It was not all but, having lost her voice earlier, she must be content to leave it at that.

"And I am grateful for your assistance. I see it is true what you say, that you have had some training in the field. Not much, clearly, but some."

"I am a doctor, yes. Although most opportunities for women physicians come in the field of obstetrics, I desire to learn the art of surgery."

"You did well enough today. Passion will take you far. But how does this go with your family?"

"I have no family to speak of, sir. I was orphaned as a young child and went on my own at fourteen. I do as I please."

"And how does society treat you, as you go about doing as you please?" He dipped a chunk of brown bread into his stew and noisily bit it off, dribbling into his bowl, his eyes still on Rose.

"I have practiced in a poor neighborhood of Chicago for five years. In such a place, society finds me quite useful."

"One need not worry in a slum, I should say."

"I am not ashamed, sir. Persons of all means today accept the wisdom of medical training for women—not only in the slums, although I am least judged there. If educated women had a choice, I believe they would prefer female doctors for reasons of modesty."

"So you wish to steal half of my business?" Dr. York said, wiping his bowl with his chunk of bread.

"I do not mean to offend, sir," Rose said.

"I am teasing," Dr. York replied. "There are patients aplenty of both genders. The fraternity needn't worry about competition quite yet. I have practiced medicine for fifteen years. I will admit that there are times when female patients come to me too late. Had they come sooner, perhaps I could have helped them. But as they are modest, as you say, they do not appear until happy outcomes are impossible."

"Precisely my concern, sir." She smiled with satisfaction at having bested him.

"I wonder, Miss Barnett," he said, "if you would do me the honor of a stroll when we reach Cairo? It has been some time since I had a lady on my arm."

Startled, Rose replied, "So I am a lady as well as a doctor?" She felt off balance again, now that the conversation had turned intimate.

"You are very much a lady, Miss Barnett. Of that I assure you."

Despite her natural beauty, Rose had never had such a proposal. She assumed she would marry someday, but between studies and work, she had found neither time nor opportunity to add gentlemen to her life. She had begun to think marriage might elude her. "I would be honored to stroll with you, Doctor," she said. The words were strange on her tongue, intoxicating and terrifying at once.

"When we dock?" said Dr. York. "Circumstances allowing?"

"Circumstances allowing," she said. She stood to leave, extending her hand. He took her fingertips in his hand and gave them a gentle squeeze.

"I shall look forward to it," he said.

As she left the mess, Rose realized she had forgotten to eat supper while there. She could not return now without embarrassing herself. She would do her rounds and ask Cookie for some bread and butter at bedtime.

At the end of the ward Rose found Roberta, eyes still closed. When Rose whispered her name, she opened her eyes in greeting.

"How are you feeling?" Rose inquired.

"Hand hurts," Roberta said.

Rose picked up Roberta's right hand to examine it, hoping this was the hand she meant.

"Not that one."

Rose set down the healthy arm. "It seems an impossibility, I know," she said.

"You saying you took my arm off and it can still pain me?"

"We are seeing this, yes."

"Meaning what, exactly?"

"It will come and go. Ideally, once you heal it will cease hurting."

"And if it don't, ideally?"

Rose took a deep breath. "Sometimes we cut a second time, higher." She worried that somehow she had caused the problem in the way she had performed her part of the operation. "You mustn't despair. It often clears up."

"Well, it's a hell of a fix."

"Ichorraemia had set in. You would have died without surgery."

"Big word for a lady. Doctor say that, or is that you bragging?"

Rose wished she had used the common term. "It is a poisoning of the blood," she said. "Would you like to talk to Dr. York?"

"Hell, no," said Roberta. "Sawbones done enough for one day."

"You can go home to your family now." Rose smiled with effort. "Where is home?"

Roberta rubbed her shoulder with her good hand, as if to rub the pain from the missing arm. "Grew up on a dairy in Ohio, but I'm all that's left of that. Pa took off for California right after Sumter. Sold the farm and said he wasn't fighting no war for the black man, anybody didn't want to go with him could make their own way, all he cared, he was gonna hit it rich and the rest of us would be sorry. He tricked us one other time, saying he was running off, but this time he was good for it. My brothers stuck with him, and Ma, but me and Sissy, we was done with him anyways." She paused and tears appeared at the corners of her eyes. "Should have went. Bank took the dairy. Callie died first winter and me, I couldn't get no decent work, not even housekeeping." She wiped her eyes on her good arm. "Tried a disassembly plant, but didn't last. Felt sorry for them poor creatures. I know we got to eat, but it ain't a fair fight in a pen like that. So I skedaddled into the army. At least the rebs have a fighting chance. My coward brothers would laugh their yellow heads off if they could see me now."

"What will you do next?"

Roberta was quiet for a time. "You ask a lot of questions."

"I apologize. You need to rest." Rose turned to go.

"No, stay. I don't mean nothing by that. I'm not the gabby type usually. Ain't got enough woman in me to gossip proper."

"Don't say that. You are beautiful and brave. Any young man would be lucky to have you at his side."

Roberta hee-hawed. "Honey, I can't get no husband. I'm halfway to husband myself."

Rose could not suppress a laugh. She had to agree that at least in her current incarnation, Roberta was an unlikely specimen for a woman. "What is there for you, then, if you do not expect a husband?" she asked.

"Farm hand, I guess. This here," she said, raising her bandaged arm, "will keep me out of that stinking slaughter house. I can milk a cow one-handed pretty good. Me and my brothers contended when we was kids. I won my share," she said.

Rose looked over her shoulder and, lowering her voice, asked, "Are you not afraid of being arrested for impersonation?"

"I've managed so far. You gonna turn me in?"

"Of course not."

"Just get me north. I'll be fine."

She might be safe from the law, Rose thought, but would she be fine? In medical college she had read of a disorder called sexual inversion. She wondered now if Roberta was a sufferer. Modern thinkers suggested the condition rested not in depravity of character, as had been thought historically, but rather in the nerves. Roberta's manner was certainly odd. She was forward and brusque, and at least under current circumstances, completely shorn of the normal expressions of femininity. Did her manner arise from her situation, or did she silently endure a nervous condition? In any event, Rose was hard-pressed, when faced with this woman's sacrifice, to find deficiency of character. She could not resist questioning her further. "Roberta," she said, "may I ask you a very personal question? You need not answer if it does not suit you."

Roberta frowned. "No, I didn't go around this way before. I just needed a paycheck."

"Of course," Rose said, feeling scolded but unsatisfied. "I am interested, is all, in your situation." She was careful not to use the word "condition." Even so, Roberta responded angrily.

"I ain't no exhibit, missy. And I don't pee standing up." She rolled over, turning her back to Rose.

Rose gently touched her shoulder. "I apologize for intruding. I shall see you tomorrow." Roberta nodded, eyes closed. A single tear ran down her cheek.

Chapter 7

W<small>HEN THE</small> *D<small>ESPAIN</small>* <small>PULLED INTO</small> C<small>AIRO, TOWNSPEOPLE WERE AT THE</small>
dock with litters and wagons to carry patients from the ship to the
hospital. Rose went ashore to ask the head nurse to make accommodation for Roberta while Dr. York examined Roberta's stump.

The matron had seen the situation once before and agreed to set aside
a private space. Rose returned to the ship and, with Dr. York's blessing,
escorted Roberta ashore. When she was settled, they exchanged smiles.

"I wish you well," Rose said. "You will be a fine one-handed milker."

"Thank you, ma'am. I'm grateful to you," Roberta replied. Then in
her straightforward way, she added, "You watch out for that surgeon."

"Dr. York?" Rose asked. "Why do you say so?"

Roberta shook her finger. "Don't you let him dazzle you, missy.
You're too smart to get yourself dazzled. You keep on your own way."

Rose was touched by Roberta's words. "Thank you," she said.
"I promise not to get dazzled."

"I mean it," Roberta said. There was an awkward silence between
them. "Go on," Roberta said finally, with a wave of her hand, and so
Rose left her, Roberta's strange warning ringing in her ears.

Across the grounds Rose saw Dr. York by a small rose garden where
a few blooms still hung tenaciously from summer. "Dr. York," she said,
"thank you for waiting for me."

"Our patient is settled?" he asked. He held a Cairo newspaper, which he now folded and placed in his pants pocket before offering her his arm.

"She is in good hands," Rose said. The next step, she knew, was to slip her hand through the crook of his elbow. She did so, almost pulling back, but he placed his other hand on hers, trapping it there. He raised his chin and began to guide her through the garden toward a path along the river. Neither spoke at first, but then both spoke at once, stumbling over each other's words and each begging the other to go first. Finally, Dr. York said, "I insist. Ladies first."

She had considered this moment all night, even losing sleep. She had decided to make safe small talk, perhaps commenting on the weather, but now that the time had arrived, she felt a desire to say something with greater meaning, something that might open up an engaging conversation. She was dismayed, therefore, to hear herself exclaim with exaggerated enthusiasm that the sky was blue.

"The weather is to your liking?" Dr. York answered. Rose noticed his eyelashes were quite short, almost invisible. Before she could answer, a gust of wind nearly blew her hat from her head. "Shall we return to the ship?" Dr. York asked. "The wind is rather demanding today."

"I do not mind it," she said, tying her bonnet more tightly beneath her chin. "I find the ship quite stifling. It is a wonder anyone can breathe on the wards."

"Do not let the Sanitary Commission hear you say that," he said, grinning. "It would distress them to think we are disapproving of their efforts."

"I do not mean to sound ungrateful. The ship is a wonder. But the ventilation is not what it should be, at least not what I had expected, for a medical facility."

"Perhaps the war is not as the Commission expected," Dr. York replied.

"We have all had surprises," Rose agreed, thinking of her walk in the hills of Vicksburg.

They came to a bench beneath an oak tree with leaves the color of leather. Dr. York gestured, and Rose smiled, accepting the invitation to sit. The wind created a gentle rustle among the leaves. He sat beside her, his shoulder but six inches from hers. From his pocket he pulled the newspaper. "The President's most recent remarks," he said, pointing to a short paragraph.

"May I?" Rose asked, reaching for the journal.

President Lincoln had lately traveled to Gettysburg to dedicate a cemetery for the Union dead. Rose read his short remarks. "'Increased devotion to our cause'?" she said. "Our president has hardened. He no longer speaks of compromise." She handed the paper back to Dr. York.

"Southerners do not want compromise," he said. "They would have the whole apple or nothing."

"The Union as well, it now seems. I am sorry for the president. He changes course so often, he must wonder if he will ever get it right."

"You may save your pity. Things will be right in the end. The South is outnumbered three to one in both men and money. Even against a country lawyer, Davis cannot prevail. The mathematics are against him. And England and France will never commit now, not since Vicksburg and Gettysburg."

To Rose the war seemed a jumble of contradictions and confusion. A victory today could prove worthless tomorrow. She could not discern a pattern to it; she certainly would not pretend to know its end. "I envy your certitude," she said.

"I am sorry to have climbed onto my soapbox," Dr. York said. "Let us speak of something less vexing. Tell me, Miss Barnett, where is your home?"

"Please do not apologize," Rose replied. "I enjoy a toothsome exchange, but I shall be glad to answer your question if you will return the favor."

"Agreed."

"I was raised on a farm near Seneca Falls," Rose said, "in western New York. Everywhere there are lakes and ponds. In winter, they freeze over and are good for skating and ice fishing."

"Ice fishing?"

"Yes, one cuts a hole in the ice and drops in a line. You stay warm by building a fire on the ice."

"You are teasing me, Miss Barnett."

Rose laughed. "I promise I am not teasing. I have not done it myself, but many people feed their families this way."

"And what magic do these lakes hold in the summertime?"

"Only mosquitoes. Or as I have heard them called here, gallinippers."

"Now, that I can believe is true."

"It is still the frontier in many ways. The Iroquois are not long gone. The towns are still small and most everyone farms. And you? Where is your home?"

"You will be surprised," he replied. "You must not judge me."

Rose looked at him with curiosity. "I cannot imagine doing so," she said, "but I shall wait until I hear to cast my lot." She heard the flirt in her voice.

"I am a Virginian," he said, "a traitor to my country."

Rose was surprised. "I would not have guessed," she said, "yet I can only judge you well for it. I understand the choice has been problematical for many Virginians. General Lee is said to have wept in resigning his commission. I believe him a patriot, deep down."

"I did not find the choice difficult," Dr. York said. "Nor did I weep." He rubbed his eyes with his fingers. His voice cracked with grief. "My tears are for my brother and cousin, lost at Laurel Hill."

"I am sorry," Rose said. "Where is Laurel Hill?"

"You see?" Dr. York replied. "They have died in obscurity. For two years they have lain, anonymous, in the soil of western Virginia." He grew silent and rose from the bench, looking over Rose's head toward the docks. "They drowned in the Cheat River. Burke, my brother, knew how to swim, but Gibb did not." He turned to look at her, his eyes narrow, his lips tight in a smirk of irony. "They were not prepared to be soldiers. No one prepared them. They were just boys. And the worst of it is their fathers sent them knowing it was a lost cause."

The wind circled them, tugging at Rose's hat again. The sky had turned cloudy, and the air had cooled. A chilling rain was likely. "Shall we turn back?" Dr. York said, lifting his chin and extending his arm. A silence, heavy with grief, enveloped them.

Taking his arm, Rose felt desperate for a new topic of conversation to distract him from his loss. "I am glad our patient can leave the army now," she said. "'Tis no life for a woman."

"I have heard of such women," he said. His voice had lost all signs of vulnerability. "But I never thought to meet one, especially in my surgery."

"What of the woman the captain keeps?" Rose asked. "She wears trousers and cuts her hair."

"The captain's companion," he replied, "is possessed of, shall we say, 'common proclivities'? While I do not condone it, it is hardly depraved." He patted Rose's hand.

Rose did not know the words were coming until they were out of her mouth. "Depravity seems a harsh assessment of one who gives an arm for her country."

Dr. York stopped. He removed her hand from his arm and said, "As such women are usually arrested, it would seem the Union feels otherwise."

Rose took a step back. "You have not reported her!"

"I am not so cruel, no. But even Joan of Arc was burned for soldiering."

"And made a saint for it!" Rose exclaimed.

Dr. York smiled. "You think our patient a saint?"

"She has done what her circumstances require," Rose said. "And served her country in the bargain. This, at least, should compel our sympathies toward her."

"I do not gainsay her sacrifice," Dr. York replied.

"In any event," Rose added, "she has told me she did not live this way before the war."

"Do not confuse my sympathy with tolerance, Miss Barnett. I suspect she does not chafe at her breeches to the extent she pretends."

"So you think her inverted, then, in the medical sense?" At last they were on common ground. "She makes an interesting case, if so, considering the exigencies of her situation. Perhaps circumstances create the impression of inversion where, in fact, none exists."

"Let us pray that is the case. Otherwise, I fear for her soul."

Rose sensed danger. "You do not see it as a medical question, Doctor?"

He replied with a question, as a professor might. "If illness it be, what is its cure, Doctor?"

Was he mocking her? "I would not bed her with a man, as some would have it! Women are not cattle." She was immediately sorry she had spoken so plainly, and she hurried to undo the damage. "I would treat the condition as any other neurosis, with warm and cold baths," she said, "preferably in a modern asylum, with separation from friends and family, lest they inadvertently trigger a recurrence. As chemical changes may be affected in the ultimate structure of the encephalon, naturally I would pursue an antiphlogistic course as well."

Dr. York cleared his throat. "And if she fails your cure?" His remark was more challenge than question. Still, Rose had already asked herself the question, and she had no answer.

"I fear, then, she will live a problematical life," she conceded. If she had hoped her concession would reestablish equilibrium between them, her effort was undone with her next breath. "Although I dare say, not as difficult a life as an inverted gentleman should endure." She was three steps on before she realized Dr. York was not beside her.

"The subject is unsuitable," he said from his distance. "I am sorry to have remarked upon it." He stepped forward and offered his arm, but Rose did not take it. He turned to face her, blocking the path. "The subject," he said, "is unsuitable." A clap of thunder rumbled nearby. He smiled and raised his eyebrows as if to say, "See, there? I am right."

Rose felt like a child being scolded. "Before you silence me, sir, I wish merely to say that a woman must, of needs, sometimes pass as a man, as there are such constraints upon her in ordinary life. But none of similar moment press upon the gentleman. For a man to pass as a woman is to yield his standing in society. No sane man would do so. Yet despite the immense risk, some do persist in inversion, or so I have read. Does this not prove that they do so from a constitutional disorder, rather than indigence of character?"

As if she had not spoken, Dr. York remarked, "I must apologize, Miss Barnett. You are quite exercised. I take full responsibility. Even as a doctor, you are yet a woman, and the subject is taxing. We have dwelt upon it quite enough."

"That is exactly what I mean," Rose exclaimed.

"You are uninformed."

"Then inform me!"

"Another time, perhaps. A storm is coming." He turned and began walking again, stopping after a few steps for her to catch up. They walked briskly and silently the remaining distance to the ship. Rose wished to mend things between them, but even if she might like to reclaim some of her words, she would not retract her opinion. As they reached the ship, she offered her hand. "I have enjoyed our walk very much," she said. "I assure you it was not the least bit taxing."

Taking the tips of her fingers in his, he wished her a good evening and left her alone on the deck.

The sky unleashed a cold, pounding rain. The thunder was no longer soft and rumbling but sharp edged and close. Rose was still standing under the main deck awning, shivering and replaying in her mind the disastrous exchange with Dr. York when Holly and Maggie appeared.

"Where have you been?" Maggie asked. "I saw Dr. York inside." She was bouncing with excitement.

Rose was reluctant to admit what had happened and keen to finish the discussion Dr. York had just cut off. Sighing loudly in frustration, she related the events of the walk.

"Inversion?" Holly asked.

"It is a neurosis," Rose said. "It manifests itself in the adoption of the habits of the opposite sex."

Holly looked at Maggie.

"Men who wear dresses," Maggie said. "And ladies in trousers sometimes, although I agree with Rose we have less to lose and everything to gain."

Holly's brows came together. "Why would a man dress as a woman?"

"That was my point with Dr. York," Rose said. "But he would not listen."

"I am sorry it went badly," Holly said, "but an afternoon stroll is for talk of the weather, not women's rights, and I dare say not whatever this affliction is."

"I merely pointed out that there can be no advantage for a gentleman to go about as a woman."

"And I agree with you, but the doctor is right," Holly said. "The topic is unsuitable for courting."

"So now we are courting?"

"Do you deny it?" Holly said.

"Not entirely. But I cannot go on about the weather forever. And I must be allowed my opinions."

"Opinions in women are not attractive," Maggie said. "They are not what men want."

Holly put her hands on her hips and glared at Maggie, who shrugged.

"I think," Rose said, "that sometimes I argue with men just to argue, to show them that I have opinions and that they must listen, lest I lose at some kind of game we are playing, one to which I do not seem to know the rules."

Holly took Rose's hands in hers. "He courts you for both your beauty and your intellect," she said. "He will tolerate much. I think you just happened upon a difficult subject. Things will go more smoothly next time."

"If there is a next time," Rose said. "I know you will not believe this, but he is the first gentleman—must I say it?—the first man I have ever walked with. I do not know how it is done."

"You'll learn," Maggie said with a grin. "I say bravo for your first time out."

"Thank you, Mags." Rose kissed her cheek in gratitude and let her friends guide her out of the storm into the ship.

The following morning, the *Despain* was underway again, loaded with recruits and ice, medicine and ammunition, fuel and blankets for the coming winter. After breakfast, Rose went to the bow of the ship to feel the first cool air to touch her skin in months. The storm had given the world a fresh start. She felt magnanimous when Dr. York appeared at her side.

"I wish to apologize," he said.

"I am sorry as well," she said, "for upsetting you."

He looked to the distance. "I was not upset," he said.

Bewildered, Rose started to object that, indeed, he had been upset, even angry, and that she should know, as she had been the target of his ire. But she had been taught in childhood that petulance was both unchristian and unattractive, and had learned from experience that it seldom made things better. In any case, the bridge had been burned. There was no gain in rekindling their argument. And so she replied, "I am glad to hear it." If he could pretend, so could she.

"There will be new surgeries when we return," he said, "if you are still of a mind."

"Excuse me?" Rose said.

"I warn you, it can become tedious."

Rose searched his face for signs of ridicule—the lopsided smirk, the raised eyebrows she had seen so often since becoming a doctor—but his face was relaxed, his eyes steady. The offer was genuine; he was inviting her into his surgery. Was this his way of apologizing? Was it a peace offering? Or did it show genuine regard for her as a physician? She wished to ask him, but there was no good answer to such a question, especially when put directly. He might even withdraw the offer. What complications could arise between a man and a woman!

"You may say no if you like," Dr. York said.

"No!" Rose exclaimed. "I mean, yes!"

He laughed. "I shall take that, in sum, as a yes," he said. "I look forward to it, then. I will see you in Memphis." Waving a large book he apparently intended to read during the return trip, he excused himself.

Rose wandered, dazed, to the top deck. There she found Maggie carrying sheets to the nurse's cabin. Holly was just leaving.

"I've news," Rose said. The three sat on a rigging trunk below the pilot house, lifting their faces to the cool breeze. As Rose told of her exchange with Dr. York, Holly and Maggie turned to her in excitement and congratulations. But Rose was not ready to celebrate.

"I am grateful about the surgery, of course," she said, "but I wonder about his motive—not to mention my own. Why did he deny he was angry when he clearly was so?"

"People dissemble when they are embarrassed," said Holly.

"Or when a woman wins an argument," Rose countered.

"Why must there be a winner and loser?" asked Holly. "This is not a game."

"Isn't it?" Rose dropped her head into her hands. She recalled Roberta's words. "I will not be dazzled," she exclaimed.

"What?" Holly and Maggie replied in unison, exchanging quizzical looks.

"I do wish to work in the surgery, more than anything," Rose said, "but I will not go there on false pretenses. He cannot buy me—either my silence or, especially, my affection."

"Pishposh," Maggie said. "Take it."

Holly agreed. "He has apologized and made a generous offer, which you have had the good sense to accept. Bat your eyes at him or don't; it is up to you. But you mustn't lose this chance out of some figment of an ulterior motive—either his or yours. The good doctor has offered you a place in his surgery. Go!"

Rose looked at Maggie, who was nodding in assent. "We will be on alert for bedazzlement, shan't we, Holly?"

Holly nodded. "Whatever that may be." She laughed.

Rose still struggled, fearful of the unknown price she might someday pay. But she had been stepping off cliffs since she was fourteen. Fear was normal. She had come this far; how could she possibly say no? She rose from the trunk and stood before her two friends. They were waiting for her to take the step they could not take. She felt excitement beginning to extinguish her doubt. Then, as if the moment had arrived unbidden, unannounced—as if the whole of it all was a complete surprise—she rose and threw her arms into the air, spinning until she was dizzy. "Surgery!" she cried. "I am going to surgery!" Lightheaded, laughing, she collapsed into the safety of Holly's and Maggie's caring arms.

Mother Pennoyer showed less enthusiasm for the arrangement. "Your absence from the wards will burden others," she said.

Rose was prepared. "I will work the same number of hours per day on the wards," she said. "The surgery shall be extra. And Nurse Lane has agreed to cover my section while I am away."

"Thereby compromising the patients in her section," Mother Pennoyer replied. "Did I not tell you in the beginning you are not to look down on the others?"

"I am not looking down! They are happy for me."

Mother Pennoyer harrumphed. She could not override Dr. York's decision.

"I promise to do my full share," Rose said. "If there is ever a time when you feel that is not the case, please speak to me, and I will set things right."

"You may be assured I shall do so," Mother Pennoyer replied.

On Rose's first day in the surgery, a new doctor arrived. He was very young. Sometimes, when a wealthy young man's pride—or his father—demanded that he make an appearance at the front, the elder would arrange a short surgical apprenticeship at home and then quietly secure a medical commission for the son. The new doctor's youth and demeanor hinted at such origins, but at least, Rose thought, he had had the decency not to slip the draft entirely.

At a morning gathering of surgeons, Rose stood nervously beside Dr. York as he introduced the new man as Dr. Adams. "In addition," he said, "Nurse Barnett will be assisting from time to time." There was whispering among the surgeons, but Dr. York ended it with a sharp whistle. Rose felt every eye on her as she followed him and Dr. Adams to a table where a frightened man lay without his shirt. He had suffered a grizzly abrasion the length of his right forearm. Less obvious was the small, oozing wound to his upper abdomen. "Your lucky day," Dr. York said to Dr. Adams. "Belly wounds, as a rule, do not leave the field."

Rose inspected the man's arm. It should be cleaned and bound immediately. As if reading her mind, Dr. York remarked, "This man has taken a bayonet. Although the wound to the arm gives the appearance of greater harm, you can see that it is clotting. No major vessels have been breached. The arm must wait for our attentions."

"Yes, sir," Rose replied. He was right, of course, that the belly wound was more dire; but were a nurse to be called now into the surgery, the binding of the arm could take place while the abdomen was tended, lowering the chance of suppuration and amputation of the limb at a later time.

"Nurse, you will please bind the arm immediately after we finish here."

A smirk flashed across Dr. Adams's face. Dr. York saw it. "Give your attentions to the patient, Doctor."

"Yes, sir," Dr. Adams replied.

Dr. York's voice became pedagogical. "Our first task is to determine whether the weapon passed entirely through the cavity."

"It did," the wounded soldier said. "I felt it!" His voice was high-pitched and breaking.

"I am certain you are an excellent witness, sir, but we must examine both entrance and exit wounds in any event." Dr. York rolled the man onto his right side so that both front and rear lesions were visible. The back wound was jagged and twice the length of that to the belly. Dr. York placed his ear to the man's back and tapped with his fingers. Straightening, he told the man to expectorate. The man spit into his hand and held it out for the doctor to examine. "Fluids are clear," Dr. York said, "suggesting the lungs are unscathed. Yet the breath is oppressed. We must conduct an experiment." He looked at Dr. Adams and pointed to the cart. "Hand me the taper." Dr. Adams lifted the candle and held it out. Dr. York responded coolly, "Else it be lit, sir, it shall tell us little." A blush rose on the new doctor's cheeks. Rose reached into her apron and offered him a match; she carried them always, to light lanterns in the wards. He lit the taper and handed it forward again. Dr. York did not take it but left him holding the lit candle like a choir boy.

To the patient Dr. York said, "Please, sir, when I give you the signal, fill your lungs and then empty them. You should feel little pain." The anxious soldier, with pinched lips and clenched jaw, nodded. "Good man." Dr. York beckoned Dr. Adams closer. "Hold the flame so," he said, taking the doctor's hand in his own and moving the flame to within an inch of the exit wound. "When our patient takes the command, keep your eye on the flame." To the subject, he said, "Now, sir, breathe in and breathe out, as deeply as you can." The man took a shallow breath and let it out. The flame remained steady. "I must ask you, sir, to augment your effort," Dr. York admonished. The man frowned but nodded his assent. "Begin," said Dr. York. This time the soldier took a deep breath. As he did so, the candle flame bent toward his body. Upon exhaling, he was seized by coughing and the flame was extinguished.

"The candle does not lie," Dr. York said. "Some think it old fashioned, but I find it a trustworthy friend. The lung has been compromised, although to what extent is impossible to discern. As the wounds do not hemorrhage, I suspect the insult is small."

Dr. Adams spoke. "Might we, sir, determine the scope of the harm through probing?"

"With what instrument, Dr. Adams?"

"The finger, I should say."

Dr. York looked at Rose. "Do you agree, Nurse Barnett?"

"With respect to Dr. Adams, sir, perhaps more damage may occur through probing, perhaps the dislodging of beneficial clotting already in place."

"Dr. Adams, what would be your approach, should the wound to the lung prove small, as I have deduced?"

"To close up the external wounds and allow the lung to heal," he replied.

"And if it is large?"

Dr. Adams paused. "The same, sir."

"Do not let care kill the cat, Dr. Adams."

"Yes, sir."

"You will mend the belly with plasters, Doctor. Nurse Barnett will close the back with silk." Then, as if balancing an invisible scale, he added, "Dr. Adams, please administer the chloroform."

The other doctors objected to Rose joining the surgery. When the man with the wounded lung developed pleuritis and died, they took their case to Captain Fuchs. As Dr. York outranked him, Rose was allowed to stay, and she stopped her ears to their whispers.

For a month she suffered ghoulish nightmares of severed digits in her morning coffee and gangrene rising in the most private of places. Roberta visited Rose's dreams twice, holding and shaking a bloody finger in vague, unspoken admonishment. Rose often was exhausted from working two shifts, but she took care not to complain. A satisfying collegiality developed between her and Dr. York. They often shared supper in the evenings, discussing their patients, political events, and the progress of the war. The subject of inversion did not arise.

One fall day Rose felt a soreness at the back of her throat that warned of a head cold. As the wards were quiet, she stayed in bed. She sent a note to Dr. York asking forgiveness from the light surgical schedule. In the afternoon, she went to the mess for a cup of tea. There she found Dr. York reading a newspaper.

"How is the invalid?" he inquired, rising and pulling a chair for her to his table.

"Still afflicted, I fear," she said, wincing as she cleared her raw throat with a tentative cough.

"I am sorry to hear it."

"Convalescing is tedious," said Rose. "I am not meant for idleness."

Dr. York reached into his pocket. "Perhaps what I have recovered from a rebel patient will cheer you," he said. He held a slim book in his hands. It was soiled and stained with blood. He slid it across the table.

"Standard Supply Table of Indigenous Remedies for Hospitals of the Confederated States," Rose read aloud. She opened the cover. "The importance of relying upon the internal resources of our own country should prompt the adoption of these remedies as substitutes for articles which now can be obtained only by importation." She looked up at Dr. York. "They have run out of drugs?"

"So it appears."

The pages of the book contained a list of plants, alphabetical by botanical name, with columns for common names, medicinal properties, dosages, forms, and quantities per batch. Rose skimmed the list. Most were remedies she had used in her practice. "Wake robin," she said, tapping her finger on one entry. "I know it as birthroot. I have used it to stimulate labor and to restart women who miss." She ran her finger across the columns. "Expectorant and stimulant to the gland system and lungs," she read, raising an eyebrow. "I have not heard of it for such a purpose." Rose browsed the column of medicinal uses with a growing sense of alarm. "For pain," she said, "they give hemlock and nightshade. And for anesthesia, hemlock again and hellebore, if used with caution." Again she looked at Dr. York. "They have no chloroform or ether for surgery, nor opium for pain."

"That's right," he said, smiling. "Another reason they will quit the fight."

"Does this not disturb you?" She found his smile unsettling.

"I am a Southerner," he said. "Of course it disturbs me. But they needn't endure it."

She pushed the book back across the table. "Let us amuse ourselves another way."

He put the book back into his pocket. "I am sorry if I have upset you. That was not my intention."

"You were not wrong to assume my interest," Rose said. "But I have seen enough."

"Look," he said, "I have a true surprise for you." He placed a tied leather scroll before her. "It is less dreary than Southern remedies, I promise. Open it."

Rose unrolled the leather to find a checkerboard and a sack containing brown and black stones. Even slightly out of sorts, she was charmed by the gesture. "I have not played checkers since I was a child," she said with a smile. "And even then I had to play both sides. As I favored black, I was seldom surprised by the outcome."

Dr. York laughed. "I am very good," he said. "You must be on your guard."

Rain had begun to pound loudly on the deck. The room was warm; the windows had fogged over from the ship's Medusa-like furnace. As Rose set up the game, Dr. York retrieved a cup of tea and placed it carefully before her. She smiled up at him. "Suddenly," she said, wrapping her arms around herself, "I feel as if the war does not exist. There is only this checkerboard."

"That is as it should be," he replied.

An hour later, Rose yawned and conceded defeat. "You have bested me today," she said, "but when I am recovered, I shall call for a rematch. Then we shall learn the true champion."

As he slid the stones into their sack and rolled up the leather mat, Dr. York looked at her with steady eyes. "I shall look forward to that," he replied. "Thank you for leaving your sickbed to enliven this dreary day. I shall be in surgery in the coming days. Please let me know when you feel up to joining us again."

"I am eager to return," she replied, "but I shall wait until I do not risk fainting, lest the others renew their complaints against me."

"You are the judge," Dr. York said. "I await your return."

Rose returned to the nurses' quarters. Despite the tea, her throat was still raw. She had enjoyed playing checkers; it was kind of Dr. York to entertain her. Still there was something odd in his reaction to the table of remedies, as if he took pleasure in the suffering of his fellow Southerners. Was this what it meant to support the war—to revel in the pain of others? If each side gloried in the other's suffering, how would the pain ever end?

Chapter 8

In December Mother Pennoyer received permission from Captain Fuchs to turn the nurses' quarters into a sick ward. It was foolish, she said, to use the large open room on the top deck for a handful of nurses when men needed well-ventilated beds during the winter season. And so it was decided that the nurses would remove to a home on the bluff across from Gayoso House.

The home had belonged to Memphis merchant Rufus Dabney, who owned the mercantile named for him near the top of the landing. He had done good business with Union troops flowing through Memphis on their way to and from the front. Dabney's sold every necessity of a soldier's life—whiskey, shaving soap, razors, coffee, tobacco. His wife made delectable caramels with fresh cream from the Union dairy on Island Ten. Three could be had, still warm from the pan, for a Yankee penny. Not least, Dabney's sold ink and paper for letters home. But on the recent day of thanksgiving and penitence ordered by President Lincoln, the shop had been looted by drunken soldiers. In disgust Mr. Dabney and his family had packed up and left to join his cousins in Atlanta. For two weeks the broken, empty store had stood like an angry schoolmaster over a naughty child. Soldiers and civilians alike lowered their eyes and crossed the street rather than pass by the formerly beloved shop. Finally, the marshal ordered it boarded up. The caramels were greatly missed.

The Dabneys' abandoned home came with a woman's touch and, in the Southern style, a name—Dabney Heights. The three-bedroom brick structure could easily accommodate the *Despain's* seven nurses, as well as three from Gayoso House. Maggie and Celia were moved to a barracks in the Negro section of Fort Pickering, freeing up their small onboard cabins for nurses covering night shifts. Able chose to go with the laundresses.

On moving day, excited nurses ran about their new home choosing bedrooms and rummaging through the wardrobes that had been only half emptied by the former occupants. Mother Pennoyer established herself in the dining room with her bed and a new large desk for paperwork. The rumble of her heavy pocket doors would signal taps at night and reveille in the mornings. The nurses were secretly gleeful at the prospect of escaping her snoring.

Behind the house stood a detached kitchen with a lean-to cabin. Unlike the house, with its flocked wallpaper and gleaming white trim, the kitchen and cabin were unfinished, with rough, unpainted walls and floors. There was no fireplace in the cabin, but it shared a thin wall with the kitchen and its iron cooking stove. Although the house had indoor plumbing, a privy stood behind the cabin.

Rose entered the room and found Holly already there, sitting on a pallet. "Look what you have found," Rose said. After the many weeks on the ship, she suddenly realized she was craving privacy. She was disappointed that Holly had discovered the cabin first. She turned to go.

"Don't leave," Holly said. "There is room for two."

"I see only one bed," Rose said.

"Mightn't we squeeze in together?"

"We could flip a coin," Rose countered.

Holly did not answer immediately but stood and walked about the tiny space. "To be honest," she said at last, "I am desperate for privacy."

"I as well," Rose replied. Seconds passed. "And so a coin would seem in order."

Holly pursed her lips and nodded. "And yet," she said, running her hand along a small chest of drawers near the door, "a coin leaves one of us among the giggling gaggle upstairs. Mightn't we each compromise a little and agree to share? Then we need only deal with each other rather than the crowd."

Sharing this tiny space could be a fair price for escaping Elizabeth's silly chatter about handsome soldiers. "Do you pledge not to giggle?" Rose asked.

"I think I could not keep such a pledge, but I can promise to laugh only at what is truly hilarious. And to respect your solitude, if you will mine."

"Then let us compromise," Rose said.

The space would accommodate one true bed and a chair, or two army cots. Rose had never shared a bed; if anything would disturb her solitude, she thought, it would be this. But cots were drafty and uncomfortable, especially compared to the lovely beds the Dabneys had abandoned. In the end, Rose's desire for a reading chair tipped the scale, and a bed was found to replace the pallet. They covered it with Rose's army blanket and the counterpane Holly had made as a girl.

Rose yawned. It was late. "Sit," Holly said, patting the bed. "I will braid your hair, then you mine. Where is your brush?"

Rose retrieved her hairbrush and sat next to Holly on the bed. Holly placed her hands on Rose's shoulders to turn her around. "My aunts braided my hair when I was small," Rose said, glancing back, "but only I have touched it since I was eight or nine." Holly pulled the pins from the knot atop Rose's head. From the corner of her eye Rose saw her fine hair flutter past her shoulders. Her skin rose in gooseflesh as Holly ran her fingernails along her scalp. Rose closed her eyes and leaned back as Holly softly counted one hundred strokes. Considerable inconvenience, Rose thought, might be endured in exchange for having one's hair brushed at bedtime.

"My turn," Holly said. "I have tricked you. 'Tis best to be second."

"I see that now," Rose said, emerging from her trance. "We shall have to even things out over time." She unfastened the large bun atop Holly's head. When the hair did not fall, she slipped her fingers into the tight brown curls. "There is so much of it," she said. "Where is your brush?"

"You must use your fingers," Holly said. "I do not even own a brush!"

Rose laughed and dragged her fingers through Holly's thick, coarse hair. Her own flesh rose again as the curly strands bubbled beneath her fingernails. She began to braid it, but it would not obey. "It is hopeless," she cried.

"Like this," Holly said, roughly separating a handful of hair. "Braid that," she said. "We must work in batches." Clump by clump, Holly's mane was tamed for the night.

There remained the matter of dressing. "Now that we are ashore," Rose said, "I think I would enjoy a walk in the evenings. Might you use the privy and dress for bed while I am out?"

"I shall run out and back before you can circle the house," Holly replied. "When you come in, I shall be in dreamland."

When Rose returned from her walk about the house and its extensive gardens, Holly was in bed, eyes closed. Rose changed into her nightgown, stepped to the bed and blew out the lantern. An urge to play came over her. Sitting on the edge of the bed, she bounced once, lightly, then harder and twice more, until Holly began to giggle. "See what fun, to share a bed?" Holly said.

"I see what I have missed in not having a sister," Rose said, smiling. She crawled into bed and pulled the blankets up.

"I like to tuck the covers around my shoulders," Holly said, tugging on the quilt and securing it about her neck. "If it bothers you, you must tell me."

"I sometimes sleep lightly," Rose replied. "I hope I do not disturb you."

"It is good you have taken the outside, then" Holly said. "I sleep like the dead—or so my sisters say." She closed her eyes.

Rose whispered, "This must have been slave quarters."

"Let us imagine it was occupied by a contented soul," Holly murmured.

"Only the walls can know," Rose replied. In seconds, she was asleep, the warmth of Holly's body enveloping her like a sweet breath.

The next night, while others slept, they seized a tapestried rocking chair from the parlor and a braided rug from the foyer. Laughing at their prank, Holly crossed her heart and spit into her palm, which she held out to Rose. Rose followed suit and took Holly's hand in hers. "Sisters," Holly said.

"Sisters," replied Rose. It was the first time she had shared spit with another person.

On the morning of Christmas Eve, a storm encased the city in a glassy mantle of ice. The *Despain* rode low in the water, creaking under the weight of freezing rain. A Christmas social was planned for the evening at Gayoso House; officers, surgeons, and nurses from across the city were invited. The women of Dabney Heights had been baking for days; with the ice, Rose wondered if they would be their own and only guests. At midafternoon the male nurses chased the women off the ship. They clung to each other as they crossed the slippery landing, squealing with the delight of children let loose from school. Along the through-road to the bluff, a line of black workers in hobnail boots, icicles dripping from their noses, handed citizens up and down the hill like buckets to a fire.

In single file the nurses trudged up the hill. At the top Holly fell, hurting her wrist. Rose lifted her to her feet. They struggled on to Dabney Heights, each with the other as ballast. Rose's cheeks stung as they entered the warm kitchen. The air was heavy with the scent of butter and sugar, cinnamon and molasses. They passed through the kitchen to their cabin, shaking the ice from their shawls and bonnets.

"Let me see," Rose said, taking Holly's hand.

"Owww," Holly cried, pulling back.

"I'm sorry, dear," Rose replied. Holly's cheeks were red from the cold. "It really must be splinted," Rose said.

Holly groaned. "Not today. I will look like a mummy at the party."

"How is it to knit if we do not immobilize it?"

"Perhaps it is not broken."

"Perhaps. And perhaps it is. Look there." A purple knot had risen on Holly's wrist. "Stay," Rose said. She went through the kitchen and opened the door to the short path that led to the main house. As she stepped out onto the icy ground, she was reminded of the shallow pond behind the barn where she had skated as a child. She stepped down and pushed her right foot forward, then her left. The path was bumpy, like the pond. Aunt Fidelia had loved skating and occasionally had joined her. Grace had come with them once, but when she fell, she said her skates rubbed her feet raw and went inside. Rose smiled at the memory as she entered the house and walked to the parlor. It was not as warm here as in their small cabin next to the kitchen. A fire burned in the parlor's fireplace, but it gave more cheer than warmth. Rose pulled her shawl close. A small pine tree had been nailed to a wooden platform; it stood in the center of the room. Rooster had cut it at the request of a German girl. She was tearing red cloth into strips to tie in bows on the branches while other nurses poked needles into holly berries, sliding them down long lengths of thread.

"Have you any more red cloth?" Rose asked the German girl.

"There is plenty, *ja*," she said. "More is in the *keller*." She pointed toward the basement.

Rose measured a length of fabric from her nose to her outstretched arm and ripped it from the bolt. "Thank you," she said, wondering how long the girl had been in America and what she thought of her new country at war.

"Are you and Holly coming?" someone asked.

"We would not miss it," Rose said. She left the chilly parlor and skated back to the kitchen, where she rummaged through boxes and drawers until at last she pulled a butter-molding paddle from a jumble of kitchen tools. Turning it over in her hand, she laid its curved neck beneath her wrist and its shallow bowl in her palm. It would work.

"You shall not be a mummy after all," she cried, waving the fabric as she entered the cabin. "I haven't a true splint, but this will do for now." She held out the butter paddle, and Holly laughed.

"If any butter needs shaping, I shall be the belle of the Christmas ball," she said. "First let me change; then you may bind my wrist." She went to the dresser and pulled a lavender gingham dress from the bottom drawer. "I wear this every year," she said, "on my birthday. My father calls it my birthday suit."

As Holly stepped into the kitchen to change, Rose pulled her green satin dress from her satchel. She had not worn it since her interview five months earlier. If the dress had led her here, to this moment, she thought, she had made a fine choice after all that day.

Holly stepped back into the cabin, a shy smile on her face. The lace collar of her dress framed her face like the wings of a dove. Her eyes reflected her dress, the candles within them floating in a sea of lilac. Rose felt a lump rise in her throat. "I have a birthday present for you," she said. From the dresser she produced a sprig of holly, which she pinned to Holly's shoulder. "I have snipped off the spines," she said, "lest they chase the boys away."

"It is lovely," Holly whispered, directing her astonishing eyes toward Rose.

"Now let us bind that wrist," Rose replied, smiling.

In the parlor a dozen nurses in colorful gowns laughed and chirped like songbirds as they flitted about the tree. It was lovely, Rose thought, to see color again. Even Mother Pennoyer wore a red ribbon tied around her black collar. At last the German girl clapped her hands, called for a chair, and climbed above to tie a candle to the top of the tree. She struck a match and lifted it to the candle. Someone turned down the lanterns in the room. The women fell silent. Rose had not seen a Christmas tree before. It was breathtaking.

They joined in a hymn, and Mother Pennoyer read the Christmas story aloud, her severe reading reminding Rose of her Aunt Grace's annual rendition of the precious story. There was a knock at the door. Elizabeth squealed and rushed to open it, revealing a phalanx of soldiers in dress uniform and hobnailed boots ready to escort them across the street to the hotel. As Rose, in her turn, took a masculine arm and stepped out onto the slippery ice, she thought of her own ice boots packed away in Chicago. Winters there demanded more of a woman.

The storm had moved on, leaving a glittering world beneath a full moon. Trees heavy with ice bowed to the ground as if personally welcoming each guest. While these women had entered the hotel without ceremony a thousand times before, now they glided up the stairs on the arms of their attentive escorts and slipped past the majestic columns of Gayoso House as if they, the wives and daughters of Northern farmers and merchants, were the embodiment of Southern womanhood itself. They entered breathless, chins high and corsets tight, ready to pretend for one evening.

Despite the weather, the huge lobby was crowded with guests—Union officers, their wives and children, patients, surgeons, and nurses. The room resounded with squeals and laughter and bombast. Rose and Holly smiled and squeezed each other's hands as they edged through the crowd to the south sitting room where tables draped in white silk bore whole roasted turkeys, slabs of beef and pork, and crystal bowls of pickles, jams, apples, and nuts. Pound cakes and gingerbreads graced marble sideboards; silver champagne urns rimmed the room. Black men in white jackets glided silently about as if they knew exactly what to do.

Soldiers had gathered around a square piano and were singing "Deck the Halls" with great enthusiasm. Dr. York was there with the others. "Wish me luck," Rose said to Holly, kissing her cheek.

"The best of luck," Holly replied, gently pushing Rose toward the piano.

As she approached, Dr. York handed her a warm drink redolent of cream and nutmeg. She took a sip but choked and patted her chest. "It smells lovely, but I cannot say the same for its taste. It is—it is practically medicinal!"

"It does boast a drop of brandy." Dr. York laughed. "We must watch you carefully."

Rose handed the cup back to him. "I do not need watching," she said. "I shall have coffee, please." She wished he had warned her of the brandy.

"I hope you do not mind if I indulge," he said, tipping the cup to his lips and signaling to a servant who held a coffee pitcher.

"A man must have his allowances," Rose replied.

"Do you mock me?"

"Only a little," she said. "Mightn't I tease occasionally?" She felt herself blush at the remark and hoped he would not notice. She had said the words from a desire to sound clever, but they had sounded more familiar than she intended.

"I suppose in our situation," Dr. York said, "some teasing is acceptable."

Rose felt, as much as heard, the word. "Our situation?"

Dr. York tipped his cup back with a jerk, finishing the nog in one swallow. "Together, as we are," he said, "in the surgery."

"Yes, oh yes," Rose said. "I have wished to thank you for admitting me to your surgery." The servant arrived with her coffee. She took it with two hands.

"You have already thanked me many times," Dr. York said.

"But I wish to do so properly. In fact," she said, "I have a gift for you." She stepped away from the piano and placed her coffee on a side table. Dr. York followed. "I have prepared this for you," she said. From a drawstring bag she had scavenged from one of the Dabney girls' wardrobes she pulled a scroll tied with red ribbon. Despite weeks of effort, she now felt uneasy about the gift. At sunrise she had gone over every word again, but still her hands shook as she handed him the paper.

"What have we here?" Dr. York said, taking the scroll in his hand. He turned his head away and coughed into his fist. "What have we here?" he repeated. He pulled the ribbon, and it fluttered to the ground. Rose clasped her hands as he unrolled the paper. His eyes moved back and forth; the corners of his mouth turned up slightly.

"*A Suggested Approach to the Treatment of Putrefaction in Wounds Resulting from Combat and Other Casualties*," he read aloud. "*Potential Efficacy of the Carbolic Acid Wash.*"

"It is just a theory," Rose said, rushing in, fearing nothing so much as a moment's silence. "I have thought to consider wound care in light of my experiences with childbirth. I imagined that you might have an interest." She heard a slight chuckle escape his throat. "And so, Merry Christmas, I suppose," she exclaimed.

"I thank you," he said. "I shall read it on Christmas morning, an edifying text for such a happy holiday." He folded the paper, rather than rolling it, and placed it in his coat pocket. The red ribbon still lay on the floor. Rose thought to pick it up, to keep it with the gift, but she left it, feeling that somehow it did not matter now.

"I've something for you as well," Dr. York was saying. He pulled from his pocket a small Morocco case of lacquered wood with leather hinges and brass clasp. She accepted it and ran her hand over its shining surface.

"It is beautiful," she said. She could store needles and threads in it, or a small comb—perhaps a brooch or two, if she ever acquired any. "Thank you," she said. "It is too much." Her fingers stroked the latch, which made a crisp clicking sound each time it slid into place. As she admired the gleaming box, it occurred to her that her treatise made a poor showing in comparison to such a personal gift. "I'm sorry…" she began.

"Open it," he said. "Open the lid." He looked from the case to her and back to the case, anticipation in his eyes.

Rose slid the latch from its place and lifted the lid. There, resting on a bed of blue velvet, lay a gleaming silver card case, wrought entirely in tiny sculpted roses. "Oh, Dr. York," she whispered, lifting it from the box. It was heavy in her hand, true silver. She had never owned such a fine thing.

Near the top of the case a tiny hinge rested among the roses. She set her thumb against the opposite edge and pushed. Like a hidden door, the top of the case opened, revealing a single white calling card inside. She tipped the card into her hand. "Colonel Yancy P. York, III, MD," she read. This was the card he would give to a servant to announce his arrival at a friend's home. When Rose had started practicing medicine, she had had a set of cards engraved with "Virginia Rose Barnett, MD," but they had sat in a drawer unused. Her friends opened their own doors.

She slid his card back into the case and snapped the lid shut. Turning it in her hand, she saw that she had been admiring the back. On the front, set down among the roses, was a circle of unadorned silver, waiting to be engraved. She ran her thumb across the silver disk, somehow beautiful in its emptiness. She tilted the case and saw her reflection in that untouched place. "It is lovely," she said. "I shall keep it as long as I live and pass it down to my grandchildren."

"May there be multitudes," Dr. York replied. "Now, it appears Christmas supper is served. Shall we?" He offered his arm. Rose slipped the case into the wooden box—itself a wonder—and placed the box in the borrowed purse. After supper, when Dr. York asked her to dance, she did not deny him.

The sleet and snow hung on in Memphis and across the South into the new year, already 1864. Combatants of both sides took cover in crude encampments of drafty wood and canvas huts. Frost formed on moustaches, blankets grew stiff with ice, and boots turned to granite overnight. War stalled as the combatants fought their common enemy. Boredom led men to drink and gamble and argue among themselves. Soldiers arrived at the *Despain* with cracked knuckles and broken noses, spewing effluvia. Fingers, toes, and even noses were the targets of the surgeons' knives now as frostbite took its due. Captain Fuchs requisitioned additional blankets but mysteriously was denied. Laborers were sent to fell the city's trees for the ship's furnace, but the green wood sent acrid smoke to every corner of the vessel. Eyes burned and coughs worsened. For some, their last breath was a lungful of soot.

Holly hated waking on cold mornings. She pulled the covers over her head and protested against returning to the smoky ship. Rose began rising early to light the kitchen stove and set water on for coffee. By the time it was ready, the worst bite of cold was gone. With a steaming mug of coffee to greet her, Holly roused more easily.

One January day, following a clear night with a steady wind, the cabin was especially cold. Ice coated the interior of the window; the floor was frosted white. Making matters worse, the water in the kettle had frozen solid. There would be no time for coffee this morning. Still, Rose lit the stove, slipped on her boots, and ran to the privy. The grass crunched like glass beneath her feet. Through the gaps in the privy walls, the wind stung her bare skin. She shivered violently as she sprinted back to the cabin. The stove had done slight work; the floor was still covered in frost. Seeing Holly still abed, Rose kicked off her boots and crawled in beside her. I am getting soft, she thought, as she drifted back to sleep.

When she woke, sun was pouring into the cabin; the room was warm. The ice had melted from the window, but Holly still slept. Her face was peaceful, like a child's. Her curly hair, escaping its night braid, framed her face. "Holly," Rose said, shaking her shoulder gently. "We have overslept."

Holly's eyelids fluttered. "It's warm," she grinned snuggling down into the blankets again.

"We have overslept," Rose repeated.

Holly's eyes opened a crack. "Oh, Mother Pennoyer will be annoyed."

"I dare say," said Rose.

"You look like an angel, with the sun behind you," Holly murmured.

"We shall hope Mother Pennoyer sees it that way," Rose replied. "Up!"

While Holly ran outside, Rose dressed and shut the kitchen stove.

"No coffee?" Holly whined when she returned.

"We shall have to beg at the galley," Rose replied. "I will leave you to dress."

"Don't go ahead," Holly begged. "That will make me the very last."

"Hurry, then," Rose said. "I shall wait in the kitchen."

Mother Pennoyer was predictably displeased, and Rose felt out of sorts all day. When Dr. York asked her to assist in surgery, she joined him but felt sluggish and cotton-headed. "Are you well?" he asked when she dropped an instrument for the second time. "You do not seem yourself."

"Too much sleep," Rose said.

"I heard you were among the missing," he said with a smile.

His teasing embarrassed her, but she was guilty and would take her punishment. "I overslept. It will not happen again."

"I should hope it would. We all are much in need of rest, especially you. If you captured some extra sleep, you are to be congratulated."

"Not in Mother Pennoyer's eyes."

"They could use some rest as well, I venture."

"Thank you. You have made me feel better by comparing me to Mother Pennoyer," Rose said, as an unbidden smile bloomed on her face.

"My pleasure," he said. They worked in silence. Their patient had been bushwhacked in Arkansas. He would walk with a crutch, but because the ball had missed the bone, he would not lose his leg. "A lucky bounce of the minié ball," Dr. York remarked. Rose smiled at his joke. "Since you are so rested," he proposed, "perhaps you would have supper with me this evening and a game of checkers after. We might discuss your treatise." At last he wished to discuss her paper. She had grown impatient waiting for his response, certain she had made a fool of herself. She longed for his impressions, but today of all days, she was not prepared to converse on its technical subject.

"I should like that very much," she said, "but I fear my misstep this morning has made me poor company. May we plan for another day?"

"Mop this," he said, pointing to a pool of blood.

Rose sponged the area he indicated. Perhaps he had not heard her. "I am sorry, I am very tired." The excuse sounded ridiculous from the lips of one who had overslept.

"It is quite all right, Nurse Barnett. Perhaps another time." They finished the surgery without speaking.

When at last she returned to her room that night, Rose stood at the window looking out at the stars. It would be another cold night. She could hear the other nurses in the house laughing and playing a game, but she could not bear the thought of joining them. When Holly entered the cabin, Rose did not turn to greet her.

"We are playing a new guessing game," Holly said. "Will you join us?"

Rose did not answer, and she could hold back the tears no longer.

"Rosie, what is it? What has happened?"

"Nothing and everything," Rose said, shaking her head. "I will survive."

"'Tis a low bar, survival. If you put words to it, you will feel better. A good friend of mine has taught me that."

Rose paced the room. At last she burst out, "Are you not ashamed to have overslept?"

"Is that all?" asked Holly. "'Twas just a mistake, Rose. We all make mistakes."

"I do not expect it of myself."

"No one expects it of you, Rosie. That is why it is so jolly. You cannot expect perfection, from yourself or anyone, Rose. I hope you do not expect it of me."

"I am hardest on myself, I know. I cannot help it." She continued to pace, wringing a handkerchief in her hands and wiping her eyes.

Holly opened her arms and caught her, stopping her pacing. "You are exhausted, else you would not have overslept."

Rose gave in to heaving sobs.

"See how tired you are? The slightest kindness brings you to tears."

Rose looked up at her friend. "I have offended Dr. York." She wept, gulping now, relieved the truth was finally out.

"So that is it. What has happened?"

"I honestly do not know. He asked me to have supper with him tonight, but I was in no mood for it. I was simply honest and declined. Is it not acceptable sometimes to say no?"

Holly's brows rose in sympathy. "He did not take it well?"

"He barely spoke to me the rest of surgery."

"Perhaps if he is so easily offended, he asks too much."

"What does he want from me?"

Holly laughed. "Surely you know what men want from women."

Rose stepped back, her voice rising in anger. "You do not know him!"

"I do know him, Rose. I do not mean to be cheap, but men desire marriage far more than they let on. It is convenient for them."

"We have not discussed marriage!"

"You may not think so, but he may. Perhaps that is where the misunderstanding lies."

"Why must there be this intrigue?" Rose cried. "I only ask for his friendship."

"Rosie, now who is dissembling? You ask far more than friendship. He has let you into his surgery. He has been very generous."

"I admit it. But did I not tell you there would be a price to pay?"

"And would marriage be such a terrible price? Not to offend, Rose, but you are of an age—and temperament, I am sorry—that even with your beautiful face, you cannot be too demanding."

Rose walked to the washbasin to splash water on her face. "I do not feel beautiful at this moment," she moaned.

"Few ladies are attractive after a good cry," Holly said. "Perhaps that is why it feels so refreshing. Come, sit."

Rose returned to sit in the rocker. Holly stood behind her. "Let your head fall forward," she said, pushing her fingers into the muscles at the base of Rose's neck and drawing them in a smooth motion out to the tips of her shoulders. "I can feel that in my toes," Rose said, rolling her head from one side to the other. "It is interesting."

"Has no one ever rubbed your shoulders?" Holly replied.

"Never."

"That's like never having tasted sugar," Holly said with a laugh. She ran her thumbs up the cords of Rose's neck and back down again, massaging the stiff muscles of her shoulders. Placing her left hand on Rose's forehead, she murmured, "Relax into my hand."

Rose closed her eyes and let her head fall into Holly's warm hand. "How did you ever learn to give such pleasure?" she whispered.

Holly laughed. "My sisters, of course. We used to sit in a circle and rub each other's backs."

"Please don't stop."

But Holly leaned down and kissed Rose on the neck. "I shall teach you how it is done, and you can practice on me, but sadly, every back-rub must end," she said. "It is the only unpleasant piece of it. Better?"

Rose rocked back in the chair, her eyes closed. "I could endure it all night."

"Yes, but we both must sleep, lest we risk a repeat of today's events."

"I had forgotten," Rose said, teasing. "And you remind me?"

"I am glad you forgot, even if for just a moment. Now we must work on having you forgive yourself."

"I shall try very hard. For you, I shall try." Rose embraced her. "Thank you, my friend."

Holly skipped to the back door. "I'll be quick."

Rose followed her outside. She had forgotten her shawl but did not feel the need for it. She felt excited, hopeful. Her missteps from the morning still stung, but they sat further back in her mind now. She must not read too much into Dr. York's actions when she was the one who was out of sorts.

She walked to the garden, where cornstalks and the tall, woody arms of parsnip flowers remained from summer. She hated parsnips. Aunt Fidelia had cherished them, calling them her winter jewels. To young Rose they had seemed more a test of fortitude than sustenance. The Dabneys had prepared the garden well for winter. Several inches of straw covered the frozen ground, keeping it cold and quiescent through the fickle moods of winter. In the corner of the garden, all was quiet at the coop as the layers slept huddled together for warmth. For a moment she envied the birds their simple lives, but a chuckle escaped her throat. Not for an instant would she trade what God had given her for life as a witless bird.

She turned back toward the cabin. Holly had forgotten to draw the curtains to their small window. She was buttoning her night-gown. The lantern behind her revealed her shape, soft and feminine beneath the linen gown. Her hair glowed. As she turned back the blankets, she seemed to hesitate and look out the window. Then she slid into bed, out of view.

Chapter 9

Rose felt a hand on her shoulder. She was dreaming of her mother and resisted waking. She heard her name in a ragged whisper. When she opened her eyes, Maggie was there, her face so close she looked like a ghost in the light of the lantern she was holding. Rose sat up. "It is the middle of the night," she said.

"Come with me. Please!" Maggie said.

"To the ship?" Rose asked.

"No. I'll show you, just come. Now."

Holly sat up on her elbows. "Are there injured?" she mumbled.

Rose gently pushed her back down. "It's nothing," she whispered. "Maggie needs me." Holly smiled and closed her eyes, pulling the blankets around her shoulders. "Let me dress," Rose said.

"Here are your shoes," Maggie said. "Just get a shawl."

"I am indecent," Rose said. "It is freezing out there. I will be only a moment."

"Hurry," Maggie implored as Rose stepped into the kitchen to dress.

As they left the cabin, Rose asked, "Now, what is it, dear?"

"My sister, Alice. In town. Where's your kit?"

"You have a sister in town?"

"Get your kit!"

Rose stepped back into the cabin for her medical bag. "Where are we going?" she whispered as they headed inland, away from the river. Snow had fallen, but the moon now peeked from behind fluffy clouds.

"To the cribs," Maggie said.

It happened less often than one expected. Confinements were expensive and disruptive to a house. While girls made barren from hard deliveries might be the backbone of an establishment, seldom were they young and pretty enough to work the front. Housemothers kept cupboards stocked with vinegar and carbolic acid, sponges and syringes. When these failed, regulation could be attempted. The better houses used French Regulation Pills, with their caution to married ladies to take care, as the pills were certain to lead to the tragedy of miscarriage. The expense of the French import, however, led most establishments to offer mugwort or slippery elm or cottonroot. When all efforts failed, there was Maggie's sister's predicament.

They walked quickly, not speaking, for many blocks. The moon lit the way. The buildings became smaller and closer together, eventually yielding to low shacks. They entered an alley that seemed to go on forever, walking and lifting their skirts over broken bottles, rubbish, and unconscious soldiers. Once they crossed a boulevard where hotels and saloons were still lit up even this late in the night. Union soldiers staggered about as Rose and Maggie dashed across into another warren of shacks and alleys.

At last Maggie stopped. "Here," she said. They were standing at the back entrance to a two-story brick building that rose above the shacks like an outcropping of red rock on a prairie. Maggie ran up the wooden stairs, gave three short raps, and then repeated the knock. A small girl opened the door.

As they stepped inside, Rose heard a woman struggling behind a door to a nearby room. The place smelled of tobacco and sweat. Union soldiers at the front door were trying to kiss an old woman in a voluminous purple dress. She pushed them, and they fell to the floor. She opened the door and kicked them in the ribs and buttocks as they crawled on their hands and knees, braying like donkeys, collapsing in laughter on the front porch. The woman turned the *Shut* sign in the window, pulled the shades, and locked the door.

She walked to the back of the house. "Stella Best," she said, offering Rose her hand. "She's having a time."

"How long?" Rose asked.

"Twenty hours, give or take." The housemother opened the door to a small bedroom lit by a single lantern. A young woman lay on a low, narrow bed covered in newspapers. In the throes of a contraction, she was pulling on a rope tied to the rusted bed frame. Despite the cold, she was naked and sweating. Beside her sat Able. She nodded at Rose.

Maggie went to her struggling sister. "I brought the lady doctor, Allie."

As a child, near her school, Rose had once seen a dead cow with the head of its bloody, lifeless calf protruding from its body. Children flocked to the scene before the teacher could intervene. Curious girls turned away, wide-eyed and quiet, but the boys chattered on all day. When one repeatedly sniggered, "Did you see its rear end?" Rose, feeling he really should be better informed, had remarked that he had been born the same way.

"I ain't no animal," the boy cried, "and neither is my ma! You take it back!"

"It's the natural way," Rose said. "Anyone knows that."

"You're crazy," the boy had sneered, turning and running from her.

Since then Rose had delivered many human babies. They never slid out as easily as they slid in.

"Look there," Able said, pointing with her chin. "Never seen that before." The mother-to-be lay on her back with her knees up; from between her legs extended a tiny hand.

Rose asked for a lamp. As ridiculous as it seemed, sometimes a hand could be mistaken for a foot. With greater light, she was relieved to confirm that the digits were those of a left hand. She pinched the palm; sometimes, upon stimulation, the arm would withdraw. Not today.

Rose had encountered a presenting arm once before. The hand and head had come together, the forearm lying beside the ear, the hand atop the head. The delivery had been quick, and other than tearing, no harm had come to mother or child. But here, where only the hand extruded and the labor did not progress, Rose feared a shoulder was lodged against the pubic brim. She recalled a lively discussion in college of whether, in such cases, to intervene or let nature take its course. Since the ancients, intervention had meant severing the delivered arm with the goal of making room for the body in the birth canal. If that failed, the mother could be saved through evisceration of the child. Her professor, being modern, had thought both techniques were barbaric and, worse, unnecessary. In his opinion, the problem lay not in the wandering arm but in the position of the opposing shoulder still in the womb. He had taught intervention, but with the hand—as for breech presentation—rather than the saw or hook.

"Has she delivered before?" Rose asked Maggie.

Maggie paused. "You will not judge her?"

"Has she delivered?" Rose repeated firmly.

"Yes."

"Was it hard?"

"No. No, it was quick."

"We are reassured, then. We need only turn the child to release it. Clean this area. Lay fresh papers, and bring hot water and clean rags." Rose rolled her sleeves above her elbows, took a small pair of scissors from her bag, and trimmed her fingernails to the quick. She took up a brown bottle with a cork stopper, turned her head, and poured chlorine over her hands, wincing as it stung her chapped skin. "What is your name?" she asked.

Maggie answered for her sister. "Allie. Alice," she said.

When the papers were laid, Rose rolled Alice onto her left side, telling Maggie and Able to hold her there. Several other women had entered the room, while the housemother stood watch over her investment. "I must insert my hand," she said to Alice. Without waiting for reply or permission, she formed the fingers and thumb of her left hand into a cone and inserted them into her patient. Alice cursed and tried to scramble away, but Able and Maggie held her. "Come around, Maggie," Rose said. "It will help if she can see you." Rose motioned for two terrified teenage girls to take Maggie's place next to Able.

A contraction began. "You must let this pain pass you by," Rose said to Alice. "Do no pushing, my friend, no matter how much you would wish to. Just this once." This last was a lie, but it would be forgotten.

Alice's gaze was locked on Maggie's; their hands were entwined—one brown, one white. Alice's eyes began to twitch. If she fainted, she might involuntarily push against Rose's advancing hand. "You must secure her attendance, Maggie," Rose said. "Slap her if you must." When Maggie hesitated, Rose leaned over and slapped Alice hard across the face. "No pushing!" she ordered. Alice nodded.

The shoulder of the extending arm was blocking the *os uteri*. To turn the child, she must enter the sacred space. Great care was required. Should the womb or placenta rupture, all would be lost. As the contraction released its grip, she slipped her fingers fully into the uterus. At this insult, Alice fainted, but there was nothing to be done. Rose swept her thumb around the child's neck, relieved to find no cord there. But the baby's pulse was dangerously erratic. She could work through three pains at most; fewer if the child was to live. The womb began to seize again. Rose opened her hand against the baby's back, that her presence there might be as slight as possible. How, she wondered, did a man's large hand ever accomplish this task? The huge muscle bore down, trapping her hand painfully. Alice, in her unconscious state, began to push. The child's pulse grew faint. When at last the womb relaxed, Rose pushed the rest of her hand into the uterus and took the buttocks in the palm of her hand. With two fingers she grasped one leg near the hip and, with the greatest possible care, turned the body one-eighth of a turn. The head dropped satisfyingly into the *os*.

Alice woke with the next contraction. Instinctively she began to push. "Stop!" Rose cried. The side of the child's head now fought for space with Rose's wrist at the *os*. "Stop her, Maggie!" This time Maggie did not hesitate; she slapped her sister who, in startled response, ceased pushing.

When the uterus relaxed, Rose pulled her hand from Alice's body. "Now, dear," she said, "with the next pain, you may push."

Relieved of restriction, Alice pushed, and the child's head emerged. Rose cleared the mucus from its nose and mouth and placed a woolen rag over its head lest it take a chill. With the next contraction, Alice pushed her child the rest of its long journey into the world, the final transit eased by a collapsed shoulder. Rose pushed the humerus into place, causing the child's first cry. The arm would trouble him, but he would learn to snap it back into place and go about his business. Of greater concern was his right foot, which upon examination showed itself to be clubbed. Perhaps it could be trained, but it would never work properly. Rose sighed with disappointment. This child would never run.

"It's a boy, Allie," Maggie cried, through tears. "A fine boy."

"Is he in uniform?" Alice asked. The two sisters burst into laughter. Maggie laid her head on her sister's sweaty, naked chest until Rose placed the child there. Another contraction began the afterbirth. Alice strained and cried. Maggie held her hand.

"You are torn," Rose said. "I shall need to stitch you. Keep your eyes on your baby." Few women could resist the urge to stare into their newborns' eyes; even so, the stitching would be difficult. She cleaned the perineum and reached into her kit for the curved needle and a length of horse hair, wishing she had thought to place a bobbin of silk army thread in her bag. She was encouraged that the vagina and bowel had maintained their separate integrities. Placing three drops of laudanum on Alice's tongue, she nodded at Able and Maggie to hold her down. Then she placed the seven painful stitches that would allow Alice to heal and return to work.

"The bleeding should last no more than five days," she said. "I shall return to remove the stitches in a week's time. Until then, take only liquids and soft foods. You must not strain."

"I am tired of straining," said Alice with a smile. "Aren't I, Lincoln?" She looked into her baby's eyes. "No more straining for Mama."

In ordinary circumstances, the boy would go to a local farm family to be raised in exchange for labor and board. If the housemother and family agreed, Alice would see him on holidays. But with the clubfoot and a bad shoulder, this child would be all burden. He would likely be sent to an almshouse. But for now he would suck and mew at Alice's breast, full with its sweet first-milk. Watching them Rose felt her own heart stir at the temporary bliss of new motherhood.

Rose left Maggie and her sister at dawn. Snow had fallen all night. The cribs and shacks glittered in the rising sun. She had never been in this part of Memphis, and despite the peaceful scene, she felt uneasy without Maggie beside her. What few shops she passed in the alleys were closed. Only the occasional hung-over soldier wandered outdoors. She passed an abandoned building marked *Forrest & Maples Negro Mart*. A spiked iron fence enclosed a large open area. Inside the pen, snow had partially covered a long wooden riser, the auction block, so that it looked like a soft feather bed. Wrapping her arms in her shawl and pulling it close, Rose moved on. She walked for an hour before finally accepting that she was lost. Her feet were numb. The wind had come up with the sun. She would have to ask directions else risk frostbite. Her dress was bloody and her hair a tangle. She stopped to tidy herself. When she looked up, a Union soldier stood before her.

"Thank goodness," she said, marshaling a sunny countenance despite her fatigue.

"Morning, ma'am," he said. He was young, a private.

"Good morning, sir. I am afraid I am in need of your assistance."

"You an early riser? Day business?"

"Sir?"

"May I see your papers, ma'am?"

In her rush the night before, she had not thought to grab her orders. Most days she did not carry them, as her business seldom took her beyond the landing. Now she sought the fine balance between showing respect and commanding authority. "I was needed in the night and neglected to bring my orders with me."

"What's the blood from, ma'am?"

"I have come from delivering a baby." She suppressed the urge to add, "Childbirth is a bloody affair," instead opening her bag to show him her instruments.

"Where's your certificate at?"

Rose suddenly realized what he thought of her, medical kit or no. "I do not possess a certificate, sir. I possess orders."

"You out in the cribs and all, looks like something else to me."

Her patience evaporated like a drop of water on a hot skillet. "Pardon me?" she said.

"The health of the troops is at stake, ma'am. Need to see that certificate."

"The health of the troops?" A derisive groan escaped her throat.

The soldier straightened his posture. He was taller than she by a foot. "I don't need talk-back from you, ma'am, just your papers."

The dangerous words felt glorious rising in her throat, rushing past her lips: "And I don't need it from you, either!"

The soldier raised his rifle. It was a startling sight, but while he might arrest a woman, he could not shoot one. Were he intoxicated, it would have been a different matter, but he was sober. "Shoot me," Rose said. "In fact, shoot me in the back!" She turned and began walking away. She did not know where she was headed, but she would not stand there and be abused by a man-child with a gun. She prayed she had not miscalculated.

"Stop, whore!" the soldier shouted.

She stopped. She turned and walked back to the soldier—her fellow-at-arms—halting an inch from the greasy barrel of his rifle. The gun was shaking, but the boy's hand was fully back on the stock, far from the trigger. He was so young, only sixteen or seventeen. She was reminded of Jimmy, but this soldier was different. Within him boiled the unstable brew of fear and bravado. She leaned into the rifle until it touched her chest. She took a step forward, forcing him backward. Snow crunched. She said, "One of your friends—or was it you?—put a baby in a girl nine months ago." She took another step forward, he another back. The gun still pressed against her chest. The soldier's fingers grew white in their violent grip of the stock. "That child will barely walk, if at all, nor likely even throw a baseball. He is lucky to be alive. I have stitched up his mother, and she will be good as new for you in just a few weeks, Private." Reminding him of his rank would either raise his temper or cause submission. She watched his right hand as she stepped forward again. His eyes grew wide as fear began to eclipse bravado. Rose continued. "If you want your womanhood waiting for you the next time you go whoring, I suggest you let me go home and get some sleep. In my bunk. On the *Despain*." With her forearm, Rose pushed aside the rifle and stormed past the boy. Unable now to see his face and hands, her own fear begged her striding legs to run until, at the first corner, they obeyed.

Several blocks later, she slipped and fell, cutting her hand on a broken spirits bottle hiding beneath the snow. Seeing no sign of the soldier, she took time to wrap her hand. Then she rose and walked toward the skyline where the road dipped toward the river.

Holly was dressed for the day when Rose entered their cabin and collapsed in her arms. "Where have you been?" Holly asked. She took Rose's hands in hers and frowned in concern. "You are freezing."

"I think I got arrested," Rose said. Giddy with relief, she fell onto the bed, laughing.

"Where were you?" Holly asked again, examining Rose's bloody dress. "Are you hurt?"

"I am not hurt—well, not badly. Maggie came in the middle of the night. You do not remember?"

Holly shook her head.

"She has a sister in town."

"In the cribs," Holly said. "I know."

"She needed delivery last night. Maggie fetched me."

"You went to the cribs?"

Rose nodded.

"Your hand," Holly said, reaching to unwrap Rose's bandage. Rose surrendered herself to Holly's care, wincing as the frozen cloth pulled at her sliced palm.

"I forgot my orders," said Rose. "A child with a gun demanded my certificate. I ran away from him, and I fell. Onto a broken bottle, of course." She examined the cut. "I think I will live."

"Your certificate? No!"

"I am afraid so," Rose said with a smile.

"It seems you are a fallen woman," Holly said, and they laughed. "Let me wrap your hand," Holly said. "You sleep. I shall make your excuses to Mother Pennoyer." Rose closed her eyes while Holly dressed her wound. As she drifted to sleep, she felt Holly's soft lips against her forehead.

Later that morning, Rose went in search of Maggie in the ship's laundry. "How is Alice?" she asked.

"I'll meet you on shore when I finish this stack," Maggie said, pointing to a small pile of sheets to be hung. Rose wondered if she should offer to help, but Maggie waved her off. "Fifteen minutes," she said.

Rose descended the gangplank and paced the landing until Maggie emerged from the ship. It was sunny but still cold outside; the snow had been packed down by pedestrians and wagons, making walking treacherous where icy spots formed. She and Maggie leaned on each other to the base of the cliff where the wind could not reach them.

"How is she?" Rose asked.

"I left her at seven. The bleeding wasn't bad."

"Does she have clean water?"

Maggie nodded. "She was thirsty as a hard-rode horse." She turned her face to the sun and closed her eyes. "It is her third child," she said.

Rose was not surprised. "Does she see them?" she asked.

"The boy died," Maggie said, still facing the sun. She paused, cleared her throat, and turned to look at Rose. "That was her first. Then she had a girl. A trader got her."

"A trader?"

"Sold, Rose. She was sold."

"Maggie, that is unthinkable!"

"That's colored," Maggie said.

Rose rubbed her temples as Maggie's situation became clear. "If Alice is your sister," she said, "then you are colored. You are colored?"

Maggie laughed. "Yes, ma'am. That would be a fact."

"But you...were you..." She could not say the word.

Maggie laughed. "You are so naive sometimes. I'm a slave, Rose. I am owned. I's just run off, is all. Till Massa Lincom ties up this here abolutionary war, I's still got me a massa, yes, ma'am."

Rose shrank from this strange person. Images from the slave pamphlets of her youth flashed through her mind. She tried to imagine Maggie on the block, naked, someone pushing back her lips to examine her teeth. It was inconceivable. "You are not a slave, Maggie."

"Beg pardon, ma'am. I is."

"Maggie, please, stop speaking in that ridiculous creole. You sound preposterous."

"That's as good a word as any for slavery, certainly better than 'peculiar institution,'" Maggie said. Her face had lost all signs of humor. "But that's not your meaning, is it? What is preposterous to you is that a light-skinned person, one as white as me, could be a slave. It is color that decides your heart, Rosie, only that. Skin color. That is what is preposterous. You would not have a black woman for a friend. Bad enough I am from the laundry."

"I do not care that you are from the laundry," Rose exclaimed. "How little you think of me!"

"Oh, don't be so delicate."

"Nor do I care about color," Rose continued. "The fight is for everyone, light and dark alike."

Maggie snorted. "The desertion rate suggests our boys are less keen to the task than you would credit them."

"They are tired, Maggie. Who is not tired?"

"A field slave is not tired?"

"I am just saying that we are trying, Maggie, dear. 'Tis as much for people like you—possibly more so—that we are fighting this dreadful war. That you should be owned is just, well, it is absurd."

"Possibly more so?" Maggie rolled her eyes. "Freedom," she said, "it for da high yella, dat's all it fo'. Not fo' dem darkies, no suh, slavery not such a shame for dem kine."

"You are twisting my words! I am only trying to say that the fight has evolved in your favor, and still we fight. Not just for the Union, but for your cause, Maggie, yours and Alice's."

"Yes, still you fight. And just what are your precious white boys fighting for, when they haven't run home? Even our president would ship us back to Africa."

"It is not a wholly irrational idea," Rose said. "Would not the darker race be more at ease where God first placed them, where less is demanded of their intellect than in this busy, modern world?"

"So we are ignorant as well."

"In America, you are disadvantaged, yes. I dare say, were I in Africa, I would be equally so."

"I see. And what of me? Where do I belong, on an island somewhere in between?"

"You could choose, of course. You and others like you."

Maggie shook her head. "Do you hear your own words, Rose? What kind of Christian are you? Do you believe God created us—all of us—in his image or not?"

"I know only that he has set variation amongst us," Rose replied, her voice shaking now. "I do not know his plan, Maggie. I am trying to understand, is all. Every day I pray for the redemption of the dark race."

"Do not hide behind God. It is unworthy of you, Rose. And we do not need redeeming!"

"I do not hide behind God! I am trying to understand his purpose in creating the races, not only through Scripture but science. I believe there is meaning in our differences and that we shall soon discover it. Mr. Darwin has offered several elegant theories to assist us."

"Assist us in what? Justifying slavery? Sending people back to Africa? You seek an excuse is all. You of all people, Rose Barnett, do not need Mr. Darwin to know that people are of equal worth, one to the other. You saw how that baby came into the world last night—just like a white baby, with wailing lungs and a pure, beating heart. You have seen our bodies, you know how we are pained and how we take ill. If you prick us, do we not bleed?" Maggie smirked. "Yes, even a colored girl can know some Shakespeare."

Rose looked down at her hands. What did Maggie want of her?

"Rose," Maggie said, "you are a doctor of women—poor women, black women. If you are a Christian, then act like one. You claim to be a scientist, but when you do not care for its truths, you retreat behind God and his mysterious purpose. The only mystery here is why you will not admit what you know is true, that the races are equal in every way. You are a hypocrite!"

Maggie walked away from the bench and stood for several minutes. Rose felt as if her veins had filled with mud. Suddenly Maggie stood before her again, shaking with rage. "Africans have worked this land for two hundred and fifty years. We," she said, pounding her chest with her fist, "we built the South, and North, with our sweat." She hit her chest again and again. "With our blood. And the blood of our children. Children, Rose! Tiny babies like you delivered last night. My mother. Her brothers. None of whom I would know if I met them on the street, by the way. Together, and all alone, one by one, we did this, all of this." She flung her arms wide and turned fully around. "And you deny us our wages just as payday dawns? Rather, I think, the whites should return to Europe. Short of that, we shall be living cheek by jowl very soon, so you had better get used to it. Now if you don't mind, I have work to do." She turned and strode toward the ship. After several steps, she stopped and turned to face Rose. "And would it have hurt you to ask after Lincoln?"

Rose frowned in confusion. "Lincoln?"

"Stella has agreed that Alice may keep him, due to his foot."

"You are not speaking of the president..." Rose mumbled.

"Oh, for heaven's sake," Maggie exclaimed, turning on her heel.

Rose spent her day distracted and tearful. She did not go to surgery. Her thoughts were on Maggie and her sister, the man at the lyceum, and her aunts' droning sermons on the sin that was slavery. She could not recall a Negro ever coming to their home or church. She had treated black women in Chicago, but they were patients, not friends. Her friends were other white women—suffragists, doctors, and philanthropists—progressives seeking to bring up fallen women of all colors through education. Was that wrong?

She approached Dr. York after supper, sliding onto a bench across the table from him. On the table was opened a year-old copy of *Harper's Weekly*, one that Rose herself had perused many times, with its illustrations of the Battle of Antietam. They said it was this victory that gave the president the courage to free the slaves.

Rose greeted Dr. York, and he looked up from the journal. "These illustrations are very fine," he said, bending again to examine a detail of one drawing. "I find them superior to photographs in every way," he said. When Rose did not reply, he pushed the magazine aside. "You appear strained, my dear. Is all well?"

She kept her bandaged hand beneath the table, not wishing to distract him. "Do you believe in resettlement of the Negro?" she asked.

"What does it matter?" he said. "And why do you ask? Is there news?" He glanced at the Harper's, but realizing it was out-of-date, shook his head and asked again. "Is there news I have missed?"

"Maggie and I had words today. It has left me out of sorts." The confession soothed her temporarily.

"On this subject? Colonization?"

"Yes."

"Why should Maggie be concerned?"

"It seems she is colored. She has a dark sister and has strong feelings on the matter."

"Well, if I must reply—and I've no desire to have words over it—I would say that, as a rule, I choose not to tilt at windmills. Therefore, I suppose, the answer is yes, resettlement is best for all concerned. Why endure of all this"—he waved his hand about—"when such a straightforward solution exists?"

"So you do not feel the races can mix?"

"Why must they?"

"But can they? 'Tis a different question."

"Perhaps a century from now. Why do you spend time with that washerwoman? She has upset you. Should I have a word?"

Rose's emotions were on a short tether. "That washerwoman is my friend! And no, I do not wish you to have a word."

"Very well," he replied, raising a hand in defense. "I did not know she was colored, but of course I see it now. Naturally the mixing of the races would be of interest to her. But it is of little consequence to us, my dear."

"Little consequence? It is of every consequence. We are at war over it!"

"We are at war over slavery," Dr. York said. "'Tis a different question from the mixing of the races. Very different."

Not wishing to quarrel with two friends in one day, Rose stood to go. "I shall leave you to your illustrations," she said, "as I know how you enjoy them."

"You are a dear," he said, appearing to miss her naked sarcasm.

Rose walked with fury back to Dabney Heights. She arrived agitated and in tears. "Dr. York can be so exasperating," she exclaimed to Holly.

"What is it?"

"I cannot put my finger on it," Rose said, "but just now when I sought his counsel on something, I felt dismissed, like a child. I do not take to being treated so."

"Nor should you. Perhaps you have asked the wrong person. On what do you seek advice, my friend?"

Holly sat next to Rose on the bed and placed her hand gently on her back.

The warmth of Holly's touch was reassuring. Still, Rose struggled with where to begin. At last she said, "Are you aware of Maggie's status?"

"What has happened, Rose? I thought this was about Dr. York."

"First it is about Maggie. We have quarreled, she and I."

"Is that why I could not catch your eye all day?"

"Did you know she is running?" Rose asked, searching Holly's face.

"I have known she is not a free person, yes. Rose, what did you say to her?" Holly's voice conveyed alarm.

"Nothing." Rose began to weep. "We argued about resettlement and the mixing of the races. She called me a hypocrite."

"And you sought Dr. York's opinion?"

"I tried, but he says the mixing of the races is of no consequence."

"It may seem so to him, but he would be in grave error."

"He offered to have a word with Maggie on my behalf."

"Ahhhh."

Rose nodded her head, grateful that Holly understood.

"I should like to see him try to have a word with Maggie," Holly said with a smile. Rose chuckled. "Once he returns to civilian life," Holly said, "I doubt Dr. York will see much of the freedman. That does not mean the matter is without consequence, even for him."

"But he will see them. If the emancipated are not resettled—and if Maggie is the measure, I am certain they would not go even if told to do so—if they do not go, then we must all live among them."

"Rather, I think, they must live amongst us," Holly said. She was quiet for a time. At last she said, "It is sad. Even the Germans have blended by now. Color is a heavy burden."

"Exactly. Nature has marked them, but why? What is God's purpose?"

Holly replied, "Perhaps this is a matter less for the mind than the heart."

"Maggie says the races are equal in God's eyes," Rose continued, "and that I must know it as a scientific fact. But I do not know it! Natural equality is a theory, only that. And if it is so, God alone knows why he designed it." She looked at Holly. "Maggie says I hide behind God."

"This is why she called you a hypocrite?"

Rose nodded.

"What if we were the slaves and they the masters? Would you not argue the races were equal?"

"Perhaps I would lack an opinion, not because I was inherently less but because I would not have had the advantage of education."

"I think you have dodged the question, but let us say you had been educated, even a little, as Maggie has. How would you answer then? Are the races equal if you are the slave?"

"Only science can tell."

"I agree with Maggie."

"That I am a hypocrite?"

"You hand the question off first to science, then to God, and back to science again. For you not to declare yourself must be very hurtful to Maggie."

Rose stood and paced the room. "I do not know what science will decide about the races," she argued. "Nor do I understand God's plan."

Holly stepped in front of her. "Rosie, you cannot hand off to science that which you must find in your heart. Maggie asks only that you love her sister as well as you love her. Science cannot tell you what to do about love. And God has already told you many times. I beg your pardon, but do you not think it a bit prideful to feel you are entitled to know God's purpose in everything? Can you not live with the simple instruction to love?" Holly stepped toward the door. "It is time for bed," she said. "Dr. York is probably correct. Racial mixing is unlikely in our lifetime. I would not trade places, to be sure, but I do not fear letting them in. You carry a poison, Rose, and you cling to it at Maggie's expense. If you wish her to love you again, you must confess it."

Rose did not sleep. The day's conversations played over and over in her head. How could she explain herself? How could she make Maggie understand? At dawn she walked to the ship. Maggie and Able stood on the landing, engaged in an animated conversation. "May we speak?" Rose called to Maggie.

"About what?" Maggie replied, but she nodded to Able, who turned an expressionless face to Rose before continuing on her way. "What is it?" Maggie asked as she walked briskly, with obvious impatience, toward Rose.

"It is about what divided us yesterday," Rose replied, "and that I hope we may be friends again." She sat and motioned for Maggie to join her. "Please, Maggie. I have thought much about it and prayed all night, and I believe I have gained a little understanding of our differences."

Maggie sat. "That is the point, Rose. We are only different if you make us so. You see our color and our circumstances, and you put yourself above us, when all along, we are as much God's children as you are."

"I do not do that! I do not put myself above you. You are my friend."

"It is not for myself I speak. It is for Alice. God does not test us with our own kind. He tests us with the other. I know you have a good heart, but it is not a perfect heart, Rose. You have much to learn." She stood to go.

"Wait!" Rose said, reaching out for her hand and pulling her back to the bench. Swallowing the lump in her throat, she confessed, "Holly agrees I am a hypocrite for not declaring against colonization."

"You are not the only Northerner to wish us out of your sight." Maggie sat again, folding her arms across her chest.

"But I do not say to send you away. I say only to consider it, from a scientific point of view."

"Science cannot save you, Rose. Do not even try with me."

Rose felt like a piece of straw in the wind, blown hither and yon, out of control. "I know it is my Christian duty to lift up the least among us."

"And we are they, the least," Maggie said. "Who has told you this? God himself?"

"I do not know what you want from me," Rose cried. "Truly I do not. I offer my Christian charity to you; it is all I have."

"Do not patronize me. I do not need you to lift me up." Maggie stood. "See? I can rise on my own." She began walking toward the ship, but after several steps, she turned and came back to where Rose sat, weeping.

As Maggie stood above her, a thought began to form in Rose's mind, a thought that she pushed away only to have it return. At last she said, "I think I know the poison." She glanced up at her friend's face, but turned away again, ashamed. "Holly said I carry a poison."

"And what might it be, Rose?"

Rose struggled, the cruel remark refusing to come forward.

"What is the poison, Rose?" Maggie demanded.

Rose looked down in shame. Her voice barely above a whisper, she said, "I am put off by dark skin."

"Now, there it is!" Maggie exclaimed, throwing her arms wide. "She is put off."

"I tell you the truth, and you mock me?" Rose cried.

"If we are ugly to you, Rose, it is because white people have made us so. You are brave to admit it. I have not heard another do so, ever, except as epithet. For that you are due credit. But it is fear that puts you off, Rose, not color. Fear is the poison."

Rose had expected Maggie to accept her confession. "Of what am I afraid?" she demanded. "Tell me."

Maggie furrowed her brow and pursed her lips. "Well, as you are not a Southerner, I do not think you fear insurrection, although I could be wrong. Afraid of Nat Turner, are you? John Brown been chasing you in your dreams?"

"Please do not make fun of me," Rose said. "I fear neither the Turners nor the Browns of this world, though were I a Southerner, I dare say I should have cause."

"Why is it," Maggie demanded, "white men can make war but black men cannot? Johnnie Reb is perfectly willing to go to war against the white Yankee, but God forbid he should have to fight the black man! Now that's just arrogance." She shook her head hard, as if she could clear it of her wrath, but then she collapsed back onto the bench. "Oh, never mind," she sighed. "I do not think it's insurrection you fear, Rose. Rather I think you fear losing your advantage. That is what 'puts you off,' as you say."

"And what advantage would that be?" Rose asked. "I am a poor woman, an orphan. I am hardly advantaged."

"Have you ever been a slave?"

"Of course not."

"Why do you say 'of course'?"

Rose struggled to answer, to find any words other than "Because I am not African," but in the end those were the words she spoke.

"Then let us start there," Maggie said, more gently now, but as if exhausted. "You are free because you are white. Because you are white, you are free. That is your place of beginning."

Rose looked away. Maggie gently took Rose's chin in her hand, turning it until their eyes met. "Fear is natural," she said. "You don't think black people are afraid of whites? If you are brave enough to go to war, Rose Barnett, you are brave enough to let the dark-skinned into your heart. All the way in. We do not bite," she said. "Generally."

Rose smiled and wiped her eyes. "Maggie, if you will be patient with me, I will try."

"You are my friend, Rose, and I believe you wish to try. But you must keep your expectations in check. I walk in both worlds. You do not. The races do not care for each other, and I doubt they ever will. We need no white woman to open heaven's door for us. If you wish to help us lift ourselves up here on earth, I am afraid we must accept, as we are very far down. But you must strike the pity from your heart and the fear from your soul. Confess your fortunate birth and give thanks to the Negro. Stop making excuses and start listening. There is unspeakable pain on one side and unholy pride on the other. Except for mending herself, not even a lady doctor can heal a wound this large." Maggie sighed and wiped tears from her own eyes. "But I do wish us to be friends again, so let the two of us, together, make a small start. Beware, I shall call out your missteps."

"Thank you, dear Maggie." Rose embraced her friend. "I had not thought myself afraid," she said.

"First you must see it. You can only begin there."

"Nor fortunate of birth."

"Then you have learned two things today," Maggie said. "Perhaps there is hope for you." She stood and extended both hands to help her friend rise.

Chapter 10

In April a fevered rebel soldier wandered onto the *Despain* and surrendered to Mother Pennoyer. She assigned him to Rose's ward until his fever broke, when he would be sent to the rebel pestilence tent. His butternut uniform was thin as a dishrag; he wore no boots. Rose imagined him in the elements of the hard winter that was still not ended, his body warmed only by its own shivering. No wonder he had taken ill. His delirium prevailed, and the fever failed to abate. When a rash appeared, measles were declared. A male nurse spread warm lard upon the rash while Rose prepared the Dover's Powder and mustard plasters that would force his fever.

Able accosted Rose. "Why do you take such care with that man?" she demanded. "You heard how Fort Pillow was done."

"'Tis the same care we give our own," Rose replied uncertainly. She and Able had spoken little since her quarrel with Maggie.

"It's bad enough we take in rebs, but a Fort Pillow reb, now that's just a sick shame, and you know it." Able put a finger in Rose's face. "There was nothing but hate in that fight. Every black man there knew it was a bullet or chains, and Forrest's men would oblige either way."

"Forrest?" Rose asked. She recalled the slave mart she had passed on her way home from delivering Alice's baby. "A slave trader led Fort Pillow?"

"Who else would nail a man's trousers to the floor and set the building on fire? Now you're cleaning up his mess." Able walked away, leaving Rose to wonder about the sick, starving man before her.

At supper she asked Dr. York what he knew of Fort Pillow. "I know it is named for a liar. Gideon Pillow was thrown out of the US Army in '48. This is undoubtedly why my countrymen have named a fort after him. But if you are speaking of the recent fight, I know only what is on the grapevine."

"That it was a massacre?" Rose asked.

"You fill up a captured rebel fort with armed black men, and you're bound to get a reaction."

"You excuse it?"

"I merely state the obvious, my dear. This is Forrest's hometown. Quite naturally he desires it returned to him."

"There were women and children in that fort. They were lined up and shot!"

"So people say."

"You doubt the reports?"

"Among the many calamities of war, one begins always with the truth, my dear. It is also said that Union officers set out barrels of whiskey to fortify their men's courage. An order like that is sure to cause mischief. In any event, it has been conceded that the stars and stripes flew throughout. Until the flag is down, it is a fair fight."

"I doubt that the showing of colors justifies murder," Rose replied. She did not care for this display of Dr. York's Southern roots.

"Given the long-standing animosities between the parties," he added, "we might expect excesses on both sides. Call it what you will—if the colors fly, men may fight on."

Not caring to debate the rules of war, Rose said, "I have one of Forrest's men on my ward."

"Ah," Dr. York replied. "Perhaps you can befriend him, and he will tell you the whole, sordid tale." He picked up his newspaper again.

"Perhaps," Rose replied. Fatigue had come over her suddenly. "I think I shall retire."

"As you wish," he said absently. "Good sleep." He bent over his supper and turned his attention to a newspaper that had sat on the table for months.

The next day, Rose found her patient sitting up, delirium and fever abated. She approached him tentatively. Was this man a murderer or a soldier? What was the difference? "Hello, soldier," she said, carefully withholding her usual smile.

"Ma'am," he replied. "Am I caught?"

"Yes, sir. You are on a Union hospital ship. You took ill at Fort Pillow."

"Paducah, ma'am. That's where I come down, south of Paducah."

"I believe you walked in from Fort Pillow," Rose said. "You were fevered; perhaps you do not remember clearly."

"I might have been there; I don't know. Like I said, I come down after Paducah. If I was at Fort Pillow, I was abed in a wagon somewheres."

Rose wished she could believe him.

"You got anything a starving rebel can eat, ma'am? I'll take scrapings."

"You needn't take scrapings, sir, but now that the worst is past, we must move you to the Confederate tent."

"What of this rash?" He pulled the sleeves of his nightshirt above each elbow. Red spots still covered each arm.

"You have the measles," Rose said. "It is not the worst I have seen, and it is nearly gone. We will keep you here another day. Do not scratch the spots, or you will have trouble you do not want."

"Yes, ma'am," he said. "I'll give it my best."

"We shall start with beef tea," Rose said. "You have been vomiting. Your stomach must be courted."

"Yes, ma'am."

When she brought his broth, Rose began with an innocent question, one she asked every patient. "Where are you from?"

"I'm a reb, ma'am."

"I think we have established that," she said. She could not help smiling at his guilelessness.

"Yanks are taking good care of me. Not what they was telling us. Don't see no horns."

"No horns. See?" Rose tilted her head downward, smiling. "So where is your home?"

"Right here, ma'am. Well, Barnett," he replied.

Rose looked up quickly. "Barnett?"

"Yes, ma'am. Just down the road. Small plantation. I was overseer there, but not since Memphis was took."

"Overseer?"

"Yessum. But the negras all up and left—even before that proclamation deal, they just took off. Nothin' to see-over no more. So I joined up. Pay ain't so good, though." He hesitated. "Probably oughtn't say that to a Yankee. Likely a war secret, our pay, even such as it is."

"I shan't say a word," Rose replied, now unable to suppress her smile. "May I ask," she said, her voice shaking, "the names of the Barnett family?" The words hung in the air as they emerged from her lips. She reminded herself that Barnett was a common name.

"Christian names, ma'am?"

"Yes, Christian names."

"The master, he was Lannis, and the mistress was Dorothy. Dotty, she goes by, Miss Dotty. Their two sons was married and lived on the place, too, but they're in the army now. Our army, not—"

Rose interrupted. "Lannis W. Barnett?" she asked.

As the soldier answered, she heard him as if listening through a door, his words plain yet muffled by a storm of emotions. "Yeah, there was a *W* in there, for Winterkill," he said. "I remember the winter killin' part, account of he was from the north. It fit him too. One year we had snow clear in May and lost the first planting. The negras said he brung it on himself account of his name. Said he had both winter and killin' in his spirit, double bad omen. Maybe, maybe not. I just know we lost one whole crop that year, and we all paid for it somehows. Now look at the place."

From her father's Bible, Rose knew that he had had a brother and three sisters. Winterkill was her grandmother's maiden name and the family name of her aunts Grace and Fidelia, who had raised her. Her father's brother carried the unusual name of Lannis, after an English ancestor. She had been given to believe that all her father's siblings were deceased, but the presence of the words "Lannis Winterkill Barnett" on this soldier's lips now said otherwise.

Her patient was gulping his tea. Reluctantly, Rose took the cup from him. "You must not take too much," she said, "lest your stomach revolt."

"Sorry, ma'am. Just hungry."

"Perhaps you can distract yourself by telling me about the plantation." Her voice shook, and the man grew suspicious.

"You trying to pry Southern secrets out of me?" he asked. "I think I'll take that move to the rebel tent, all the same to you."

"I am seeking to pass the time, is all," Rose replied, returning his tea.

As if the cup were a magic talisman, he began to speak again. "Like I said, negras all but gone, full two year now. Mistress, she's a tough bird. Solid secesh, that one."

"Where is it," Rose asked, "the plantation? You said it was near here. How near?"

"Barnett? Just ten mile northeast."

Barnetts were New Yorkers. The farm where Rose had been raised had been allotted to her grandfather for service in the New York militia during the Revolution. Even before then—when New York was still New Netherland—the Barnetts had farmed along the Hudson River. Rose's father had been sent south to Mobile during the 1812 War. There he had billeted in the home of a local family, romanced the middle daughter, married her, and taken her north. As a child, Rose had filled in the details—a lavish wedding, Mobile's elite gathered to celebrate the handsome couple's new life (even if the groom was a Yankee), her grandfather presenting them with a new four-in-hand for the long trip north. Rose had imagined her mother's sorrow at leaving her family, her sisters throwing rose petals at the carriage, weeping their good-byes, promising to write. As an adult she had learned that the Mobile of 1815 was little more than a mosquito-infested military fort, but the revelation had done nothing to unseat her fantasy of her parents' romantic beginnings.

Now she asked her rebel patient, "Is it possible for one to visit Barnett Plantation?"

The soldier handed back the cup. "Ain't safe for Yankees, ma'am. Nothing out of Memphis safe for Yankees, even ladies."

"I suppose you are right," she said. She did not wish to appear overly curious. "Have a good day, Sergeant." She turned to leave the ward.

"How about some of them peaches I seen around here?" he asked. "I'll settle for juice."

"I believe we could safely try some peaches at supper," Rose replied. "Whole ones." She would not give scrapings to this rebel.

Rose found Holly and shared her news. "Your uncle?" Holly gasped. "Flesh and blood cousins?"

"Yes!" Rose exclaimed.

"Reb cousins," Holly said.

"Slavers," Rose admitted, but she was already formulating a plan.

"You are not going out there," Holly said. It was half question, half remonstrance.

"I can take Sergeant Mann. I will get him oathed."

"Oh, Rosie, no," Holly said.

Rose continued as if Holly had not spoken. "I can put him in farmer's overalls. We will be a poor man and his wife. My cousins know him. He will soften the blow."

"Rosie, you don't know this man. You cannot go riding around the countryside with a rebel soldier. What if he decides to hold you for ransom?"

"Holly, do you think the Union would pay one copper for me? If I am kidnapped, I am sure to be on my own."

"Two ambulances were ambushed last week."

"Yankee ambulances, full of opium and bandages. We will be two country folks in a farm wagon. I am sure we will be fine."

"Sure enough to risk getting gobbled by rebs."

"I promise I will not be taken hostage. They are my family, Holls. Assess the man yourself if you like, but I am certain I will be safe."

Holly embraced her. "Of course you must go, but I shall be worried sick until you return. And, yes, I shall assess him. I will not hand you over to a scoundrel."

Rose clapped her hands together and hugged Holly. "Cousins!" she exclaimed.

She slept poorly that night. In her dreams her Southern family members were the Fort Pillow rebels and the sergeant was General Forrest. She rose before sunrise, exhausted. Holly was already gone. Rose found her on the ship in the mess.

"Bad dreams," they said in unison. "Tag, you're it," Holly exclaimed. "You owe me a kiss." She tapped her cheek with her finger.

Rose laughed and kissed Holly's cheek then grew somber. "Is this a good idea?" she asked.

"You cannot sit in Memphis wondering, Rosie."

"But now I am frightened."

"Perhaps a Union escort is better."

"'Tis not guerillas that worry me, but my own flesh and blood. Why do you suppose Fidelia and Grace never told me about them?"

"Perhaps you are about to find out," Holly replied.

Later that morning Rose settled herself on her stool beside Sergeant Mann's bed. He was enjoying a bowl of canned peaches. "Thank you, ma'am, for saving a starving reb," he said.

"Do not eat them too fast, sir. You would not enjoy them nearly so much a second time."

"That'd be my luck," he said, setting the peaches aside. "Ain't never had much luck."

"Why do you say so?" Rose wondered what role Barnett Plantation played in this man's fortunes.

"My ma and pa just had a acre," he replied, "with a shack and six kids. Ma died with Caleb. I was nine. 'Tween me and Pa, we didn't spare no rod. I was on the receiving end a good bit myself. Anyway, no Mann I know of ever had no plantation. We just one step up from slave, to be honest." He added, "At least we got that."

"So you became an overseer?"

"I look at it like this, ma'am. In God's own book there's slaves and not slaves, and if you ask me, God is darn well partial to those that's slaves, always bringing them out the bonding and all. When the work was offered me at Barnett, I had those babies on my mind, and Pa. I just done my job. Figured God, he gonna take care the slaves, I gotta watch my own."

"How old were you when you went to work for Mr. Barnett?" Rose asked.

"Fifteen, sixteen. Overseen the place near about ten year before Yankees come through. That's when I joined the Tennessee. Our Tennessee, ma'am."

Rose intended to put her plan to him one step at a time, beginning with his loyalty. If he would not swear, she would never get permission from the marshal. "If you took the oath," she asked, "would you mean it, in your heart?"

"Well, now, I been chewing on that for some time, ma'am. Seems to me you can't put Jenny back in the bottle. Union been holding most the Mississippi for goin' on two year. South is hungry. Downright starvin', most of it." He was thoughtful for a time. Rose waited, wanting his words to be his own. "Slavin', that just didn't work out, far as I can see. Never did for us poor folk and now not for planters neither. Negras, they just seem to got the Lord on their side, like I said."

"Where is your family?" Rose asked. Even if he was not at Fort Pillow, were his kin among the guerillas terrorizing the countryside?

"Pa, he's dead a while, before the war. Sure glad he didn't see this mess. My brothers went north, joined the Union. Can't say why, other than the pay being regular. They always did take the low road on things, those two. One sister married off to a cowboy somewheres, the rest are gone."

"I am very sorry," Rose said. "Have you heard from your brothers?"

"Nah. I expect they're pretty sorry soldiers. Neither one of 'em did a lick of work around the place. I think Pa just worked himself to death while them sons of, you know, sat on their tails. Said workin' was for negras. All that money I sent, ten years I was overseein', it just washed down their gullets, my guess." He paused. "Probably Pa's too, if you want the truth."

Rose stood to leave.

"What about that oath?" he asked.

"So you are interested?" she replied.

"Reckon so."

"I shall see what can be arranged," she said, pursing her lips to prevent the smile trying to bloom there.

Holly made her own inspection of the sergeant the same day. "He did not molest me," she said to Rose at supper.

"Now who keeps a low bar?" Rose laughed.

"I think he goes with the wind. He told you he is willing to swear?"

"He did."

"He knows it will keep him from jail."

"I think 'tis more than that," Rose replied. "He has cared for a family. I think he is, at heart, a good person."

"Rosie, he is an overseer."

"He was driven to it," Rose said, hearing the hope in her voice but not the irony in her words.

"Ask the marshal," Holly said, throwing up her hands.

"I intend to," Rose replied.

"Will you tell Dr. York?"

"He will not care for it." Rose groaned. "But I will tell him tonight."

"What of Able and Maggie?"

"Able is already angry. She thinks Sergeant Mann was at Fort Pillow. He says not, but I doubt she will believe it. But I shall tell them as well; I cannot think of hiding it."

Dr. York was passing through the mess with a book under his arm and his supper on a plate. "Never put off until tomorrow..." Rose said to Holly, rising and calling out to him.

"Good luck," Holly whispered.

As she caught up with Dr. York, Rose realized he must not think she was asking his permission to visit her family. She kept her words short and declarative. He listened and nodded, glancing toward his food as it grew cold on the plate. She was relieved when his objections amounted to nothing more than the obvious admonition to be safe.

She found Able in the nurse's cabin below, preparing for a night shift. "So he says," Able replied when Rose told her Sergeant Mann had slept through Fort Pillow.

"I believe him," Rose said. "I have questioned him, and he seems to know nothing of it. I cannot say he is not lying. If he is guilty, he might say anything to save himself, but more likely, I feel, he would brag of it. But he does not. He was brought to my ward the day after, already in delirium. I believe he slept through the fight."

"That was no fight. It was a massacre."

"Conceded. But can you agree that his story is plausible?"

"He's still a reb. What else has he done? And just why do you care so?" Able's voice had grown heavy with suspicion. She hugged the Bible she was holding close to her chest with both hands, like a shield.

Rose knew that after the word "overseer," Able would hear little else, and so, as if preparing a patient for difficult news, she began with words of warning. "You will not like what you hear," she said. Able's face grew hard, her eyes narrowed. The face always protects the heart, Rose thought.

"Say it," Able said. She needed to know. Knowing was better than suspecting. Still, Rose took the long way around.

"He has told me that he worked for a man near here, on a plantation. From what he has said, I believe the man, the planter, to be my father's brother. My uncle." In taking such care, Rose could feel herself becoming even more afraid of delivering the full prognosis, something her professors had warned against. Was she protecting Able or herself? In any event, she must get to the whole truth. "The soldier was my uncle's overseer, and I intend to meet my cousins," she blurted out.

Able scoffed. "What else would a white man be doing, he works for a planter?" She did not wait for Rose to answer. "I thought you had no family, except the two that raised you."

"I did not know my uncle was alive."

"A planter."

"Yes, a planter. I must meet them, Able. Can you understand?"

Able threw her Bible on the bed. "You want my blessing?"

"I thought to tell you as a courtesy."

"Listen," Able said, "don't come tiptoeing around me with your business. You do what you have to do. What you can do. Do you think I don't understand family? This whole war is about family! Children sold off their mothers, wives from husbands. Well, God bless you, orphan girl. You've found your flesh and blood. Go to them. I would do the same if only I could."

"Please don't be angry, Able."

"I'm not angry, Rose. I am just sick and tired." She turned her back and jerked her head toward the door. Rose quietly left the cabin.

Maggie's response was similar. "Add it to your ledger of white blessings," she said. "Blood kin. Lucky you." Rose did not argue.

She put her proposal to Marshal Spalding that afternoon. "I have little family, sir. I should like to meet those I can claim."

"It's not safe out there for a lady," he replied. "I've no escort for you, and I have a city to run."

"I am aware there is much to attend to."

The marshal turned to the corporal at his side. "Why must I deal with whining women?" he complained. "I have watered the streets." The clerk laughed at his superior's wit. The marshal was reading a thick report. Rose could see over the desk that its title related to banking and currency exchange. Behind her stood a room full of citizens and soldiers seeking passes, permits, and adjudications.

"I know you are busy, sir. I seek only a pass."

He looked away from her as he said, "I have been petitioned by Dr. York to deny your request. I am inclined to defer to his judgment."

Rose's breath stopped in her throat. "I am sorry, sir. Who did you say?"

"I believe you know Dr. York?"

"Yes, sir, but he does not speak for me."

"He said you would aver as much, but he felt it his duty."

"Duty?" Rose repeated. The marshal smiled at her and went back to his reading. Rose cleared her throat and he looked up at her again. "I know, sir, that you need your men here. I do not ask for a Union man to accompany me. I have another solution."

The marshal set down the banking report and fully looked up at her at last. "And that is?"

"I shall take a reb, sir."

"Dr. York mentioned that as well." Again he smiled up at her, his head tilted to one side as if that was the end of the matter.

Despite the fury growing in her breast, Rose pushed on. "There is a rebel soldier, sir, recovering from measles. He is willing to swear."

"And how is it you know he will do so?"

"We have discussed it, sir."

"You have not made promises," the marshal stated, his voice rising. It was not a question.

"No, sir, I have made no promises. Yet in my conversations with him, I have determined him to be of sound character."

"He is a rebel, Nurse. And according to Dr. York, he was at Fort Pillow, for God's sake."

"He was ill through Fort Pillow, sir. Dr. York is mistaken."

"York said you would say that too." The marshal leaned back in his chair. "Nurse," he said, "I work hard to keep the people in this city safe. Why is it you are so determined to abandon its comforts?" He threw open his arms as if to emphasize what a lovely home he maintained just for her.

"They are my kin, sir."

"Yes." He leaned forward, listening at last. "And what evidence do you have that these people will welcome a Yankee?"

"I will send a letter first, of course. The rebel patient, Sergeant Mann, was the overseer there before the war. I believe they might welcome him, which I hope will ease my way."

"Are you familiar with the work of an overseer, young lady?"

"I was well taught as a child, sir," Rose said. "And yet, when I speak with Sergeant Mann, I find it difficult to fit the glove to him."

"People do what they can get away with, Nurse. Do not be too quick to forgive, especially in war."

"That is sound advice, sir. But I do believe the sergeant will protect me, and I pray he may help my family open their hearts to a Yankee."

"They are the enemy, for Chrissakes. Excuse me." He lifted his eyes heavenward and turned away from her, staring at a large map of the Southern states on his wall.

"Sir, may I just say," Rose offered, "that perhaps with closer family relations, things would not have gotten out of hand as they have." She knew her remark was naive. War was a world of grays and shadows—noble deeds and nefarious acts, private grudges and public wrongs. Yet in the end, one either went to war or one didn't. Who could say what small kindness might have blown the final straw from the donkey's back?

The marshal slammed his fist on the desk. Rose jumped. "Our nation," he shouted, "is at war not because Aunt Milly failed to ask Cousin Jack to tea! We are at war over fundamental questions of right and wrong. Fundamental!" He hit the desk again. "If we must pay our labor, so must they!" His eyes moved back to his report, but he did not appear to be reading the words. "We shall have to wrestle these bastards to the ground, inch by inch," he said, as if speaking to the document.

"So it is said, sir."

He looked up from his papers and, as if seeing her for the first time, said, "Send me your rebel sergeant, Nurse. If I feel you will be safe with him, you may have your pass." He shook his head as if in disbelief at his own words.

Rose was startled by his sudden acquiescence. "Thank you, sir," she said, smiling broadly. She wondered how much of his permission was intended as a message to Dr. York not to interfere with the marshal's affairs.

"I make no promises," he said.

"Of course," Rose replied.

She left the marshal's office in search of Dr. York. She would rather have run to Holly, but this chore could not wait. She found Dr. York near the surgery. "How dare you speak to the marshal in my place?" she whispered. He took her by the elbow and led her out to the deck. She shook her arm free. "You do not speak for me."

"You are acting impulsively. You do not know these people, Rose. You especially do not know this rebel soldier. He is of the lowest class. You could be killed."

"Do you think I am unaware of the danger? Do you think me that stupid?"

"You are anything but stupid, my dear, but you are being foolish. You are blinded by the thought of these strangers somehow being your family and that you shall have a charming reunion. I apologize if I have embarrassed you. But it had to be done."

"Is that what you think concerns me, that I am embarrassed? Yes, I was embarrassed before the marshal, but more importantly, this is not your affair."

"What is the difference, so long as you are safe?" He said this gently and reached out to take her hand, but she pulled away.

"The difference is great, and if you do not appreciate it, 'tis greater still!"

"I will not apologize for protecting you."

"You need not apologize. I do not seek it. Nor do I seek your protection."

Rose left the ship and went home to write a letter of introduction to her cousins. Her hands shook with both anger and excitement, and the letter was almost illegible. That evening, she copied it over.

The next day, as she returned to the ship from posting the letter to her cousins, she was met by a contrite Dr. York. Rose was weary. She had played their exchange over and over in her head all night while graphically imagining every unsettling reason she should take his advice. Her stomach knotted at the sight of him.

"May we speak?" he asked.

"Must we?" she said. "I do not feel well."

"I am sorry to hear that, but I did not sleep last night. If I could have a moment of your time…"

Rose felt some satisfaction at the image of him tossing and turning as she had. "So we are both exhausted," she said. "I suppose we must talk, then, if only to share our common misery."

"I admit my error," he said. "'Tis not my place to direct you. I should not have spoken to the marshal."

Rose took a deep breath. She was surprised by his contrition. "I know you went to the marshal out of concern for my safety," she said, "but do you not see, first, that it demeans me, and second and more importantly, that I am able to judge the risk for myself? I must know that you understand both parts of it."

He was quiet for some time. Rose wondered if he was going to tell her again not to go, that it was too dangerous. It was her experience that in apologizing, many people simply hoped to reopen the argument; that the words, "I am sorry," were often followed by some form of the revealing "but."

"As a man, and a doctor," he began, "I am accustomed to being heeded." Rose tried to speak, but he put up a hand—the irony of which seemed to escape him. He continued, "It seems that if we are to be friends, I must become less bullheaded."

"Are you teasing me?" Rose searched his face for meaning.

He took her hands in his and looked into her eyes. "I am not teasing you, Rose. Far from it. I pray you will take me back into your heart, at least for a game of checkers now and then."

Rose laughed. "Now you are teasing."

"We are two small creatures in a vast conflagration," he said. "Mightn't we lean upon each other to get through?"

Although desperate for equilibrium between them, Rose still needed reassurance. "I value your advice, but I must make my own choices."

"And I must be allowed to state my opinions. We shall not always agree."

"In this case we shall agree to disagree," she said cautiously.

"So it would seem," he said.

But Rose was not yet at ease. "You will not go around me," she said.

Dr. York sighed. "I shall not go around you."

She wanted to believe him. "Then, yes," she said, "let us enjoy some checkers."

A letter arrived at Dabney Heights the following week. With Holly at her side, Rose ran her finger under the seal. The paper appeared to have been cut from a book. She skimmed the letter and smiled.

"Tell me!" Holly exclaimed.

Rose read aloud:

My Dear Miss Barnett,

Regarding yours of late, if—as you say—you are the child of my husband's brother, you will indulge me by answering the queries below. One cannot be too careful today. Upon satisfactory response, I shall make a determination.

First: Please advise as to the maiden name of your paternal grandmother.

Second: Please name the place where your parents met and married.

Yours,
Dorothy Barnett, Mistress
Barnett Plantation

"I know these things," Rose said. "I know them!" She hugged Holly and went to pull her stationery kit from under her bed. Holly cleared a space on the top of the dresser. Rose's hand shook as she wrote:

Dear Mrs. Barnett,

Thank you for your kind reply. My father's mother was Caroline Winterkill. Her husband, James Barnett, was born in Saratoga, New York, and fought in the Revolutionary War. My father, James Jr., was born and raised in western New York. He was sent to Mobile, Alabama, during the latter days of the 1812 War. There he met my mother, Virginia, whom he married before returning home. My father's brother is Lannis Winterkill Barnett, whom, through information recently made known to me, I now surmise to be your husband.

I was orphaned at a young age. I am at your mercy if I am to know my family. I pray we may meet that we may be united at last.

With utmost sincerity and hopefulness, I am yours most truly,
Rose Barnett

The invitation that followed a week later was formal and curt.

Your presence is requested at Barnett Plantation on the fourteenth day of May, eighteen hundred sixty four, for dinner at twelve o'clock noon, invitation to be presented upon arrival.

Holly and Maggie examined it. "It looks like an invitation to a ball," Holly said.

"Typical," said Maggie. "Probably thinks she's a queen."

"'Tis not a ball," Rose replied. "Sergeant Mann says the place does poorly now. I shall hope for a cup of tea, nothing more grand than that."

"It is not for the tea you are going," Holly said.

"No, 'tis not for the tea."

Chapter 11

May fourteenth dawned clear but cold. At nine thirty, Rose and Sergeant Mann left Memphis for the ten-mile ride to Barnett Plantation. "What will you do while I am with my aunt?" she asked. She wondered if he was feared by the slaves and whether any that remained would welcome him.

"Look around, I suppose."

"Reminisce?" Rose asked.

"Not too many good memories," he replied.

He was a small man. He would have needed every tool of the trade to do his job. "Will the Negroes welcome you?"

"Not likely, but they're mostly gone, far as I hear. To where, I do wonder. The fight, some, but women and children, I suppose they'd be in the contraband camps just waiting this thing out. 'Less they've come back. I hear sometimes they do that, come back. Them camps ain't too easy, especially for house folks."

One question had been on Rose's mind from the beginning. She had put off asking, but it could wait no longer. "What can you tell me of my uncle?" she asked. She felt afraid of her own words. "Is he…a sympathetic man?"

Sergeant Mann whistled through his teeth and looked to the horizon. "You sure you want to ask me that?"

"I am certain I must know one way or the other. I will take it as opinion, not gospel. And I shall not repeat it."

He slapped the reins against the horses' backs, taking time before answering. "Slavin' is a hard business, ma'am. You and me's just lucky we're born white. Don't never want to be no slave." Rose nodded and waited for him to continue. Even soldiers who liked to talk sometimes needed acres of silence around them. At last he continued, "Your uncle, he puts out good cotton." He stopped, effort on his face, as if he was in physical pain. At last he said, "That kind of cotton takes everybody working together, if you know my meaning." He looked Rose in the eyes until she turned away in silence.

Two hours from town, the road became a footpath and then disappeared entirely. Fields of green foliage led to every horizon. "This here is Barnett land, ma'am," the sergeant said. They made their own way through the abandoned fields, following only the occasional footpath.

"It is beautiful," Rose murmured. "What is growing here? Is this cotton?" she asked.

Sergeant Mann laughed. "No, ma'am, that ain't no cotton. That's jimson weed mostly, and morning glory. A little cotton here and there underneath, but mostly jimson. And crabgrass in them rows, or what used to be rows." He shook his head.

"Will you show me?" Rose asked. "May we get down?"

"We shouldn't be stoppin', ma'am."

"Sergeant," said Rose, "we are in the middle of a flat plain. We can see for miles. Surely we can get down for a moment. I wish to be conversant when I meet my family."

Sergeant Mann pulled on the reins. "Just for a minute, ma'am."

Rose slid down from the wagon. The field grew wild; it was no longer a tended place. Mounding weeds formed redans as great as any army might build. Vines slithered through rows of woody shrubs, jumping from plant to plant, as if nothing less than total conquest would do. Beneath it all lay the soft white bolls Rose had seen only in books, a last harvest abandoned to the silty soil that once had grown the best cotton in the world.

"Mr. Barnett, he had the touch," Sergeant Mann said. "He picked cotton from July clear through September, even into October some years. Like I said, takes discipline."

"So it is a summer crop?" Rose asked.

"Yes, ma'am. This time of year, this field should be knee high, furrows strawed to keep the weeds down. Ought to be in candle now, but look at this junk. All nonsense now."

"Candle?"

"These bushes," he said, lifting the invading vines to show the woody stalks that came to Rose's waist. "That's your cotton. First it puts out the square, then the candle—sort of like pods, those are. Then the bloom comes—pretty little thing, starts out white and turns scarlet—then the bolls. When the bolls pop, you got cotton for picking. Assuming bollworm stayed home."

"How long does all of that take?" Rose asked.

"One hundred forty days, give or take."

Rose was astonished by the plant's elaborate mechanism just for coming into the world—and all before it was picked, ginned, spun, dyed, and woven into usefulness. "I think I shall never take a piece of cloth for granted again," she said. Her eye was pulled to a tall bush with long, dangling seedpods. "What is that plant called?" she asked, pointing. "It looks something like corn." The plant stood shoulder high and grew in ragged patches across the field.

"That there's millet. Africans got a taste for it. Make their bread and mush, that sort of thing out of it. Mr. Barnett, he let the field hands grow it long as they kept it out of the cotton. Wind and birds been spreading it, you can see."

"I should like to taste it sometime."

"I doubt you'd tolerate it, ma'am."

"Perhaps not."

"Look at this sorry sight," he said, shaking his head. "We got to go now."

They returned to the wagon. Rose looked across the ruined cotton field. She imagined it in bloom, clean white cotton bolls pushing sunward in arrow-straight rows, dark Negroes in bright colors gathering the soft crop into billowing sacks, teaching their children the beautiful Negro spirituals. She wished she could have seen it, but no sooner had the thought completed its fleeting journey through her mind than she thought of Maggie and Alice. It was not as if she didn't know better. Her aunts had warned her. "When you hear those things, those pretty stories," they had said, "stop your ears. Do not let those pictures take root in your heart. They are lies, and you must call them out as such." Now she recalled that the burs were sharp, that they cut and scarred a picker's hands. She imagined a child on her first day of picking, startled when a bur sliced the pad of her tiny finger, staring at the oozing blood, complaining to her mother that she did not like this work, and the mother hushing her before the overseer heard. She imagined women with toddlers tied to their backs, bending for hours in the steaming heat, and newborns left in cabins, fussing at the dry breasts of old women until mothers came from the fields with breasts exploding with milk, choking the infants so they left the breast early, beginning a vicious cycle of hunger and frustration in their tiny souls. Rose rubbed her eyes hard with her fingers. A slight whimper escaped her throat.

"You all right, ma'am?"

"Just trying to make sense," Rose replied.

"That can be hard to do, ma'am."

They entered a thick copse of birch trees. Several had been cut down, but the stand was still substantial, standing in straight rows, apparently planted as a crop. A narrow road led through the trees. In the distance Rose saw a square two-story clapboard house that, even at a distance, was in clear need of whitewashing. A lean-to hung from one side. The house sat on a low mound with a single willow tree at its base.

"That's it," Sergeant Mann said. "That's Barnett Plantation."

"Are you certain?" Rose said, looking from him to the structure in the distance. "It seems a common farmhouse." The pale green leaves of the weeping willow glowed in the morning sun, as if boasting of their comparative beauty.

"Real sure, ma'am. You were expecting a Georgia mansion, I suppose. Folks out here, ma'am, they not established like the deep South. Different worlds. Your uncle, he's just a farmer, you get down to it."

She had expected, if not a mansion, certainly more than this simple structure, but she knew this would not be her last surprise of the day. She straightened her skirt, dusted her shoulders, and checked the pins in her hair. "I have come this far," she said, smiling at Sergeant Mann, who clicked his tongue and snapped the reins.

The mound was larger up close than it had seemed from the woods. It was in fact a broad hill with a road that spiraled from its base to the top. The road had once been paved with crushed rock but now was rutted and dusty, the rock thrown off to the sides, no one to rake it back. As they reached the top, Rose looked out over the field below, beyond it to the copse of trees like a miniature forest, and beyond that to the abandoned fields they had just crossed. Like many things in life, they were more beautiful at a distance than up close.

Sergeant Mann pulled the wagon to a stop in front of the house. An elderly black woman sitting in a rocking chair on the veranda called out to them. "Who you be?"

Rose replied, "We are invited to dinner with Mrs. Barnett. I am Rose Barnett." She climbed down from the wagon.

"I ain't never heard of no Rose Barnett," the woman shouted.

"It's okay, Hattie. It's me, Mister Mann," said the sergeant.

"Mister Mann?" the woman called. She stood and clapped her hands several times. "You bring the chapel wagon?" She did not look down at the sergeant but out into the blue sky. Rose wondered if she was blind. The front door opened, and a tall woman with red hair fixed in a large knot atop her head emerged. She was dressed in black.

"That's enough, Hattie," she said. "Hush." She placed her hand on the woman's shoulder and pressed her down into the rocker. The black woman began to mumble, "Mr. Mann, Mr. Mann. Chapel wagon."

"Well, so it is, Hattie," the woman said, approaching the wagon. "I thought you'd be dead by now, Robert, or in jail."

"No, ma'am, I ain't neither."

"Looks like you gone Yankee on us. That's worse than dead."

"I have brought you your niece, ma'am."

"My supposed niece, Robert." She turned her gaze on Rose standing next to the wagon. "Let me take a look at you." She descended half a dozen wooden stairs from the porch to the dusty road.

Rose held out the invitation she had been told to bring. "I don't want that," the woman snapped as if Rose had offered her a dead rat. She looked closely at Rose's features, leaning in until Rose could smell the mint leaves packed in her cheek. "You do favor Lannis's side. Turn." Rose turned slightly. The woman's thumb and fingers grabbed her chin and yanked her head to the side. Rose reflexively brushed at the woman's hand, but the fingers continued to pinch. "Yes, that is surely a Winterkill nose," the woman sighed at last, letting go with a wave of her hand.

Rose rubbed her sore chin. "Winterkill was my grandmother's name," she said with far more gaiety than she felt after such a humiliating introduction.

"I know that," the woman said. "Well, there's nothing to it but to own it," she sighed. "Always knew we had Yankee in us. Never expected it to turn up." She turned and stepped to the porch. Rose held back, not knowing what the woman expected of her. "Do you wish to meet your cousins?"

"I do, very much, ma'am."

"Then follow. Robert, we shall be two hours, no more. If you need refreshment, you may go to the back. Don't bother the cabins."

Rose looked at Sergeant Mann.

"Go on," he said. "This is what you come for." He flicked the reins. "Git up." The wagon rumbled off.

Rose followed her aunt up the stairs into the house. She had not expected to be grabbed and twisted in such a fashion; the encounter had left her neck with a slight sprain, which she rubbed.

A parlor and piano were to the left. On the right was a small dining room, its table set for a meal. A hallway ran through the center of the house. At the far end, her aunt led Rose through a door into a plain sitting room. The sloping ceiling revealed that they were in the lean-to. Two other women were there with several children. A fireplace heated the space against the chill of the spring day.

"Close the door behind you," her aunt ordered. "We're trying to save the furniture." Recalling the forest of birches, Rose thought it would be some time before they had to use their chairs for fuel.

"Yes, ma'am," she said, latching the door.

"These are my daughters-in-law, Charlotte and Margaret Barnett," said the woman. "I am Dorothy Barnett. You may call me Miss Dotty."

"And I am Rose Barnett. It is such a pleasure—an honor—to meet you," she said. To Margaret she added, "You look familiar. Do you ever come into Memphis?"

Margaret fluttered a fan before her face. "When I must," she said. "But I doubt we have met."

"I am certain we have not met," Rose said, studying Margaret's cloud of russet hair and pale green eyes, "but I thought perhaps I had seen you near the landing or at Dabney's."

"The Dabneys have left town," Margaret said from behind her fan.

"Perhaps I am mistaken," Rose said, feeling sorry she had mentioned the little shop but no less certain she had seen Margaret before. "And who are these lovelies?" she asked, addressing two young girls who looked at each other and grinned.

"Stand up," Margaret said to the girls, "and introduce yourselves properly."

A tow-headed blond stood and held out her hand. "I'm Elizabeth, but I like Lizzie best," she said. She extended the sides of her skirt and dipped slightly. Her hair hung in carefully crafted ringlets.

"How do you do, Lizzie?"

"I do fine, ma'am, thank you. I'm eight."

"That is very clever of you," Rose said with a smile. Lizzie twisted back and forth. "And who is your mama?" Rose asked. The child pointed to Margaret.

"I see," Rose said. She turned to the other girl child. "What is your name?"

"I'm Adelaide," she said, performing a curtsey that involved elaborate bobbing and spinning until her grandmother finally called a halt.

The woman named Charlotte lay her hand gently on Adelaide's shoulder and spoke softly to her. "Offer your hand, Adelaide. That's a good girl." Mother and daughter shared the same light-brown hair. Adelaide's fell in a thick braid to her waist; her mother's was twisted tightly at the base of her neck.

Rose took the girl's tiny hand. "And how old are you?"

"Seven, ma'am. I shall have a birthday next month, though." She wiggled as if full of dancing grasshoppers.

"Will you be caught up to Lizzie, then?"

"For a little while," Adelaide replied, flashing a look of triumph her cousin's way. Lizzie stuck the tiniest tip of her tongue out at her cousin, but only after carefully turning her back to her grandmother.

"And who are these fine gentlemen?" Rose asked, turning to introduce herself to two boys. They were Roscoe and Boyd, both age six and gap-toothed. Another boy, about thirteen, stood in the corner, apart from the rest. When Rose spoke to him, he turned away.

"That's William," Lizzie said. "He ain't ours."

"Isn't," said Margaret, "he isn't ours." To Rose she said, "William's parents have passed." Her eyes went wide as if sharing a scandal. "He wishes more than anything to run away to become a drummer." William slumped against the wall, staring at the floor.

"Well, it is a pleasure to meet you all," Rose said. To the children, she explained, "I am the daughter of your grandfather's brother." They looked at her quizzically. "It is difficult to get straight, isn't it?" she said. "You may just call me 'cousin.'"

Adelaide stepped close and tugged at Rose's skirt. Rose smiled down at her. "Yes, Adelaide?"

"Grandpa Lannis shot himself," the child said. The corners of her mouth turned down and her brow furrowed. Her eyes began to tear.

"Adelaide!" The two mothers and grandmother admonished her at once, and the child burst into sobs. Charlotte took her daughter by the elbow and marched her from the room. The other children were silent, watching. Then Lizzie spoke.

"It's true. He did. Right over there in the barn," she said, pointing out the window. "Didn't want no Yankees getting him."

Margaret advanced on her daughter. "'Any Yankees,'" she said as she pushed Lizzie out the door.

"Now you see your Southron kin," Dotty said to Rose. "We are a sorry lot in these troublous times."

The irony of having found her father's brother only to have him snatched away made Rose weak in the knees. "May I sit?" she asked.

"Of course," Dotty said. "You have had a shock."

"I am sorry to hear of my uncle's passing, especially in such manner."

"Never mind Lannis," said Dotty. "The child is right. He could not abide a Yankee."

Rose did not protest that he was, in fact, a Yankee himself. He apparently had made a thorough conversion.

"You need tea," Dotty said. She opened the door and called Hattie's name several times before the old woman finally appeared. One steady blue eye was clouded with a thick cataract. The other wandered idly.

"Yes 'um?"

"Hattie, would it be too much to ask for a pot of tea?"

"Tea, ma'am. Yes, ma'am, I would like that."

"No, Hattie. Can you please bring some tea here, to our guest?"

"That would be nice," Hattie replied.

"Never mind, Hattie. Go back to the porch. I'll get it," Dotty said. "Damned things. We keep them in their dotage, and they still can't make a cup of tea. Boys, entertain your new cousin."

Dotty shooed Hattie toward the porch and called to Charlotte and Margaret for help before descending a set of stairs in the corner near the sullen William.

Rose was alone now with the three boys. The six-year-olds were whispering to each other. "What would you like to know?" Rose asked them.

"How did you know?" Roscoe said, glancing at Boyd, whose eyebrows shot up. "How did you know we were talking about you?"

"You were whispering. I thought it might have something to do with me being a Yankee."

The two boys looked at each other and erupted in giggles.

"So I was right?"

"Have you got horns?" Boyd burst out in laughter, covering his mouth with both hands. Roscoe slapped his thigh and guffawed.

"Would you like to check?" asked Rose, bending down so they could see the top of her head. At this they fell to the floor, kicking their feet in fits of hilarity.

"That wouldn't be polite, ma'am," Boyd said when he came up for air. "Least not from what I hear."

Rose straightened, wondering where on her body these children had been told she grew horns. She felt it best to leave the question unexplored. She stepped to join William. "How long have you lived here, William?"

He still leaned by the window near the kitchen stairs. He did not look back at her but said to the outdoors, "A year."

"You have no people?" Rose asked.

"Something like that," William said. He was a plain boy. He was taller than normal for thirteen but still had his baby fat. He would be a large man when fully grown.

"I did not have family either," Rose said. "Until today." She made an attempt to put cheer in her voice, only to hear her error before she even finished.

"Lucky you," William replied.

"I was clumsy," she said. "I am so sorry."

He jerked his head in acknowledgement but did not look at her or reply.

Rose thought of Grace and Fidelia. Why did she say she had no family when what she meant was her parents were deceased?

Dotty was climbing the stairs from the kitchen. As she entered the sitting room, she stopped to catch her breath. Behind her came her daughters-in-law carrying tea paraphernalia. Their chastened daughters followed, with Adelaide bearing a plate of molasses cookies.

"What trouble are you two in?" Dotty asked Roscoe and Boyd as she crossed the room to sit in a broad wooden rocking chair. They scrambled to their feet. "None, Miss Dotty," they said in unison.

"That I highly doubt. Take a sweet and go. You too, William. The ladies will have their time."

Grabbing their cookies, the little boys dashed from the room. A screen door slammed. William left silently, closing the sitting room door gently behind him.

Dotty addressed her granddaughters. "That was not a very good start, was it?"

"No, ma'am," each said in her turn.

"However, it had the virtue of being true," Dotty observed, still addressing the children. "If there's one thing I cannot abide, it's dissembling." She turned to Rose. "We are unashamed of our struggle, Miss Barnett, whatever its manifestations." She motioned for Charlotte to pour the tea and turned back to the children. "'I am sorry to say that your dear uncle has been gathered to the angels.' That is the proper way to inform another that a loved one has passed. One does not expound upon the details."

"I am sorry for your loss," Rose said. "I had hoped to see something of my father in your husband."

"But for the nose, you do favor the Barnett side," Dotty said. "My dear Lannis was fair, as you are."

"I see it in Lizzie," Rose said, stroking Lizzie's white-blond hair. "It has come down through the genes."

"You are a Darwinist," Dotty stated.

Rose replied carefully. "I find trait inheritance an intriguing phenomenon, that is all."

"You do not suggest we are monkeys," Margaret said, one hand over her mouth, her fan fluttering again.

"We are not monkeys, no," said Rose. "I mean only to say it is of interest to me that my fair hair and eyes should repeat themselves in your lovely child. That is all I meant by it." She would not mention her Winterkill nose.

"Mr. Darwin's ideas gain little purchase here," Dotty said. "We live too close to the apes as it is."

Rose ignored the crude remark. "How is it," she asked, "that there came to be Southern Barnetts? I knew my mother was from Mobile, but I thought my father's family was entirely in the North."

"Yes, Lannis was the black sheep—well, gray," Dotty said. "I will not go all the way to black. His mother never forgave him for leaving New York, although I do not recall a great gnashing of teeth over his sister running off to Ohio with that Indian fighter. Regardless, when the Tories attacked, Lannis and your father joined the federalist army. They fought in Canada first, then in Mobile toward the end of the conflict. They earned land grants here in Memphis for their trouble. Your father traded his for Lannis's interest in the family farm in New York."

"After marrying my mother in Mobile," Rose said.

"Yes, dear." Dotty took a noisy breath through her thin nostrils. Her eyelids drifted closed, fluttering as she spoke. "They were newspaper people."

The remark from this arrogant and frightening woman washed over Rose like a warm rain. It pleased her to think of her mother's family as newspaper people, perhaps especially if her aunt had disapproved.

Charlotte spoke. "You are a nurse?"

"I am. I serve on the *Despain*. We are docked at the Memphis landing."

"I have not been to Memphis since the Yankees came," said Charlotte. "Do the shops still sell European things?" She looked at Rose, suddenly animated.

Margaret interrupted. "You could go if you had a backbone," she said. Charlotte's eyes dropped to her hands in her lap.

"Memphis is still bustling," Rose said, "although you would probably find it much changed. There are not the European things there may once have been, of course, due to the blockade. But it is still a busy place."

"Crawling with Yankees, she means," Dotty said to Charlotte. "Dirty Yankees. Why, the cribs have multiplied like rabbits!" Her eyelids fluttered closed as she lifted her tea cup to her lips.

Margaret burst out, "The evils Yankees inflict upon us!" She fanned herself.

"I will not defend Union vulgarities," Rose said. "I have seen the neighborhood myself. We take advantage, it is true, especially of the poor."

Dotty put her teacup down with a bang. "The neighborhood?"

"I assure you my visit was quite necessary," Rose replied.

Charlotte interjected, "Please tell us about New York." She looked into Rose's eyes and smiled broadly, but the fingers of her clasped hands were white with tension.

"No, Charlotte," Dotty continued. "I will have my say. That business on Beale Street has soiled all of Shelby County." She turned toward Rose. "The Barnett name will play no part in it."

Rose allowed a small hum to escape her throat. She would not be bullied, but she would hear this woman out in her own home. She had come to learn, after all.

"Take the Churchill girl," Dotty said, turning toward to her daughters-in-law who nodded in acknowledgement if not assent. "Her mother is pulled to pieces in all of Memphis. What was the girl thinking? I admit her father is a banker. Still, she is not white trash. Even the issue of a common street merchant knows better than to hatch a child before one's vows."

Margaret emitted a tiny shriek and shielded her face with her fan. Dotty turned to her. "You are anything but common, dear." Then as if unable to leave bad enough alone, she added, "Nevertheless, you know you have been fortunate in your union." Margaret lowered her eyes and nodded. Dotty turned back to Rose. "I lay it directly at the feet of the Yankees. Our young people are in an unnatural state of urgency."

"It is true, Cousin Rose," said Margaret, her eyes on Dotty. "Things have become coarse." Dotty patted her hand, and Margaret smiled.

"I pray for both mother and child," Rose said. It was hopeless to try to raise their sympathies for the poor subjects of the gossip, but she would speak up on their behalf regardless.

"Well, this spawn shall have its waters smoothed," Dotty said, growing red-faced. "The girl sat with it in the front pew only last Sunday."

Charlotte ventured, "Mightn't we be glad she repents?"

Dotty turned to Charlotte, her voice rising to a shrill. "With half the churches closed," she said, "and Yankee preachers in the rest, we do not need sinners like her taking up space." Charlotte did not reply.

"Yankee preachers?" Rose asked.

"It seems our traditions must be preached out of us," Dotty sneered. Her lips pressed against her teeth. She turned her head away from the group and sniffed audibly. "Our pastor has been spared," she whimpered, "but with that wretched child in the front row, I do not know how much longer I can endure."

Rose replied, "I often find such women repentant." She exchanged smiles with Charlotte.

Dotty's head snapped back toward Rose. "How is it you occupy yourself, Miss Barnett?"

"Birthing is something I am trained for that the surgeons are not," Rose replied. "I have only been called to it once so far in Memphis, but I have been blessed to bring many children into the world at my dispensary."

"You are a midwife?" Charlotte asked with enthusiasm.

"I am a doctor, actually," Rose said. To a poor woman in Chicago, these words carried the ring of hope, but they often confounded those with the means to nurse their sick and deliver their children at home. Men especially tended to see her as either a midwife or an abortionist. Her years of study—of diagnostics, anatomy, and remedies, of cause and effect, of contagion and sanitation—were hidden beneath the mask of her femininity. Now she must try to clarify regarding her nursing duties on the *Despain*, guaranteeing even further confusion. "I am first a doctor," she said, "but I am learning to become a nurse. I have introduced many babies to the world."

"First the nursing of Yankees; now midwifery," Dotty said.

Rose locked eyes with her. "I have an interest in diseases of the lungs and heart. I hope to become a chest surgeon."

Dotty pulled in her chin and frowned.

Margaret asked, "Do you percus the chest?" Her fingertips fluttered about her neck, which grew splotchy.

"I do," Rose replied. "The practice is quite useful to the trained ear. It takes but a few taps of the fingers with the ear placed firmly upon the chest, or a trumpet if one is available. I could show you—"

"I think not today," Dotty interrupted.

"—if you like," Rose finished.

"I said, not today," Dotty repeated. Footsteps echoed in the hallway. "Ah, the gentlemen have come to right the ship," she declared. "Charlotte, get the door."

Charlotte rose dutifully, but before she could reach the door, it opened, revealing two older gentlemen and a young man about Rose's age.

"Princess!" the first man crowed, taking Charlotte in his arms and kissing her noisily on the cheek. "Where's the Yankee?"

"Daddy!" Charlotte blushed.

Dotty cleared her throat. "Good afternoon, gentlemen. May I introduce the only child of Lannis's brother, James? This is Miss Rose Barnett." She pointed at Rose.

"I hope I did not embarrass you, Miss Barnett," said the man who seemed to be Charlotte's father. "Quentin Bakker," he said. "I am honored to stand before such loveliness." He bowed toward her and came up grinning. He was a rotund man with long, white hair. Around his head, like a headband, was a brown stain from the leather hat he held in his hand. Below the stain his face was saddle-brown; above it, white as a hot summer sky.

"'Tis a pleasure to meet you as well, sir," Rose replied before turning to greet the others. All three men were clean-shaven, in contrast to most Union men, especially ill or injured soldiers. Eli Culpeper, Margaret's father, was a slim man draped in sartorial overstatement. He wore a turquoise silk vest and cravat, sharply pleated but frayed silk trousers, and highly polished black shoes.

The third man, much younger, was Eli's son and Margaret's brother, Skip. Of medium height, he was missing all but six inches of his right arm. He wore a short, brass-buttoned jacket of storm-cloud gray with a black standing collar. A stripe of the same gray embellished the sides of his black trousers. Wounded rebels arrived in Memphis in all kinds of garb, usually made of light gray or butternut fabric, often threadbare, torn, and sun-faded. This man, she guessed, was in regimental dress; he had fought early, before the sides had claimed their colors, before the South had turned to homespun. As his right sleeve was pinned up, Rose offered her left hand in greeting, as she had learned to do with her patients, but he did not return the gesture. She lowered her arm to her side and turned away, feeling all eyes upon her.

Dotty broke the silence. "Sit down, gentlemen." She pulled a ribbon and key from her bodice and handed it to her daughter-in-law. "Margaret, pour the sherry. Charlotte, get Hattie moving downstairs. Girls, out, out, out." Lizzie and Adelaide clasped hands and walked backward from the room, seeming reluctant to miss a single moment of the drama.

"May I help?" Rose offered.

"Never, my dear," Dotty said. "You are our guest. If the Yankees had not had their way with us, none of us should have to serve. But such is the state of affairs. We are sorely tried."

Quentin, Charlotte's father, spoke. "You are James Junior's daughter?"

"Yes, sir. My mother passed in my birth, and he died when I was four."

"I am sorry for your losses, my dear. I do recall hearing about your father's passing from Corky—James, that is—Charlotte's husband, rest in peace. He was named for your father."

Rose turned to Dotty. "You named your son for my father?"

"Lannis would have it," Dotty said.

"Thank you, ma'am." Rose did not know that thanks was the appropriate rejoinder, but she felt the urge to offer them nonetheless.

Eli asked, "Do I hear you treat the wounded, Miss Barnett?"

"Yes, both Union and Confederate, sir."

"Free Confederate? Or oathed?"

"We attend to all the injured who come, sir. Once they recover, the oath is their choice, or not, as they see fit."

"And if they do not see fit," said Skip, "it is the warehouse."

"Those who choose not to swear are held, yes, until there is a prisoner exchange."

Skip snorted. "If they live that long."

Rose would not debate prison conditions with this man. Neither side could claim honor in that regard. Instead she said, "The gentleman who brought me today was one of my patients. He once worked here as overseer."

"That so?" asked Skip. "Would that be Willie Mann?"

"Yes. He came to the ship with camp fever but has recovered. He is the one who told me about the Barnetts. He is here, somewhere." She looked to Dotty.

"Wandering the grounds," Dotty said. Turning to Skip, she added, "No doubt having a poke in the cabins."

"Now, Dotty," Quentin admonished. "Let us not shock our new cousin."

Eli said, "I didn't know there were any coloreds left here, Dotty."

"A few have come back. I cannot abide their insolence; they work only when the spirit is in them, and that is seldom, let me say. They keep the vegetable garden a bit and run the chickens, those they have not eaten. Hattie never left, but she is all burden." She looked to each of the gentlemen in the room and spread her arms wide. "I have not turned her out, have I?"

"No one says you haven't done well by Hattie, Miss Dotty," Eli said.

"That devil Garrison says so," Dotty replied, her voice rising in both pitch and volume. "Whores, he calls us, every one of us," she said, pointing around the room. "Babylon itself, he says." She looked at Rose. "There are two sides to every story, young lady. We are entitled to our opinion. And respect." She turned away as if holding back tears. "Hattie's damned lucky to have a roof over her head. All I put into her, and her going downhill like that." The room was silent.

Charlotte opened the door, announcing that dinner had been laid in the dining room. The gentlemen stood, motioning to Dotty to lead the way. Rose wondered if Dotty would retrieve her composure on the way to the dining room or whether she was just getting started.

The table was set with bone china, tarnished flatware, and small crystal glasses that had been half filled with sherry. A fire had been laid in the fireplace, but the room retained its chilly air. In one corner, Adelaide and Lizzie ascended stairs from the basement, carrying corn bread and gravy. The buffet held roast chicken and carrots. Rose wondered who had killed and cleaned the fowl.

Margaret lit the last few inches of white candles that stood, dust-covered, in crystal candelabras on the table. The little girls placed their contributions on the sideboard and stood at attention. Roscoe and Boyd were absent, as was William.

"That will be all, girls," Charlotte said to the children. They left the room, lingering beside the open door until their grandmother shooed them away.

"My own grandchildren, servants," Dotty sighed.

"They enjoy the kitchen," Charlotte said. "Lizzie cut the corn bread herself. And Adelaide likes to peel carrots."

"Hush," Dotty said. "Everyone sit. Quentin?"

Charlotte blushed deeply and took her chair.

Quentin prayed, "Lord, thank you for this bounty and for bringing our cousin, Rose, to us in the midst of our trial. Keep her safe when she is away from us and award us soon the victory you have ordained. Amen." Even accounting for the prayer's assumptions, Rose felt a shiver run through her as this man invoked God's protection on her behalf. She smiled up at him in gratitude as she echoed, "Amen."

"We shall have to pass," Margaret said, as she and Charlotte rose to retrieve the platters from the buffet. She handed the carrots to Quentin at the head of the table opposite Dotty. He passed the dish to Rose on his right. She took the warm bowl from him just as tears began to sting her eyes. With trembling hands, she placed a spoonful of carrots on her plate. As she passed the dish to Skip, her first tear just missed falling into the bowl.

"Rose?" Charlotte said.

All eyes were now on her, and Rose lost her battle against the flood. "I beg your pardon," she said, looking around the table. She attempted to laugh, but her tears would have their way.

"My dear, my dear," said Quentin, taking her hand. "What is this about?" He slid his chair back and turned to look directly at her. Crow's fee made his blue eyes appear to smile gently. Rose trusted him.

"It is nothing," she said. "I am just happy to be among you."

"Well, of course you are," said Margaret. "Anyone would be."

"I should go collect myself," Rose said, rising.

"I'll go with you," said Charlotte. Quentin stood and pulled out Rose's chair. Charlotte put her arm around Rose's waist and led her from the room.

In the sitting room, Charlotte wrapped both arms around Rose, causing another wave of weeping and hiccupping, which proved quite contagious. Soon they were laughing through their tears together.

"I don't know what has overtaken me," Rose said.

"Nor I myself," said Charlotte. "I feel as if a dam has burst."

Rose wiped her eyes with her napkin and blew her nose. "Oh, this is your good table linen," she cried, sinking into the wooden rocker.

"Blow away," said Charlotte. "The old biddy."

"I shall wash it before I go."

"Do not worry. It is such a pleasure to have you here. I cannot tell you what a delight it is to see a fresh face and hear a kind voice."

"We are all captives in our own ways," Rose said, thinking how lovely it was to be away from the ship. "Perhaps you and I can meet sometime in Memphis."

"I am afraid of the pickets, but I might suffer them to visit you," Charlotte replied. She kissed Rose on the cheek and with her fingers gently wiped the last of Rose's tears away.

Rose smiled. "Shall we return to the coliseum?" Charlotte laughed and nodded.

In the dining room, Dotty had become agitated again. "It is true. I learned it from Mildred Beeves herself last week. A Negro—in uniform, no less—walked right into her home and demanded his wife and daughter. Mildred showed him the bill of sale. But this"—she looked at Rose, who was retaking her seat with Quentin's help—"I shall not say gentleman, this individual, insisted they be given up. What of Mr. Beeves's investment?"

"Such are the times," said Quentin, resettling into his own seat. Charlotte silently returned to her chair next to Dotty.

"The man had a sword in his hand. What was Harold to do?" Dotty continued.

"Acquiesce, I suppose," Quentin said, slipping a juicy piece of chicken skin into his mouth. Fat dribbled down his chin.

"It is theft, any way you look at it," Dotty declared. She turned her attention to Rose. "Welcome back, my dear. You are worn out," she said. "A woman's constitution is not meant for war."

"I am overwhelmed from the joy of meeting you," Rose said. "'Tis nothing more than that."

Skip spoke, his eyes on his plate. "I should think you would be overwhelmed with the burden of caring for all that Yankee flesh." Margaret tittered in response.

Rose replied, "As I have said, we care for Yankee and Confederate alike. Lately we have had a run of measles. Contagion is indifferent to politics."

Eli remarked, "I would say that politics itself is a contagion." He laughed heartily at his own joke. "As a businessman, I prefer the ledger to the legislature." He chuckled to himself this time, as if he held a secret.

Skip was cutting his chicken by rocking the side of his fork back and forth upon the slice of dark meat on his plate. Arm amputees ate this way, unable to use more than a single utensil at a time. "I would be ashamed to be felled by contagion," he said. "I would rather what

I have." He put down his fork and, again using his only hand, shifted his chair closer to the table before taking up the fork again. He did not look at the others.

"Illness abounds," Rose said. "The southern clime is more susceptible, it seems, to agents that travel from one person to the next."

Skip turned to face her. "And how do you find the South, Miss Barnett, aside from its unhealthfulness?" He spoke more loudly than necessary, as if addressing Dotty at the far end of the table rather than the person next to him.

"I did not mean to offend," Rose said. "I find the South beautiful. In fact, on the way here, I was admiring a cotton field."

"Not much to admire these days," said Eli. "Gone to seed. Our own foolishness saw to that. Burning our cotton was not our finest hour. From a businessman's perspective, I say."

"May I ask," Rose ventured, "why you do not plant vegetables and grain where once there was cotton and trade among yourselves?" Rose asked.

Skip snorted. "You may have noticed, there is no labor." He raised his left arm, pointing toward the cabins. The stump of his right arm followed naturally and he blushed.

"Mr. Lincoln suggests we might each prosper from our own labor," Rose said.

Laughter broke around the table. "Rose, dear," said Quentin, reaching for her hand. "If you are to be a Barnett, you must grasp the basics of capital and labor." He winked at Dotty who closed her eyes and shook her head. "This whole unpleasantness," he continued, making a circle with his fork, "could have been avoided had the North just invested in its labor. Why, labor is the original form of capital. The most ancient form. The Romans knew this. As with the Romans, we seek to secure our investments, nothing more sinister than that."

Eli broke in. "Let us say two gentlemen dicker over a piece of land. The land is neutral, is it not? It cares not who owns it."

Rose felt about to be trapped, but she nodded.

"Because the land is silent, the deal remains between equals, and in that way the fairest price is reached. Labor, as a type of capital, is similarly neutral. It is an asset to be purchased, or not, as a producer requires."

Quentin shrugged. "The auction is fair to all," he said. "Pass the jam, please, Margaret. We've no objection to the black man, you see. He is essential, but he must be seen as the investment he is."

"You liken workers to land," Rose repeated carefully.

"A quick study," Eli declared. Quentin nodded and sipped his sherry.

"I confess I had not thought of it so," Rose said. "Do you believe investment, as you say, in labor, should be taken north, to the factories?"

"It has been suggested, yes," said Eli.

"A house divided and all that?" said Quentin. "We must choose one way or the other. Why not the Southern way? The Constitution provides for it, after all."

"I have seen Northern factories," Eli said. "They differ little from plantations, save in what they produce. It is not a far stretch to ask industrialists to invest in their people just as planters have. Of course, they must be in it for the long term. They must feed and clothe their workers, as we do here, and care for them in their old age. None of that is in place yet, but I believe it is possible, if capital would just take the long view."

"Instead," Margaret whined, "we have this ridiculous proclamation. Why can't they just leave us alone?"

"The Miscegenation Proclamation," Dotty sneered. "I would note, for the sake of our new cousin, that the edict does nothing for the servant in Memphis or Maryland. But then, we all know the thing is meant as a gauntlet to the deep South, not a life ring to the black man."

"It cannot be enforced," Skip said. "Mr. Lincoln doesn't control the Confederacy. We're a sovereign nation."

"The thing is lawless even in the Union," Quentin said. "The right to one's property goes back to the Magna Carta."

Rose ventured, tentatively, into the discussion. "You do not agree, then, with the Declaration of Independence—that we are created equal?" The unpleasantness with Maggie came to mind. Was this all she had been trying to say?

Everyone began speaking at once. Quentin raised his hand, and they yielded. "The phrase, my dear," he said in a voice he might use with a child, "is a meaningless *fleur de lis*. Pretty words, but they are not the law. That our own man wrote the silly thing is an embarrassment, I grant you." He looked around the table before adding, "But I am certain Mr. Jefferson would pull it back if he could see the suffering it has wrought. The Constitution is the law, and it expressly accommodates bonded labor. Congress so ruled seventy years ago."

Eli turned to Rose. "As with the colonials, my dear, at its heart this is an economic matter. The North will soon realize it cannot exist without our cotton and the tariffs it sucks from the Southern bosom."

"Daddy!" Margaret exclaimed at his vulgarity.

"Which is why we shall win this thing," Eli concluded with a shrug.

Quentin spoke. "No, Eli, I disagree. More is at stake than tariffs."

Eli compressed his lips into a tight grin, as if accustomed to being corrected by his better.

Quentin began poking the table with his index finger. "Under natural law," he declared, "any state may dissolve the political bands which bind it to another." His voice rose to a commanding volume, almost a shout. "We have done nothing more than the colonies did! Why, the abolitionists themselves have been calling for New England to secede for twenty years. Everyone knows it is a natural right."

Rose noted that, after having just denounced the essential premise of the Declaration of Independence, Quentin was comfortable relying upon it to justify secession. Perhaps that was why his ears had grown scarlet.

"Abolitionists haven't the cheek to secede," Dotty scoffed. "They hide behind their printing presses, name-calling and inciting insurrection." She sniffed hard, and her voice took on a high pitch. "We are a forbearing lot, but enough is enough. Do they not know the worry they cause us as women? We are merely defending ourselves, while your president puts rifles in the hands of our Negroes." She was not finished. She pointed a finger at Rose, who reflexively took up her fork, as if to defend herself. "And let me tell you something, young lady. The English flag flew at Jamestown thirteen years before the Pilgrims ever laid eyes on Plymouth Rock. If one considers Roanoke, the advantage is greater still. The South has given this country its best men. My ancestors built this country!"

Rose noted that Dotty still seemed to feel very much a part of the United States, even as a secessionist. How wretched it must be to feel cut off from one's own country, estranged from one's ancestors and all they had built. But if Dotty felt cut off, what must Maggie feel?

Quentin was speaking, arms extended in conciliation. "As for bound labor," he declared, "it is, like the magnolia, both gift and curse." Around the table heads bobbed, as if they had heard the metaphor many times. "It requires constant attention and cleaning up after, Lord knows." He shrugged and raised his eyebrows as if helpless in the matter. "God has given us the black man. Despite the challenges, we must husband the gift bestowed upon us."

"I see I am among the devout," Rose replied. How could both sides believe God was with them? To cast war in holy terms could only make it more intractable. But then, holy wars were as old as time.

"Devout we are," said Dotty, "which is why I, for one, will never take that blasted oath. I would not take it for a sea of fresh-picked cotton at three Yankee dollars a pound."

"It's not a true oath, Miss Dotty," replied Margaret, "if you reserve yourself in your mind. That is how many take it."

Dotty's face went cold. With hooded eyes, she turned to Quentin. "How things have changed," she said. "One's word means nothing today. Is this what we have raised, Quentin? Liars?"

Margaret blushed and lowered her eyes.

Quentin was aggressively sucking on a drumstick. "You needn't fret, Dotty. You may stand by your principles until your dying day. To reenter the Union—and God forbid we ever shall—but to reenter the Union, a state need swear only ten percent of its people. I think you may safely disappear among the ninety percent, should it come to that. But Margaret is right. The Yanks have broken every promise in the book. Why shouldn't we?"

"How low we have fallen," Dotty said, shaking her head. "Yankee low."

Rose looked at Charlotte across the table. She sat with her hands in her lap, her eyes downcast. When Dotty repeated herself, "Yankee low," Charlotte burst out, "Can't we just stop this? I am so weary of war! We fight amongst ourselves more than with the enemy. Why must we fight at all? Is there not another way?"

"And be murdered in our beds?" Dotty snarled.

Charlotte began to weep. "I am exhausted from fear, Miss Dotty, and not fear of being murdered. First it was our own men setting fire to things, now it's the Yankees and guerillas. I am tired of bandits and Yankees and, yes, rebs keeping me locked up in this house."

"You needn't be," Margaret said.

Charlotte glared back at her.

"Truly we are afflicted," Skip remarked, watching the sisters-in-law bicker. To Rose he turned, demanding, "Are you really a Barnett? Or a Yankee spy?"

"I should be going," Rose said. "I did not mean to upset anyone." She pushed back her chair.

"Now, dear, you stay right here," said Quentin, taking her hand and restraining her from rising. "It is the nature of the times, is all. Until we work out this labor question, most families are bound to be at odds occasionally." To Skip he said, "Fear not, son. I am quite certain we are not in the hands of the enemy." He patted Rose's hand, smiling.

Skip snorted and turned his chair so his back was to her.

"Hattie," Dotty shouted without warning. Everyone at the table jumped. "Hattie!"

When the old woman did not appear, Charlotte sighed. "What is it, Miss Dotty?" Rose pitied Charlotte, under her mother-in-law's thumb, helpless without her, yet losing a bit of her soul every day she lived under this woman's rule.

"Hattie!" Dotty called, ignoring Charlotte. "Near blind and just as deaf. And yet I keep her. I am certain that would not be the case up north. Hattie!"

Charlotte rose. "She is napping, Miss Dotty," she said. "I will make the tea. Margaret, you will help me, won't you?"

Her sister-in-law sighed and pushed back her chair. "I hate serving," she pouted. "It's degrading." Nevertheless, she stood to go.

"May I help?" asked Rose, beginning to rise.

"Sit," ordered Dotty. "We have not forgotten how to treat a guest." With an artificial smile, she added, "Now, tell us about your branch of the tree, dear."

Rose had only taken a breath when Hattie stumbled into the dining room.

"Better late," said Dotty. Even the false smile she had given Rose was gone.

Hattie approached Quentin. "I seen him!" she cried. "I seen my boy." Her clear eye darted around the room, her head following it wildly.

Dotty shouted down the stairs. "Margaret! Come get Hattie."

"I seen my boy," Hattie repeated, tilting toward Quentin, as if she might fall. "The one Missus sold off me. I seen him." She shuffled toward the other end of the table where Dotty sat. Rose saw the matriarch grow rigid as the color left her cheeks. Dotty was afraid—afraid of her slave.

Hattie wobbled past her mistress to the top of the kitchen stairs. There she sank to her knees and began stroking the finial on the banister. "Oh, Tig. How you now?"

"Margaret!" Dotty shouted again.

Eli rose from the table and knelt beside Hattie. "You've been dreaming, Hattie. There's nobody named Tig here." He put his hand on her shoulder, but she threw her arm back, striking him in the face, causing him to fall backward.

"Hattie!" Dotty jumped up, but she froze in place as Eli put up his hand to stop her. He tried to grip Hattie's shoulders, but she struggled, weeping.

Dotty raised her arm as if to strike the old woman, but Quentin stepped forward and arrested it in midair. "Get her out," Dotty growled. "Get her out of here." She wrested her arm from Quentin's grasp. Her pale lips were turned down, the muscles of her jaw pulsed. Rose thought she might be about to expectorate.

Charlotte and Margaret ran up from the kitchen. Charlotte knelt beside Hattie and whispered in her ear. The old woman nodded. Gently Charlotte lifted her to her feet. Eli and Quentin stepped aside.

"Get her remedy," Dotty ordered Margaret. "Double it." Charlotte led Hattie from the room toward the front porch. Margaret retreated down the kitchen stairs.

Dotty, seated again at the head of the table, lifted her chin and pressed a handkerchief to her eyes. "I do wish she would stop picking that scab," she said. "What does she want from me?"

Margaret returned with a tray. "The cookies are a little dry," she said to the gentlemen. "We are low on molasses."

"Never apologize, my dear," Dotty said, smiling and slipping the handkerchief up her sleeve. "It just draws attention. Now, Cousin, tell us about your life with the enemy."

Chapter 12

"I'VE SEEN WORSE," MAGGIE SAID, WAVING HER HAND BENEATH HER glistening neck. By the time of Rose's return, the day had turned hot. The air hung over the ship like a dirty bedsheet. Somewhere behind a dingy sky, the sun, as if exhausted, was trying to set.

"Can we not rescue Hattie, at least?" Holly asked. "Bring her in to Memphis?"

"Leave her be," said Able. "You don't want an old woman in a camp."

"Dotty will go inland," Maggie said. "I'd bet a week's pay on it."

"But will she take Hattie?" Holly asked.

Maggie spoke. "If I know white ladies, she'll not leave her behind."

Able nodded.

"Even demented, Hattie is hers," Maggie said. "Once she leaves that land, Hattie is all the property Dotty's got. She won't let go of that."

"Well, I do not see Dotty going inland," Rose said. "She is as stubborn a woman as I have ever met."

"Will the men not force the issue?" Holly asked.

"They are not her men. They are the fathers of her son's wives. Dotty makes her own choices."

"At least the cabins have cleared out," said Maggie.

"Most of them," Rose said.

"The women are probably right here on Government Island," said Able.

Maggie shrugged. "Or in the cribs."

"Oh, let us hope not the cribs," exclaimed Holly. "I worry for their souls, those poor women." She turned to Maggie, adding, "Poor Alice."

Able exchanged looks with Maggie. "If you all are going to get into the working girl's soul, I'm going below," Able said. "I am glad you met your people, Nurse Barnett, even considering."

Rose smiled in gratitude. She had once proposed to Able that they use Christian names between them. Able had agreed but never made the change. When asked if she wished to be addressed formally, she had declined, waving her hand. "Habit," she said. "I don't swim upstream unless I have to." Apparently, despite her earlier objections, Able now felt Rose's family relations were no longer worthy of an upstream swim.

As Able left, Maggie turned to Holly. "Please stop fretting about Alice. In the balance of things, I think she will do just fine at the pearly gates."

"But mightn't she work on the ship?" Holly replied.

"Do not judge her!" Maggie exclaimed.

"I do not," Holly said. "I only worry for her health."

"You just invoked her soul," Maggie replied, "and that is not your business!" Rose had never seen Maggie raise her voice with Holly; when Holly began to cry, Maggie relented. "I swear," she said, taking a seat beside her. "You two could worry the skin off a mule." She put an arm around Holly. "Shhhh," she said. "I haven't forsaken you. Either of you." She looked up at Rose. Then with words as common as air and as sharp as razors, she began.

"I was light," Maggie said, "so I was in the house, but Alice was in the field. I got some lessons, not much, but I learned to talk white. I can read a little. The driver, well, he just wouldn't let up on Allie. He was on her every which way. Now there's a bunch going to hell—drivers. Turning on their own. Anyway, we were south of Louisville. We didn't have to get far, just across the river. I stole a penny here and there from the house until we had the money to pay a man to take us across. We knew he would turn around and charge our missus twice as much to tell her where he dropped us. That's how it worked. But then the driver got in a fight and was shot, and in the hullabaloo, we were overlooked. That or our missus just let us go because the war had started and her man was gone. Maybe she didn't have the money to fetch us. Who knows? I don't care. Alice was nineteen and I was sixteen. We got clear to Indianapolis, and we talked about Canada, but we could never make ourselves go." She shook her head. "Something about crossing that border just didn't seem fair. Alice worked for different houses. She'd learned plenty from the driver. She wouldn't let me get started in it, though. Since I could pass, I worked in a laundry. I went to market and such for the house. We made out okay for a year, but it seemed like that winter would never quit. Probably the real reason we never got to Canada."

Rose smiled, remembering the cold winters of Chicago and New York.

"When the Union grabbed Memphis," Maggie continued, "Alice said there would be cribs galore, so we snuck back into Dixie. Can you believe it? One minute Canada on the horizon, and the next, we're slipping into Memphis just to get warm." She shook her head. "Able knows what I mean. Anyway, Alice got me the job on the ship."

"But why did she not take one also?" asked Holly. "There are colored women in the laundry, even on the wards. Look at Able."

Maggie laughed. "Holly, dear, do you know the silver they make at those cribs? Even with the house cut, it's three times what the army pays me to wash bloody sheets. Plus whatever she can lift off a drunk soldier." She bent over and whispered, "White men like her. A lot."

Holly turned away, flushed, but Rose held Maggie's gaze. "You are not thinking of joining her," she said.

"We've talked about it." Maggie shrugged. "I'm of an age now, if there is an age in that line of work. I've seen ten-year-olds at it. Now, that's a crime."

"No, Maggie," Holly moaned. "You mustn't."

"And you needn't," Rose said.

Maggie grew serious again. "I needn't go to the cribs, Rose? Why? Because I look white?"

Rose swallowed the urge to defend herself. "When I study it, yes, that is what I was thinking."

"And what would be the flip side of that coin?"

"That black women belong in the cribs?" Rose asked.

"She is a fine pupil," Maggie said to Holly, her humor returned.

"I take the point," Rose replied. "But may I continue?"

"You may, as long as you admit there are plenty of white girls in the same predicament."

"All I want to say is that it is dangerous, and you must do everything you can to stay out of it."

Maggie sighed. "Alice says the same."

"Because she loves you," said Holly.

"Relax, ladies. I am not going to the cribs. That would take the fun out of it!" She grinned broadly.

Holly's eyes grew wide.

"I am hardly the only one," Maggie said, throwing her arms wide. "Look at Elizabeth."

Rose had heard rumors. Where men and women were together, nature took its course, like a river sought the sea.

"But you do not take money," Holly said cautiously.

"Have no worry, Holly, dear. I am not for sale. I am done being for sale."

"It is a kind of slavery," Rose added, "isn't it, when money is paid?"

"Yes. Yes, it is," Maggie said.

"What if you get pregnant?" Holly demanded.

"I did have to do something once, and I won't lie, it was not nearly so pleasant as the rest of it. But it was only once. Since then, my luck has been holding."

"Maggie, you may be infertile," Holly cried.

"Maybe," Maggie said with a shrug. "But I have not seen that childbearing improves a woman's lot, especially a poor woman's. If you wish me ill or dead, then wish me children."

Holly groaned, but Rose understood the truth of Maggie's words. Her married patients in Chicago had been exhausted from childbearing. If they missed their monthly, they begged her to restart them. Ergot of rye was affordable and effective but treacherous for the mind. One of her patients had hanged herself after taking it, leaving seven children behind. Her husband, in despair, shot the children in their beds and then himself. Rose had not used the drug again.

"At least a married woman has the comfort of Scripture," Holly said.

"My dear, sweet Holly," Maggie said, with evident impatience, "I do hope to find a good man someday, I do, and to become an honest woman. We will settle down on a farm with Alice and, who knows, perhaps the Lord will send me a child. One child. That would be nice. Alice will have no man again once she is free. In fact, I expect her to grow righteous, like the two of you." Maggie winked at Rose. "So I must have my fun now." She stared out at the river, as if seeing the farm and her child calling to her from the far shore. Then she sighed. "Who knows if I shall have the chance to grow old? Do not begrudge me my youth."

A shy smile came to Holly's lips. "It is pleasant," she said, "once one becomes accustomed."

"You see?" Maggie exclaimed to Rose. "Holly knows. She has been a married lady." She tickled Holly until she begged for relief.

"I must go," Holly exclaimed. "I cannot take more of this." She rose and kissed them both on the cheek. "I love you, Maggie. I begrudge you nothing. But take care."

"Yes, Mother," Maggie said.

As Holly left them, Rose turned to look at Maggie, this wise woman ten years her junior. "I am blessed to know you, Mags," she said. "I am book-taught but horribly ignorant of some things. You help me find beauty in the world as it is."

"There's nothing wrong with book-taught," said Maggie. "I could use more of it myself. Most of what I know is from scrapping."

Rose heard the words before she knew it was she who spoke them. "Maggie, may I ask you something? It is something I should know, I confess, but I do not know it and cannot find it in a book, not really."

"Goodness, Rose, I am curious."

Rose wished to say that it was nothing after all, but more words came of their own accord. "'Tis about men, Maggie," she said, a crack in her voice. Maggie's eyebrows shot up. Rose ran her hands nervously over her skirt. "It is just that they are such curious creatures," she said, watching Maggie's face in the twilight. "They are soft one moment and hard the next."

Maggie's eyes widened and she burst out laughing.

Rose looked away, embarrassed. "You know my meaning," she said.

"Oh, yes," laughed Maggie. "Yes, I do."

"Do not tease me," Rose pleaded. "What I mean to say is, can you tell me what it is like—to be with a man?"

Maggie looked at Rose. "So now you wish to hear all about it? What happened to 'Oh, your mortal soul, dear Maggie'"?

"Please," Rose begged. "I must know."

"Has Dr. York proposed?" Maggie smiled broadly.

"No!" Rose exclaimed, looking over her shoulder, fearing they might be overheard. "But I feel that if he were to do so, I should want to know what I was getting into."

"You really mean it, don't you?"

"I have neither mother nor sister to teach me," Rose pleaded. "I've only textbooks, and they are wholly inadequate to the task. Please, Maggie."

"What of your patients in Chicago? Did you learn nothing from them?"

"Even poor women keep certain things to themselves."

Maggie took Rose's hands in hers. "Dear Rosie. I am sorry for you. Let me see." She worked her lips, pursing them, clenching them, clearly straining to contain a smile or, worse, laughter, but Rose waited, mortified but relieved the answer to her most private question was finally within reach. "I don't know if I can say it with words," Maggie began, "first you do this thing, and then you do that. That is not the way of it at all. It's more like time stops, and at every step, you are simply pulled along. It is natural, very natural, and fine."

"And is it often, I mean, must it be?" Rose asked.

"If you are lucky," Maggie said, smiling.

"Please be serious," Rose begged.

"Yes, ma'am," Maggie said, dramatically clearing her throat. She paused then raised a finger into the air. "You know morning glory? On a ship full of soldiers, you cannot have missed it."

Rose's thoughts went to the flowering vine before she grasped Maggie's meaning. "That is but a full bladder," she said. "So I was taught." She had sometimes found her eyes straying in the direction of this astonishing and common display of biology beneath the blankets.

"Perhaps it is just the bladder," Maggie replied. "In any case, it does nicely. With just a little kissing, a woman can be equally ready and both are satisfied."

"Every morning?" Rose asked.

Maggie laughed. "I'm sorry, Rose. You are just too dear. I have not been married. Perhaps you should ask Holly."

"I can think of nothing more mortifying," Rose said. "Please, you must know."

"All right, my friend," Maggie conceded. "As far as I hear, it is not every morning, except possibly in the beginning. It can be enjoyed any time of day, you know."

"Of course I know that," Rose said, blushing deeply.

"Enough for now?" Maggie asked with a smile.

"Yes," Rose said. "Enough."

In early June the provost marshal's clerk approached Rose on her ward. "Marshal will see you, ma'am." It was less request than summons.

"The marshal?"

"Yes, ma'am."

"I must relieve Corporal Tucker of his breakfast," she said, indicating her patient. "I shall come when I have finished." Although the corporal had not eaten in three days, still Rose and Mother Pennoyer had concurred that an emetic was in order.

Maggie was passing by and remarked, under her breath, "I am glad I am a laundress." She and Rose exchanged smiles.

The clerk seemed annoyed that Rose had turned her attention from him. "You stay out of it," he said to Maggie. To Rose he said, "Fifteen minutes." Then he turned and walked away.

"I will do my best," Rose mumbled, having the last word, even if it was only with herself.

Corporal Tucker had not spoken since coming to the ship two days earlier. No physical wound afflicted him, but his commanding officer had sent him to the ship under escort. His handler had left him with Elizabeth, the first nurse he saw. "What is his injury?" she had asked.

"War," the guard had said.

Rose was nearby at the time. "I'll take him," she said. Her interest in the nostalgic had deepened. She noted that their invisible wounds were revealed through a set of shared behaviors—paralysis, agitation, muteness, mental distance, and visions. She and Dr. York often disagreed on the disposition of such patients; he tended to see malingering. Knowing the neurotic could harbor an imbalance of chemicals in the brain, Rose felt they should be treated with vigor lest the illness spread to the spine. She wondered now if such was the case with Corporal Tucker. He had lain paralytic for two days, neither eating nor eliminating except from his kidneys, which was done without remark, from a supine position. He seemed feverish by appearance, but when Rose placed the back of her hand on his brow, it was always cool. She feared a hidden fever, perhaps indicating infection of an internal organ. Mother Pennoyer agreed that, despite the ban on calomel, purging could force the fever, if it existed, to announce itself.

Rose combined the medicine with water and a teaspoon of molasses. She gathered a bucket, a glass of pure water, and two damp towels before approaching the unfortunate soldier. She called Elizabeth to assist. "Corporal," she whispered. His eyes were open, but he did not seem to see. She wondered if the suspected infection was of the brain itself, which would suggest mania.

"Sir," she said, "I am concerned by your condition. I should like to conduct a procedure that may relieve your suffering. Shall we begin?"

The man did not respond.

"Excellent. Please sit up." Rose indicated for Elizabeth to assist her in pulling him to a sitting position. When he was upright, she ran her hands along his back, pressing gently. She could feel his viscera quivering within him. "Can you swing your legs over the edge of the bed, please, sir? It will assist."

Again the corporal neither resisted nor complied, so Rose pulled his legs over the edge. She handed him the cup. "Drink," she said, bringing it to his mouth and tipping it gently at first to see if he would take it on his own. The bitter taste of the medicine caused him to use his hand to push the cup away, a sign that the brain might be less involved than she had thought.

"You must drink," Rose said firmly, and without waiting for reply, she trapped his head in the crook of her arm, took hold of his chin, and poured the liquid down his throat. A shudder shook his body, but his eyes remained glazed. "I apologize, Corporal," she said. "That is the first step, and you have accomplished it admirably." She assisted him in lying back down on the bed. Within moments, he began to shiver and roll about, until suddenly he sat up on his own. Rose placed the pail beneath his chin. In three great heaves, the procedure was done.

Rose gave him fresh water. He took the cup in his hand and spit into the bucket. That he did so of his own accord was a good sign. She cleaned his lips with one of the damp cloths and wiped his neck and cheeks with the other. He still had not spoken, but he was calm. She laid him down and sent Elizabeth for a blanket. Before she returned, the soldier was asleep. Rose covered him and touched his brow. It remained stubbornly cool. "We must allow time," she said to Elizabeth. "Please check him for fever every fifteen minutes while I am gone." Elizabeth nodded. While she remained a silly, vacuous girl, she had learned well how to watch a fever.

The usually crowded marshal's office today was quiet. Only the marshal and his clerk were present. "Your cousin is moving provisions for the enemy," the marshal said. "And communications." He stared at her over his spectacles.

"My cousin, sir?" Memphis was crawling with spies. It was not out of the question that Skip, with two good legs, was moving supplies and information. The fire burned in him. "I do not wish to be placed in the middle, sir."

"We can turn an eye to the forage, but the letters must stop."

Rose recalled the vitriol Skip had directed at her. "Surely someone from your team can approach him, sir. I barely know him. And to be frank, I doubt he would listen to me." A new possibility occurred to her. "I hope you do not wish me to get close to him, sir. I am a nurse, not a spy."

"I don't know how many rebel cousins you're owning to, Nurse. Perhaps we should have a longer conversation."

"Sir?"

"I am speaking of a woman, Nurse Barnett. A Margaret Barnett."

Relieved he was not referring to Skip, Rose could not suppress a smile. "Margaret?" she said.

"She has been at it for some time. It occurs to me you can return the favor I have recently granted you."

"For how long, sir, if I may ask, has she been so engaged?" She regretted that her visit may have brought the family to the marshal's attention. If Margaret was smuggling food, she was only providing for the family. As a soldier, Skip would be suspect, and Charlotte was afraid to come into town. Certainly Dotty would not stoop to gathering groceries. She would starve to death first. If food was needed, it would be Margaret who secured it. "I hope I have not endangered my cousins, sir."

"As I said, the provisions can be overlooked, but the movement of information is another matter," he said. "She has been at it for some time, but I only now have put two and two together. I am asking politely that you speak to her, but I can order it." The threat in his voice was real.

"What is it you suspect her of transporting?"

His face turned scarlet. "Information, Nurse. Information!"

Rose thought it best not to annoy him further. "Yes, sir. I will speak to her."

"Speak firmly, else she will face the full wrath of the Union army," the marshal warned, waving Rose away.

Rose now knew where she had seen Margaret before—near the landing and strolling among the shops on the bluff. Why did she come to town so often? Within the week she saw Margaret speaking with a gentleman near the boarded-up Dabney's. Rose watched for a few moments—spying, she realized. When the two parted, she called Margaret's name and crossed the street.

"Hello, Cousin," Margaret drawled.

"Hello, Margaret. May we speak?"

"Why, of course we may." The drawn-out drawl and sugary tone of Margaret's voice told Rose this would not be an easy conversation. She stepped toward a bench near the shuttered store, but Margaret remained standing near its door. "Do you not wish to rest your feet?" Rose asked.

"I am content. How may I help you?"

There was no point in beating about the bush. "The marshal says you are smuggling," Rose said. "Is it true?"

Margaret widened her eyes and pressed a gloved hand to her breast. "Rose, dear, I know we have our differences, but this is simply too cruel." When Rose did not reply, Margaret added, "I should have known that Yankee marshal would pit kin against kin. Sending you to do a man's job. Pitiful. No Southern man would use a woman this way."

"So you are smuggling. That is why you seemed familiar to me. I have seen you here before."

Margaret fluttered her fan.

"Well, stop it," Rose said. "You could get hurt. Or worse, one of the children could get hurt. Or Charlotte or Dotty. Just stop."

"What do you know about it?" Margaret snapped. "The army feeds you very well, from what I am told."

"You would be surprised what I know," said Rose, bluffing. "It is not the provisions they mind so much as the letters. They cannot abide the communications."

Margaret smiled. "You would deny our Southern boys the simple joy of a scented epistle from their sweethearts? A few lines of comfort from their mothers?"

"And those Southern generals the Union troop movements from their spies?"

Margaret looked at Rose with what seemed to be satisfaction, crossing her arms and smiling. "That bothering the marshal?"

"Just stop it," Rose snapped. She turned from her cousin and walked away. She was agitated but also charmed by Margaret's boldness. She had heard Southern women both praised and cursed for their grit. It was no surprise that a species that had been pampered and petted for generations would take the bit when the opportunity arose. Still, Rose worried for her family if Margaret should cross the marshal in a serious way. It was not unheard of for the Union to jail troublesome Southern women. Rose hoped she had persuaded Margaret, but she knew it was unlikely. Margaret was probably regaling her friends with the tale already, laughing at her naive Yankee cousin.

As she entered the ward, Rose saw that her paralytic patient was sitting up and taking beef tea from Elizabeth. "It is good to see you recovering," she said, to no reply. She felt his forehead. It was still cool. It seemed that infection raged neither in his brain nor in any other organ. His face now held expressions that changed from instant to instant, as if he were seeing something in his mind that his eyes did not see. To Elizabeth she said quietly, "I think we shall call his family."

Elizabeth nodded and set the tea down.

"Let him finish his tea," Rose said. Elizabeth dutifully picked up the cup and held it to the man's lips.

A few days later, eight thousand Union troops went in search of General Forrest in northern Mississippi. Holly convinced Rose to join her and other cheering nurses in sending the men off. It took hours for the cavalry to pass, followed by the infantry and, after the crowds had melted away, supply wagons manned by twelve hundred colored troops. Ten long days passed. The weather turned hot and rainy. Memphis grew tense. Finally, exhausted Yankees began staggering back to town—most without their weapons, many shirtless and barefoot. All were ravenous, having been on half rations for days. At a crossroads deep in Mississippi, hungry and lost and utterly without order, they had been greeted by General Forrest's well-fed and rested cavalry. The boys in blue had retreated in chaos, struggling through extreme heat, mud, and rain, with Forrest and his men nipping at their heels. Only at the edge of Memphis had Forrest pulled back.

The citizens of Memphis had a good laugh as the Yankees dragged in, but their smiles faded a day later when two hundred colored troops marched down Beale Street, colors flying and bloody bayonets glinting in the sun. Called upon to defend the rear flank, the cooks and drivers, it was said, had not hesitated.

As the Fort Pickering colored hospital was full of chickenpox patients, the wounded among the newly minted warriors were assigned to the *Despain*. Mother Pennoyer called the nurses together. "The Lord has sent these brave men to us," she intoned. "Nurse them as you would any other. Courage, ladies!"

Able stormed out of the room.

In the surgery Dr. York delivered similar encouragement to his surgeons. "Why must you say that?" Rose asked as she cut through a soldier's muddy pant leg.

"Would you rather I say nothing and let these brave men take whatever comes their way?"

"I would rather it should not need saying."

"Someday, perhaps, but not today," he replied. "I believe we must take the knee."

That afternoon, as Rose changed the man's dressing, Able approached. "Same color on the inside," she said.

"I have just thought the same," Rose replied.

"Seeing is believing."

"I am sorry for Mother Pennoyer's remarks," Rose said.

"It may need saying," Able said, "but I'll be damned if I'm going to listen to it."

Just then the marshal's clerk appeared at Able's side. She looked him up and down.

"I think he is here for me," Rose said, feeling a knot rise in her belly.

"Marshal wants you," the aide said to Rose.

"Go on," Able said. "I'll take over here." Rose's patient offered Able a broad smile as if the two of them shared a secret.

Rose followed the clerk off the ship. At the marshal's office there were no pleasantries. "I want your cousin frisked," the marshal said.

"Pardon me, sir?"

"All the way to her drawers. Beyond her confounded rebel drawers, if you must."

"Frisked, sir? Margaret? Is that really necessary? I will talk to her again."

"If not you, I'll have one of my men do it. Right here in this office. I will not have our men taken by that bastard Forrest because a damned secesh woman is passing secrets!"

The knot in Rose's stomach tightened. "Sir, I do not know when I shall see her next. Give me a week, sir, please. I will find her and be more forceful in my appeal."

"You can appeal to her right now," he replied. His voice was high-pitched with ridicule. He jerked his head toward a door behind his desk. "Be as forceful as you wish, Nurse. But you frisk her or I will. I want everything she's got. Especially the bodice." He blushed. "Under her shirt," he grumbled. "You know what I mean."

"Now, sir? She is here?"

In response, the clerk opened a side door and with his eyes indicated for Rose to enter. The building had once been a cotton warehouse. Rose had never been behind the foyer where the marshal conducted public business, but she knew the Union had turned most of it into a jail for prisoners of war and deserters. Surely Margaret was not in a jail cell with soldiers. Rose grew anxious as the clerk led her down a musty hallway lined with desks, a soldier at each one, others milling about. They looked up as she passed. "Let 'er rip," one shouted. "Need help?" another asked, leering at Rose's bosom. She crossed her arms over her chest. They knew. They all knew what she had come to do.

At the end of the hallway, they turned right again, passing through a locked door to a row of jail cells. The smell of latrine met her nostrils. She tried to hold her breath but gasped at what met her eye. Each cell held dozens of prisoners, most shirtless, a few naked. Some were chained to iron rings in the floor, which was covered by human filth. Vacant eyes stared from fleshless faces. The prisoners did not call out; the hall was eerily quiet. Now Rose grew truly afraid for her cousin.

They passed through another set of locked doors. On the other side was a door to a room that the clerk unlocked and pushed open. There on the floor sat Margaret, her blue hooped skirt surrounding her like a lake. Her hair was mussed, but she sat with perfect posture, her nose high.

"Thank you, Sergeant," said Rose. "I shall take care of her."

"Yes, ma'am, I hope you do that." He closed the door loudly behind him. The lock turned. She knelt and tried to put her arms around Margaret, but she pulled away. A tiny corner of paper peeked from her bosom.

"Are you spying for them now?" Margaret spat.

"Margaret, dear, please. What have you done? Why are you here?"

Margaret took Rose's shoulders into her hands, squeezing them until they hurt. "Supporting your family!" she said, pushing Rose backward onto the stone floor.

"Stand up," Rose said, getting to her feet. "Let's get this over with."

Margaret glared at Rose and stood. As she did, a clanking and rattling arose from her skirt.

"Must I undress you, or will you save yourself the indignity?" Rose demanded.

"I will do no such thing," Margaret replied. "I am no traitor." She closed her eyes and crossed her arms over her chest.

Rose sighed and stepped behind her cousin. With shaking fingers, she began to unfasten the worn silk buttons that ran halfway down Margaret's skirt. Humiliation rose in her throat and the buttons blurred as her eyes filled with tears of embarrassment and frustration. On the sixth button she opened the skirt and told Margaret to step out, but Margaret stood still as a statue. Angry, Rose took the fabric in her hands and pulled the skirt apart at its seam, ripping it and dropping it in a pile on the floor. Her eyes now took in Margaret's secret. "Oh, Margaret," she whispered. "This is," she placed a hand over her mouth. "This is actually rather wonderful!"

Her anger vanished. Two canteens, a pair of men's boots, a salt sack, and a leather cartridge box hung from the stays of Margaret's sheer linen crinoline. Most impressively, to each of Margaret's narrow hips was strapped a slab of fatback. Rose stood back in wonder. "However do you stand, let alone walk?" she asked. Margaret took a few exaggerated steps like a bow-legged cowboy, the contraband swinging between her legs.

"Why do you think Southern women walk so slowly?" Margaret said. "It is not from the heat, dear cousin."

"I admire your daring," Rose confessed. How many women like Margaret were proving similarly useful to the Confederacy or, for that matter, the Union?

"Well, Charlotte will not forage. That girl has the nerves of a mouse."

"The fire does not burn in her as it does in you."

"She is a coward," Margaret said. "At least I come to town. And as long as I am here, I may as well be useful. I've a permit for the salt, by the way."

Rose smiled. "I do not think that shall help in this case," she said. "I must take an inventory." She looked closely at Margaret's bodice. "And I really must have what is stuffed into your bosom."

Margaret pulled away. "You shall have to take it," she declared.

"Let us start with the underskirt," Rose offered.

Margaret folded her arms and turned her head away.

"So, you will make me do it," Rose said with a sigh. "You are a stubborn woman, Margaret Barnett." She stepped forward and released her cousin's hoops, which fell to the ground with a clatter. She knelt and untied the ribbons that held the contraband in place. In the cartridge box she found a bottle of quinine.

"That is for the family," Margaret said, "or do you care?"

Rose replied by roughly untying the pork, jerking it down over Margaret's drawers, and kicking it aside.

"Remove your shirt," she ordered, turning away as much to calm her own temper as to give her cousin privacy. But Margaret made no move to comply. Through unwelcome tears, Rose stepped forward and began unfastening the tiny covered buttons below Margaret's trembling chin. As she stripped the shirt away, several letters fell to the floor, but more lay beneath the corset. Rose stepped behind and yanked at the lacings. One snapped off in her hand, and she threw it across the room. As the corset opened, letters peeked from Margaret's waist. "Shake it," Rose said, but Margaret had become as still as Lot's wife. Rose stepped around to face her and with shaking fingers opened the small metal clasps that held the corset together in front. At last it fell to the ground, releasing a shower of dispatches and Yankee dollars, and leaving Margaret naked as a jay, save her drawers.

Rose fell to her hands and knees to scoop up the damning evidence. She threw Margaret's skirt at her feet. "Cover up," she said.

"You have torn it," Margaret whined.

"Make do," Rose snapped. "Like the rest of us." Wrapping the money and letters in her apron, she went to the door and pounded on it until a guard came. She did not care that he would see Margaret in her shame. Later that day Margaret was ordered released, banished from Memphis, a bounty on her head. Rose delivered to the marshal one of the Dabney girls' dresses for Margaret to wear on her journey to the interior.

Chapter 13

BEFORE DAWN ON A STEAMY AUGUST DAY, THE NURSES OF DABNEY Heights woke to the sounds of gunfire and the rebel yell. They gathered at the front windows as a band of Confederate soldiers rode frantic horses up the stone steps of the Gayoso House, through its broad front doors, and into the lobby itself. It was the first time the nurses had seen the enemy at work; there was excitement—even giddiness—among them. Holly and several others followed Mother Pennoyer to the basement, but Rose was among those whose curiosity exceeded their fright.

The raid was the talk of the ship that morning. It had been led by General Forrest and, according to rumor, had as its purpose the capture of Union generals and the release of the unfortunate souls held at the Irving Block prison. But when the Union took a stand at the State Female College, the rebels decided to turn back. By the time the sun was fully up, they were gone, taking with them a herd of horses and a clutch of half-dressed Yankees still warm from their beds. They had released no prisoners from the Irving Block nor captured any generals, but they had taken hostage the uniform of Union General Cadwallader Washburn. He, in turn, had run to safety in his nightshirt, taking with him, some said, his reputation for all time.

Rose was not surprised that General Forrest was behind the raid. Since April he and General Washburn had engaged in a war of words, charges, and countercharges, first over Fort Pillow and then the ambush in Mississippi. In July the marshal had replaced the city's mayor, judges, and aldermen with Union men. As Dr. York had pointed out, this was Forrest's hometown; he must answer or be called a coward.

That afternoon Rooster approached Rose on her ward. "Reb lady's asking for you," he whispered. "Says she knows you."

It could not be Margaret. She was on the run in rebel territory, and she could never have gotten past the pickets today. Who was asking for her? Rose went to the deck and scanned the landing but recognized no one. A woman raised her hand and timidly called her name. It was Charlotte. Short tufts of baby-fine hair encircled her face. Above her ears she was completely bald. Rose ran to embrace her, and Charlotte began to weep. "I look like a plucked chicken," she sobbed. "I forgot my bonnet, and now my poor, defenseless head is sun-cooked." She wiped her eyes. "This is a real handkerchief, by the way," she said, waving it at Rose, "not a table linen." She smiled, revealing she had lost one of her front teeth. Rose's eyes went to the hole, and Charlotte placed her hand self-consciously over her mouth. "I had a bad tooth," she said. "Dotty pulled it."

Rose consoled her. The thought of Dotty pulling Charlotte's tooth infuriated her. She wondered if the tooth had really needed pulling or whether Dotty had just wanted to torture her daughter-in-law. As if reading Rose's mind, Charlotte said, "It needed doing."

"All right. I will take your word," Rose said. It must have cost Charlotte considerable pride to have come to her this way; Rose would not quibble over a lost tooth. She guided Charlotte to sit on a bollard. That this timid woman had made it past the pickets, today of all days, was testament to her desperation.

"What has happened?" Rose asked.

Charlotte began to sob. "Why I stay with that woman grows less clear to me every day," she said. "We will lose the land; everyone knows it. She is holding onto a ghost."

"Dotty is making her stand," Rose said. She thought of how stubborn Margaret had been in the jail. "How is her health?"

"She has not gone bald, if that's what you mean."

"Hunger treats us all differently."

"She's still rough as an old barn board. I'm not here for Dotty. I wouldn't come to town for her."

"The children?"

Charlotte turned her swollen eyes to Rose. "Boyd is still in his shoes from two years ago. I think he has stopped growing. Our friends have all gone to Richmond. It is so lonely!"

Rose put an arm around Charlotte's bony shoulders. "What are you eating?"

"The last fresh meat we had was the chicken I cooked when you visited."

"You killed your last chicken for me?"

"Don't worry, he was a mean old rooster," Charlotte said. It was encouraging that she had retained her sense of humor. "I am used to no meat or salt, but the last milk the children had was before Margaret left." She paused for a long time before confessing, "I fear it has taken Adelaide's health. I should have come sooner."

"'Tis Adelaide that brings you, then?"

"She can't keep anything down." Charlotte began to weep in earnest.

"What have you given her?"

"Green tomatoes, small ones. And some corn, but it's worm-eaten. And it comes right back up. She takes clay best." She raised her bloodshot eyes to Rose.

"You are feeding her soil?"

"It stays in her."

"You mustn't, Charlotte."

"I know," she wept. "I know. Please, come."

Rose had no desire to see Dotty, but she would go for Charlotte and the children. "I will have to get a pass," she said. "It may be difficult after this morning."

"The pickets gave me a hard time," Charlotte said, blushing deeply. "What has happened?"

"General Forrest dressed up as a Yankee and slipped a thousand men past the pickets," Rose said. "They rode their horses right up the steps of the Gayoso and into the lobby itself!" Charlotte chuckled, and Rose smiled with her. While the raid had seemed serious at the time, she realized now it had been meant to embarrass, not to conquer. "Come along. Let us see about those passes."

The marshal was only slightly less sanguine about the morning's events. "Are you prepared to engage General Forrest, Nurse Barnett?" he asked.

"I doubt I am his next target, sir," Rose replied.

The marshal sighed. "I doubt it too," he said. He dipped his pen to write their passes. "Out and back today," he said. "Take that reb sergeant with you."

"Yes, sir. That is my intent."

"Sundown, no later." The marshal looked at Charlotte. "How did you get past my pickets? Oh, never mind." He handed Rose the orders.

"Thank you, sir. And may I take provisions? They are starving."

"Whatever you want," he said. "Just come back in one piece." Rose thought she heard genuine concern in his voice. Whether it was for her or her cousins, she did not care.

In the kitchen at Dabney Heights she packed salt, flour, fresh and tinned milk, and a brick of desiccated vegetables. She sent Sergeant Mann to the Gayoso for quarts of beef tea and peaches. It exasperated her that people were starving so close to the city, where the army kept a flourishing dairy and cattle herd, and where soldiers complained of the tiresomeness of oysters.

Dr. York appeared while she was loading the wagon. "Aiding the enemy?" he teased.

"They are kin," Rose said. It would not hurt for a certain surgeon to experience for a day what her cousins had endured for three years.

"Do you wish me to accompany you? I am a genuine Southerner, remember," he said.

"Hence a traitor," Rose replied, casting a false smile his way. She had no desire to defend her family to him. "Thank you for the offer, but Sergeant Mann will be with me."

Dr. York lifted the bag of flour into the wagon. "I would like to examine the child myself," he said.

Rose set down the box of peaches. In her hurry, she did not choose her words carefully. "She is not in need of surgery, Doctor. She is in need of diagnosis and tending. Such are my bailiwicks."

"I thought you might say that."

"Then why did you ask?" Rose sensed the thunderheads of a quarrel rising between them. Why did they struggle so?

"Might I not be your assistant for a change? Besides, I should like to meet your family." He stood before her and took her hands in his. "Would that be acceptable?"

Rose's breath caught in her throat. Such a request could only mean one thing. But was he introducing himself to her cousins or scrutinizing them? Was this a proposal or a test? In either case, why the pretext over examining Adelaide? She did not have time to decipher this infernal code.

"Another time," she said. "Thank you just the same. I shall report in when I return."

Dr. York sighed and turned to go. "Another time," he said over his shoulder as he walked toward the landing. Relieved, Rose finished loading the wagon, making a bed for Charlotte in the back.

Charlotte was asleep before they left the city. On a hill north of Memphis, Rose and Sergeant Mann looked down upon a small group of Union soldiers engaged with a guerilla group.

"They all look alike from here," Rose remarked as Sergeant Mann yee-hawed the mules around the skirmish.

"They're all just boys, ma'am. Some mother's son, every one."

"And I shall be writing letters to some of those mothers." Rose sighed.

"No doubt, ma'am."

At the plantation, Sergeant Mann unloaded the supplies while Rose and Charlotte took a quart of beef tea straight to Adelaide upstairs. She lay in a dusty bed, atop a sodden, gray sheet. Like Charlotte's, her light brown hair had fallen out, but in irregular clumps. Her mother had cut it short, leaving her looking like a spotted dog. She was asleep and feverish and bone thin. Her wet gown clung to her tiny chest.

"How long has she been fevered so?" Rose asked.

"It is intermittent, over two weeks," Charlotte said. "It clears up, but then it returns."

Summer fever always suggested malaria. The intermittency was typical, but the length of time it had persisted and Adelaide's starved condition were concerning. Suddenly Rose realized she had forgotten the quinine. She had set it out but somehow left it behind. She thought of Dr. York; did she blame him for distracting her? She forced the distracting thought from her head, opened the quart of tea, and held it to Adelaide's mouth. The salt would be beneficial if she could keep it down.

"Should she be bled?" Charlotte asked anxiously. "I'll allow it if you say so." Her voice was a mere whisper, choked with tears. Rose knew she was frightened of both the disease and the cure. Although she had been taught to eschew bleeding, Rose knew the practice was still in vogue in many areas of the country.

"'Tis not bleeding she needs but quinine."

A look of worry came over Charlotte's face. "Margaret used to bring quinine, but we haven't any now." Rose remembered the medicine she had seized from Margaret and groaned.

"What is it, Rose?"

"Nothing."

"Hattie used to brew fever bark," Charlotte said, "but we haven't any of that, either, now that she's gone."

Rose looked up from Adelaide in astonishment. "Hattie is gone?"

Charlotte nodded. "She walked off."

"Did no one go after her?" Rose was alarmed for the old woman's safety, alone in the chaos of war.

"Dotty wouldn't allow it."

Maggie had been wrong. Dotty had let her last piece of human property escape. "There is no word at all?" she asked. "When was this?"

"No, no word," Charlotte said. "It was after your visit."

"I am so sorry." Rose felt with the weight of remorse settle on her heart. The roasted chicken had been the least of the damage. She had taken medicine from a child and unmoored an old woman. "War," she muttered angrily. "Why do we fight like this?" She turned back to Adelaide and placed the back of her hand on the girl's forehead. "We will make the infusion ourselves, then."

"Our fever tree died when the pond dried up last year," Charlotte said.

"You have willow. Have the boys cut six or eight inches of bark and deliver it to the kitchen. They must cut deeply, into the green layer. It is a hard bark but a sharp machete will do it. Perhaps Sergeant Mann can help them. We've no time to dry it properly, so chop it as best you can and toast it in a fry pan. Pour hot water over it to steep. Do not let it boil."

Charlotte nodded and left without a word, seeming relieved to have someone point the way. Rose fed Adelaide another few drops of the beef tea then left her to sleep. Outside in the garden, she searched for vegetables for this seemingly helpless family. How could a people starve in this warm, damp climate? She recalled the freezing winters and short summers of her youth, the verdant kitchen garden her aunts had kept, and her tiny plot in Chicago. She had never known hunger. Her Southern cousins, meanwhile, were starving on three hundred acres.

Rose gleaned the neglected garden. Besides a few green tomatoes, she found two early ears of mealy corn and half a dozen onions that had gone to seed. In the cool basement kitchen, she rolled the meager harvest onto a table. Charlotte was chopping bark. She shook her head when she saw what Rose put on the table. "I am no gardener," she said. "I have always had servants."

"We will make soup," Rose said, beginning to chop the tops of the onions. "It will taste mightily of onion, but it will be soup nonetheless."

Charlotte grinned. "In New Orleans, on our wedding trip, Corky and I tasted onion soup at the hotel. We thought it would be odd, but it wasn't—it was lovely."

"I cannot promise anything lovely," Rose replied. "In fact, I have forgotten more than the quinine. I brought you the makings of biscuits but have left the leavening behind." She groaned with frustration. "Haste makes waste," she muttered.

"Then we shall follow our cousins the Jews," said Charlotte, pulling a bowl from the cupboard and opening the bag of flour. "But you must show me how."

They worked until a simple meal emerged. Rose placed her arm around Charlotte. "Adelaide will be fine," she said. "Now let us call dinner."

Charlotte blinked back tears. "To the lions," she said with a tenuous smile.

The children gulped the fresh milk as if they were at their mothers' breasts again. The biscuits were like hardtack, and the rehydrated vegetables had turned the soup thick and gray, but no one complained. Not even Dotty refused the meal, as Rose had feared she might.

"God has sent our Yankee cousin to succor us," Dotty intoned, holding up her bowl. "Thank you."

"You are welcome," Rose said before realizing she had fallen into Dotty's trap.

"I was speaking to the Lord," Dotty said.

"Of course you were," Rose replied, unable not to smile. "I cannot stay long," she added. "I must be at the pickets an hour before sundown."

"Those pickets are coming down soon," Dotty said. "Memphis will be returned to the bosom of Dixie at last. It is only a matter of time."

"Perhaps," said Rose.

"Do not underestimate General Forrest," Dotty said, sniffing loudly. "Today was but a taste."

"I underestimate neither your generals nor ours," said Rose.

Without warning, Dotty slammed her spoon on the table and pushed away her empty bowl. "What did you do to Margaret?" she demanded. "Boys, Lizzie, leave the room. I have business with your cousin." The children scrambled to obey.

Rose had been waiting for some kind of remonstrance from Dotty, some reaction to the situation with Margaret. "Do you mean when she got herself arrested?" she replied.

"You practically raped her," Dotty cried.

"She was smuggling."

"You needn't have used force. You could have asked her politely."

"I did!"

"I don't believe you. You're a Yankee spy, and I want you out of my house! You abused my son's wife, and now she is on the run. Your Yankee devils have driven her near to madness. She cannot sleep in the same place twice in a week. And look at us. We are left to starve." She opened her arms wide. Rose wondered if a slap was coming her way. She sat forward, ready to take whatever Dotty had in store. She was glad Dr. York was not present, that he would neither witness the blow nor protect her from it.

Rose was surprised when Charlotte spoke. "That's not true, Miss Dotty. Margaret has been at Mayfield for weeks," Charlotte said, "swimming in their bathing pond and playing euchre, and flirting with all the generals that pass through there. Bathing with strange men, that's what she's doing. She has probably never been happier."

Dotty turned to Charlotte, spittle flying from her mouth as she rebuked her daughter-in-law. "Mind me, young lady. She is your sister, and you are a guest in this house. Unlike Margaret's, your husband is dead. There is precious little left for you here."

Charlotte lost her nerve and began to cry.

Rose stood up from the table. "You are a cruel old woman," she said. "I am going to give Adelaide her medicine, and then I shall be out of your way." She beckoned Charlotte to come with her. In the hallway, she embraced her. "Get the willow tea," she said gently. Charlotte nodded, still in tears. Rose climbed the stairs to Adelaide's room with rage in her heart. She did not understand her aunt's stubbornness. The embargo had been slowly starving the South for three years. Dotty had lost a husband and a son to the conflict. That she took a stand for herself was one thing; that she let her grandchildren suffer was unforgivable. If the situation were reversed, would she fight as hard for the Union? Could she sacrifice a child for a nation? Was it a nation Dotty was fighting for or something else?

She placed the back of her hand upon Adelaide's small forehead. The few sips of beef tea had stayed down, but while the willow bark had been steeping, the fever had worsened.

Charlotte arrived with the willow tea. "Is she poisoned?" she asked. "From the soil?"

"'Tis the ague is all, dear. It will run its course. Raise her up for me."

Charlotte slipped her arm behind Adelaide's back and lifted her. Adelaide's eyes opened wide. She seemed not to recognize Rose, who said, "Sweetheart, this will taste wicked, but you will forget it once you are well." In a single motion, she pulled open Adelaide's jaw and poured the bitter tea straight toward her tonsils. Half made its mark and entered her throat before she shook violently and spit out the remainder.

"Good girl," Rose said, smiling up at Charlotte. "She must have it every two hours. You see how to deliver it; she will fight it otherwise.

Keep giving her the beef tea; her body needs strength for the fever to work. Send one of the boys if she worsens."

Charlotte nodded.

Rose went from Adelaide's room to the wagon. Sergeant Mann was waiting. She wondered if he had heard their family quarrel through the open windows.

"You ready, Miss Rose?"

"Yes, Sergeant. Take me back to the army."

"Yes, ma'am. That would be the Union Army, now, wouldn't it?" he said with a smile. She nodded, grateful for his friendship.

September came. On an evening when tupelos and cypresses glowed in the late sun, Rose walked with Dr. York into the Memphis hills. A bald eagle glided over the river, its white head and tail alight against a bruise-purple sky. Rain was coming.

"They say Atlanta is fairly won," Rose remarked.

"By what rules do you say 'fairly'?" Dr. York replied. "A hundred thousand federals have overrun and fired the town. A hundred thousand more are chasing Early up and down the valley. The Union no longer fights. It stalks."

Throughout the summer, news from the South had been somber indeed. On General Grant's direct order, its breadbasket, the Shenandoah Valley, had been stripped of its crops; its livestock had been driven off, its barns burned. Now Atlanta had been torched, and foot soldiers in the hundreds of thousands were hunkered down in trenches around Petersburg and Richmond. Grant's hard hand of war had been clenched, and the blows kept coming. Rose was not surprised Dr. York was angry.

He looked toward the horizon. "I cannot do this anymore."

"Would that everyone felt that way," Rose said.

"I have been transferred."

"Transferred? From the *Despain*? Ashore?"

"To the surgery at Jeffersonville." His eyes remained on the horizon.

Rose stepped around him to look up at his face. "You cannot look at me and say this?"

"You think me a coward," he said.

"You are far from that. Yet you would tell me this without so much as a glance?"

Now his eyes did meet hers. "Glancing at you has been the sole joy I have taken from this dreadful place. I do not fear to look at you, Rose. I fear not looking at you."

"Can you not refuse them? I know surgery is infrequent now, but still we need a head surgeon. Did you say this to them?"

His gaze traveled back to the horizon. "I requested it," he said. "I intend to move west. They say I will not be denied a discharge. I will go to Jeffersonville in the meantime."

He was not leaving the *Despain*; he was leaving the army. He was leaving her. "One does not just walk away," she said, her words soaked in both anger and disdain.

"I have lost my taste for war," he said.

"We all have lost our taste for war, if we ever had it! Why suddenly is this assignment so intolerable to you?"

Dr. York took her shoulders in his hands. "Rose," he said, "do you love me?"

Now it was she who looked away. She had imagined this exchange a thousand ways but never as an ultimatum. "Are you asking me to go with you?" she asked in a choked whisper.

He lifted her chin with his finger. "More than anything," he said, "I wish you would agree to come with me."

Not, "Will you marry me," but "I wish you would agree." He would leave it to her, then, to say aloud what they both had known for some time—that such an agreement was impossible. She did not know why she struggled to accept the love of this man, but struggle she did. She took his hands in hers. "I am sorry," she said. "I do not understand it fully myself, but I cannot."

He stepped away, as if at attention. "My orders are to leave with the next transport. It is any day."

Rose looked at his inscrutable face. "I do not mean to hurt you," she said. "You have been my teacher and my friend." The words came truthfully from her heart as she added, "I will miss you."

"And I you," he said. He bent and touched his lips to hers, their first kiss. Rose allowed him to linger a moment before pulling back. He turned and walked alone toward the ship.

Rose watched his shape recede in the distance. Tears came, yet even in her regret, no inclination to call him back rose within her. As the sun set over the river, the sky turned to the pale yellow of ordinariness. The rain cloud had moved on. When at last she traced her way back to the house, night had fallen. She sat beneath the magnolia until Orion and his sword hovered overhead. Silently she entered the cabin, undressed, and slid into the warmth next to Holly.

The next morning, Rose was dressed and waiting for Holly to finish pinning her hair when she told her of Dr. York's decision.

Holly dropped the handful of curls she was twisting. "Leaving? The ship?"

"Yes, the ship and Memphis. Leaving the army."

Smiling broadly Holly asked, "Did he ask you to marry him?"

"Indirectly," Rose said, stepping into the kitchen for coffee. She returned and handed a mug to Holly. "He said that he wished I would go with him."

"Is that not the same thing? Tell me you are to be Mrs. York at last!"

"'Tis not the same thing at all, dear Holly. How can I become Mrs. York when he has not proposed marriage?"

"Surely he did not suggest you follow without sacrament."

"No, he did not suggest that."

"What did he say? Please, do not play with me." She reminded Rose of a child waiting for a present behind her favorite uncle's back.

"He said, 'I wish you would agree to come with me,' and this only after I asked if he wished it."

"Rosie, you had only to agree and you know a proposal would have been next on his lips. How can you not feel his words were a proposal of marriage?"

"It was odd, as if he felt obliged to declare himself, but rather than propose marriage—rather than ask a question—he chose this ambiguous remark. I will not push him into marriage."

Holly slammed her cup onto the dresser, spilling her coffee. "I do not understand you, Rose Barnett. Forgive me, but any woman of your age is fortunate to receive such a 'remark,' as you call it. Many of us will be without husbands for the rest of our lives."

"Do not be angry with me, Holly. I could hardly propose to myself."

Holly would not be pacified. "You shall not have children without marriage, Rose. You saw your aunts' lives. Is that what you wish?"

"I am not my aunts." Rose shrugged. "Perhaps it was their lesson that leaves me unafraid to be alone."

Holly softened. "Oh, Rosie. Why did you deny him?"

"I have told you, 'twas not a genuine proposal. If he had wished me to marry him, he would have used the word. He did the best he could, but I found myself unwilling to ask if such was his meaning."

"Pride goeth before the fall, Rose. Can you not change your mind?"

"I do not wish to. I feel content with the outcome. It was not pride that held me back."

"What, then?"

Rose looked out at the morning, thoughtful. "Perhaps I do not feel we are suited."

"You are perfectly suited," Holly exclaimed.

"Then perhaps I alone am not suited. To marriage."

"How is that possible? You are a fine, beautiful woman."

"I wish to be a surgeon, Holly. To become one will take study and travel abroad. How could I realize my purpose once children started arriving?"

"You cannot be in two places at once, Rose. I fear you ask too much of yourself."

"Dr. York apparently shares your fear," Rose replied. She was thoughtful for a time. "I believe him when he says he wishes I would go with him, but he and I both know it is not a practical arrangement."

"So you will not be his wife?"

"I shall not be his wife."

"Nor anyone else's, if your reasoning holds."

Rose looked down at her hands. "I shall pray for a companion who will tolerate my peculiarities."

"I am very sorry, Rosie, for you would have been a loving mother, and I am certain a convivial wife."

"There is a fine store of fish in the sea," Rose said.

"Not so fine as there used to be," Holly replied, shaking her head.

The following day a transport arrived. Rose watched from the top deck of the *Despain* as Dr. York went aboard. He turned and looked up at her. They each raised a hand in farewell before he stepped inside the cabin and was gone.

On a hot fall night, Rose and Holly sat up talking until almost sunrise. Neither was scheduled to go to the ship that day. Only when cool air finally arrived near daybreak did they go inside to sleep. When they rose a few hours later, a day of leisure stretched before them. Rose proposed a picnic.

Holly replied, "My mother says that every picnic basket must hold a chocolate cake. She makes one whenever we carry our supper to the river. I still have the chocolate she sent at Christmas." She began to dig through her apple crate. "Here," she said, pulling a lump wrapped in brown paper from her jumble of treasures.

"A cake from chocolate?" Rose replied.

"You will like it, I promise," Holly said.

Rose grinned. "You rob the henhouse, and I will light the stove." In the kitchen she dipped flour and sugar from their barrels and pulled butter from the crock.

Holly returned with a dozen eggs. She filled a pot with water for the stove and placed a second pot, holding her lump of chocolate, above it. "Stir that as it melts," she said. "Do not let it burn." She turned to crack eggs into a bowl. Their yolks were orange as persimmons from the hens' diet of summer grass.

Rose stood over the chocolate. As it began to melt, its bitter scent rose to fill the room. Soon Holly came with the bowl—eggs, sugar, and butter combined. "Add it," she said, "all of it." Rose poured the river of chocolate into the bowl while Holly stirred. Streaks of chocolate meandered like the Mississippi through the yellow batter until the whole thing turned a deep, glossy brown. "Taste," Holly said, dipping a finger into the batter and holding it to Rose's lips. The chocolate had turned sweet and rich, beyond anything Rose had ever tasted. When she reached for another sample, Holly grabbed her hand. "Oh, no you don't," she scolded. "You may lick the bowl when the cake is in the oven." Into Rose's hand she placed a chunk of hard butter from the crock. "Warm that up and rub it in the pan." Rose smeared the butter with her fingers onto the side and base of a square pan. She had never greased a pan this way; her aunts had used a greasing cloth. The feel of the fat on her skin, under her nails, where it did not belong, somehow pleased her.

While the cake baked, they packed a crate with peaches and a blanket. An hour later, they pulled their steaming accomplishment from the oven. Nurses in the house came running. Holly had thought ahead, having gathered extra eggs and saved back a piece of her chocolate. "Extra makings are there," she said, pointing.

Rose wrapped their cake in a towel and placed it in the crate. As they left the kitchen, a clap of thunder rumbled nearby. In an instant heavy rain descended. "No!" Holly cried. "We have missed our chance."

"Nothing shall keep me from that cake," Rose declared. She pulled the blanket from the crate and spread it on the floor of their cabin. Holly laid out their picnic. In the rich light of the storm, the colorful fruit and deep brown cake glowed against the blue blanket.

"We've forgotten a knife," Holly said, rising. Rose grasped her hand.

"We are camping. We must make do." Rose smiled mischievously and pushed two fingers deep into the warm cake. As she placed a bite onto her tongue, her eyes drifted closed with pleasure. "Your mother is right," she murmured.

Holly followed suit, her eyes drifting closed and her head nodding, as she tasted their creation. "I think I have never tasted anything as delicious as this," she said.

Rose opened the jar of peaches, retrieved a half peach, and placed a bite of cake in its center. This she held to Holly's lips. Holly lapped up the sweet, wet bites. Peach juice ran down her chin. "You are a messy eater," Rose said gently. She wiped her thumb across Holly's chin and held it up for her to lick clean.

"And you are a fine baker," Holly replied. She pulled a piece of cake from the pan and held it to Rose's mouth. In return, Rose placed a bite on Holly's waiting tongue. Their eyes met. Someone in the kitchen dropped something, and they both jumped. Rose broke off another piece of cake and poured peach juice over it. Holly leaned forward to take the slippery bite in her mouth.

Rose pulled a cloth from the crate and wiped Holly's chin, tracing her lips. The symphony of the storm mingled with the soft, feminine hum from the kitchen next door.

Taking the cloth from Rose, Holly smiled gently. "You are tidier than I," she whispered, dusting a crumb from Rose's mouth. Setting aside the cloth, she ran her fingers across the scar on Rose's forehead, down the bridge of her nose, to Rose's lips. Rose felt her body being pulled forward. Holly's face became a blur of soft features and sweet breath and, for an eternal instant, their lips touched.

Rose jumped back as if she had seen a snake. "You are my dearest friend," she whispered, her eyes drifting toward the storm outside.

"And you are mine," Holly replied.

"I hope we have not spoiled it just now."

Holly dropped her eyes. "Are lady companions not allowed a kiss now and then?" she murmured.

"I suppose they are," Rose replied, although she did not actually know what she supposed. She rose and stepped to the bed, sank to the floor, and leaned back against the mattress. When Holly joined her, Rose felt her pulse rise. Their shoulders touched. Rose did not pull away. The feel of their arms together in shared balance caused a lump to rise in her throat. And as when one notices a noise only when it ceases to roar, Rose felt fear leave her like a sigh.

A mosquito buzzed Rose's head, and Holly protectively waved it away. "I have never told this to anyone," Rose said, wiping away inexplicable tears. "You are the first." She smiled and shook her head. "When I was small, I believed there was a special place in Hell for children whose mothers died in childbirth. It wasn't quite as hot as real Hell. It was more like a steamy summer day, like today, with swarms and swarms of mosquitoes. If you were very good and did not scratch your mosquito bites, your mother would come down from heaven once a year, on your birthday, and hold you, right there in Hell. The mosquitoes would go away, and the air would be cool for the rest of the day. The following day the heat and mosquitos would come back until your next birthday."

"That is a heavy burden for a child," Holly said. She reached up and tucked a piece of Rose's hair behind her ear.

"Our barn was a falling-down Iroquois longhouse with a swampy old pond behind it. On my birthday I would go there and let the mosquitoes eat me alive. In case my mother should come, I did not scratch all day. I wanted her to see how good I was. It was agony." She laughed at the memory, jostling loose a tear, which she wiped away. "My aunts would scold me, but they did not know why I did it. Of course later I would scratch the bites until they bled. What child does not? They always became scabbed and horrid." The lump in her throat gave way to a genuine laugh. "I still love a good mosquito bite."

"What a child's mind contrives," Holly said, laughing.

"I hope I was wrong about mosquito Hell," Rose said, "but I would go there today if I could see my mother for a day."

When Rose opened her eyes the next morning, the memory of the kiss quickened her heart. Even though the sun was just rising, Holly was up and dressed. "You were right about the picnic," she said. "It has cheered me. Look at me, up at such an hour. I have decided to go immediately to the ship." She stepped out into the dawn before Rose could reply.

Rose lay back on her pillow. It had been a brief kiss—a peck, really—well, softer than a peck, but still, so light and brief. Holly being from Maryland, with its Southern ways, perhaps ladies there did kiss so, not just on the cheek but on the lips, so long as they did not linger. Rose rolled over and curled into a ball, dozing until the sun's rays entered the room, insistent that she rise.

She went straight to the surgery. The surgeon who had taken Dr. York's place allowed her only to trim gangrene. It was tiresome work the other surgeons were glad to hand off, but today she welcomed the task. She worked alone with her sleeping patients and her runaway thoughts—of Holly, the picnic, the kiss; of Maggie's worldliness, Roberta's inversion and her aunts' sisterly companionship; of God's first and greatest commandment, to love one another; and of her brief kiss with Dr. York, a kiss as different from Holly's as hope from despair. But Holly had been a married woman. Clearly it was she, Rose, who had trespassed. She would apologize, and things would be right again.

Rose spent the rest of the day whispering words of contrition to herself—practicing, polishing—even as her mind wove a confusing web of exhilaration, fear, and wonder. She entered the cabin that evening exhausted and with a nervous stomach. Holly sat in the rocker, reading. She smiled at Rose as she entered and set the book aside. "I am not really reading," she said.

"You appear to be reading," Rose answered, willing to parry, content to postpone the reckoning.

"I am thinking of yesterday," Holly said. "It was a lovely day, clear to the end. I think we are such pleasant companions, don't you?"

"Companions," Rose replied, her resolve to apologize melting like snow in summer, helpless before the fact of the sun. "Yes, we are the best of companions," she said leaning over and kissing Holly gently, briefly, on her miraculously soft lips.

"That reb lady's back," Rooster said to Rose one afternoon in November.

"I see her, Rooster. Thank you." Rose looked across the ward to the deck of the ship where Charlotte stood, and walked toward her. As she drew near, she saw Adelaide peek from behind her mother's skirt. Rose embraced her cousins. Their clothes were damp. "You are looking much better than the last time I saw you," she said to Adelaide, wondering what Charlotte was thinking, bringing the child into town. "Your hair has returned. You look a lady again. So does your mama."

Adelaide grinned. "I don't remember when I was sick," she said, hugging her mother's leg, eyes wide as she stared at the ship full of soldiers.

"That happens sometimes," Rose said. "I am glad you have forgotten it." To Charlotte she said, "It is not healthy on board. Let us go ashore." In the months since she had seen her cousins, the typhoid that had sickened Adelaide had infected most of the surgical patients on Rose's ward. Half had died, leaving Rose with the doleful task of writing to parents that their brave sons had succumbed not to the enemy but to disease. Adelaide had been lucky.

They crossed the landing to the benches by the cliff. Both Charlotte and Adelaide carried satchels. "It is good to see you," Rose said, "but it is rather a cool day to be out. Are you here for supplies?"

"Miss Dotty went to Richmond," Adelaide said. "She took Boyd with her."

Rose looked at Charlotte, who nodded and began to weep.

"Ma misses him more than I do," Adelaide said.

"Charlotte, tell me what happened," Rose said.

"She can't," Adelaide said. "She ain't talking."

"Adelaide, what is going on?" Rose asked.

"We were two nights in the field. Can you make mama talk?"

Rose brushed the child's baby-fine new hair from her face. "Tell me what has happened," she said.

"Miss Dotty and Miss Margaret and Roscoe and Boyd and Lizzie all just up and went to Richmond," Adelaide said. Her chin began to quiver. "It wouldn't be so bad if Lizzie didn't go." She began to cry.

"When did they leave?" Rose asked. "They just left you behind?"

"I think more than this many days." Adelaide held up both hands, fingers spread wide.

"Is that when your ma stopped talking?"

"No, she went quiet when we begun walking in."

"Why did you and your ma not go to Richmond?"

"She had a fight with Miss Dotty, and Mama said, 'Who will stand with me,' and nobody would stand with her, so finally I did, because Boyd, he said he wouldn't be no damn Yankee, so Miss Margaret hugged Mama and said she would take care of Boyd and would write and then it was just me and Mama." Rose imagined the scene, wagons loaded, the two women quarreling at the last minute—probably over the whole scheme of escaping to Richmond, something that likely had long been decided against Charlotte—and her finally taking her stand, even as it cost her a son.

"Well, you have had a long walk, haven't you?"

"Yes, ma'am, we have. Miss Rose?" Adelaide said.

"Yes, darling?"

"I'm pretty near starved."

"Then we must feed you, mustn't we? Have you ever eaten in a café?"

"No, ma'am," said Adelaide, grinning.

Rose led them up the through-road to Maynard's ladies' lunch shop. She ordered soup with buttered bread and coffee. Mother and daughter ate hungrily. Adelaide picked up her bowl to drink the last drop. "Be a lady, Addie," Charlotte said. Adelaide began to protest but then, realizing her mother had spoken, broke into a grin.

"Mama! Are you talking again?"

Charlotte looked at her own almost empty soup bowl, as if trying to read her fortune in its dregs. "I suppose I am going to have to," she said. She looked at Rose with tears in her eyes.

"You have had a shock, losing Boyd," Rose said.

"I couldn't go, Rose. I don't know if it is just Miss Dotty or this whole self-righteous place, but I see no profit in being a Confederate anymore."

"So you are here to take the oath?"

"Yes."

"And then return to the plantation alone?"

Charlotte looked at Rose as if pleading for forgiveness. "I gave it away," she said. "The Negroes have it."

"You gave away the plantation?" Rose cried. Heads turn toward them across the cafe.

"Well, Miss Dotty didn't want it," Charlotte whispered. "The day she left, slaves started coming out of the woodwork. They moved back into the cabins and even the house. I decided they had more right to it than I did. I mean, I married it, is all I did. At least they know how to farm it."

"Are you returning to your own family, then?" Rose assumed Charlotte was from a nearby plantation, although she realized she had never asked. "Where is your home?"

"Richmond," Charlotte said.

"Richmond? Your family is in Richmond?"

"I know what you are thinking, but I am not going home. My mother passed last year, and Daddy went off with the army. He was

254

only in Memphis for business the day you met him. Who knows if I shall ever see him again?" Her voice cracked and more tears fell.

"Quentin enlisted?"

Charlotte nodded. "They put the draft up to fifty. He's fifty-two, but he went anyway."

Rose had a difficult time imagining the round old gentleman in battle. "But your home is in Richmond—your friends, other family. Do you not have sisters and brothers?"

"I have lost my brothers," Charlotte said, "and my sisters have married."

"But there is a house for you there. A roof over your head. Over your child's head. Boyd is there. What are you thinking?" Rose was concerned for Charlotte's state of mind.

"I do not expect the house to be waiting for me once I have declared my loyalties."

"Then do not declare them!" Rose replied. "Charlotte, you must either go to Richmond or back to Barnett Plantation. You cannot live safely in Memphis, even once you are oathed."

"We're moving to Chicago," Adelaide declared. "We are independent women, like you."

The story was growing more fantastical by the moment. "Oh dear, Charlotte," Rose said, "I am afraid that is more easily said than done. Could you not go back to Richmond at least until the war is finished?"

Adelaide interrupted. "Mama? You said Cousin Rose would take care of us."

Charlotte slid her hand along her child's back. "Shhhh," she said. To Rose she replied, "Dotty said the same, of course. I could have returned to Richmond, but it is likely to be burned to the ground once the Yankees go through. I do not wish to see that."

"I fear you overestimate the comforts of the North," Rose said. "There will be other challenges. It is cold, you know," she said, teasing.

Charlotte would not be distracted. "Look around you, Rose. The South is destroyed. I have no man to care for me, no land, and a child to raise." She took a deep breath and held it for a long time, as if gathering strength to say what she had needed to say for years. "I will not raise my daughter here, Rose. I have lost Boyd, but I still have

Adelaide. I will not have her grow to think she is owed more than she works for, that she is of greater worth than others in God's eyes. And I will not have her grow up helpless. We are going North. Must I beg you for your help?"

Rose reached across the table and took Charlotte's hand in hers. "Of course not. I respect your decision. I am proud of you. But it shall not be easy."

"I'm sorry we are so pitiful," Charlotte whispered, lowering her eyes, their lashes heavy with new tears.

"You shall have to work, you know," Rose said.

"We will work, won't we, Adelaide?" Charlotte turned to her child, who locked eyes with Rose and nodded in wide-eyed silence.

"Have you any money at all?" Rose asked.

"Only Confederate, and you know what that is worth. We are awash in Yankee counterfeit, though."

"Do you have jewelry or silver? There is a shop here that trades for greenbacks, real ones. The owner is miserly, but it would be a beginning."

"Miss Dotty took everything except my wedding ring," Charlotte said. From her bodice she pulled a ribbon that held a narrow gold band.

Rose sighed. "Let us leave it as insurance for now. The first task is to visit the marshal and get you sworn."

"I have been looking forward to that," Charlotte said.

Rose left Charlotte and Adelaide at the marshal's office and returned to the ship in search of Holly.

"She did what?" Holly cried.

"She wishes to become a Yankee," Rose said. "She is in line at the marshal's now."

"I fear she shall make a poor Yankee. She has never worked."

"What am I to do with her?" Rose said.

"How in the world did she get this idea?"

"I am afraid, perhaps, from me. She says she wishes to live independently."

"Few women live well independently," Holly said, "especially with a child in tow."

"We might delay her departure," Rose said, "if we find work for her here."

"Perhaps in the laundry?" Holly suggested.

"Yes, let her start there," Rose said with a sigh. "Meanwhile we must impart to her some nursing skills that will allow her to move up."

Rooster agreed to the plan. Charlotte and Adelaide joined the laundry and moved with Maggie to the fort. Adelaide followed both Maggie and Holly about like a duckling after two mothers. One evening Rose entered the cabin to find her with Holly laughing and clapping to a nonsense rhyme. "Juba this and juba that," the two of them sang, their hands flying in and out to the rhythm. "Juba 'round the simmon vat!"

Rose smiled at the sight of the new friends at play. "What's a simmon vat?" she asked. She removed her apron and hung it on a nail next to the dresser.

"Slave beer," Adelaide said with a shrug. "Hattie taught me and Lizzie." A cloud came over her face, and tears pooled in her eyes. "Lizzie's really good at rhymes," she said. "Miss Dotty doesn't like it, but we do it anyway under the porch." Holly took Adelaide's hands in hers and gently resumed the game. "Sift the meal, give me the husk. Bake the cake, give me the crust," she sang. In a few moments, Adelaide was laughing again.

Rose sat in the rocker. It had been a long day, and she was tired. As she watched Holly and Adelaide, she realized the game was not nonsense at all, but the story of a slave's life—a life where clapping games sustained a people who somehow, day after day, bore the un-bearable, a life where children learned to accept the crust. Far from being nonsense, the rhyme was a window on a world as sensible and rational as any other, a world she would never fully know but could only glimpse.

Chapter 14

As Christmas approached, frequent rumors of peace were answered with more fighting. Significant battles were far to the east and north. In Memphis flu and pneumonia turned the *Despain* into a sick ward. The thought of spending another winter in Memphis tending sick men, with no clear end in sight, was hard for Rose and her friends to bear. A gentleman traveling to Washington City entertained the dispirited doctors and nurses with images of California thrown by a magic lantern onto a wall at the Gayoso. The shadowy shapes of waterfalls, mountain peaks, and gleeful gold miners caused people to pine with both delight and dismay. When Maggie complained of malaise the following day, Rose wrote an order for "Rest and California."

"I will go there someday," Maggie said, placing the order in her pocket. "You will see."

For Rose, talk of "someday" led to thoughts of Holly and the conversation they never seemed to have. Rose had long planned to take surgical training in Europe after the war. Holly spoke modestly of returning home but with Rose's encouragement had sent inquiries to several of the new nursing colleges in the North. What these plans meant for their friendship, neither had dared ask aloud.

On a dark December afternoon, word came that a Philadelphia nurses' college would be honored to admit Holly as a student. She flashed the letter at Rose, glowing with excitement.

"You see?" Rose said. "Before long you will be the teacher." She took Holly in her arms and kissed her forehead. "My little professor."

"It is just an acceptance to study," Holly said, blushing and pulling away. They were in their cabin; the evening stretched before them. "Rose?" she said.

"Yes, professor?"

Holly smiled and set aside the letter. "I think it shall be very hard to say good-bye." She had tears in her eyes.

Rose pulled her close again. "Yes," she whispered. The warmth of Holly's body brought a lump to her throat, and she could say no more.

"But we are together now," Holly said brightly, stepping back. "So let us enjoy it." From her pocket she pulled a triangle of chalk normally used for marking the dead. Rose watched with curiosity as she drew a pattern of squares on the cabin floor. "Have you played this game?" Holly asked.

"I saw boys play it in Chicago," Rose replied, content to postpone again talk of separation.

Holly dropped the chalk into the first square. "You must skip over the box with your marker and place only one foot per box." She jumped to the second square and hopped about the pattern, returning to pick up the chalk at the start. "Since I did not fall, I am allowed another turn, but you go. Use this." From the dresser she snatched a cast-off button and placed it in Rose's palm. Rose dropped it into the first box and hopped about. When reaching for her button, she lost her balance, falling into Holly's arms.

"What is next?" she asked languidly, not truly wishing to know. Holly grinned and wriggled free.

"This," she said, tossing her chalk into the second square. "You work your way around the pattern until you have covered all the squares. It becomes harder to make the throw as the squares become farther away. If you miss your toss, you lose your turn."

When it was Rose's turn again, she dropped her button into the second square, but Holly snatched it, holding it back and away. "You rascal," Rose cried, reaching for the button. Holly dove under Rose's arm, skipping across the room, taking refuge behind the rocking chair.

"Come and get it," she teased, waving the button at Rose, only to snatch it away when Rose came near. They chased each other, giggling like children, until at last, out of breath, Rose relented.

"I surrender," she said. "I am your prisoner."

Holly took Rose's hand, dropping the button gently into their joined palms. Rose whispered, "Do you know how beautiful you are? Dance with me." She raised their joined hands, only the button between them, and wrapped her other arm around Holly's waist.

"We've no music," Holly demurred.

"We shall make our own," Rose said. She waltzed Holly about the room, whistling the melancholy love song "Lorena"—a tune so liable to lead to desertion its singing was banned in both armies. Now Rose knew why. Their waltz slowed and they pulled each other close. Holly took up the tune, softly singing the haunting words of pledge and longing. They rocked from foot to foot, their limbs interlocked, moving as one.

"We fit," Holly whispered, but before Rose could reply, Holly stepped away. "I think it is time for bed," she said.

"I could sleep right here, standing up," Rose murmured, reaching out to her, but the spell was broken.

Holly shook her head. "Shoo," she said, pointing to the door. "Take your walk."

"Yes, ma'am," Rose said, gently chucking Holly under the chin. "Thank you for the dance."

Rose slept poorly. Rising at dawn, she lit the stove, and ran to the privy; then, despite her intention never to do so again, she crawled back into bed, tucking up behind Holly, indulging in her warmth. Holly murmured and scooted backward into Rose's body. Rose pulled the blankets around their shoulders. Then slowly, dangerously, she slid a hand under one of Holly's breasts. Her fingers closed instinctively around the soft, full globe. She lifted it slightly and lowered it again. The weight of it in her palm caused a shudder to run through her body. Holly stirred, and Rose rolled away. She stared at the rough timbers of the cabin's roof, her heart racing, every nerve alert. She slipped out of bed and went into the kitchen to dress. Trembling, she pulled on her stockings and drawers. How had she gotten here? As she struggled with her corset she wondered why she had refused Dr. York, but no sooner had the words formed in her brain than she dismissed them. He could not save her, not then and not now. She was on her own. Still with quaking hands, she made their morning coffee and took a cup to Holly. "Time to get up," she said. "I am leaving early." She placed the coffee in a surprised Holly's hand, turned, and left.

In the mess her cereal grew cold as she stared into the gray dawn. Holly did not arrive at the ship until past her scheduled time. When Rose remarked upon it, Holly burst into tears and ran from the ward. They did not speak the rest of the day, and Holly missed supper. As Rose crawled into bed, Holly clung to the edge, facing the wall. The moon cast hard shadows across the room. Rose listened for Holly's breathing to slip into the even tempo of sleep. When it did not, Rose finally spoke.

"Why are we quarreling?" she asked.

Holly did not reply.

"Are we quarreling?" Rose tried to pull Holly to her, but she would not come. "Can I not comfort my friend?" she asked. She sat up and turned toward Holly. "Something has disturbed you. What is it?" She grew hot with shame at her dissembling.

"It is you!" Holly cried, to the wall. "You have disturbed me."

"I am sorry I snapped at you. You were late, you know." Rose forced a chortle from her throat, knowing her sin only grew worse.

Holly rolled over at last. Their eyes met in the moonlight. "I felt you take my breast in your hand this morning," she said.

Rose looked away, relieved at having finally arrived at the truth thanks to Holly's courage. "Do you not think I am disturbed as well?" she cried. "Your closeness pulls at every nerve in my body." She turned back to look at Holly, to drink in her magic eyes and gentle face. "But you are a wife, or have been. And will be again. I will not spoil you for that. You've a right to be angry."

Holly sat up and leaned against the wall. "I am not angry with you Rose. I am in love with you. I have been in love before. I know the feeling."

The extraordinary words enveloped Rose like a warm blanket. A sob rose unbidden in her throat. Still, she reached for the closest shore. "You cannot mean it," she said. "We have been reckless, is all. Lonely and reckless."

"Perhaps I have been reckless, Rose, but I am not lonely. I am never lonely with you." Holly smiled. "It does seem unusual. But I will stand with it if you will love me back."

"It is not just unusual," Rose said. "It is illness. Inversion. You saw Roberta."

Holly laughed. "I am not about to cut my hair, Rose, nor don a pair of trousers!"

"There is no cure for it," Rose said.

"Why must it be cured?"

To this Rose had no answer. "I am afraid," she said.

"I am a little frightened too," Holly replied, "but mightn't we endure together, so long as our hearts allow it? It is a private thing. Others need not judge us."

Rose looked into Holly's innocent face. "Life is seldom so simple," she replied. But it seemed her body would argue the point, for she leaned forward with a will she could neither comprehend nor deny. As if bending to the scent of a perfect rose, she closed her eyes and surrendered. They came together gently at first, as they had before, and then without restraint. As Holly's tongue moved past Rose's lips, a shiver ran through Rose's body. Holly's hand at the base of her spine caused a pleasant rush of pulse Rose had not felt before. But the fierce rising of her hips that followed startled her, and she pulled away. "Let me think," she said, rising from the bed.

"This is not something that yields to cognition," Holly said, teasing. "Come back to bed and be with me. I think I know how it is done. I was a married woman, remember?"

"How what is done?" Rose exclaimed, anger suddenly filling her well of fear. "It is base!"

Holly's smile dissolved. "I love you, Rose. It is only that!" She rolled over, and began to weep, but Rose did not go to her. Instead she stepped to the rocker and, folding her arms to steady her trembling body, sank down to be alone. She shut her eyes against the tears rising there, and having not slept the night before, yielded to fatigue and the blessing of sleep.

She dreamed of a garden at dawn, the sun's rays raking through the cornstalks like the Lord's fingers. As her bare feet touched the earth, a shaft of light pierced the thin fibers of her nightgown, revealing the shape of her legs. From a tomato bush she plucked a leaf and held it to her nose. Eve, she knew now, had sinned not for the apple, but for this. She picked a tomato as large as her fist. Its firm stem rose from a deep green star nestled in undulating purple shoulders. Raising and lowering her hand, she savored the weight of the fruit in her palm. She passed a soldier vigorously working the handle of a pump. When he winked at her, she smiled and ran a thumb along the tomato's swollen flesh, so silky she wept.

Rose woke feeling warm. Sometime in the night she had crawled into bed with Holly. She sprang from bed, afraid she had overslept, but dawn was just beginning. Her head was foggy, the dream still with her. Something was amiss. What was it? She slipped on her boots and stepped outside. In the cold air she snapped awake and remembered Holly's declaration and their kisses. She dropped her head into her hand and rubbed her temples hard as she walked across the icy ground to the privy. When she returned to the cabin, she went to the kitchen to start the stove and lay out the coffee. Even as doubt and confusion fought for her attention, a smile bloomed on her lips. Holly loved her! She had said so. But what did it mean?

She walked into the cabin, pulled her father's Bible from the shelf and returned to the rocker. She began with the familiar words of John and Matthew, instructing Christians to love one another as they loved God, fully and fearlessly. She read Ruth's gentle pledge to Naomi, to cleave to her until death bade them part. From Genesis, where all things began, she read softly aloud the words, "male and female created he them, and God blessed them, and God said unto them, Be fruitful, and multiply." She turned to the rhythmic words of Solomon, the allegorical love song between the Lord and his bride, the church, but the words of longing, of sweet kisses and a woman's breasts caused her to blush. Closing her eyes, she whispered the Lord's Prayer—first as it had been given to her, and then backwards as she had taught herself as a child, that she might have a private conversation with God. Finally, without answers, knowing only that another day lay ahead—a day filled with the blessing of Holly's companionship—she went to wake her friend. She would apologize first thing. This time it would be a true apology, full-throated and unconditional, and they would return to the way they had been, equilibrium restored.

As she bent to peck Holly's cheek good morning, a cloud of warm, moist air rose to meet her. She pulled back. Perspiration covered Holly's forehead. Wet tendrils of hair clung to her neck. Her cheeks were flushed. Rose shook her gently and called her name, but Holly slept on.

Rose's heart went to her throat. Fever could take a dozen paths. Influenza season had begun; it could be hard, but not like typhus or measles. Any rash would not appear for at least twenty-four hours. Still she checked behind Holly's ears, but the skin was smooth and healthy. She tucked the blankets tightly around Holly's shoulders and crossed to the main house. The doors to the dining room were open, and Mother Pennoyer's bed was empty. She climbed the stairs and banged on the first door at the top. A nurse from the Gayoso answered. "Holly is ill," Rose said. "Please, will you go to the ship and get Mother Pennoyer?" She took blankets from the nurse's bed and returned to cover Holly. She opened the windows and doors in both the kitchen and cabin. As cold air swept in, Holly endured a long, wracking cough. Even so she did not wake.

Mother Pennoyer arrived. "Was she ill before? Could it be scarlet fever?" she asked.

"She has not been ill before, no. It came on in the night." Rose thought of the deep kiss they had exchanged. "And now this," she said, as if Mother Pennoyer could follow her train of thought. She was startled by her own remark, and for a moment stared blankly at Mother Pennoyer.

"Rose, are you all right? You are not sick also?" Rose shook her head. "We forget we are human too," said Mother Pennoyer. "I have Dover's Powder, and Rooster will bring a plaster."

Rose went to Holly's bedside and wiped her forehead and cheeks. At last Holly opened her eyes. "Hello, there," Rose said.

"Kiss," Holly whispered.

Rose grew hot at the suggestive word. "Yes, you are sick," she said, as if speaking to a child. "We will give you Dover's Powder—you must drink it all down, and some tea as well."

Holly nodded and was taken by a series of dry coughs. Rose held her until the coughing passed then lay her gently back on the pillow. The thinnest smile graced Holly's face before she closed her eyes again.

"You may stay with her," Mother Pennoyer allowed, "but it may be long. You require your own rest, and there are men to care for. We may need to move her across the street."

"No, please, no," Rose said. The nurse's ward at the Gayoso was a gossip nest of idle women. She would not see Holly put there.

"Let us see how she progresses," Mother Pennoyer said. "I will allow three days. I fear for you as well, young lady."

When Rooster brought the mustard plaster, Rose felt a rush of gratitude toward the old man so deep and sudden it brought tears to her eyes.

"She'll be fine," he said gently, and Rose could only nod her thanks.

Holly had grown restless, mumbling and throwing off the blankets. Rose placed the poultice on her chest, but its vapors burned even Rose's eyes. Holly thrashed and pushed it away until Rose removed it. Even without the plaster, the fever continued its work. Sweat covered Holly's face. Droplets collected beneath her lower lip, the lip Rose had kissed only hours before. The cabin grew frigid, and as the sun went down, Rose went in search of more blankets.

She was in the kitchen when she first heard the unmistakable sound. She ran to find Holly sitting up, her body heaving with sharp, ragged coughs, one after the other. Her eyes were wide with fear as she struggled to take air back into her lungs. When at last she caught her breath, the dreaded whistle—the whoop—confirmed Rose's fear. Twice more Holly struggled, and twice more the high-pitched whooping sound filled the cabin until at last the cough receded and she fell back, exhausted.

Rose had been visited by *tussis convulsiva* as a child; she knew Holly's fear. "You must relax," she said. "When your heart is racing, the demand on your lungs is too great. If you are calm, your air will return more quickly." Holly closed her eyes, senseless to Rose's advice. Rose put her ear to Holly's damp chest and heard the soft rush of air flowing peacefully through her lungs. How could a body seize so violently one minute and relax so completely the next? This was an illness that hid in plain sight.

Holly was seized by another spell, this time followed by vomiting. This would be the pattern, for weeks or months. She would grow accustomed to it, learning to cough, purge, and go on her way. Rose placed a slop bowl next to the bed. "Good girl," she said to her insensible patient. "You have escaped the emetic." Vomiting would clear away the secretions of Holly's cough and relax her larynx, but where the action was spontaneous, induction of additional retching could only lead to mischief. With Holly purging on her own, Rose would not risk adding to her misery with unnecessary inflammation or, worse, a torn esophagus.

The fits came every fifteen to thirty minutes. Holly emptied her lungs until Rose thought surely she could cough no more, but still she coughed and whooped until her breath finally, miraculously returned. With each episode, she grew blue in the lips, her frantic heart demanding more than her lungs could deliver. That afternoon a rash appeared on her chest and spread quickly to her arms and legs. Instinctively, still mad with fever, she scratched. Throughout the night, as Rose held the slop bucket to Holly's chin, she gently pulled Holly's fingers from her body where, if not watched, they scratched until they drew blood.

As the sun entered the open window the next morning, Rose stepped into its feeble rays. Fatigue closed her eyes. She breathed deeply, feeling the exquisiteness of God's simple gift of oxygen. She turned to look at Holly. Was she not a blessing too? Of all the people she could have loved, Holly had chosen Rose. Could such a gift be refused?

Holly mumbled, and her eyes fluttered open. Rose approached her and kissed her forehead. Although still evident, the fever was less.

"I do not feel well," Holly murmured.

"You are doing a fine job of sweating a fever," Rose replied.

"My throat hurts."

"You have been coughing," Rose said. "And vomiting, I am afraid. You do not remember it?"

Holly shook her head, and as if on cue, a series of ragged coughs came over her, ending in dry heaves. "I hate vomiting," Holly whimpered.

Rose smiled. "I know," she said gently. "Let me warm some beef tea. At least then you will have something to bring up." Diluting her stomach acid would make Holly's plight more bearable and hopefully hold inflammation in check.

In the kitchen Rose warmed a cup of tea for each of them. They exchanged shy smiles as they sipped their breakfast. Before they could finish, Holly's cough returned, and the tea came up. She groaned in despair.

"Let us bathe you," Rose said gently. "It will lift your spirits." Holly's gown and bed clothes were soaked in blood and filth. Rose moved her to the rocker and changed the bed linens. She rebraided Holly's hair and fetched a fresh nightgown. Handing Holly a cloth and a pan of warm water she said, "If you can manage, I think I will take my walk." Holly nodded with a weak smile. When Rose returned, she was fast asleep.

In the hours since Holly had taken ill, Rose's confidence that an apology could restore equilibrium between them had flagged. How could they return to the way things had been before? A bell once rung could not be unrung. Beyond words of apology, what else could Rose offer? Whether regret or concession, she did not know, but it must be one of these. There seemed to be no middle ground.

The following day, Holly's fever abated. She sat up in bed. "May I have breakfast today?" she asked. "I cannot live on beef tea forever."

"You may have cereal," Rose said. "Oats or grits?" Porridge of any kind was not to Holly's taste—"fodder," she called it—but it was easily digested, especially after a fever.

"Oats," Holly said with a pout. "Bring lots of sugar."

"Yes, ma'am," Rose replied. In the kitchen she dipped the oats from the bin and put water on to boil. With Holly awake, things needed to be set right. She had been ill, Rose would tell her. She could not have meant what she said. It was the fever talking. As she stirred the oats, Rose tried to imagine the rest of the conversation, but always it ended in this same place, with her denying the one thing that felt most true. She scooped the thick, warm cereal into a bowl and placed it on a tray with a pot of tea and two cups. When she reached for the sugar bowl, it slipped from her trembling hands and broke. "Damn it!" she exclaimed.

Holly called from her bed. "Is everything all right?"

"Just spilled the sugar," Rose replied with a nonchalance she did not feel. "Forgive my language." She swept up the mess, filled a cup with sugar, and carried Holly's breakfast into the cabin.

"I have never heard such language from your lips," Holly said with a smile.

"I apologize," Rose said. "I seem to be turning into a sailor."

Holly laughed as she drenched the steaming cereal in sugar. "Looks delicious," she said, wrinkling her nose.

"Do not gobble it down," Rose cautioned.

"There is little danger of that, now, is there?" Holly replied with a grin. She carried a spoonful of oatmeal to her mouth. Despite everything, a purr of satisfaction rose from her throat. While Holly ate, Rose sipped her tea. A delicate dance of glances arose between them. Rose offered more sugar. Holly shook her head and smiled. Rose lifted the teapot. Holly held out her half-full cup. Rose straightened the things on the breakfast tray. Holly placed her empty bowl there. Rose offered more tea. Holly declined. With each exchange, their eyes met for half a beat, and they looked away.

Finally, when Rose offered another cup of unwanted tea, Holly replied, "Do you see how we are, Rose? How we could be? It would not be only about the one thing but about making a home, about caring for each other."

"I am sorry for what I said before," Rose said, relieved they were underway at last, again because of Holly's courage.

"I was too bold," Holly replied.

"I was cruel, and that is unforgivable."

"I forgive you, Rose."

With apology given and pardon granted, silence settled over them again. As she struggled to find words, Rose remembered Dr. York's ambiguous declaration that he wished she would come with him. The remark—not a question but a statement—had allowed them to reach an honorable resolution, a middle ground of sorts.

Perhaps if she merely spoke of her desires—not to say what must or mustn't be, but what she, Rose, wished and hoped for, simply what was true for her, perhaps if she did that, she and Holly might end in a righteous place. "I wish—" she said, but then she stopped, unable to finish. Unlike Dr. York, she realized, she did not know what she wished.

"Do not fret," Holly said, waving a hand as if brushing away a fly. She touched a handkerchief to the corner of her eye and laughed softly. "Go," she said. "I need my nap."

Rose rushed to reply. "We must talk again!" she said. "We must talk about what we wish." She kissed Holly's forehead and carried the dishes to the kitchen.

Moments later, when a long string of coughing and whooping came from the cabin, she resisted the urge to run to Holly. Her cough would be with her for many weeks. She needed to learn to handle it on her own. But when the coughing stopped suddenly and was followed by a loud crash, Rose ran to the door. She almost stepped on Holly who had left her bed, knocking over the crate that held her water and slop bowl. Now she lay at Rose's feet, her eyes huge with fear. The cough was silenced; she held her hand to her throat, her mouth opening and closing like a fish's. She was choking. She had vomited her breakfast and pulled the sticky cereal into her lungs.

Rose folded her over, delivering several sharp blows between her scapulae while scolding herself for allowing solid food, but Holly's breath did not return. With her ear to Holly's back, Rose could hear the melancholy moan of obstructed lungs. Holly's lips were blue, almost purple; her eyes were wet with tears. Rose raised Holly's hands over her head. "Jump!" she ordered. Holly took a small hop but collapsed to the floor. Rose pulled her up and made her jump again, but this time Holly fainted. Rose put a finger down her throat. She gagged but brought up nothing. Rose carried her to their bed. Perhaps gravity would dislodge the plug. Laying Holly on her back, with her head hanging over the edge, Rose pressed her fingers against her throat, massaging the airway. "Please, please relax," she whispered, but Holly's discolored mouth and rolled eyes told her that without a miracle, the only rest now would be with the ages.

Rose's own throat ached from the words she had held back, words that unless released would if not kill her, surely keep her from living. "I love you, Holly," she wept. "I do love you. Don't leave me. Not today. I am not ready today!" Holly opened her eyes briefly and smiled. She raised a finger to Rose's lips as if to quiet her. Rose kissed her forehead, and held her close until the last beat of her perfect heart. A moment later, Holly jerked violently, her body seeking its last gasp, but even that most holy of breaths was denied her.

Someone had closed Holly's beautiful eyes. Rose tried to open them, but Mother Pennoyer had hold of her hands and was pulling her away.

"We must wash and dress her," Mother Pennoyer said, "to prepare her."

"Prepare her for what?" Rose asked. She shook off the older woman's grasp and sat beside Holly again. She touched Holly's mouth. It was the wrong color; it was cold. Something was amiss.

She heard Maggie's voice. "She must be undressed, Rose. Would you like me to do it?"

Rose turned to Maggie, kneeling beside her, and saw her pink lips. Now she knew what the problem was. She fell into Maggie's waiting arms and wept.

Maggie helped her up and led her to the chest of drawers. "Get her things," she said gently.

Rose pushed her away and opened the drawer in which Holly kept her clean underclothes. It was January; she pulled out Holly's heavy leggings. From the bottom drawer, she took the lavender dress with its lace collar. She draped the clothes over the back of the rocker.

"Can you bring some warm water, Rose?" Maggie said.

Without speaking, Rose went to the kitchen and poured hot water from the kettle into a large bowl. She added cold, that Holly not be burned, and dropped a clean dish towel into the bowl.

In the cabin, Holly's soiled nightgown lay on the floor. Maggie had covered her with a sheet to her neck. Did Maggie know?

Maggie reached to take the bowl of warm water from Rose's hands, but Rose held it against her belly. "Do you want to do it?" Maggie asked.

Rose did not answer. She tightened her grasp on the bowl. Maggie waited. Finally Rose said, "May I wash her face?"

"Of course you may. Just give me the bowl for a minute."

Rose felt Maggie pulling at her fingers.

"Rose, you must let go."

"Must I?"

"Yes, dear, you must."

She gave up the bowl and sank to her knees beside Holly. She reached up and brushed Holly's hair from her face. "You look a mess," she said, smiling.

Maggie handed Rose the steaming cloth, wrung tight. Wouldn't it be lovely, Rose thought, to bury her face in its warmth? She imagined the damp heat flowing into her pores, rising through her nostrils to her lungs. She would rub her swollen eyes, scrub her neck. How light she would feel as the moisture evaporated. She might cry into the towel, hide in it, come out only when she woke from this ghastly dream.

Maggie placed her hand over Rose's and guided the towel across Holly's brow. Rose paused to rub Holly's temple then took the towel to herself and dipped it into the water again. Twisting the cloth, she watched the steam rise in whorls. The beauty of it was something Holly would enjoy, another of God's simple gifts. She washed Holly's closed eyes, her cheeks, her nose. She pulled the towel slowly behind Holly's neck, stopping to massage the cords there. She draped the towel around her index finger and dipped it into the water. Tears came in earnest as she traced Holly's discolored mouth with her finger, the cupid's bow of her top lip, the corners of her mouth where she smiled, the mouth Rose had kissed. Finally, she wiped a speck of vomitus from Holly's chin. Then she stood and handed the towel to Maggie.

"Call me when she is dressed," Rose said. "I must take my walk."

Rose sat alone with Holly overnight. She covered her with blankets and her counterpane, tucking the linens around her shoulders, as she liked it. She watched Holly's face in the lamplight, looking for signs that a terrible mistake had been made, that the patient was cured and would rise. But sometime in the night, in a moment Rose could not identify, hope yielded to memories—of those magnificent eyes, of how they had shared a bed as sisters, of their first kiss and those that had followed, growing from innocent to knowing, ripening from sisterly to passionate, their meaning ultimately unmistakable. She thought of her own betrayal, and she wept.

In the morning two soldiers arrived with Mother Pennoyer and a wooden casket. Rose placed Holly's counterpane in the bottom of the box. At a nod from Mother Pennoyer, the men lifted Holly's body into the box and stepped back. Rose tucked the blanket around her and pulled her braid forward over her shoulder. Suddenly she remembered the child in Vicksburg. "Wait!" she cried. From the dresser she retrieved her green satin ribbon, the one she had worn on her first day with the army. She tied it to the end of Holly's braid. There could be no mistake. Holly was loved.

Rose leaned in and kissed Holly's forehead, and then she ran to the kitchen. At the sound of the first nail being driven, she collapsed with her hands over her ears, cries rising from a place she had not known existed.

Holly's body was sent by transport to Jeffersonville the next day. Her family would come from Maryland when they could. It was winter; there was no rush. Mother Pennoyer released Rose from duty for three days but cautioned her not to wallow. Rose returned to work on the second day, finding the distraction better than her ruminations in the empty cabin. Maggie and Charlotte gave her knowing smiles and hugs as they passed on the ship, offered to sit with her at supper, and left her to her thoughts when she asked for privacy. She was grateful to them both, but Adelaide was her best medicine. Unlike the others, she was not afraid to mention Holly. One afternoon she climbed into Rose's lap and leaned her head on her chest.

"Why does God take people away?" she asked. "It's not fair."

"God is always fair," Rose replied, reciting what had been said to her in her own childhood. "Perhaps he needed Holly in heaven."

"Is there a war in heaven?" Adelaide asked, alarmed.

Rose pulled her close. "No, sweetheart, there is no war in heaven, ever. I think God must have missed Holly, just as we do. He has been without her a very long time, ever since she was born. We have only been without her a little while, and we miss her so very much. Consider how God was feeling." Comforting the child did not ease her own pain, but it allowed her to say Holly's name out loud.

On Christmas Eve, Holly's birthday, Rose developed a cough and fever and was put to bed by Mother Pennoyer. Maggie and Charlotte were moved to Dabney Heights to care for Rose and a half dozen other ill nurses. Idleness and fever led, inescapably, to impulsive musings—the taste of Holly's kiss, the feel of her breast. Rose's senses caressed her as she drifted in and out of her dreams. Only her wretched cough woke her fully from these private moments, reminding her of her loss.

When the fever left her, she was flooded again with grief and confusion. Had they been reckless, or had they loved? For a year and a half Rose had watched as Holly calmed frightened soldiers, mothered young nurses, and skillfully appeased Mother Pennoyer. Only Holly's clear-headed fortitude had kept Rose from succumbing to despair over Parrott's fate and Quaker's suicide. Rose had worked and slept next to this good woman, taken her warmth, laughed with her, confided in her and accepted her compassion. The picnic, the game, the dancing had led to a handful of gentle kisses and one fiery kiss that had begun with Holly's declaration of love. Was it possible that what Rose had called recklessness was in fact the opposite? It occurred to her that with Holly's death, she might avoid answering this troublesome question. And in an episode already overfull with shame, Rose recognized this fleeting thought for the disgrace that it was.

Chapter 15

EIGHTEEN-SIXTY-FIVE BEGAN WITH THE UNIONISTS OF EASTERN
Tennessee convening in Nashville to abolish slavery. The greatest har-
mony and goodwill obtained among the three hundred delegates,
and when the matter was put to a vote of like-minded Tennesseans
two weeks later, it passed by a landslide. In Confederate Memphis,
people could only laugh. The war persisted like a stubborn winter
pneumonia, the patient neither alive nor fully dead. A peace confer-
ence attended by the president himself failed. When Sherman reached
Columbia—a capitol city of broad boulevards, stately homes, and
stunning gardens—its mayor surrendered rather than see his city burn,
but Union troops looted and burned their way through town anyway.
Sherman, feeling his boys needed to let off a little steam after the long
walk from Savannah, turned his back.

Rose wondered what Dr. York thought of the destruction in
the South and the chances for peace. She missed their tête-à-têtes.
Charlotte was disinterested in politics, and Maggie turned every mention of the war into a lesson. When Rose remarked that it was a shame
Columbia had burned, Maggie replied, "Dear me, the hard work of
all those slave carpenters and slave gardeners, reduced to rubble!" Able
was nearby, and the two exchanged smiles and suppressed laughter.
Rose felt she would never get it right. She felt alone.

In missing Holly, Rose spent hours alone in the cabin. Sleep eluded her. One night she wandered to the ship, where she found Able in the mess. Able spent most days in the contraband camps now.

"It is nice to see you," Rose said. Able pointed to the other chair at her table.

"Trouble sleeping," Able said.

Rose nodded. They sat in silence. Although they had never grown close, she would miss Able after the war. At last Rose asked, "Will you go back to Boston?"

Able shook her head. "I'm staying here, in the camps."

"I admire you."

"You could stay."

The remark carried the bite Rose had learned to expect from Able, but they both knew Able could do ten times the good Rose could do now. "If I am ever to go abroad," Rose said, "now is the time. Surgeons in Vienna and Paris are having success opening the chest. I hope to learn their methods."

"A lady surgeon."

"Yes, ma'am. That is my intention."

"Takes pluck to be a girl sawbones, but you don't seem lacking there."

"Please, not a sawbones," Rose replied, groaning. "I have had enough of amputation. I want to heal, not mutilate."

Able laughed. "Fair enough," she said. "You know, when you get down to it, pluck is nothing but uppity, whitewashed. I know something of uppity." She smiled. "You keep your pluck, and you'll get your surgeon's stripes."

"I have your blessing?"

"Yes, ma'am, you do. But wouldn't it be something for a black woman to be a surgeon of the chest?"

"Yes, yes it would," Rose replied.

"You do that," Able said. "One thing at a time right now. Got to clean up these camps and teach these folks how to live in town. Their country ways need some tamping down."

"Camp Dixie, Boston of the South," Rose replied, smiling.

Able laughed. "Do you know I deliver a baby a day in those camps?

And every one of those children comes free into this world. Now that's a miracle."

"Yes, it is," Rose replied. "Able, speaking of miracles, may I ask you a question? It is about the races. You needn't answer if you don't care to."

"Am I not done with you yet?" Able huffed with a friendly shake of her head. "Feels like we'll be schooling white people till the Second Coming."

"We have a lot to learn," Rose said.

"Ask away," Able said with a sigh. She took a swallow of coffee as if to fortify herself.

"Maggie believes the races will never get along, that we will never reach incorporation. Do you feel the same?" Rose asked.

Able stared into her cup and raised one eyebrow. "I expect trouble to come our way, if that's what you're asking. South and North alike. It will look different in the two places, but we'll be scrapping for some time, no doubt." For the first time in Rose's presence, a tear ran down Able's cheek. She wiped it away. "If only they would just let us be," Able exclaimed. Rose heard both anger and despair in her voice. She moved to comfort her, but Able waved her off. "One day at a time," she said with a thin smile. "Think of all those children born free."

"Why did we have this war, Able? Why could we not find another way?"

Able frowned and cleared her throat. "Some think God brought this down on both sides," she said, "as punishment for slavery."

"The president says so."

"I know he does. He's a fatalistic man, Mr. Lincoln. But to my mind, the Lord just sets the finish line. It's in our own free will how to run the race. The ways and means of things, those fall to man's ledger. If this be punishment, then it's us holding the lash, not the Lord. There was a peaceful way to end slavery; we just didn't choose it."

"What was that? Buying out slaveholders?"

"Lord, no. That's just paying off the devil, and you don't get peace trading with him. You might get quiet for a bit, but you don't get peace. If anybody should get paid it's the African, for two and a half centuries of hard labor. No, I mean something bigger than buying our way out. Much bigger."

"Aside from planters just giving up their slaves, what else was there?"

"That right there," Able said. "The South could have freed the slaves."

"They would never do that."

"You asked."

Before the Emancipation Proclamation, only radicals had argued for the wholesale release of the slave population. Rose had thought the idea impractical, ridiculous even, but for a moment she let herself languish in the vision—a country peacefully transformed, united; its people free, paid for their labor; children in schools instead of fields; a nation growing, rising, untouched by war.

"I'm not saying it was ever likely," Able continued. "I just say it was one way. Every one of those slave owners could have gotten down on his knees, begged God's forgiveness, and cried, 'Lord, I have sinned. Where do I sign?'" She made a flourish with her hand, as if signing a slave's manumission papers. "But no. They'd rather die—not fighting the black man, mind you, but fighting other white men. It had to be whites. God knows they would never stoop to fighting us straight on. They knew we'd take them. Pitiful."

"What stops us from choosing peace, Able?"

Able answered without hesitation. "Pride."

"As simple as that?"

"Pride is not simple. Pride got Lucifer tossed from heaven, remember?"

"His was the first sin," Rose said.

"Yes, ma'am. Before Eve ever set eyes on that apple, Lucifer's pride came first. But pride is two-edged. On the one hand, it's a gift from God; dignity and self-respect, they're our birthright. But misuse your pride and you end up in Lucifer's spot. His mistake was putting himself over God—thinking he was prettier and smarter than God—just like the white man does the Negro. Pridefulness, that was Lucifer's sin—and mankind's eternal curse. Take any war, even our own revolution, and you'll find somebody's Luciferian pride mixed up in it. King George couldn't let us go. What would the other kings think?"

Rose laughed. "My cousins think the North is prideful," she said, "and arrogant in the things we say about the South. They say they only want respect. And to be left alone."

Able snorted. "They don't think slaves want respect? And left alone? Ha!"

"I admit they have probably not considered things from your perspective. They think they are entitled to their point of view."

"Look, somebody owns someone else, that's not a point of view, that's just evil. I'm sorry, as I know you care for them, but except for the lady who brought her child to the ship, your kin can jump in a river. That's my opinion."

Rose laughed. "This may surprise you, Able, but I agree. I do not think they will reform. But the North has been prideful, too, hasn't it? Perhaps not so much in the way my cousins think, in words on paper, but in having looked the other way. Or was that just greed?"

"Pride goes before greed as before any other fall," Able said.

"As it goes before war?"

"Yes, ma'am. Mind you, we took a great length of time getting to this war. Slavery came to Jamestown in 1617. Quakers waited fifty years to speak out. The Founding Fathers disgraced themselves with their dillydallying." Able pushed her chair back. "One thing I'll say for Mr. Lincoln—at least he stood and fought. Good night, Nurse Barnett. It's been nice talking with you."

Rose stayed at the ship, unready to go to her empty bed. Was Able right that pride was the rootstock of war? She would have said fear and greed, but even these were firmly rooted in pride. Yet pride, dignity, and self-respect were at the core of what it meant to be human. Without pride, the black man would not have known he was enslaved. Only his God-given self-respect had sustained him until this moment in history. "Pride is two-edged," Able had said. The sin of war sprang not from pride itself but from pride misused. Yet it seemed to Rose that such a passion was unlikely to yield to a force as blunt as war. She recalled from her days of teaching that a naughty child corrected in private was likely to reform but one called out and humiliated before his peers only grew more stubborn and devious. The North had been a harsh schoolmaster. She feared for the South.

The wards of the *Despain* had become a jumble of civilians and soldiers, women and children, blacks and whites, Confederate and Union. The surgery was empty; Rose spent her endless days tending fevers and ordering bodies moved to the death-house. In the east, the war ground on.

In late March Mother Pennoyer became ill. She took to bed for the first time in four years, only to die the following day. The loss of the gruff old woman was a cruel reminder that the conflict was not yet over. Rose took her place, taking on her administrative tasks and offering solace and balm to the bruised spirits of those around her, even while nursing her own wounded heart.

Maggie came to Rose's room one evening asking permission for a laundress to return home. "Why cannot we all go home?" Rose replied. "It is ridiculous to waste another life on this conflict when it is already won."

"You would cast the South free, then, slaves and all?"

"Of course not."

"Then it is not so ridiculous."

"You are right, Maggie, of course. Lives lost now just seem so wasteful."

"And those of a year ago? They were worth more?"

"I confess it makes no sense. Do not scold me!"

"I am just teasing," Maggie said. "You are easy, you know it?" She threw a pillow at Rose.

She caught it and pulled it into her chest. Memories of holding Holly washed over her. "Yes, your friend may go home," she said with a sigh.

"Thank you," Maggie replied. "She will be pleased. She has a proposal waiting." She cleared her throat. "Sit down, Rose."

"What is it?" Rose sat on the bed. The look on Maggie's face was a mixture of bemusement and concern. "What?"

"I did not come just for the laundress," Maggie said, "nor to tease you. I've something to say, and you must listen. I know you are still tender, but you must hear me out." She knelt before Rose and took up her hands. "I know," she said.

"You know what?" Rose said, growing afraid in the face of this sober talk from Maggie. She tried to pull away, but Maggie held her hands firmly in her own.

"That you loved Holly."

"Of course I loved Holly."

"I mean that you were in love with her, just as you were not in love with Dr. York." Rose did not answer, but turned her head aside. Maggie reached up and gently turned her face back. "Who better to know you than a woman?" she asked softly.

"It is not what God designed. It is not the natural way."

"Rose, did you not scold Dr. York for saying exactly that?"

Rose knew only too well what she had said on that dreadful first walk with Dr. York. Perhaps she had been arguing merely to argue; perhaps she did not know then, and still did not know, what she believed. "At the time, it was a hypothetical question," she said.

"It is hypothetical no longer," Maggie said.

Rose groaned.

"Look, Rosie. You are always talking about God's design. Can you not imagine that he made you this way? That for you this is natural? That the other is unnatural in your case?"

"I try to live by God's laws," Rose said. "Even as a scientist, I believe."

"And what commandment did you and Holly break? Neither one of you was married, so there cannot have been adultery in it. There was no coveting that I can figure, as you had eyes only for each other. Did you steal something—besides Holly's heart? Okay, maybe fornication, but I am pretty sure there must be a man in the room for that."

Despite herself, Rose laughed. "Maggie, please. We were companions."

"Companions in love," Maggie said.

Rose's tears came without warning. "I turned her away," she wept. "Twice I said no!"

Maggie wrapped her arms around Rose. "Shhhh," she whispered as Rose sobbed. "She just knew first, is all." When Rose nodded, Maggie added, "You can be a stubborn woman, Rose Barnett."

"Prideful," Rose answered.

"That too," Maggie said.

Rose pulled back. "How did you know?"

"I only saw it toward the end," Maggie said, "but it became hard to miss."

Rose wondered if Dr. York had seen it, but she let the thought drift by unexamined. It did not matter. "And you do not judge me for it?" she asked Maggie.

"I do not judge you, Rose. The world is full of people who will, but I am not one of them."

Rose wiped her eyes. "Thank you, Mags," she said. "I think I would like to be alone now."

Maggie stood to go. "War is no place to make attachments," she said. She bent and kissed Rose on the cheek and chucked her under the chin. "But cheer up," she said. "There are many mermaids in the sea."

Rose grabbed the pillow and threw it, chasing Maggie from the room. She sat up late into the night. If Maggie was right, her time with Holly had not been reckless at all but had followed the pattern that was right for them, beginning in friendship and growing with respect and trust through a thousand kindnesses, two people of similar desires moving inexorably, naturally, along the long road to romantic love. She remembered Able's words, that God sets the finish line and man, through his free will, chooses how to run the race. If God's commandment was to love, was it up to her to choose how? In Maggie's view, she had no choice; God had already chosen for her. Perhaps her choice was simply to trust, or not, in what God had made. Perhaps in order to love him she needed first to love herself.

On April 9, 1865, Robert E. Lee surrendered his fifty thousand men to Ulysses S. Grant. When news reached Memphis, the streets filled with ecstatic Yankees and Confederates alike. Rose stayed indoors avoiding errant minié balls. Surgeons would be digging lead from soldiers and civilians alike—even from children—in the days to come as people took up arms to celebrate the end of bloodshed.

Rose had seen too much guerilla activity to believe that the South, especially here in the west, would follow Lee into the shame of surrender. Many in Memphis, even while celebrating, were calling Lee a coward. President Davis was on the run and known to be gathering troops. Johnston and Sherman were still fighting each other in the Carolinas. Forrest had not been heard from, and Confederate ships were still at sea. To Rose's mind, the surrender of one general, even one as great as Lee, was unlikely to persuade the South that its cause was lost.

Five days later President Lincoln was murdered. Memphis grew tense. The locals went indoors as Union troops patrolled the streets in numbers that had not been seen since the embarrassing raid by General Forrest. Nurses gathered in small huddles, weeping in shock and fear of what might be next. While Lincoln's funeral train chugged toward Illinois, Union soldiers chased his killer, and President Johnson—a Southern Unionist—ordered the fight to continue. But the lure of peace proved irresistible. By the end of the month, Confederate generals across the South surrendered their commands.

Quietly and without celebration, people chose to carry on their lives. Maggie and Alice had decided to claim their 160 acres of free land in California. On a cool April day, they prepared to board a westbound train. Rose went to say good-bye. Alice's faithful binding and stretching of little Lincoln's clubfoot had made it possible for him to stand upon its edge, and he now wobbled about enthusiastically, knowing no other way. He would walk after all. The arm Rose had dislocated to pull him from his mother was prone to falling from its socket, but both Alice and Maggie, who shamelessly spoiled the child, were adept at replacing it. His young body had endured a terrible crucible, but he had survived. Like the nation, he was imperfect but whole. Knowing he would not have lived but for her effort, Rose allowed herself a private moment of satisfaction before asking God to protect him.

She turned to Maggie. "How do I thank you?" she asked. Her heart ached at this parting, almost as it had in losing Holly.

"Love yourself," Maggie replied. "Love Rose."

Rose smiled at the deep wisdom of her friend—one who, but for a dreadful struggle, would have been lost forever to the purgatory of slavery. At every turn Maggie had held up the mirror to Rose. It was Maggie who had shown her, truly for the first time, that every child was born perfect, with neither more nor less claim to dignity and righteous pride than any other child of God. It was Maggie who, through uncommon patience and good humor, had led Rose to the irreducible truth that one's sins are judged not by how one loves but how one hates.

"I shall try," Rose replied, wrapping her arms around her friend. "I shall try to love Rose. And If I succeed, I will have you to thank." She turned to Alice and, running her hand through Lincoln's soft curls, wished them good luck on the farm.

"Yes, ma'am," Alice replied. "I know how to work a field." Rose smiled and nodded. She hoped their money would hold out and that Alice would never again know a day as dark as those she had known until this day.

At the conductor's insistent call, Rose kissed Maggie's cheek and stepped aside. At the door of the car, Maggie blew a kiss and then disappeared.

The army had given Able a cottage at the edge of Camp Dixie. She was busy whitewashing it and scavenging for kitchen tools. She was eager to cook again, she said. Already she had turned the soil and planted potato sprouts she had nursed through the winter. Rose helped her move a bed from Dabney Heights, along with the rocking chair from the cabin. It pleased her to think of Able retiring to the rocker at the end of a long day. Otherwise they left the Dabney home as they had found it.

Charlotte and Adelaide were bound for Chicago by steamer and train. Rose's dispensary partner, Chloe, now managed a small settlement house and hospital and had agreed to take them in. Adelaide would go to school and help with the cleaning and laundry while Charlotte learned dispensing. Before heading to Europe, Rose would make a quick stop in Chicago to ensure they were settled, but first she had promised Rooster she would prepare the ship for decommissioning.

One rainy night shortly after Maggie had left, Rose walked Charlotte and Adelaide up the gangplank to the transport *Samuel K* bound for Cairo. The ship was crowded with men released from

Southern prison camps. Their hollow eyes and emaciated frames frightened Adelaide, and she clung to her mother's skirts. "Please come with us, Cousin Rose," she pleaded.

"I must put the *Despain* to rights," Rose said. "I shall join you very soon." Adelaide stuck out her lip in a pout. "Do not let that fall off," Rose said with a gentle smile. She led the way through the woeful men, asking them to clear a place against the gunwale for a mother and child. Settling her cousins there, she told Adelaide to keep her eyes on the sky, to count the stars. "I shall want to know the number when I see you in Chicago," she said. She hugged them good-bye and pried a giggling Adelaide's fingers from her neck before leaving her new family to their journey.

The ship weighed anchor at midnight. In two days' time, Charlotte and Adelaide would be in Cairo, where they would board a train to Chicago. Rose watched the lights of the ship until it was out of sight, and then she returned to the *Despain*. She and Able spent an hour cleaning and packing, readying the ship for decommissioning. Rooster and a handful of male nurses were still aboard, as were a few patients. One surgeon remained. He was young. Rose had not even bothered to learn his name. She let Rooster tease her about staying behind to have the doctor to herself.

Rose and Able retired to the former nurses' cabin on the Texas, each retaking her old bed. The room was well-worn, its shiny paint now chipped and dull, its gauzed windows torn and burned from flying cinders. Still, Rose felt pleasure at laying down her head in the gilded space where she had spent her first night in Memphis.

It was still dark when something rocked the ship. In nightgowns and shawls, Rose and Able ran barefoot to the main deck, where Rooster and others had already gathered. A bright light lit the northern sky. Captain Fuchs, in silk pajamas and spyglass in hand, was last to arrive. "The *Samuel K*," he said. "Boiler finally blew."

Rose's knees buckled. Able caught her, saying, "The *Sam K* left hours ago."

"With that load and this current," Captain Fuchs replied, "she was making less than a knot when she came in. I would put her at about Mound City right now."

Rose regained her legs and stood to face the captain. "You do not know it is the *Samuel K*, or any other ship, for that matter."

"Guerillas be my guess," ventured Rooster, "blasting a cache while they still can. Just playing." Rose was grateful for his calm surmise.

The young surgeon, still in awe of his superior, asked, "What shall we do if it is a ship, Captain?"

Rose shrieked at him. "It needn't be a ship! And we certainly do not know it is the *Sam K*!"

The captain looked at Rose with hooded eyes. "Of course, Nurse Barnett. We do not know. We shall have to wait, shan't we?"

"Send a tug," she cried, pointing into the night. "Find out what has happened. Go to the rescue!" The northern sky was still horribly, unnaturally alight.

"So it may be a ship after all?"

"Even a blown cache makes for casualties, Captain." She would not miss this petty, arrogant man.

"You needn't worry, Nurse. I have already dispatched a tug. Perhaps it will reach the accident, or whatever this is, within the hour. It is always hard to judge distance with fire. Tricky." He put the glass to his eye.

Rose wanted to jump into the river and swim toward the eerily lit horizon.

Able took Rose by the elbow. "Burns will be coming, regardless," she said. "The cotton wool must be unpacked and the ointments mixed." To Rooster she said, "Go to the Gayoso. Tell them we have burns. While you are there, get lead oxide and lime; we've plenty of linseed already."

Rose worked beside Able in a stupor of worry, unpacking bandages, making beds, and mixing ointment, thinking only of Charlotte and Adelaide. The *Sam K* had stopped in Memphis because its boiler had needed repair. She had encouraged Charlotte to take the ship, the sooner to reach Chicago. Now…she could not think of now.

Near dawn the sternwheeler *Boston* appeared. Its deck was a hideous sight. Burned men lay everywhere, cloth and skin melted together in peeling black shards. Their eyes held the blank stare of the dead, yet they were not so. Not yet. Shouting and chaos broke out as sailors from the *Boston* began carrying the wounded onto the *Despain* and men from the *Despain* rushed onto the *Boston*. Rose forced her way on board. Grabbing the arm of a sailor bearing a burned man on his back, she demanded, "Are these men from the *Samuel K*? Sir! Is this the *Sam K*?"

"I don't know, lady. Some ship blew up near Mound City. We come on it sometime after—not much is left. Bodies hanging in trees, whole river's on fire." He slumped away from her, grumbling about the war's endlessness.

Rose pushed on, exploring every corner of every deck. "Have you seen any ladies?" she begged. "Is there a woman here? Have you seen a child?" No one replied. She heard Rooster calling her. She was needed in the surgery. Numb with fear, she returned to the *Despain*. She worked through that day until dawn of the next, first in the surgery removing torn limbs and then on the wards pulling off burned skin and painting raw flesh with the foul-smelling ointment. At last she collapsed on a bed beside a dying soldier and slept.

Shortly after daybreak another ship brought more victims. Able woke Rose so that a new patient might have the bed. Again she went aboard the rescue ship, pleading, "Is there a woman here? Is there a child? Have you seen a child?" It was Rooster, with a man on his back, who finally pointed and said, "Look there, missy." In a corner of the stern, a girl child huddled, her hair burned off, her body covered in coal-black soot, but otherwise seemingly unharmed. It was Adelaide. Beside her lay Charlotte's body. Rose rushed to embrace the child.

"Cousin Rose?" Adelaide cried. "I can't find Mama. I've called and called."

Rose lifted her tiny cousin, her Southern kin, into her arms. "One step at time," she said, as she carried her to the *Despain*. "One step at a time."

Epilogue

Rose was in Chicago when word of Jefferson Davis's capture came, a month after Lee's surrender. Fighting had continued in Texas, and rumors still flew of Confederates regrouping in Mexico or Canada or Cuba. Things remained tense in Indian Country, where a Cherokee Confederate general continued the fight, perhaps for reasons only he and his people understood. Although the president's assassin had been found and shot in Virginia, General Forrest was still silent.

Rose heard a newsboy shouting "Extra!" and ran to the street with her nickel. "Ignominious Surrender," read the headline. The Fourth Michigan cavalry had surrounded the Confederate president's party in Georgia where, it was reported, he had been caught sneaking out of camp in one of his wife's dresses. A thirty-nine-year-old company clerk named Andrew Bee was credited with the capture when he shouted, "There goes a man dressed in woman's clothes!" The Fourth had been led to the camp by a former slave pulling a cart through the woods. His name, Rose noted, was not recorded. In the adjacent column, a headline announced that Nathan Bedford Forrest had ordered his troops to stand down.

Rose sat on the stairs, absorbing the news. With both Davis and Forrest in hand, she let herself believe that the war was over, and it felt splendid. An apple tree bloomed across the street, its white buds swelling against a blue sky. Flooded with the joy of God's many gifts, Rose gave thanks for peace.

Shortly before his death, President Lincoln had said that the fight might continue until every drop of blood drawn by the lash was matched by one drawn by the sword. While the words were poetical, Rose had thought them reckless. There was no evening-out to be had here. Blood did not cleanse blood; it only deepened the stain. Worse, Mr. Lincoln seemed to imply a quest for vengeance in the Negro, when all that was asked were the natural gifts of freedom—the right to choose where to live, whom to marry, how to work; to live with one's own flesh and blood, to rear one's children; and to reclaim the God-given gifts of pride, dignity, and free will. These were not dreams of vengeance. Nor had Rose agreed that only God could end the war. She thought that, just as Maggie and Holly had once accused her of doing, the president had handed off to God that which was man's responsibility. In light of his fatalistic remarks, she wondered if he had done all he could to keep the peace among his people. Failure in this regard would be a heavy burden to bear through eternity, although he surely would not bear it alone. Rose shook her head to clear the sad thoughts of the lost president from her mind. The war was over. The nation was delivered. The scar was deep, but the body was mending. Let the president—and the patient—rest.

The following day, they would leave for Seneca Falls where Rose would present Adelaide to Grace and Fidelia as her ward and the grandchild they had thought they would never have. She would ask their forgiveness for her youthful willfulness and, more recently, her long silence. And she would seek their wisdom—for although she had been Adelaide's guardian for less than a month, already Rose felt the sweet, thorny weight of the child's future on her shoulders. She could think of none better to guide her than the two sisters who had turned a brokenhearted little girl into a bold young woman who went to war and believed she could become a surgeon. After Seneca Falls, she and Adelaide would sail for Europe, where Adelaide would attend the Paris school for the blind while Rose studied surgery at the Université de Paris.

Rose stood and ran up the stairs to the flat above the dispensary, calling Adelaide's name. She found her in the parlor, her unseeing eyes bright with excitement.

"What is it, Cousin Rose? What has happened?"

Rose placed the newspaper in Adelaide's lap and guided her palm across its inky surface. "There is good news at last," she said. "The best of news. Come. We must make a chocolate cake to celebrate."

Acknowledgments

MANY GENEROUS INDIVIDUALS GAVE OF THEIR TIME AND TALENTS TO help me bring this story to life. Thank you to readers Tom Edwards, John Hayhurst, Sue Hayhurst, Olivia Bartlett, Sandra Mico, Greg Mico, Virginia Cornyn, Kathleen Brugger, Charlotte Schwartz, Cindy Stewart-Rinier, Judy Cherry, Bill Cherry, Neeley Wells, Kim Heron, Karen Oehler, Stephanie Sherman, Steve Baker, CD Redhawk, Merridawn Duckler, my classmates at The Attic Institute, and the good people at Indigo Editing & Publications. Special thanks to the residents of Holladay Park Plaza for their unflagging enthusiasm; Roger Paget for his profound friendship and scholarship; Delia Bayley for the maves; and Gary Rogowski and Barney for the pizza. Last but never least (because they are, in the end, everything) thank you to my family, especially Anne, Scott and Dick, for keeping the horizon in view and picking me up when I stumbled, every single time. You are my sunshine.

CPSIA information can be obtained
at www.ICGtesting.com
Printed in the USA
FFOW03n0220061117
43306538-41873FF